The *USA Today* Bestselling Author
ALYSSA J. MONTGOMERY

Return to Hope Creek

HOME IS A PLACE TO HEAL

Serendipity, 51 Gower Street, London, WC1E 6HJ
info@serendipityfiction.com | www.serendipityfiction.com

First published in the US in 2024 by Escape Publishing, an imprint of
Harlequin Enterprises (Australia) Pty Limited, a subsidiary of HarperCollins
Publishers Australia Pty Limited | www.romance.com.au/escapepublishing

Print ISBN 9781917163705
Ebook ISBN 9781917163712
Set in Times.

ABOUT THE AUTHOR

Alyssa lives with her husband and three children on a five-acre property nestled into a mountain range south of Sydney, Australia, and enjoys having the space for gardens, a dog, horses, goats and chickens. Visits from the native wildlife (echidnas, wallabies and a variety of native birds) are particularly welcome… although visits from native wildlife with scales and fangs aren't met with quite as much enthusiasm!

She continues to work in her private practice as a Speech-Language Pathologist. Previously she's done a stint with Qantas Airways as an international flight attendant, completed her Master of Science degree, and has also been a professional pianist.

If you'd like to know more about Alyssa, her books, or to connect with her online, you can visit her webpage or like her Facebook page https://www.facebook.com/AlyssaJMontgomery

Alyssa loves to hear from readers and can be contacted at alyssaj.montgomeryromance@gmail.com

CHAPTER ONE

Leaving a cloud of red dust in its wake, the four-wheel drive bounced along the short stretch of unsealed road to Hope Creek Station – the place that'd become Stella's home eighteen years ago.

She bit down on her lip as a rush of memories assailed her.

Don't cry.

When she'd been a vulnerable twelve-year-old making this same trip to meet her new foster parents, she'd repeated the same words as a mantra.

Then, she'd battled grief and the uncertainty of not knowing what awaited her.

Now, her yearning to be back with those she loved most in the world was a physical ache in her chest. She couldn't wait to cocoon herself in the haven of Hope Creek Station and ground herself in everything that mattered most. It was time to heal, regroup and to pursue her new direction.

Things will work out.

Be strong and put on a brave face.

The first time she'd come to the cattle station it'd seemed like she'd journeyed to the ends of the earth, even though the station was a part of the small community of Hope Creek and only a forty-five minute drive from the rural township of Lancaster.

'Nearly home, love,' Blue told her as he navigated carefully around a large pothole in the road.

Home.

Again, Stella told herself firmly to keep her tears dammed.

Although she'd only lived here permanently for six years, Hope Creek Station was definitely home and this wasn't going to be her usual flying visit, crammed into her previously hectic international schedule.

This time, she was coming home indefinitely.

This time, she had plans to make a home of her own here – had been forced into it, really, as the life she'd lived for the last twelve years had come to an abrupt and brutal end.

My life hasn't ended, she assured herself. *It's just the beginning of a new chapter.*

She made a valiant attempt to keep her voice steady but couldn't stop the waver when she agreed with the elderly ringer, 'Yes. Almost home.'

'Jim and Margaret are so excited. The boss was disappointed he couldn't make the trip to pick you up.'

It'd been decided that Blue would come because her foster parents might be recognised at the airport and blow her cover.

'Jim says he's been keeping well, but I know he'd tell me that anyway so I didn't worry. No more angina?'

'No. That heart attack was a warning. He was lucky it was a mild one.' Blue gestured towards the land to their left that was part of Hope Creek Station. 'Nothing much has changed.' He'd never been much of a conversationalist, but he continued talking in an obvious attempt to ignore the circumstances that had forced her to return. 'We've put in a few more improved pastures, but life pretty much continues as it did before you left. Marg is still making her famous scones for smoko and Jim still breaks out his harmonica every now and then to play us a tune.'

With a glance at her watch, Stella smiled. Her flight from Geneva had landed in Melbourne as dawn broke over the city and she'd slept for most of the car trip, but Blue must've set a cracking pace. 'Of course, you've timed our arrival nicely for smoko, Blue.'

'No flies on me, love.' His face, weathered from long days spent in the sun, broke into a broad, crooked-toothed smile as he took his eyes off the road for a second to wink at her.

Stella's laugh turned into a gasp as she caught the sudden movement in her peripheral vision. Her body stiffened and her fingers cramped around the car door handle. 'Roo!'

The large Eastern Grey kangaroo bounded out onto the road right in the path of the vehicle.

Stella broke into an instant sweat and braced against the dashboard, expecting impact with the animal. But, as Blue swerved, the roo maintained its path and jumped clear of them and into the bush on the other side of the road.

For a few moments, Stella couldn't breathe. Sitting back, her hands clenched into tight balls and she pressed her fingernails into her palms.

I'm completely safe.

I'm in Australia and I'm almost home.

But she couldn't dispel the images that gnashed through her brain.

Blinding camera lights flashed into the car from all angles as the vehicles of the paparazzi surrounded them in a frenzied swarm – all trying to get the shot they wanted. Relentlessly and recklessly, they hung out of their cars or rode their Vespas, yelling questions at her as their cameras clicked away.

Like bloodhounds they'd scented a story.

They'd spotted Stella leaving the venue early – and in tears – when she should've been celebrating her success.

Now, they wanted the scoop. A photo for the front pages of the tabloids would ensure them a big payday.

Even as she held her clutch bag high to hide her face, she dreaded the headlines.

'Idiots!' The driver cursed, blasting his horn.

'Slow down!' Stella demanded from the back seat as the driver increased his speed.

'I can lose them.'

'No! It's too dangerous.' Peeking out from behind the bag, she saw the Parisian footpaths were bustling with tourists and locals. 'I don't want to cause a crash.'

'We're not going to crash.'

'Slow down. I insist.'

The driver ignored her and weaved through traffic at an alarming speed, pulling away from the photographers on either side of the car as he shot through a gap between two other vehicles, only narrowly avoiding side-swiping one of them.

Horns blared.

The driver gave a cocky laugh as he took his hands off the wheel and sent a rude gesture towards another driver.

Bracing herself against the seat in front of her as terror coursed through her veins, she screamed at him. 'Stop! Please!'

Stella thought fleetingly of her parents, killed by a drunk driver in a head-on collision on the open highway in Australia.

Then, tyres screeched.

The driver slammed on the brakes.

There was a loud bang and the scream of tearing, twisting metal. A jarring collision that threw her back forcefully against the seat.

She cried out in excruciating pain before the blessed dark curtain of unconsciousness was drawn.

'Stella.' Blue's hand on her arm jolted her from the horrific memories. 'Stella!'

Opening her eyes slowly, Stella felt dazed and disoriented. She frowned as she became vaguely aware that Blue had stopped the car on the side of the road.

'Deep breaths, Stella.' She heard the note of panic in the old ringer's voice and tried to do as he urged. 'We're both fine.'

It was a struggle to get her lungs to work against the constriction of her chest, as she willed her heart to stop its rapid assault against her ribcage.

'You're okay, Stella,' he assured her again.

It was a few moments before she could speak.

'Yes. I… I'm okay, Blue. I…'

'I get it, love.' He rubbed one callused hand up and down her bare biceps in a soothing action. 'You've been through…' His voice broke. 'You've been through a hell of a lot.'

She let her head drop forward so any anguish on her face would be concealed by the curtain of her long, dark brown hair. Hearing the emotion in Blue's voice nearly broke her because she knew she was genuinely loved by everyone at Hope Creek Station. Although none of them were her blood relatives, they were all her family. They'd all been with her in spirit every step of the way, rejoicing in all her triumphs. Now, they were all feeling her trauma as though she was their daughter, or sister, or niece.

They'd been everything to her and she owed it to them to be strong.

'I… it was the roo. I just…'

'There's no need to explain, love. I'm so sorry you were startled like that. I should never have taken my eyes off the road.'

There were a lot of kangaroos in the valley, but they were generally more of a risk on the roads from dusk until dawn.

'Please, don't mention this to Margaret and Jim.' Her parents were worried enough about her and she didn't want anything adding to their stress.

He raised his fingers to his lips and made a zipping motion. 'Mum's the word.'

Stella rolled her shoulders to try to ease the stiffness that had knotted the muscles across her back.

'I'm glad you're home, Stella,' the old ringer said. 'We're all glad.'

'Me too.' Seeing the sheen of moisture in his eyes, she put her hand on his wrist for a moment before she said, 'How about we get going? We don't want to be late for smoko.'

'That would never do.' The words were spoken lightly, but she didn't miss the considering look he gave her.

Stella forced a smile. 'I'll be right as rain when I get home.'

Blue's mouth twisted a little in doubt, but he nodded as he restarted the car and pulled out onto the road.

Stella closed her mind to all her uncertainties and focused solely on the beauty of the land around her.

Nestled in the Lancaster Valley, with access to the wide and ever-flowing Dundee River, Hope Creek Station wasn't a remote cattle station in the harsh, unforgiving Australian outback. The land had been settled by migrants during the Australian gold rush. Very little gold had been discovered in the area, but some of the settlers had stayed to farm. The land was very fertile with its rich, red soil, and these days the farms in the valley were a mix of sheep, cattle – both beef and dairy – and crops and vineyards.

Marg said farm stays had become popular, and tourism was bound to grow because Jim had said that a golf course was being built on the other side of Lancaster.

Lancaster had its own agricultural university campus and a space observatory; but Hope Creek itself was still a small community, and everyone knew everybody else's business.

Everyone in the area certainly knew of her accident, but then it'd been international front-page news. People across the globe had been shocked and distressed. Stella had been touched by the amount of support that'd flooded in from all corners of the world while she'd been recovering in France and then in Switzerland.

'There she is!' Blue proclaimed warmly. 'Home sweet home.'

As they crested the hill and the homestead came into view, a sob parted Stella's lips.

Originally built in the 1850s, the homestead's sandstone block walls had been built by convicts – in fact it'd been one of the last buildings in the nation to have been made by convict labour. The pitched roof had been replaced several times and heritage green Colourbond steel had replaced the corrugated iron. The wide verandahs surrounding the house were like warm, welcoming arms reaching out to Stella, wanting to enfold her in their embrace before ushering her inside to the heart of the home.

Blue beeped the horn a couple of times to announce their arrival.

Almost instantly, and before any of the human family could respond, Ned Kelly and Ben Hall – the family's border collie dogs who were named after two famous Aussie bush rangers – came racing around the side of the verandah barking excitedly while their tails wagged furiously.

'No surprise that the two boys are first out to greet you,' Blue said as he pulled up at the gate to the house yard, turned off the engine and got out.

Stella stayed where she was for a few moments, trying to calm herself as a whole host of memories and feelings coalesced inside her.

Much the same scene had greeted her when she'd arrived as a child. At that time, the Richardsons' two dogs had been named after the famous Aussie explorers, Burke and Wills, and she'd loved those dogs to bits. Sadly, they'd long since passed away, but she'd met Ned and Ben on a few of her brief trips home and they were just as friendly.

She was looking forward to taking Ned and Ben for long walks, longer every day until she could keep up with them again.

'Welcome home, Stella!' Margaret called out as she and Jim emerged from the home, faces wreathed in smiles.

'Quiet down, boys,' Jim told the dogs firmly as they raced back and forth along the fence, anxious to be let out to greet Blue and Stella. 'Heel!'

Her parents' appearance spurred her into action. Unclasping her seat belt as Blue opened her car door, Stella couldn't wait to give the couple huge hugs. In her excitement, she completely forgot her new limitation. Thankfully, she managed to grab on to the car door to steady herself, because she lost her balance and stumbled awkwardly the instant her artificial foot hit the ground.

CHAPTER TWO

'Steady now,' Blue said from beside her as his hands shot around her waist. 'Easy does it.'

Her cheeks heated and she looked down at the ground to hide from the pity she expected to see in his eyes.

'I'm sorry,' she mumbled. 'I... I forget sometimes.'

'It's only been a few months. It'll take you a while to adjust.'

A few months...

It'd been almost five and a half months. Long, fraught months of rehabilitation where Stella pushed herself every step of the way.

Jim and Margaret must have put their running shoes on when they saw her stumble, because they were through the gate and at the car when she looked up again.

Damn. *Damn!*

Frustration at her new limitation bit deep and she tried to keep her emotions under control.

Her resolve was in danger of crumbling when she heard the strong support in Jim's deep, bass voice. 'Easy does it, Stella.'

'I'm sorry.'

'It's okay,' Jim said quietly.

Then Blue guided her over and she was in Jim's crushing embrace.

'It's so good to have you home,' Margaret said as she stood at Stella's back and joined in for a group hug.

There was so much Stella wanted to say, but it was impossible to speak.

Every breath jerked into her lungs and was let out with the same irregularity.

Tears that'd been building like heavy clouds behind her eyes finally burst and rained forth in a deluge of unstoppable sobs.

'Oh, darling Stella!' Marg cried along with her.

Everything around Stella receded as she soaked up the comfort of her parents' love.

Ever since the accident – maybe for even longer – she'd lived for this moment.

Ached for this moment.

Her world had been turned upside down and inside out, but now she was back home with the people she loved and who loved her in return.

The people who would never let her down.

Overwhelmed by the need to be comforted, she let her mask slip and allowed all her emotions pour out without fear of judgement. She wasn't sure how much time passed before she summoned the strength to grit her teeth together, will her tears away and pull out of the hug to wipe her cheeks with the back of her hands.

On a long outward breath, she told them, 'I needed that.'

Jim's voice was thick. 'I needed it too.'

'I hope you've got the kettle on, Marg,' Blue said gruffly.

Margaret sniffed loudly and wiped her eyes. 'Kettle's always on, as well you know,' she told him wryly. 'But your timing's perfect because I've just taken the scones out of the oven.'

'Now, that's what I like to hear,' Blue said.

Margaret put her arm around Stella's waist. 'Come on in, darling.'

Stella took care to lift her right leg a little higher so her prosthesis didn't drag and cause her to trip. She always had to take more care with her walking when she was fatigued.

The dogs were well trained but Ned started to whine. He was impatient to be greeted by Stella.

'You'll have to wait for a while, boy,' Stella told him. 'If I'm not sitting down when I pat you, you'll probably knock me off balance.'

'He can wait,' Jim said. 'Last thing we want is them underfoot.'

Especially the artificial foot.

'We're expecting Morgan home for dinner,' Margaret said quickly, as though she'd read Stella's mind. 'Naturally, she's anxious to see you.'

'But we won't wait dinner for her,' Jim said.

'No damn way,' Blue put in. 'She's been home late every night this week with one medical emergency or another.'

Margaret shushed him before admonishing, 'Morgan's out there helping to save lives and that's more important than being home on time for dinner!'

The Richardsons had fostered Stella, Morgan and Callie one after the other and the three girls regarded each other as sisters. Morgan was a pilot for the Royal Flying Doctor Service and flew from the RFDS base in Lancaster. She'd moved into her own home in Lancaster a few years ago, but was currently back living at the homestead while her bathroom and kitchen were being renovated.

'I spoke to Callie before I left Switzerland,' Stella said. 'She said she'd be home on the weekend.'

'Yep,' Jim confirmed. 'She'll be driving up from Melbourne straight after work on Friday afternoon. She would've been at the airport this morning to greet you but we told her you'd be keen to get in the car and get going.'

'Morgan's arranged to have the weekend off so we can have a proper family reunion,' Margaret said.

It would be great to have everyone together again.

'You said the therapists are pleased with your progress?' Jim asked.

Stella nodded. 'I used a wheelchair to get through the airport – but that was largely so that I'd blend in with the crowd and none of the paparazzi...' She shuddered as she uttered the word. 'That was so my photo wouldn't be taken by a photographer – or someone with a phone – and put on the cover of a tabloid.'

Jim let out an angry hiss. 'Damned media. I wish they'd mind their own bloody business!'

While Stella also craved privacy, she understood that fame and public interest went with the territory. 'People are curious and most want to hear a happy story of my recovery.'

'Did people recognise you?' Margaret asked.

'I doubt it!' Blue said. 'What with that baseball cap and those sunglasses, I almost walked straight past her.'

'As far as the press are concerned, you're still at a Swiss rehabilitation facility.' Although Jim spoke confidently, Stella was a lot more cynical.

While she was pleased she'd been able to make the journey to Hope Creek and not have to face a barrage of photographers as she made her way through the airport, someone was bound to have recognised her.

When she'd presented her travel documents to check-in staff at the airline and custom's officials, they'd instantly recognised her name and taken a second look. She doubted her return home would go unnoticed for long. Sooner or later she was going to have to give an interview so that she could satisfy everyone's curiosity and become yesterday's news.

'You boys stay outside,' Jim told the dogs. 'We'll let you in for a bit when Stella's settled.'

'I'll take your bags to your room,' Blue said as they entered the homestead.

'Thanks, Blue.' She stopped and breathed in the familiar scent of home – and the aroma of the scones she knew would be cooling in the kitchen.

At the side table in the entryway, Margaret had filled a vase with an arrangement of native plants from her garden. A colourful display of yellows, oranges and reds from the various callistemons, grevilleas and melaleucas were an instant homecoming welcome.

'The flowers are beautiful and the scones smell divine.'

'You'll love the rose garden, but that's for tomorrow. You've had such a long trip, you're probably dead on your feet, but—' Margaret broke off and clapped her hand over her mouth, her wide-eyed embarrassment palpable. 'Oh dear!'

'Oh Lord!' Jim muttered.

The elephant in the room had to be addressed.

Stella couldn't help but smile at their mortified expressions. With an exaggerated shake of her head she said, 'Golly, you two really know how to put your *foot* in your mouth, don't you?'

Instantly, they all laughed.

'Honestly, though,' she said as they sobered, 'the last thing I want any of you to do is pussyfoot around me.'

They looked at her again with their eyebrows raised and she realised that she'd unwittingly made another foot reference. This time it was her turn to clap her hand on her forehead. 'See what I mean? It's incredible how many expressions there are and that we use when we're trying to avoid a word or topic. *Cold feet. Best foot forward. Finding my feet.* I've groaned inwardly each time I've thought this is the perfect place to come and get *back on my feet*!'

Jim reached out a broad hand and ruffled her hair just the way he'd always done when she'd been a kid. 'Glad you haven't lost your sense of humour.'

Sobering, she looked away from them for a moment, remembering the mess she'd been in the weeks immediately following the accident. 'We all know I did lose it, but I'm happy to tell you I've regained it.'

Her parents nodded sagely. They'd been by her side through her darkest hours.

'You've had huge adjustments to make. Give yourself time,' Jim said.

There were some scars she was certain she'd carry for life. 'Nevertheless,' she said cheerily, 'I'm going to have a quick shower, then I'll come out and treat myself to a scone or two. I'll be as quick as I can.'

'No rush,' Jim told her.

'Ha!' She wagged a finger at him. 'I'll be quick or I know you and Blue will demolish all those scones between you!'

It was good to hear their laughter as she turned away and made her way down the wide hallway and to her bedroom because she knew the shock of her accident had taken a toll on them.

They'd known about her fate – about the end of her career – before she had, because they'd been with her in Paris. Regulars in her player's box for the finals of all the Grand Slam tennis tournaments she'd played in, they'd been in the centre court box at Roland Garros to watch her win her thirty-fourth grand slam tennis title.

They'd been at her side when she'd turned up for the celebration dinner but hadn't known she'd worn a smile to cover her turmoil after a life-upending conversation.They were still celebrating later, unaware she'd dashed away from the event in tears.

Margaret and Jim had been at her bedside in the hospital when she'd regained consciousness after the accident and the subsequent surgery to amputate her right foot – too badly mangled in the crash to save.

'You're alive,' Margaret had kept telling her. 'That's all that matters.'

It was more than could be said for the driver of her vehicle who'd taken it upon himself to play cat-and-mouse with the paparazzi.

The Richardsons had known before she'd even regained consciousness that she'd never again pick up a racquet and stride out onto centre court.

Never again keep the crowds enthralled with her diverse array of shots and the most powerful serve women's tennis had ever seen.

Never again hold one of the big four trophies aloft.

They'd been there through all her tears, shedding tears right alongside her and dealing with their own shock and grief.

It'd been Jim who'd broken the news to her that she'd lost her foot, but he'd left the room when Margaret had broached a different but very sensitive subject with her.

Even though Stella remembered every word of the conversations with her foster parents and the doctors, the memories were surreal. For hours she'd been numb. Hours had ticked by where everything had seemed like she was lost in a thick fog – as though she was having a nightmare and would wake up and find none of it was true.

As her losses had finally registered, the tears had been unstoppable.

Nothing could've prepared her for the shock of discovering she was an amputee. She hadn't even known how to start coping with it. There was a period of anger – demanding an answer from the universe as to why this had happened to her.

As if it hadn't been enough to cope with the aftermath of her accident, she'd had to do it without the one person she'd come to rely on most. Her fiancé, Steve, had been the person who'd been a constant in her life for twelve years – the one who'd been with her every day supporting her and mentoring her and – she'd thought – loving her. Her engagement was one more thing that lay in tatters – one more thing to come to terms with, although, surprisingly, that loss had been a mere blip on the radar in the scheme of things.

Jim had been rational. 'Yes, it's the end of your career, but it's not the end of your life.'

Margaret was all love and reassurance. 'We're here to do whatever we can to support you.'

Life had stretched in front of her as a giant void, but somehow, through her misery, Stella realised her parents were right. There were far worse things in life than losing a foot and a fiancé.

When she finally worked through the shock and denial and anger, it was guilt that ate at her for having been so self-absorbed rather than counting all of her innumerable blessings.

The Richardsons had travelled with her from Paris to

Switzerland to settle her into the rehab facility. Her prosthesis had been fitted and she'd begun to learn to walk with it. Callie had also managed to take leave from her job in Australia and had flown to be by her side, and Morgan – who hadn't been able to get leave – had phoned her every day. But as the first two months had dragged and Stella had seen a counsellor to work through her initial grief, she'd sent her foster family home and kept them up to speed about her progress through daily videocalls.

There'd been one other visitor from Hope Creek to see her while she'd been at the rehab facility.

Liz Burton, the Richardson's close friend and neighbour, had been in Europe promoting her latest book. Making a special detour to Switzerland so she could visit Stella, Liz had been more than supportive.

Understanding Stella would be feeling hopelessly lost, Liz had made her a business proposition that had provided an exciting, new direction.

Stella had signed on the dotted line before Liz had left Switzerland, and tomorrow she'd re-visit Hope Creek Farm. She'd already made concrete plans for how she wanted to develop her new investment, and the Development Application had been fast-tracked through Lancaster Council. Earthmovers would roll in as early as next week to grade the land, then the builders would start the following week.

It was all happening.

She was determined to move forward with her life.

CHAPTER THREE

The door to Liz Burton's farmhouse swung open.

'Stella!'

Faced with broad shoulders and six feet five inches of muscle-packed athlete's frame, Stella's eyes widened. She stood statue-still, her heart the only thing in her body that appeared to be functioning – and it pounded so furiously it would surely crack a rib any second.

No!

It can't be!

But there was no mistaking his deep, attractive voice with its soft hint of American accent.

No denying the familiarity of those broad shoulders and the memory of how his strong arms had held her against his oh-so-divinely masculine chest.

She didn't want to look up into eyes she knew were as deep blue as the Pacific Ocean, but there was no escaping them.

No way could she run and nowhere to hide from this encounter.

No way she could ignore the little frissons of awareness that danced up and down along her spine.

'Mitch.' Her sharp intake of breath was jerky.

What is he doing here?

His life was thousands of kilometres away.

Thousands of kilometres away from her.

Why on earth had he chosen now to come and visit again?

They stood staring at each other, then both started talking awkwardly over the top of each other.

'I didn't realise you were home.'

'I... I had no idea you were visiting your aunt.'

Liz hadn't given Stella any warning that her nephew was back in Australia when they'd spoken on the phone earlier and arranged for her to drop by.

Why hadn't Margaret or Jim warned her?

They must surely have known Mitch was back for a visit?

Heavens, the whole of Hope Creek must know.

His gaze lowered to the shoe which covered her prosthetic foot. 'I was shocked to hear about your accident.'

Her vocal cords seized up completely, so she simply nodded.

Had it really been ten years since they'd seen each other?

In this moment, it seemed like yesterday, and although Stella thought she'd moved on,

her heart suddenly felt as though it was caged in barbed wire.

She swallowed as she drank in the strong, square jaw and well-defined cheekbones that were so familiar to her – familiar yet, somehow different? She struggled to identify the change. Perhaps the planes of his face were a little harsher? Or was it the sexy stubble along the jaw line that made the difference? He'd always been clean-shaven at college.

Don't just stand there gawping. Say something!

'I... sorry. I'm...' He shook his head. 'I wasn't expecting to see you at the front door and I've forgotten my manners. Come in and have a seat. Liz is on the phone to her agent at the moment, but she's already been talking for a while, so she shouldn't be long.'

'I phoned her this morning. She knew I was coming.' Her words sounded defensive to her own ears as he gestured for her to go ahead of him into the house. 'She didn't say anything about you being home.'

All the while she spoke, she took care to lift her right foot up off the ground properly. The last thing she wanted was to stumble in front of Mitch who still epitomised masculine physical perfection.

'I wasn't told you were back, either. I thought you were still in Switzerland.'

So, he'd known that much about her, she registered as she continued into the room and sank into a comfortable armchair.

When he sat down opposite her, it was an effort to speak because she found herself drinking in every detail of his appearance. It was hard to grapple with her reaction and realise that after such a long lapse of time she was still so aware of him.

Not just aware.

Mitchell Scott was still the most handsome guy she'd ever met and her blood seemed to flow faster through her veins just from her being in the same room with him.

How could she still react this way when he'd betrayed her so badly?

'How's the football going?' The words were stilted – uttered because she had to say something and it was better to talk about him than have him ask her questions she didn't want to answer.

'I retired at the end of last season.'

It wasn't anything she didn't know. She just didn't want him to know she knew.

Maybe she was a masochist at heart because she hadn't been able to help but follow his amazing career all this time.

'I see.' She shifted a little in the chair. 'So, what's next for you?'

I'm only being polite. I don't really care.

'Now I'm no longer tied to football, it's time to settle down.'

The barbed wire cage around her heart pulled tighter, cutting into her as she thought of Mitch settling down.

Once, they'd planned to settle down together after their professional sporting careers had ended.

They'd planned to have a family...

As far as she was aware, there were no indications in the media that he'd been in another serious relationship since his divorce. Had he kept a new lover under wraps?

Was he planning to remarry?

'How long are you here?' She told herself she was only forcing out another polite question and that she didn't really want to know.

'Actually, I've moved to Hope Creek.'

Stella's eyes widened and she felt her jaw go slack again. 'Here? You've moved *here*?'

'Yep.'

That couldn't be right. 'But... why? What will you do here?'

The edges of his eyes crinkled as he smiled and she realised he was amused by her gaping disbelief. Annoyed, she clamped her teeth together.

'It hasn't been announced yet, but I bought the old pub from Bill Hickson and I plan to run it.'

No.

He couldn't be serious.

'I...' Words failed her.

'Probably about time I put my economics major to some use,' he added.

Why hadn't anyone told her Mitch was back – that he now owned the pub, for heaven's sake?

'I can't believe it. Jim and Margaret... Liz... nobody told me.'

He shrugged those broad shoulders of his. 'It's only just a done deal. Although I've been in contact with Bill for a while, I only signed the dotted line yesterday. Bill's wanted to keep it under wraps until he makes the big announcement this Saturday night, but you're right – it's amazing word hasn't already travelled through the town, although I've been sticking close to the farm since I arrived.'

Stella's mind spun with the news.

It was bad enough that he'd decided to move back here but even worse that he'd bought the pub. Hope Creek was such a small community and the hotel was pretty much the heart of the place – where everyone met and mingled.

If she was going to be a member of the community, there was no way she could stay away from the hotel, which meant there'd be no way of avoiding him.

'If you plan on moving back here, it looks like we'll be neighbours again, Stella.'

Her eyes narrowed. 'Members of the same community,' she asserted. 'We'll hardly be neighbours with you living at the hotel.' A deep sense of foreboding accompanied the unease that skittered down her spine. 'At least, I assume you'll live in the manager's residence at the pub?'

'No. I've bought into Hope Farm, so this will be my home.'

Her head jerked back so sharply it's a wonder she didn't get whiplash.

'No.' She shook her head as she frowned at him. '*No*,' she repeated more firmly. '*I've bought into Hope Farm*. This is going to be *my home*.'

'What?' His confusion mirrored hers.

'Actually, you've both bought Hope Farm,' Liz announced casually as she walked into the room. 'Hello, Stella.'

'Liz?' Stella was so confused, she didn't even think to acknowledge the greeting from the slender, brunette woman. 'What's going on? What are you talking about?'

'It's simple.' Liz perched on the arm of a different armchair. 'You each own fifty per cent of the farm.'

Stella repeated the words in her head, sure she couldn't have heard Liz correctly.

When Stella looked at Mitch in question, she saw he looked shell-shocked. Then, he jumped to his feet and glowered down at his aunt. *'What the hell?'*

His quietly grated words were more effective in communicating his fury than if had he boomed them.

'I told each of you I was only prepared to sell you a fifty percent share of the farm,' Liz said calmly.

No.

No. No. *No.*

Denial beat a steady tattoo through her veins.

'I assumed, when you offered me a half-share, you weren't prepared to sell me the property in its entirety,' Mitch said tightly, 'because you wanted to keep half for yourself!'

'Both of you wanted Hope Farm. This way, you both have it.' She made a sweeping gesture with her arm towards Stella. 'You get to build your tennis courts and develop part of this property as a tennis centre for under-privileged kids while you,' she gestured to Mitch, 'have always wanted to live here, so you get to enjoy the quiet lifestyle Hope Creek offers.'

Mitch wanted a quiet lifestyle?

Since when?

When they'd been teenagers, they'd both said they wanted to return to Hope Creek one day, but that'd been a long time ago. That'd been before he'd returned to the land of his birth and become a famous quarterback.

He had no business returning here.

Besides, he'd used some of the extraordinary wealth he'd accumulated from professional football to establish a chain of exclusive nightclubs in major cities all through the United States and even in Europe and the United Kingdom.

As a multi-millionaire and with a nightclub empire to run, how could he live in Hope Creek?

'No way!' Mitch vented as one hand sliced through the air. 'This is not on. I can't believe you've tried to pull a stunt like this.'

'It's done, Mitchell.' There was neither remorse nor smugness in Liz's tone.

Being careful with how she moved so she didn't pitch forward unsteadily, Stella stood. 'This can't be legal, Liz.'

'It's all perfectly legal.' Mitch's aunt folded her arms across her chest. 'You both knew you were buying a fifty per cent share in the farm. You both have the right to develop your half of the property as you see fit. If it doesn't work out harmoniously after two years, you each have the right to negotiate buying the other person out. If no agreement can be reached at that point – either each of you keeping half the title, or one of you selling to the other – I have the option of buying you both out for the market value of the day and regaining the entire property. It was all outlined in the contract.'

'But I thought *you* owned the other fifty per cent,' Mitch pointed out to his aunt.

'My contract didn't mention Liz's name directly. It referred to 'the other party'.' Stella shook her head at Liz. 'I did assume it was you, Liz. There was no mention of Mitch owning the other half.'

'You're right, specific names weren't mentioned, but what's the difference who owns the other half of the property?' Liz demanded a little impatiently. 'You're both adults. You've known each other for years. Are you telling me you can't share the ownership of Hope Farm amicably?'

There was a challenge in her voice and it had Stella squirming, but Mitch wasn't backing down.

'You know very well it makes a difference because you know Stella and I were more than friends and that we didn't part *amicably*.'

Stella had to swallow down on all her regrets as she remembered their final meeting.

'That was over a decade ago.' There was an edge of exasperation In Liz's words. 'For heaven's sake, you were barely out of your teens. You've both grown up since then. Don't tell me you haven't moved past that time in your lives?'

'Of course we have,' Stella interjected rather too quickly. 'But—'

'If you didn't anticipate either of us would have a problem

with this arrangement, why didn't you tell us straight out that we'd be co-owners?' Mitch demanded.

Liz wasn't at all cowed. 'Because I know you're both stubborn as hell and don't know what's good for you!'

'It was always my understanding I'd either inherit or buy one hundred percent of Hope Farm. That was always our arrangement, Liz.' One of the veins in Mitch's neck became more prominent and Stella guessed he was keeping a very tight rein on his fury. 'You always said you wanted to keep it in the family.'

'You're an owner, Mitchell.' Liz didn't appear fazed in the face of Mitch's arguments. 'It's still in the family.'

'You can't—' Mitch started to protest but Liz cut right across him.

'I can and I have. You're both adults who love this farm and this community. Once, you loved each other.' She pointed her finger at each of them as though she was a teacher addressing two errant students. 'Do yourselves a favour and make it work!'

Before either of them could respond to the outrageous declaration, an exuberant sandy-haired boy ran into the room with a scruffy brown puppy hot on his heels.

Having seen photos of the boy on the internet, Stella recognised him in an instant and her heart twisted painfully.

'Dad! I think the goat's about to have her kid!'

CHAPTER FOUR

Mitch's demeanour changed instantly – every ounce of aggravation evaporating. 'That's awesome!'

'Oh yes! The vet said she'd be due about now,' Liz answered as she stood up. 'It might even be twins. How exciting you're going to be here to welcome them into the world.'

The ten-year-old started to tell his great-aunt about the moans the goat was making when the puppy noticed Stella and started barking.

The boy's eyes widened when he followed the dog's gaze. 'Stella Simpson!' He looked questioningly from Stella to his father and to Liz.

'Hello.'

Mitchell cleared his throat and told his son, 'I think I've told you Stella grew up at the station next door.' Moving closer to the boy, he put a proud – maybe even protective? – hand on his son's shoulder. 'Stella, this is my son, Kade.'

His son.

Kade.

The boy whose conception had ripped them apart.

Say something, Stella.

'It's nice to meet you, Kade.' Manners forced the reluctant words through her taut vocal cords.

'Kade's enjoying exploring the farm, aren't you, buddy?' Mitch's expression was full of warmth as he looked at his son.

'I love it!'

'Why don't we go out and check on the nanny, Kade?' Liz suggested quickly. 'We don't want to miss the birth and sometimes it can all be over quite quickly.'

'Um…' It was clear Kade was torn – wanting to stay but not wanting to miss the birth. 'Will you be here for a while?' he asked Stella.

Absolutely not.

The faster she got out of here the better.

'I'm not sure.'

'If she's not, I'm sure you'll be seeing her around, Kade. Hope Creek isn't a big place.' As though Mitch had read her thoughts, his words warned there was no escaping the inevitable.

'You've moved back here?' Mitch's son looked delighted at the prospect.

'Yes.'

'I guess I'll be seeing you then,' the boy said hopefully.

Stella's heart sank and she had to force a smile as she made a non-committal, 'Probably.'

Was the universe enjoying kicking her while she was down?

Liz didn't give Kade a chance to say anything more. She chatted to the boy about the goats as she ushered him and the exuberant pup out through the back door, ignoring Mitchell's warning. 'Don't think this is the end of our discussion, Liz.'

Once they were gone, an awkward silence stretched between Stella and Mitchell.

She raised one hand to her temple and exerted a bit of pressure on the area that was starting to thud. 'I need to sit down.'

He glanced at her prosthetic foot. 'Of course.'

It wasn't her prosthesis that was causing her need to sit. It was sheer shock – one shock after another, actually.

'Can I get you a glass of water?'

'Thanks, but I'm okay. Well, as okay as I can be in this

situation. I have no idea what to say about what Liz has done,' she told him when she was sitting again. 'I can't believe any of this.'

'She's finally flipped!'

Stella doubted it. 'No. The way she worded our contracts and kept our names out of it, she's thought this out.' As embarrassing as it was, it had to be acknowledged. 'She's trying to... force us together.'

'Her motives are all too embarrassingly transparent, but we're not characters from one of her romance novels. She's living in the past.'

Stella felt the heat sweeping from her chest to her cheeks. It was beyond embarrassing. She'd been fifteen and Mitch had been sixteen when they'd started dating.

Liz had done everything she could to support their relationship.

Five years later, when Liz had found out they were splitting up, she'd been straight on the phone to Stella trying to see if she could get them back together. For years, every time Stella had come home to Hope Creek, Liz had broached the subject of a possible reconciliation – regardless of the fact that Mitch had married Kade's mother and Stella had become engaged to her tennis coach.

Mitch was right.

Stella had read some of Liz's romance novels and this was shaping up to read like a plot line from one of her best-selling books. An incurable romantic, Liz had obviously hatched this plot and thought she'd force a happily ever after ending.

'We've both moved on,' Mitch said firmly before he demanded, 'Why did you buy into the farm? You knew I always wanted this property.'

Truth was, she hadn't even stopped to think about Mitch when Liz had offered her the deal. Now she felt guilt bubble up inside her as he regarded her accusingly. Reacting defensively, she let out an exasperated huff of breath. 'Oh, come on, Mitchell! That was something you talked about in your teens. It was another lifetime ago.' She made agitated gestures with her hands as she spoke. 'You're American. I can't believe you're serious about settling here.'

'I'm serious alright.' He gestured towards her. 'You know I've always been an Aussie at heart.'

'But your life is in America.'

'I didn't grow up there. My life's only been in America for the last thirteen years, and only because of the football.'

She was about to point out that he had parents and an ex-wife and son who lived in the US, but didn't get a chance.

'Why are you settling here? I can't believe your fiancé is happy to move here permanently.'

Mention of Steve pulled her up short. Her right hand moved subconsciously to cover her left hand and the diamond ring she still wore on her ring finger. She really needed to take it off now she was home and wasn't in any danger of being besieged by photographers.

'He always struck me as a big city lights kind of guy,' Mitch continued. 'Surely, he's going to be bored out of his skull here?'

Stella shifted uncomfortably in her chair.

Their breakup would probably emerge in the next six months, but she had no intention of revealing the truth to Mitchell now. As for Steve being bored here, Mitch was right. There's no way he'd settle here. He'd always referred to it as a 'backwater.'

'Is he in Hope Creek with you?'

'Not at the moment.' Ignoring Mitchell's one raised eyebrow, she said, 'This is obviously an untenable situation for both of us. What are we going to do about it?'

He didn't hesitate. 'I'm going to buy you out.'

'I'm not sinking money into the development only to have you buy me out at the end of two years.'

'I'm not talking about two years. I'm talking about right now.' His strong, tanned hand slashed through the air as he underlined his stance.

Despite being worth millions in her own right from all her tournament wins and sponsorship deals, Stella knew Mitchell was substantially wealthier. But she didn't want to be bought out and she didn't even think it was possible at this point.

She'd pinned her future on Hope Farm. It'd been the motivation for her to get through her rehab as quickly as possible. 'My development application has already been approved. I have earthmoving contractors rolling in here on Monday and construction starting the following week.'

'Developers? Hell! Why the bloody hell didn't Liz tell me?' He paced back and forth a few times before he sat opposite her. Although he appeared to be trying to calm himself, his expression was so intense she felt as though his blue eyes were pinning her to the chair. 'I want this farm, Stella, and if you're fair, you'll admit I have more claim to it than you do. It's been in my mother's family for four generations.' He raised his large, tanned hands and wiped them down his face in a gesture of exasperation. 'I should've been consulted about this.'

'Obviously, Liz kept both of us in the dark.' She still held on to the slim hope that this was all some warped joke. 'But you can't be serious about settling in Hope Creek.'

'Why wouldn't I be?'

In contrast to the sharpness of his words, she tried to keep her voice light. 'You talk about Steve missing the bright lights, but you've been based in L.A. for years. This is a far cry from there. I wouldn't have expected Hope Creek to be your pace.'

'We haven't seen each other in a long time.' There was a flash of hostility across his features. 'It's presumptuous of you to assume you know my *pace*.'

She took a deep breath, reasoning that perhaps she'd never truly known the real Mitchell. She'd thought she'd fallen in love with an honest, straightforward guy who loved and cherished her. Her discovery of his betrayal had left her gutted. 'I've heard you own a string of glitzy nightclubs all through Europe and the US. This area has absolutely no nightlife.'

'My nightclubs were a good investment. It doesn't

mean they represent my lifestyle.' His gaze bored into hers. 'Anyway, I'm in the process of selling them.'

Oh.

A terrible thought struck her. 'Oh, good grief, Mitch! Hope Creek Hotel is nothing like your nightclubs. I hope you're not going to try to turn it into something flash. The Hope Creek community will never stand for it.'

The exasperated roll of his eyes told her she was mistaken. 'Restore it to its former glory? Yes. Modernise it and lose its charm? No way,' he said in defence. 'Apart from a fresh coat of paint and some new carpet, there's nothing I want to change about the hotel. Hell, Stella! As if I'd try to change the flavour of the local drinking hole!'

Every vertebra in her spine locked into place in indignation. 'It's more than a drinking hole. It's a place for the whole community to gather. It's got history and…'

'Exactly. If you ever knew me at all you'd know I value this community and its way of life. It's the reason I'm back.' He shook his head. 'When Liz told me Bill Hickson was trying to sell the pub but hadn't been able to find a buyer, I jumped at the chance.' He looked at her intensely again for a moment. 'You know I was never into nightclubs.'

No. He'd never been interested in going to nightclubs.

He'd never been a huge drinker either.

Except for the one night that had changed their lives forever.

Don't go there, Stella.

The past is past.

Leave it there.

'I know this farm belonged to your mother's parents but—'

'It belonged to them and it's special to me. Liz always promised she'd give me the first option when it was time to sell.'

His words made her feel guilty, yet it wasn't her fault Liz had broken her word to him.

'The older I get, the more I realise that I identify more

with the Australian half of me than I do with the American half. I've continued to visit because of Aunt Liz and because I've always loved the Australian lifestyle. The lifestyle in California isn't as real to me.'

'I'm sure your father wouldn't like to hear that.'

'It's the truth and I don't give a damn what my father likes.'

Stella was surprised at the vehemence in his words. She knew he and his parents had never been particularly close, but there was genuine hostility and even a trace of bitterness to Mitchell's words – the way he'd uttered the word 'father' had made it sound as though he despised the powerful man who was now speaker of the United States House of Representatives.

With less hostility he said, 'If you remember, I always maintained Hope Creek felt like home to me.'

It was true, and probably unsurprising since he'd spent his childhood moving from one country to another every two to three years as his father had taken up various diplomatic posts. Hope Creek had been his one constant throughout his childhood and adolescence.

Why hadn't she considered this?

Probably because Mitch had returned to the United States to play American football when he'd been eighteen, and he'd spent all his life there since. Challenging him, she stated baldly, 'There's no Grid-iron in Australia, and I know you didn't want to play Aussie Rules football.'

It was why he'd chosen to play rugby union when he'd left school here in Australia, even though the state of Victoria was mad keen on the Aussie Rules code.

'American football was my career and it's over. But it's only a part of who I am. It's not all of me any more than tennis is all of you.'

She knew him well enough to understand exactly what he meant, although his reference to her tennis struck a raw nerve.

'Hope Creek is full of happy memories for me.' He looked

away from her for a moment and she wondered whether he was remembering all the happy times they'd spent together. When he met her gaze again he added, 'It was here I came to understand what family was all about.'

Her heart ached for him because she knew he'd felt unwanted by his own parents.

Growing up as the only child of career diplomats who'd transferred from one part of the world to another in the pursuit of furthering their careers, Mitch had been flown to Hope Creek each school holidays to stay with his Aunt Lizzie. It was during her first year with the Richardsons that Stella had met him.

Even though he'd been thirteen to her twelve, and a boy to her girl at an age when awareness of the opposite sex was starting to kick in, they'd become firm friends and spent almost every waking moment together out of school hours.

Then, when his parents had been transferred to the American Embassy in Iraq, Liz had persuaded his mother – her sister – to send him to school in Australia to finish his education. It was during those years, when they were aged sixteen and fifteen respectively, that their friendship had developed into a teenage crush.

Mitch had been her first boyfriend.

The first boy to hold her hand.

The first boy to kiss her.

Momentarily, she closed her eyes, her mouth dried and all her limbs went weak as she remembered the surreal experience of that kiss.

Oh Lord.

A few years later, when she'd finished her final year at high school and followed him to college in America on a sports scholarship, he'd been her first lover.

Oh no! Eyelids snapping back open, her cheeks burned even hotter and hot arrows of awareness rushed much lower when she saw him looking at her lips.

Was he remembering their kisses too?

Doubtful.

The legendary NFL quarterback had surely kissed too many lips over the years to remember hers?

'You wanted to develop a tennis centre here?'

His question jolted her.

'I *have approval* to build a tennis centre. I'm going to run camps for talented but underprivileged kids to have expert coaching. It's why I now own half the property.' She waved her hands in front of her in exasperation. 'The plans are already in motion!'

'It's out of the question.' His lips twisted. 'I know this farm is right next door to where you grew up, but apart from that, you could buy any property, anywhere, to develop this idea.'

'But Hope Creek is a special community. It's my home. You know as well as I do that land rarely comes up for sale here, so finding somewhere else close by will be next to impossible for me. Local land is mostly passed on to the next generation of farmers.'

'Exactly. I'm the next generation. That's why it's only fair that I own Hope Creek farm and keep it in the family.'

An impasse.

Her conscience told her she should cede.

No!

Mitchell Scott had destroyed her dreams for the future once. She was damned if she'd let him do it again.

'You can't need the whole farm for commercial reasons and I don't need to put tennis courts over the whole property. We could agree for you to keep to your half and I keep to mine.' It was less than ideal. She'd rather he high-tailed it back to America, but if he was determined to settle here…

'Are you proposing we'd avoid each other?' he asked.

'We can hardly do that if we're both living in a place the size of Hope Creek,' she admitted. She immediately consoled herself with her belief that Mitch wouldn't settle here permanently. He was used to fans chasing him for autographs and selfies. Used to glowing accolades and attention. He'd get bored here soon enough.

You're used to the same level of attention, but you couldn't wait to leave it all behind, her inner voice pointed out. *Why should it be any different for him?*

'No.' His tone was adamant.

'I don't even need half the farm,' she added quickly. 'I just need enough for half a dozen tennis courts, some cabins, a gym and a swimming pool.'

'Geez, Stella.' His jaw firmed.

'The relatively small parcel of land I need would have hardly any bearing on the running of the farm.' She focused on a vase of daisies that were on a lace doily in the middle of the coffee table between them, rather than looking into his eyes. 'Planning this has been front and centre of my mind ever since Liz came to visit me in Switzerland. Everything is in place and it's going to be so good to give back to the tennis community.'

What she didn't say, but what she thought he would understand, was that this had motivated her to finish her rehab. It didn't matter that she'd made so much money she didn't have to work again. She needed a project to put her heart and soul into.

'If you and your fiancé are adamant about returning to Hope Creek, speak to Jim and Margaret. I'm sure the Richardsons can set aside enough land for your project.'

She ignored his reference to Steve and forced her gaze to meet his as she told him firmly, 'I want to stand on my own two feet.'

Oh damn!

His gaze dipped towards her artificial foot, then he cleared his throat and his eyes focused back on her face. A flush ran under his tanned skin, as though he was embarrassed to have looked there.

'It's important to me to be independent,' she rushed out. 'It's why I bought this land. It keeps me close to my family but still able to live separately.'

'Co-ownership isn't going to work,' he stated. 'I'll talk to Liz and make her see sense. If she doesn't budge, I'll contact my lawyers this afternoon and see what can be done about buying out your share. Meanwhile, I suggest you cancel the earth movers and either speak to Margaret and Jim, or approach Bob and June Lynch.' He referred to the owners of the property that bordered the other side of Hope Creek Station. 'See if they'll sell you a parcel of land for your tennis centre.'

She gritted her teeth and stood up. Mitchell had always been stubborn and once his mind was made up, that was the end of it. In fairness, he did have a moral right to the ownership of the entire farm.

Darn Liz and her interference!

'Clearly, there's nothing more to say at this point,' she grated out.

* * *

Mitchell nodded and followed Stella to the front door.

Damn, but she'd always turned his insides to mush and sent his libido into overdrive. She was still as attractive as hell – hazel eyes burning with fury and back ramrod straight as she made her exit.

Stella Simpson had always managed to get under his skin and right now he wanted to take her in his arms and kiss her senseless – partly to get rid of that anger that seemed to be fusing her spine together and partly because he just wanted to give in to this need that thrummed through him. He wanted to reacquaint himself with every heavenly inch of her beautiful body.

Hell.

A decade on.

Ten years of separation and what seemed like a lifetime of different experiences that they'd had individually, yet there was still a strong need in him that yearned for this woman who'd been his first lover.

She's not yours anymore.

It was true, but it didn't stop him feeling as though she was the other half of his whole – as though none of his life had been as meaningful since the day Stella had broken up with him.

She's engaged.

Engaged to a man who didn't deserve her.

What sort of guy let Stella, who must surely still be feeling vulnerable after her accident and the loss of not only her foot, but her career, travel to Australia alone?

If Stella had been Mitch's fiancée, he would not only have married her years ago – he'd be at her side right now supporting her as she made this transition to life outside her professional tennis career.

Stella dumped you.

Stella put her tennis career before your relationship.

Yeah. She had.

It still rankled.

He'd always wondered whether her feelings for her coach had been developing even while she'd been going out with him.

Then again, he'd never liked Steve Carter. From the moment Stanford University had appointed the guy as Stella's coach there'd been an undercurrent of dislike between him and the slightly older man. It'd seemed to Mitch that Steve had done everything he could to keep boyfriend and girlfriend apart – arranging for Stella to play tournaments when Mitch was at home between football games, then opting out of tournaments so she could resume her studies when Mitch was away.

In retrospect, his suspicions didn't seem far-fetched.

It might be fanciful but Mitch had always suspected Steve had angled for their breakup. Carter struck him as an opportunist. He'd stolen the limelight, intimating that Stella's meteoric rise to the top and her continued successes since she'd reached the top had been all his doing.

The guy had an ego as big as Mount Rushmore.

No way was her fiancé going to be happy playing coach to a bunch of underprivileged kids at a rurally located tennis camp. But how was Mitchell going to cope living here when Stella and Steve were a stone's throw away? Constantly running into them was going to be sheer, bloody, torturous hell.

His lips tightened and he raised his palms and ran them over his face.

His gut roiled.

When Stella told him it was over, he should've done more to persuade her they were meant to be together. He should've never let her go.

You were a fool, Mitchell Scott.

But even as he told himself that, he had to acknowledge that her breaking up with him had been easier on him in the end and the way things had turned out, it'd saved her from a lot of heartache and left his path clear to do what he'd believed was the only thing he could do in the circumstances.

CHAPTER FIVE

'You're a fool, Mitchell Scott,' his aunt railed at him when she returned to the house after leaving Kade with the newly born kid triplets and the energetic Jax.

'You're the one who's being foolish, Lizzie. The teenage first crush between Stella and me was over when we were still at Stanford.'

'Rubbish!' Liz marched back and forth across the worn wooden kitchen floorboards while shaking her head vehemently. 'You two were destined for each other.'

Mitchell groaned. 'You've written too many romance novels and you're starting to blur the lines between fact and fiction. You can't write a part for real people and expect them to play it.' Staring her down, he had to stop his fists from clenching at his sides when he thought of Steve Carter. 'You're also forgetting that Stella has her future mapped out with someone else.'

A small smile tugged at Liz's mouth before she pressed her lips together and raised both eyebrows. 'Has she?'

'Reality check, Liz,' he bit out in frustration. 'She's engaged.'

'No. She's not.'

What?

The normally strong, steady rhythm of his heart skipped a

beat and his breathing became shallow before reality crashed back.

This was not one of Liz's books where she could change the outcome for someone with the stroke of a pen or a few taps on her keyboard.

'She's no longer engaged,' Liz emphasised as he stared at her.

Instant denial sprang to his lips because it would be too hard to believe what Liz said only to find out she was wrong. 'Despite what you may wish, she's engaged to Steve Carter. We were just talking about him moving here.'

He pulled himself up trying to remember what she'd said. His heart beat a little faster when he realised she hadn't actually addressed the issue. She'd simply deflected the conversation onto Mitch's plans to settle here.

'They're not engaged anymore,' Liz insisted.

'Then why is she still wearing his ring on her finger?' The bloody huge diamond had sparkled tauntingly at him every time she'd gestured with her hands as she'd argued with him in Lizzie's sitting room. The first mention of her fiancé's name and the fingertips of her right hand had flown to the ring as though she was seeking a closer connection to him.

'Because she doesn't want the press to know. She wants some privacy as she heals.' Liz muttered something derogatory about the paparazzi under her breath before she said sympathetically, 'Stella needs time to get her life back on track before the world realises her engagement to that low-life opportunist is over. Last thing she needs now is for the press hounds to come looking for her again.'

He felt his jaw slacken. 'You're certain she's broken up with Carter?'

Liz's mouth twisted a bit and she leaned against the kitchen bench before she said, 'I probably shouldn't be repeating this because Margaret told me in absolute confidence but…' She drew in a breath and it whooshed out as she said, 'The relationship is most definitely over.'

Even as he was pleased to hear it, he felt gutted for Stella because he was certain she and Carter had definitely been an item when she'd taken to the court at Roland Garros.

'When? Don't tell me the bastard dumped her after her accident.' As if Stella wouldn't have had enough to come to terms with given her amputation and the end of her career, without coping with the end of her relationship as well.

'It ended that night, yes.'

He swore.

Against all logic his mind said, *You should've been there for her.*

When he'd heard the news of Stella's horrific accident, his first instinct had been to grab a bag, throw some things together and race to the airport so he could jump on a plane and fly to France to be by her side.

He'd reached his bedroom door before he'd come to his senses and reminded himself that Stella wasn't his to care for.

Wasn't his to love.

It was totally out of the question – completely irrational – that he go haring off to Paris to be by her side.

'What a bastard to break up with her then,' he grated through clenched teeth.

'According to Margaret, Stella knew it was over just before the accident.'

'He didn't break up with her because of her amputation, then?'

'Apparently the relationship had been... well, I won't say any more except that it would've been over even if there'd been no accident.'

That announcement made his eyes widen. 'They looked as though they were still a couple at the French Open.'

'I've already said more than I should've,' Liz continued, 'but I'll tell you one more thing. Let me just say that she'd finally discovered his true colours right before she went on her ill-fated taxi ride through Paris.'

Mitchell found his next breath easier to take. It was as

though a vice had been squeezing his lungs since he'd first opened the door and seen Stella, and now the pressure was easing.

'Did she break it off or did he?'

Liz hesitated. 'She told him it was over, but... no. I won't say more. If you want to know, you'll have to ask Stella.'

Damn!

Why is it so important you know? his inner voice demanded.

His inner voice knew the answer.

Stella may not be engaged but that didn't mean she wasn't still in love with Carter.

He thrust his hands into the pockets of his trousers as he turned Liz's bombshell over in his mind.

'Why did—?'

'No more questions.' Liz put her hand up to stop his question. 'If you want any more answers you'll have to get them from Stella. All I'll say is that the door is well and truly open for you.'

He opened his mouth to deny that he wanted the door to be open but his mind flashed back to his reactions to Stella.

Liz started to fill the electric kettle. 'Cuppa, Mitch?'

'I should go and check on Kade.'

'Kade's fine and perfectly safe. He's fascinated with the kids and he knows not to go too close to them while they're with their mother.' She reached for the cannister of tea. 'Have some tea, then you can go out and share in his excitement.'

Mitchell nodded. Then he was quiet for a moment, turning everything over in his mind.

Yes, he was still attracted to Stella but she hadn't shown any signs she was feeling the same way.

Could he rekindle what they'd had?

You're a fool, Mitchell.

What you had was an illusion.

She let you down badly the one time you needed her most.

He didn't want to put himself in that position again,

especially now he had Kade to consider. Yet, the attraction he felt for her...

Shaking himself, he told himself he was a realist, not a romantic like his aunt. 'What you've done with these property contracts is wrong and misguided. It's ancient history between Stella and me, Liz.'

Ticking her points off against her fingers as she spoke, his aunt launched her defence. 'What I know is that Stella was completely heartsick when you moved to Melbourne to play rugby union the year after you finished school, and she was heartbroken when you moved to Stanford.'

'Oh, for goodness sake! We were kids – hardly old enough to feel real love.'

Liar, he told himself. The connection he'd had with Stella had been there right from when he'd met her in his early teenage years. No, they were too young then for it to have been love, but they'd certainly clicked instantly and over time their feelings – their trust – had deepened until they'd become closest friends. They'd spent so much time talking together – sharing all the little things in their lives as well as their fears and their dreams. They'd discussed their happy and sad times and opened up to each other in a way Mitch had never been able to open up to anyone else.

As hormones had kicked in, so had attraction and it'd been the most natural thing in the world for them to eventually become lovers.

Desire still held him firmly in its grip and he had to exert phenomenal control to banish those memories and stamp out the flames of sexual need that licked through him.

The sex between them had always been amazing.

Nothing since had even come close to being all-consuming and all-fulfilling. He'd believed making love with Stella had been a blending of hearts, bodies and souls.

Yes, he was a fool.

He'd believed a lot of things.

He'd believed it was fate that'd brought them together.

It'd seemed predestined that the two of them had met in Hope Creek, and both had dreams of becoming sporting champions. Neither of them had wavered in their commitment to those dreams. They'd shared the understanding of the degree of training, focus and discipline it would take to turn those dreams into reality. They'd spurred each other on.

Mitch had dreamed he might take after his paternal grandfather – a legendary quarterback in the NFL – and Stella had wanted to honour the memory of her parents by holding the Wimbledon trophy aloft and fulfilling their dream of her becoming number one women's tennis player in the world.

Both of them had succeeded and become internationally recognised sporting stars but if it'd been destiny, then destiny was sure having one hell of a laugh at them now.

'Are you listening to anything I'm saying, Mitchell?' Liz's accompanying foot stamp got his attention. 'Stella was over the moon when she got the scholarship to Stanford.'

'But you were the one who orchestrated that, too, weren't you Liz?'

'No. I facilitated it.' She took a couple of brightly coloured mugs out of a cupboard. 'I didn't orchestrate it. She wanted it with every fibre of her being.'

He looked beyond her and out through the kitchen window where a magpie had landed on the verandah rail and now appeared to be listening to every word they were saying. 'It was an adventure as well as a golden opportunity for her tennis,' he said half to Liz and half to the magpie. 'Having me – someone she already knew – at Stanford only made it easier for her to pack up and travel halfway across the world.'

He looked back at his aunt and was startled by the ferocity of her expression.

'I've never heard such rubbish.' Liz glared at him. 'If it wasn't compulsory to wear a helmet in gridiron, I'd think you'd had too many blows to the head, Mitchell Scott! Yes, she wanted to pursue her tennis but the scholarship was all-important because it was the only chance she had of being with you. That's why she wanted it.'

He broke eye contact with Liz, unable to believe his aunt's convictions.

Wanting to be with him hadn't been enough for Stella.

Something had changed between them at Stanford.

He hadn't been enough for Stella anymore.

Tennis had meant more to her.

He'd spent sleepless nights looking back over their relationship and trying to pinpoint when things had changed – what signs he'd missed.

He'd drawn a blank.

'Whether or not she'd come to Stanford, our relationship would've ended. It has ended.' He shook his head. 'Don't meddle, Liz. Accept that it's over.'

'I don't believe it. Can you look me in the eye and tell me you didn't feel any connection today?'

He couldn't. In fact, he actually had to stop himself because he was already beginning to turn away from his aunt in case she guessed how affected he'd been today. 'Have you forgotten Stella was the one who broke off the relationship?'

'My instinct always told me that she broke up with you because she knew about Deanna.'

'Impossible! There was no Deanna to know about.'

Liz put her hands on her hips, raised her eyebrows and cleared her throat pointedly. 'Your ten-year-old son says differently.'

Frustration bit deep as he sat down on one of the old kitchen chairs and rubbed one hand against the nape of his neck. 'There was no relationship with Deanna. It was…' God, but he wished he could tell her the whole truth. 'I've told you before, it was a one-night stand I don't even remember having.'

Regret was pointless.

There was no travelling back in time.

He loved Kade. Mitchell would do anything for that kid.

Because he'd felt unloved and unwanted by his parents as he'd grown up, the most important thing in his life had become saving Kade from a similar fate.

Liz stopped pacing and dragged a chair out so she could sit beside him. One of her hands closed over his wrist and she was all compassion as she said, 'Kade's the one good thing to have come out of that dark time, but I don't think you've ever stopped feeling guilty for being unfaithful to Stella.'

Mitch pulled his hand away. 'Don't, Liz. You don't know anything about it.'

His aunt shook her head then continued. 'You obviously acted out of character. You'd just been told your parents had been in a terrorist attack, were presumed dead. Nobody could blame you for turning to your friends and hitting the bottle with them. I think Stella would even have forgiven you for taking Deanna to bed when you were drunk, because she would've understood your grief and your very human need for comfort. It's said that having sex is a way we reaffirm life in the face of loss through death.'

Stop it! he wanted to scream. *It wasn't like that.*

'I hear you trying to make excuses for me, but you don't understand.'

'Make me understand.'

'No.' He held his hand up to stop her when she was about to speak. 'It doesn't matter what the circumstances were, to have gone to bed with Deanna would've been unfaithful.'

'All I'm saying is, that there were extenuating circumstances and you acted completely out of character. You need to forgive yourself. Not everyone gets a second chance, Mitch.' She gestured upwards. 'The stars are all aligned.'

He shook his head. 'Not everyone has a happy ending.' As soon as he spoke he wished he could recall his words as he saw a shadow of sadness in Liz's expression.

Damn it!

Liz knew first-hand that happy endings weren't guaranteed.

Her husband had succumbed to cancer when they'd been married for only three years.

Before he could apologise for his thoughtless insensitivity she said, 'Real life is often stranger than fiction.' She gave a knowing tap of her finger against her temple. 'And true love is even more wonderful when it's fact rather than fiction. It's worth fighting for, Mitch.'

Love.

He'd spent years wishing his parents had loved him.

He'd spent years coming to terms with Stella not loving him.

The shrill ring of the house phone broke through his thoughts.

'That'll be June Lynch,' Liz said. 'I'm expecting her call about the stall we're organising for the CWA fair.'

It was, no doubt, only a temporary reprieve because Liz would probably be offering more advice the instant she got back.

His aunt was wrong about rekindling his relationship with Stella.

Too much time had passed. And, in all that time, the wound she'd inflicted on his heart still hadn't fully healed.

As much as he was still attracted to her, Mitchell wasn't about to open up his heart to Stella again for another battering.

He thought back to the events leading up to finding Deanna in his bed...

Even though he hadn't had a close relationship with his parents, Mitchell had been devastated when word had come that there'd been a terrorist attack on the US embassy in Tehran where his parents had worked as diplomats.

He'd watched the news coverage in horror, glued to the screen and wondering how anyone who'd been in the building would've been able to survive.

During their infrequent telephone calls, his parents had told him they rarely left the building due to safety concerns.

For the first few hours after the news had broken, he hadn't called Stella. He'd sat glued to the TV screen in shock and also hadn't wanted to be on the phone in case officials called back to give him more information. But as the coverage continued, imagining his parents buried under the debris of the bomb blast had been too much to cope with and he'd phoned the person he loved most.

The person he believed loved him as deeply.

But he hadn't been able to reach Stella as her phone had been switched off.

When he'd phoned Carter in a desperate bid to contact her, the coach had told him he was being selfish to expect her to come back to Stanford to be by his side when she was due to play in the semi-final of a WTA tournament in Cleveland. Carter had been adamant she had to concentrate on that and said that if Mitchell really cared about her, he wouldn't ring back – he'd man up and deal with his crisis instead of using Stella as a crutch.

The words had found their mark and stung.

Mitch had felt guilty and weak.

He hadn't argued when Carter refused to pass on Mitch's message.

Every hour, though, Mitch had looked at the clock, expecting Stella to call.

She had to have known about the bombing. It'd been all over the news, playing in an endless loop, and it was all everyone was talking about.

Stella hadn't called him.

It seemed as though she'd turned off her phone and refused, through her manager, to take his call.

The message was clear. The tournament and her ranking points were more important than his personal hell.

Without thinking, Mitch placed his right hand up over his abdomen as he recalled the clawing nausea that had accompanied his anguish.

Knowing she wasn't prepared to be there for him was even

worse than the thought of having lost his parents. He was broken. Empty. Confused.

Had the situation been reversed, he knew he would've dropped a game – not only breaking his contract but also letting his team mates down.

Nothing and nobody had been more important in his life than Stella.

After Mitch had got off the phone from Carter, his teammates had found him staring at the TV screen, red-eyed. They'd assumed all his emotion was for his parents, but in truth he'd been gutted that Stella had let him down so badly.

Unprepared to receive the final confirmation about his parents' deaths, he'd turned off his phone, gone out with his friends and drowned his sorrows. Nursing an almighty hangover the next day, he'd awakened with Deanna naked in bed beside him.

From that point, his life fast became a nightmare.

When he'd turned his phone back on, he'd received a couple of missed calls but no messages from Stella. He'd phoned her back six times before she picked up and to this day he remembered every word of their conversation.

'Mitchell.' There was an emotional waver in her voice as she uttered his name.

'Stella. I've been trying to reach you.'

'I… I called you too.'

'It's Mom and Dad…' His voice broke. 'Have… have you seen the news?'

'I have.' There was a long pause before she said. 'I'm sorry, Mitchell. I… this must be awful for you.'

'I need you, Stella.'

'No!' The word was almost savage. 'You don't need me. I'm certain there are others you can turn to for support.'

Mitch heard the resolution in her voice and… anger or resentment?

Did she really resent him for asking her to come to him at such an uncertain point in his life?

Almost robotically – as though she'd memorised her lines – her voice was flat as she said, 'I'm not coming back to Stanford so you'll just have to find someone else to support you through this crisis, Mitchell. These WTA points are all-important to me, and I can't pull out of the tournament or I'll lose the opportunity to gain points, plus I'll probably never gain another wild card entry.'

'Stell—'

'I have to go, Mitchell. Goodbye.'

She'd disconnected the call.

The only relief had been that his parents had still been breathing when they'd been pulled from the debris by rescuers two days later.

They'd been flown back to the States and he'd had a brief, formal reunion with them that'd made him yearn for Stella even more. Their lack of warmth had made him crave and appreciate the love he and Stella shared more than ever.

By that stage, Stella had flown to a tournament in Tokyo, but she was acting strangely.

He'd flown straight to Tokyo to see her to try to sort out why she was ignoring most of his calls, and being preoccupied – almost distant – when they did connect. She'd lost the Cleveland WTA semi-finals playing what commentators said was the worst game they'd ever seen from a professional tennis player.

They'd said she was 'disconnected' and making shots 'almost absentmindedly' which was nothing like the Stella he knew.

He hadn't been certain whether there was something more troubling going on or whether she was regretting her decision not to be with him, but he'd been determined to find out.

His unannounced trip to Tokyo had backfired in spectacular fashion.

'Mitch!' For a split second there was joy on her face when she opened the door. It quickly evaporated and he didn't

recognise the cold set of her features. 'What are you doing here, Mitchell?'

'I'm worried about you. You're hardly answering my calls and when you do, you're distant.' Not to mention he'd thought she was crying a couple of times. 'What's wrong, sweetheart?'

Blinking, she looked as though she was fighting back tears, yet the young woman who spoke to him was a stranger because she had a voice like an ice princess. 'What's wrong is you! I need to focus on my tennis, Mitchell, and I can't do that when you keep ringing me every five minutes. This has to stop.'

'What the hell?'

'If I'd known you were flying this great distance I would've told you not to bother, because there's no point.'

'I don't understand. What's happened?'

'Nothing,' she denied quickly. 'Nothing except I realise that tennis is the most important thing in my life and I don't have time for a relationship if I'm going to make it to the top. I don't have time for you.'

As shocked as he was, he demanded, 'Is that you talking or your coach?'

'My feelings for you have changed.' She didn't meet his eyes as she said, 'I don't… I don't love you anymore. Maybe I never did.'

'What?' He shook his head. 'Stell, you can't mean that. Please, let me in. Sweetheart, let's sit down and talk about this.'

'There's no point, Mitchell.' There were tears in her eyes now. 'Please don't make this difficult. Just accept my decision, respect my decision and move on with your life.' Her lower lip had started to tremble, but now it grew firmer. 'Find a new girlfriend, Mitchell. I'm sure it won't take you long to replace me.'

'What the hell? Stella! I don't want a new girlfriend. You're the only girl for me.'

'Really?' Her sarcasm stung and confused him. 'Well that's tough because I don't want you to be my boyfriend anymore.'

She slammed the door and he stood in shocked silence for

at least a minute wondering what the hell had happened. Then he started knocking on the door, pleading with her to open it. How long he knocked, he wasn't certain but she didn't open it and he ended up being removed from the premises by two beefy security guards.

He hadn't even had a chance to tell her he'd been drafted into the NFL. Although, at that point, his excitement for his football career had waned. There hadn't seemed much point in having a promising future when his personal life was in tatters.

He'd written to her begging for an explanation and telling her that they were meant to be together. They were both driven to succeed in their sports and they each understood the other better than anyone else could. He'd argued they could make allowances, make compromises, but they were meant to be together.

The letter had been returned unopened and she hadn't even sent a congratulatory message when the NFL draft had been publicly announced.

Swallowing now against the swirling, crushing emotions those devastating memories still evoked, Mitch realised his hands were clenched at his sides. Relaxing his hands, he made himself take a few steadying breaths then stood up to finish off Liz's task and make the tea.

'All organised!' Liz declared as she rejoined him. 'June and I are going to have the best stall at the fair.'

'What's the stall selling?' He asked out of politeness.

'Christmas crafts.'

Christmas loomed on the horizon. 'Wonderful,' he said without any real interest.

He carried both cups over to the table and they sat opposite each other.

After one sip, Liz said, 'I've never met two people better suited than you and Stella.'

Her eyes were suspiciously bright as they pleaded with him. 'You're still young. Hopefully you've got many years ahead of you with a lot of living to do.'

Mitch reached across the table and enveloped her hands in his. 'You still miss Uncle Pete, don't you?'

With a small sigh she moved her hands so she held his and gave them a light squeeze. 'Every day. He was my great young love and was taken away from me way too soon.' After pressing her lips together firmly in what seemed to be a determined effort to regroup, she squeezed his hands again. 'There was nothing I could do to avert the outcome, but you and Stella…' Her forehead wrinkled. 'I could shake the two of you and am tempted to knock your heads together until you see sense. You're both the loves of each other's life. Oh… sure… some people are lucky enough to find someone else to love and want to be with after their spouse has died, but that's rare.'

She hesitated for a moment.

A different energy – a lighter, happier energy bounced in his direction, but it was only brief.

Liz seemed to discard whatever it was she'd been going to say before she said, 'Don't blow it again! Talk to each other and work out what went wrong or leave past hurts behind you and forgive each other. You need to enjoy all the future has to offer because life is too short. Use whatever time you have left and work your way back to each other.'

She let go of his hands and picked up her cup to cradle it in her hands.

'Things are different now, Liz.' He picked up his cup and drank a few mouthfuls. 'Kade is my number one priority.'

'Kade could do with a decent mother figure in his life.' She cast a glance at the back door to make certain Kade wasn't about to burst in on them. 'God knows that woman who gave birth to him didn't have a single motherly bone in her body!'

Mitch understood why Liz felt that way, but there were circumstances she didn't understand. Circumstances he couldn't discuss without revealing the entire truth and he wasn't ready to do that yet.

For all her faults, Kade's mother had been an insecure

young woman who'd been scared witless when she found herself pregnant. Kade had been a bargaining chip – used by Deanna to secure marriage to Mitch, who by then was the youngest quarterback in the NFL and rated as one of the most promising of all time.

'The ink on the contracts for Hope Farm is well and truly dry.' Liz's tone was less bossy – more persuasive. 'I suggest you might like to help Stella move her things into the caretaker's cottage. I've had it refurbished in the last twelve months and she'll be more than comfortable there.'

'The cottage?'

She nodded. 'Unless you'd prefer to live there with Kade and let her move into this house?'

'I—'

'Your contracts don't say you have to live under the same roof – just that you have to both live on the property for two years.'

He leaned back into the chair. 'You know it's unfair to go ahead with this ridiculous scheme of yours. If she sinks the money in to develop her... tennis complex... she's hardly going to want me to buy her out at the end of the two years. The way the contract stands, without Stella and I being able to reach an agreement on the buy-out, you'll be able to buy the whole property back from us. It makes no sense, Liz.'

'Won't happen,' Liz stated calmly. 'You'll find a way to make this work. I have confidence in both of you. More to the point, I have confidence that love will guide the way.'

Mitch let out a big hiss of pent-up frustration. 'You're not going to see reason and let me buy her out here and now, are you?'

'I'm not going to pretend to be sorry this is causing you angst. I'm not.' Her chin jutted forward a little in stubborn determination. 'Ultimately, you'll both thank me.'

Feeling every muscle in his body tense in frustration, Mitch decided he needed to put some space between himself and his aunt. He wouldn't be able to find a workable solution to the problem while he sat there and listened to her nonsense. 'I'll finish this down at the goat pen and take Kade a bottle of water.'

'Don't be cranky with me, Mitch,' she said as he stood up to leave. 'You know I love you.'

As frustrating as she was, he knew it was true. 'You are infuriating but I'll always love you,' he told her as he bent to give her a kiss.

As he straightened, a sudden realisation hit him and made dread course through him.

'Liz! It's just occurred to me that you've completely sold the farm.' He'd been so flummoxed finding out Stella owned the other half, that he hadn't stopped to think about the fact that Liz didn't.

'I have, so you'd be quite within your rights to boot me out today.'

As if he'd ever do that.

'Why didn't you keep a share?'

She straightened. 'I'm moving to Melbourne in the new year.'

His eyes widened. 'Why all the secrecy?

Life is short...

'Please tell me you're not sick.'

'No, no.' She smiled as she shook her head. 'I'm well and happy. In fact, I haven't felt this good in years.'

Trying to read between the lines was impossible.

'What aren't you telling me?'

'Well...' Her cheeks dimpled. 'I've met a man and we've bought a place together and we're moving in together in January – just as soon as the lease expires for the current tenants.'

Mitch sat down. 'I knew you'd been making quite a few trips to Melbourne lately but I thought they were all work related – that you were in meetings with the head of your publishing house.'

'Yes and no,' she admitted sheepishly. 'Connor is the CEO of the company.'

'Connor.' It sounded like a young name. 'How old is he?'

The trill of laughter that tripped from her lips made him worried.

'Liz, you're a very wealthy woman. You need—'

'Oh, darling, thank you for caring enough to worry about me, but Connor earns more than enough for himself as CEO. He's not interested in my royalty cheques.' The denial was absolute. 'And... he's a bit younger than I am but neither of us thinks it's important and he makes me happy. That's all I'm saying at this point.'

Mitch was both happy and concerned for her. 'When do I get to meet him?'

'He's tied up now until Christmas and then I'm presuming you'll let me ask him to share Christmas with us here and stay on until New Year?'

'You presuming? Never! When have you ever been presumptuous, Liz?' he intoned with light sarcasm. 'Or pushy for that matter.'

His agitation made him slosh some of his tea as he carried it and the water bottle to the goat pen. Yet he couldn't help but turn over Liz's suggestions in his head.

Having Stella live in the cottage would be like living next door – virtually the same as if she lived in the homestead with the Richardsons.

When she'd suggested they go ahead and live on the farm together, he'd refused point blank. He acknowledged, now, that it was the thought of having Stella living so close by with Carter that'd been the clincher. No way could he ever have entertained the idea of having that guy living at Hope Creek Farm.

But... if it was just Stella...

They'd been friends once. Could they be friends again?

Surely they could both manage living close by civilly?

He mocked his own thoughts.

Stella probably wouldn't have any difficulty with it. She wasn't the one who was nursing any angst.

He'd have to keep his distance though. This morning had proved that she could still disturb his equilibrium like no other woman could.

Darn Liz for creating this situation!

He felt himself swaying from his initial, determined stance to fight Stella's co-ownership.

Hell! What a mess.

CHAPTER SIX

'G'day, Jim.' Mitch got out of his car at Hope Station later that afternoon and bent down to pat the two dogs that ran towards him.

'Heel, Ned. Heel, Ben.' The dogs instantly obeyed their master as he walked forward, pushed the brim of his Akubra hat back and extended his hand to Mitch. 'Good to see you again, Mitch.'

'It's good to be back,' he told Stella's father as they shook hands.

'Stella said she'd seen you this morning – and that you've bought the hotel from Bill.' He shook his head in disbelief. 'Word usually travels fast. I'm not sure how you've kept that news under wraps.'

'Most of the negotiations were done over the phone while I was still in the States. I only finalised the deal with Bill two days ago when I arrived back in Australia. We signed the paperwork yesterday and I take ownership on Saturday.'

'That was another surprise.' The corners of Jim's eyes wrinkled in amused bewilderment. 'Your arrival seems to have gone unnoticed.'

Mitch laughed. 'Must be my greatest achievement ever – flying under the Hope Creek grapevine!' More seriously he added, 'Bill is planning to make the announcement this Saturday night at the pub, so keep it under your hat, will you?'

'Will do.' Jim leant down and patted the dogs. 'You say you arrived two days ago?'

'That's right. I've been planning the move here for a while though.' He looked again at the stately and well-kept homestead and saw nothing much had changed. 'I'm here with my son, Kade, and we've been recovering from jet lag. He's been happy to explore the farm with me or I would've been over earlier to see you.'

It'd been quite difficult to persuade Kade to stay at the farm with Liz. His son had wanted to come and see Stella again and meet their neighbours. He'd flip out completely if he knew there was a possibility Stella might move to the cottage.

Jim straightened. 'Heard you retired from football.'

'Yep.' He looked again at the homestead and wondered whether Stella was home. 'Played my last game back in January.'

'You had quite the career. I followed your progress – I think the whole town did. In fact, Bill subscribed to a sports channel just so he could stream your games – although we all had a hell of a time trying to work out the rules!'

Mitch was touched. 'I had no idea.'

'Yeah, it kind of seems right that after the interest he's taken in your career, you'll be the one who's allowing him to move on with his retirement.' He let out a low whistle. 'It's incredible to think that Hope Creek has produced two world champions. Well,' he shifted a little on his feet, 'we like to claim you as one of our own, anyway.'

'That's fine by me. It's the one place I've always called home and that's why I'm back now. I want Kade to be raised right, and to grow up knowing the sense of community Hope Creek offers. I don't think the city life was doing him any favours.'

'They do say it takes a village to raise a child.' Jim raised his hand to shoo away an annoying fly.

Mitch had to do the same as the fly buzzed in his direction.

'He'll learn a lot about values here that are vastly different than those in the area of LA where he lived.'

'Well, it's good to have you home,' Jim told him. 'Come on in and say hello to Margaret, and next time, bring your young whipper-snapper with you. It'll be good to meet the lad.'

At least that was one of the Richardsons who was happy for Mitch and Kade to be here.

Mitch figured he could expect a warm, but perhaps a wary, welcome from Margaret. Stella's sisters were likely to be openly hostile.

Liz had called the girls Hope Creek's own version of the three musketeers – all for one and one for all. They were fiercely loyal to each other and he guessed that even though Stella had broken up with him, they wouldn't look kindly on him for having married soon after – particularly when they must've heard Deanna was pregnant when he'd married her.

Following Jim towards the homestead, he asked, 'Is Stella home?'

'Sure is.' Jim stopped and turned back to him. At six foot four, Stella's foster father was almost as tall as Mitchell and the men looked each other directly in the eye. There was a warning light in Jim's eyes. 'She's pretty upset at Liz right now.'

'She's not the only one, but I'm hoping Stella and I will work our way through it.'

'We're close to your aunt. She's been a good friend all our lives and we think highly of her in most things, but she can be a bit single-minded sometimes.' His lips twisted. 'Margaret means to give her a serve about her meddling.'

The news of the joint property ownership would probably be all over Hope Creek in no time flat.

'It's high time someone did,' Mitch agreed. 'I can't get through to her.'

Jim merely nodded. 'Come on in and I'll give the ladies a yell.' As they walked the remaining distance to the house, Jim kept up the easy conversation. 'You must've been pleased to end your career on a high note and been part of the winning team again for the Super Bowl.'

Ned and Ben walked at their heels, and sat obediently when Jim told them to stay out on the verandah.

'I certainly had a good run,' he agreed as they entered the house and the flyscreen clattered shut behind them.

Marg's woman's touch was everywhere, making the house a welcoming home.

The fresh native flowers in the vase on the hall stand, the smell of furniture polished with beeswax combined with whatever delicious meal that was cooking in the oven – it was all familiar and reassuring in its constancy, bringing back many happy memories of the days he'd spent here in his youth.

This was the first place he'd ever experienced a sense of home and family.

Oh, Liz had welcomed him and been loving and warm in a way his parents had never been, but it'd just been the two of them at Hope Farm as Liz's husband had died before Mitch had ever met him. It'd been the Richardsons that'd really given him his taste of family with all its consistency even during times of chaos, its fun and laughter and most of all the undeniable love and caring that'd been so palpable here.

'Stella! Margy! We have a visitor!' Jim called.

Margaret emerged from the direction of the kitchen, wiping her hands on her floral apron. 'Mitchell Scott!'

Her hair had gone a lovely silver colour since his last visit home, and she seemed a little bit shorter than he remembered, but her smile was still as warm as a summer's day.

'Stella said you were back in town. It's lovely to see you.'

As Margaret reached up to him for a huge hug, Stella emerged from the living room and looked anything but delighted to see him again.

'It's great to see you, too, Margaret,' he said as he returned the hug and looked over the top of Margaret's head at Stella. 'Hi Stella.'

'Mitchell.'

Pulling out of their hug, Marg looked beyond him. 'You didn't bring your son with you?'

'Not this time. Liz had ordered in the *Harry Potter* Series for him to read and she gave them to him right before I left, so he's busy.' He didn't add that the books had been brought out as an inducement for Kade to quit complaining about having to stay.

'Stella's told us all about Liz's plotting.' Margaret had always been no-nonsense and straight to the point. He guessed that now she knew Kade wasn't with him, she felt free to speak. 'I'm going to be giving her a piece of my mind when I see her.'

'Jim told me as much and I support you one hundred per cent.'

'I love her to bits, but I think she's been writing those novels for too long. In fact, I read all of them and this very much resembles a plot she wrote a few years ago where a couple were forced to take joint ownership of a property to fulfil the will of a dying old man – not that Liz is dying, of course.'

Mitchell cleared his throat. 'Well, Liz's machinations are why I've come visiting this afternoon. As much as I've been l looking forward to catching up with you and Jim, I've actually come to see Stella to see if we can find a way to work through this co-ownership Liz has set up.'

'Good idea,' Margaret declared. 'Why don't you both go on through to the gazebo out the back? But, before you go, can I get you a cuppa or a cool drink?'

'There's a beer in the fridge on the back verandah if you'd like one,' Jim put in.

'Nothing for me, thanks,' he said.

'Well, if you change your mind, just help yourself 'cause I'm going out to check on some stock.' Jim went to Marg and gave her a quick kiss. 'See you at dinner, gorgeous.'

Charmingly, Marg blushed a little. 'Are you hoping calling

me gorgeous will get you served up some of your favourite apple pie?'

'A man can live in hope.' He winked at Mitch whose mouth was already watering as he remembered having been served Margaret's apple pie with great dollops of thickened cream and scoops of icecream.

* * *

Stella could hardly rail at her foster parents for being so friendly. It was the country way.

'Let bygones be bygones,' Jim had always told them as they'd grown up.

'No time for living in the past,' Margaret had said. 'We have to move on and live in the present.'

Besides, as far as they knew, she'd got over her feelings for Mitchell years ago.

Seeing Mitchell this morning when he'd opened Liz's front door had been an absolute shock to the system, but seeing him in her home now was another thing entirely.

He'd visited her at the homestead countless times – stood right where he was standing now. He'd been her friend then her boyfriend, but this was the first time he'd visited as her ex and his presence did weird things to her insides.

'Stella?' Mitch's deep voice was like melted chocolate but instead of soothing her nerves with its warmth, it only made them buzz with hyper-awareness.

Oh dear. Marg was looking at her pointedly, expecting her to play hostess, but nothing about this situation was normal.

'Come through.' She led Mitch down the long hallway lined with a load of family photos that attested to the special times she'd shared with her foster sisters and parents.

Once through the back door, she had to navigate the four steps leading from the verandah to the garden path. She held on tightly to the railing – trying hard to not look as though she needed to hold on tightly.

In the days when they'd been friends and lovers, he'd always been super sensitive to her needs. That much didn't seem to have changed as he asked, 'Would you like a supportive hand?'

'Thanks, but I'll be right,' she replied stiffly.

She was still underconfident with stairs, having to navigate them carefully with her new foot, and still relying on her eyes to tell her she was placing her foot in the right spot. The sensation of his hand on her arm would most likely throw her off balance completely by shattering her concentration.

Ned and Ben must've heard the back door close. She heard them tearing around the verandah and suddenly they were right underfoot.

'Heel!' Mitch commanded as his hand shot out to Stella's elbow. 'I've got you.'

A burst of anger made her heart pump harder.

She wasn't angry with the dogs or with Mitch but at her need for Mitch's steadying support.

Maybe Mitch realised she was cranky about her shortcomings because he said casually, 'Marg and Jim look well.'

He released his hold on her elbow when the dogs were behaving, but remained close enough to catch her if she tripped.

'They're going okay.'

When they were sitting opposite each other at the table in the gazebo, Stella found herself completely tongue-tied.

How did any man get to be so divinely handsome?

Thankfully, Mitchell got straight to the point before she could dwell too much on his lethally good looks.

'I've spoken to Liz and there's no changing her mind about the terms of the agreement.'

Focusing on a gardenia bush so she didn't have to meet the depths of his blue eyes, Stella let out a pent-up breath. 'I suspected as much.'

'I've also called my lawyers and, although they've

promised they'll go over the contract again with a fine-tooth comb to find a loophole, they believe the contracts we signed are quite legal and will be watertight.'

'I've had the same conversation with the lawyer Jim and Margaret recommended.' She dragged her gaze away from the fragrant white flowers as she added, 'However, he did say that if he can't find a legal loophole, we may be able to make a case of it being deemed unfair because the terms were not wholly transparent.'

'*Wholly transparent*?' he scoffed. 'That's the understatement of the year. There was nothing transparent about them at all. It was wilfully misleading.'

Even with the slightly bitter twist to his mouth, his lips were inviting.

Sensuous.

His kisses had been sensational.

Oh my gosh. Stop it, Stella!

She had to clear her throat before suggesting, 'We may be able to mount a joint legal challenge to the validity of the contract.'

'By the time the case went to court, the two-year time period Liz has specified would probably be up, not to mention the publicity the case would raise given all three of us have very public profiles.'

Damn it.

He was right.

Famous former US superstar quarterback, former number one women's tennis player and a current *New York Times* bestselling author. The high-profile case would definitely attract media attention, especially with it being public knowledge that Stella and Mitch had been an item in high school and at college.

Ned and Ben had been sniffing around the gazebo, but now they came to sit at Stella's side, Ned resting his head on top of her lap for a pat. Thankful for the distraction, she scratched behind his silky soft ears.

'I've been turning everything over in my mind. When Liz came to me in Switzerland and offered to let me buy into the farm, it was like a salvation because I'd had no idea what I was going to do with my life.' It shouldn't matter, but somehow it was important to her to let Mitch know she hadn't been in on Liz's scheme. 'I truly hadn't entertained the idea that you'd still want the farm. Now I know you do, I see how unfair this is to you.'

'Thank you for acknowledging it,' he said quietly.

'Now it's sinking in, I realise I'll have to look for somewhere else to build my tennis centre.' As she spoke her shoulders rounded and she immediately sat straighter so her body language didn't give away how defeated she was feeling.

'You could look elsewhere.' He nodded as he rested his strong, tanned forearms against the table and leant towards her. She had to tear her attention away from the masculinity of those arms to focus on his words as he suggested, 'Or, we could follow Liz's stipulations for the moment, then at the end of the two-year period, I buy you out—'

'But I would've—'

He held up a hand. 'Hear me out, Stella. The contract only states that one of us can buy the other out. What I propose is that in two years, I buy you out in total. I then have full control of the farm so nothing would stop me from subdividing the land and selling you the parcel of land you've developed.'

'You'd consider that?' She tilted her head to one side. 'I thought you'd completely ruled out any ownership by me?'

His dark eyebrows raised slightly. 'How much land would you need for your development?'

'The development application was for five acres.'

'That'll hardly make a dent in the property.' He rubbed his hand along his jawline in thoughtful contemplation.

Since she'd learned about Liz's deception, Stella had oscillated between anger and disappointment. Now, she found herself hopeful yet wary.

'When I left the farm a few hours ago, co-ownership wasn't something you were prepared to contemplate. What's made you change your mind?'

His voice seemed to come from a long way away – as if he was lost in his own memories. 'There was a time when I imagined we might live at the farm together permanently.'

Was it her imagination or did his words hold an edge of regret?

Stella had to swallow hard. They had made plans together to make it big in their respective sports and then to retire to Hope Creek and raise a family.

'We were just kids.' The words and her tone were dismissive.

'Yeah. That was before you broke up with me.' He matched her tone. 'A time when we were both still in throes of *'adolescent infatuation'.*'

That he threw her very words back at her after all this time told her they'd made a lasting impression.

Eyes narrowed, she stared at him unflinchingly as she tried to read his expression – his mood.

Yes. She'd broken up with him but only after she'd walked into his college room – unexpectedly and unannounced – and found him sleeping next to another woman.

The woman who happened to be Kade's mother.

'It was a long time ago.' She hated the stiltedness of her words.

'You're right.' He straightened and became more businesslike. 'We've moved on, and presently Liz has outmanoeuvred us both.'

Focus on Liz, she told herself. *Direct all your energy to this quandary and don't think about the past and how much Mitchell broke your heart.*

'I still can't believe Liz has done this.'

* * *

Hearing the anguish in her words, Mitch scanned Stella's beautiful but troubled features and couldn't suppress the memory of having traced his fingertips over each one of them countless times. Her perfectly arched brows were the awning to hazel green set in almond-shaped eyes. Her cheekbones were high and her chin had always struck him as being determined.

Realising his fingers were itching to trace over her features once again, he forced himself to sit back against the cushions on his chair and to focus on the problem at hand. 'It's a shock Liz manipulated us both when we placed our trust in her. I could never have seen it coming.'

'She doesn't see it as betrayal.' Stella sighed. 'Everything about the situation is wrong, yet as Margaret acknowledged to me, and we both know, she has a heart of gold. I think her intentions were good. *Unrealistic*,' she underlined hurriedly, 'but well intended.'

'What's the expression? "The road to Hell is paved with good intentions?"'

She buried her head in her hands for a few moments and he watched her, noting the way the sunlight highlighted some chestnut in her dark brown hair. He'd always been fascinated by the way the sunbeams played with the natural variations of colour in her silky hair – mostly dark brown, but with some lighter brown and this gorgeous chestnut.

She lifted her head and looked directly at him. 'You're serious about this offer to subdivide?'

'It merits consideration, especially as you've already had your DA approved, and have everything in place.'

'You could live with a tennis centre at Hope Farm?'

He nodded. 'I think it's commendable you want to do something for disadvantaged kids, and now I've had time to think about it, it's good to think Hope Farm can be part of their experience.'

'Thanks.'

He was about to tell her how he hoped other kids would

find her tennis centre changed their lives for the better as the farm had changed his, when she broke the silence.

'I need to think about my options,' she said slowly as she interlaced her fingers on the table in front of her. 'You're right that there are other properties in different areas I can buy.'

'There are, but I feel badly that you've had your heart set on Hope Farm and already have your plans in motion, and there's another reason I'm making this offer...'

Crunch time.

Unclenching his teeth he said, 'Remember that our contracts say that if we fail to live at the farm with the co-owner, or can't reach an agreement at the end of the two years, Liz buys back our shares.' His teeth clamped together for a moment before he confided his concern. 'Liz is under no obligation to allow me to buy the farm back from her at any point of the future.'

Her gasp was audible. 'Oh Mitch! Surely she wouldn't stop you from buying it if she knows how much you want it? She's not vindictive.'

'I don't think so either, but it's not a chance I need to take if you'll consent to living there and going ahead with your plans.'

Stella looked miserable.

Ned sensed it and whined next to her.

Mitch watched as she rocked back and forward a little in the armchair in a self-comforting action as she patted the dog. He knew she was weighing up of the enormity of the situation for him.

'We can find a way around this.' Her rocking stopped when he said, 'We can sign a separate agreement.'

Wariness clouded her eyes as she looked at him.

'In our agreement, we both live at the farm, as stipulated by Liz,' he repeated. 'At the end of the two years, I buy you out of your fifty per cent, then I re-sell you the land you've developed. On your part, you also renounce rights to claim any more than the specified five acres.'

'That sounds fair.'

'But?'

Her perfectly even top teeth rested for a moment on her lower lip.

He recognised the action in a heartbeat as being the way she reacted to being put on the spot and having a worrying decision to make.

God, he'd missed all these little things about her.

Had Steve Carter ever known Stella the way he had?

Had he ever appreciated these little gestures Stella made the way Mitchell had held every one of them close to his heart?

Stella sighed. 'There's a lot of history between us, Mitchell. I know we've both moved on, but... I don't want to live so close to you if there's likely to be any... awkwardness between us. I have to give this some thought.'

'Do you need to talk to Carter about this?' He fished.

If Stella had seemed a little uptight previously, his question ramped her tension up several thousand notches. As soon as Carter was mentioned, she stiffened and looked away from Mitch while the colour bleached from her cheeks.

Although he hadn't wanted to make her uncomfortable, Mitch wanted to confirm she wasn't with her fiancé any longer. He was making the offer on the premise that Carter was definitely out of the picture, but he didn't want to come straight out and ask her.

He probed again. 'Would he be happy to live on the property when I'm there too and, as you pointed out, there's history between us?'

'Steve won't be living in Hope Creek.' The words were flat and final.

His gaze went to her left hand and he noticed that now, the ring was missing.

'Not at all?'

'No.'

Mitch didn't feel he could push her any further, and the

way her lips had clamped firmly together, he read that the topic wasn't up for discussion.

While he didn't want to think Stella was nursing a broken heart, surely Liz was right and Carter was her ex-fiancé? Marg would hardly have told Liz they'd broken up if it wasn't true.

He cleared his throat. 'You'd be living at the caretaker's cottage – which Liz showed me after you left. It's had a complete makeover and has been modernised and made very comfortable.' He moved his hands expansively. 'If you can put the past behind us, I really need you to do this, Stella. I'm willing to do whatever it takes to make this work because otherwise I might lose all rights to the farm. I don't want that to happen. It's important to me because one day the farm will be Kade's – if he wants it.'

* * *

Kade.

He wanted the farm for his son.

'How long will Kade be holidaying here with you?'

God, she hoped he wouldn't be here for long.

It was one thing knowing that she'd run into Mitchell around Hope Creek – that she'd most likely see him every darn time she went to the hotel to meet up with friends and neighbours – but another thing entirely to know she might come face to face with the evidence of Mitch's betrayal for as long as his son was here.

'I've had permanent custody of Kade since March. He's not here for a vacation. We've both moved to Hope Creek permanently.'

Everything in her screamed out in denial.

Hope Creek was her home.

It was her special place.

Yes, Mitch had lived here too at one point as had his mother's family, but to bring his child here to the place where

Stella and Mitch's friendship had deepened into love, was like a giant kick in the gut.

Pain seared through her brain and her stomach churned.

This was one more betrayal – almost a desecration of the place she and Mitch had shared such happy times before everything had become so complicated.

How could he be so insensitive?

She wasn't sure how much of this she could take.

CHAPTER SEVEN

'Oh,' was Stella's only response to his declaration.

If he'd thought she'd paled only moments ago, now he watched as she blanched even more dramatically – so dramatically that Mitch would have sworn she was in physical pain.

No.

He was imagining things.

Stella was long past reacting to anything he had to say.

Stupidly, because he'd been so irrevocably in love with her, he'd almost felt relieved for her sake that she'd been the one to call it quits – that he'd been the one left broken-hearted rather than him having to have hurt her a little over a month later when he'd received the shattering news that Deanna was not only pregnant, but was claiming the baby was his.

How was it that all this time later, he still felt an inexorable pull towards his first love?

First love?

Shit.

Stella had been his only love.

Now, she was sitting opposite him, co-owner of Hope Farm.

Coming face to face with her again...

Nothing had prepared him for this.

Stella shifted uncomfortably in her chair, closing her eyes briefly.

'Stella is your… foot bothering you?'

'My *artificial foot* is not currently causing me any bother, thank you.'

Mitch felt awkward. He hadn't known exactly how to refer to her prosthesis – how to be sensitive and politically correct. But, as well as correcting him, had her tone insinuated that he was the one who was bothering her… or had he read too much into it?

'This is such a bind.' There was fatigue in her voice now – even a note of defeat.

Since when had Stella ever given into defeat?

Her determination to win tennis matches had set her apart from her rivals. Even when she'd been a set and a half down, at times, she'd managed to claw her way back and claim a win.

'Believe me, I've looked at this and had the lawyers look at it from all angles. There's no other way to protect my rights to the property.'

'I'm sorry.'

'It's not your fault.' He rested his forearms on the table again and leaned forward. 'But I will tell you that while I've always wanted to come back here, I'm here right now because of Kade. He's been through a really rough time. I've been there for him as much as possible since Deanna and I divorced, but I was always coming and going during football season. We had shared custody and I didn't realise Deanna was… well, she was neglecting him emotionally. Turns out he went through quite a lot and he needs to heal.'

* * *

Stella felt a sad smile tug at her lips because she could relate to what Mitch was saying. It was one of the reasons she'd returned. 'No better place for healing than Hope Creek.'

Lucky Kade.

He'd been brought to a community that would embrace him whole heartedly. He also had his strong father there for him.

Protecting him.

Loving him.

Stella wished…

'Which is why I bought into the farm.' He moved his large hands expansively. 'This is everything the part of LA we lived in is not. This is community. It's real. People have good, solid, honest values – the type I want Kade to grow up with.'

Stella's sigh was part resignation. As much as she didn't want to see or get to know Mitch's son, it looked as though there was no avoiding it. 'You won't hear me disputing the virtues of living here.'

'Then you understand why this move is important for me.'

Yes, she did. 'My foster family and all those things you mentioned are exactly what draws me back here.'

The silence between them became uncomfortable.

Stella's conscience bit deeply as she recognised the healing she'd already experienced as a child when she'd come to live in Hope Creek. And it hadn't just been her. This had been a place of healing for her sisters, too.

It was something she hoped she could help other kids achieve through her tennis centre.

How could she resent any child – even Deanna's – coming here to work through whatever demons were plaguing him?

Part of her wanted to ask what Kade had gone through, but the larger part of her didn't want to know.

'Will you at least think about my suggestion?' he asked quietly. When she nodded, he continued, 'Apart from this farm ownership fiasco, how are you doing, Stella?'

She didn't meet his eyes. 'I'm okay.'

'I can't imagine—'

'I doubt anyone can,' she cut in quickly. Then, she shrugged. 'It wasn't the way I wanted to finish my career.'

'I understand. No professional sports person wants their career finished by injury.'

The magnitude of being forced to retire through injury

was probably something only other career sports professionals could understand.

'You were fortunate you were able to end your career on your terms,' she said. 'I think I read somewhere that you remained free of major injuries throughout your entire career?'

* * *

Crazy, but his heart lightened to know she'd bothered to read about him. 'I was lucky.'

Her hazel eyes were gorgeous as they met his gaze. 'You were extremely talented. I know they say you were one of the greatest quarterbacks who's ever played in the NFL.'

He'd had a lot of praise from countless people over his career, but none of the verbal accolades had ever registered. Strangely, the note of pride in her voice made pride swell in his chest.

Even after their acrimonious parting, that they could still feel pride in the other's achievements counted for something. Didn't it?

'I heard commentators say that you only escaped injury because you had a high game intelligence – being able to move around the pocket and read the defence. I remember one commentator said you had incredibly focused mental acuity.'

Yes, there was definitely admiration in her eyes and it warmed him right through.

'You watched my games?'

A shutter drew down on her features and she bit her lip as though regretful she'd revealed so much. 'Sometimes, I had jet lag when I arrived at a hotel on the other side of the world.' She moved one hand in a bored way. 'I saw a little from time to time as I flicked through the channels.'

For all that her words were dismissive, he recognised her 'tell'. The way she pressed her lips together as soon as she finished speaking had always been a dead giveaway to him that she wasn't being completely honest.

Instinctively, he knew she'd watched more of his games than by a sheer fluke of flicking through the channels and happening upon them.

Good. Because he'd watched every single one of her grand slam finals and a whole lot of her other matches that'd been televised.

'I saw some of yours too,' he said casually.

More recently, Kade had started watching them with him.

Neither Kade nor Mitchell would ever forget her last match in Paris. It'd been obvious she hadn't been well. The heat had definitely affected her because she'd lost one crucial point at the end of the first set as she'd had to race off the court to be physically ill. It'd caused an absolute stir and stopped play.

The crowd had risen to its feet and given her a standing ovation when she'd taken to the court again rather than forfeiting the match when the umpire had called time.

Always a crowd favourite, the spectators had been behind her even more when they saw she struggled to hold it together and play each point.

Kade had cheered in their living room as she soldiered on. His son had been so impressed, continually commenting on how she must be digging into her reserves to return to the court and keep hitting those shots back over the net.

Mitch had been proud.

It hadn't been a resounding victory. It'd been a hard-fought match, with none of her usual brilliance but all of her tenacity. Instead of her normal repertoire of winning shots, she'd basically just kept hitting the ball back to her opponent and waited for her to make a mistake.

The crowd had been up on its feet – almost as one – celebrating each time she'd won a game as though she'd won the match. They'd hung on every point and ultimately celebrated her victory, not realizing at the time that they'd witnessed her last professional tennis match.

Mitchell had never successfully shut Stella out of his life.

He confessed as much now as he told her, 'You had an amazing career. The most powerful serve in the history of women's tennis, and you hold the record for the longest streak of undefeated matches not once or twice but half a dozen times, I believe?'

There was a flare of surprise in her eyes before she murmured, 'I'm sure it will be a record soon broken.'

'You always did brush off your achievements.' Their gazes locked and Mitch found himself taking a deep, steadying breath as an almost tangible current of connection ran between them. His voice softened. 'I'm really glad your dreams came true, Stella.'

Her slender throat worked up and down. Just before she tore her gaze away from his, he glimpsed sadness bracket her mouth and a slight glistening of moisture in her eyes.

His heart twisted.

Everything in him wanted to take her in his arms and kiss her. Everything in him longed to make her happy and see her beautiful smile.

'I'm glad for you too, Mitch.' As she stood, he noticed she put more weight on her left foot. 'I… I'll think about what you've said. Right now, though, I really need to rest. I'm still on Swiss time and today's been a bit of a strain.'

He understood, yet he didn't want to leave.

He wanted to stay.

He wanted to stay and catch up on everything that'd happened since they'd parted.

You're a fool, Mitchell Scott.

She broke your heart once. Do you really want to let her do it again?

He really was a fool, because Stella was already taking a couple of steps to leave the gazebo and telling the dogs to heel so she could make her way back to the house.

It was clear she had no desire to bridge the gap, yet something made him push the possibility they could be friends.

In a couple of long strides, he was beside her. 'We

were friends once, Stella, and even though there are years of experiences we haven't shared, do you think it might be possible for us to recapture our friendship?'

The scars he carried when he'd walked away from their relationship still ran deep.

Did she have any regrets at all?

'Stella?'

'There's a lot I'm working through, Mitchell. I'm not certain I'm at a point where I want to re-establish friendships with anyone right now.'

'I'd like for us to get to know each other again.' He watched her closely as he asked, 'Would you come out with me one night in Lancaster for dinner?'

'I… I can't.'

He looked away from her, unwilling to let her see his disappointment.

'The media still thinks I'm in Switzerland,' she explained hurriedly. 'I don't want to be seen out and about.'

Hope flared and his gaze locked on to hers again. 'What about lunch then? A picnic lunch by the creek or on top of Shady Hill, just like we used to when we were kids?'

* * *

Just like they used to…

Alarm bells clanged.

It seemed so simple, but they weren't kids anymore.

Everything was more complicated now. Yet, despite everything, she still liked Mitchell.

Once they'd gone their separate ways, it'd felt like something vital was missing from her life.

Could she let him back into her life as a friend rather than wanting him as a lover?

Trying to sound as pragmatic as possible she said, 'You're right. We shared a lot together over our formative years.' Honestly, apart from her sisters, she'd never had another person she felt as close to. Never known another person with whom she could simply be herself – unreservedly herself – without any fear of judgement. Not even Steve. 'Let's have that picnic together sometime soon.'

'Stella! Mitch!' Marg called from the house. 'June and Bob have popped in. Come on up. They'd like to welcome you both home.'

Stella's chest tightened.

She knew they'd be receiving a lot of visitors in the next week to say hello to her and she knew everyone in the community would be coming out of genuine warmth and caring rather than out of curiosity and a need to gossip.

But the way Marg had phrased it – like she and Mitch had come home as an item…

The way she'd linked their names together…

It made her breath stall in her throat.

CHAPTER EIGHT

'We were friends once. We could make this work,' Stella rationalised out loud to Morgan and Callie the next day as the three of them sat out on the large swing seats that were suspended from the beams of the verandah.

'I think you've got rocks in your head,' Morgan pronounced almost savagely.

'I think you should go for it,' Callie disagreed. 'Hope Farm is ideal. It's right next door so you're still close to home without actually living at home.'

'You're being lazy,' Morgan told her. 'You don't need to be right next door to the station.'

Margaret joined them, carrying a wooden tray of glasses that were full of iced-cold, home-made lemon cordial. 'Morgan's right,' she said as she handed out the drinks to their chorused thanks. 'Although we'll be happy to have you so close, you don't need to live right next door. But if you do choose to live anywhere in Hope Creek, then make sure you're moving back here for the right reason. I've always said it and I still say it – Hope Creek is a place to heal, not to hide.'

Clutching her glass in front of her, Stella leaned against the cane backing of the swing seat and set it rocking.

Had she come home to heal or to hide?

In truth, she knew it was a combination of both. She didn't want to be exposed to the prying eyes of the press or the public – gawked at as she tried valiantly to walk without the slightest hint of a limp. Even now, on this hot summer's day, she wore light trousers while her sisters were dressed in short pants, and Marg had on a short, summery dress.

She wasn't sure she'd ever not be self-conscious about her artificial foot.

'I've already signed the contract and everything is on track for the development to start on Monday.'

'I'm sure there'll be a loophole. Liz wasn't exactly giving full disclosure, was she?' Morgan argued.

'You were happy enough for Stella's project to go ahead before you heard Mitch owned the other half of the farm,' Callie commented. 'I don't see what difference it makes – unless one of them still has feelings for the other?'

Stella was aware of Margaret's scrutiny.

Oh.

Not just Margaret's scrutiny.

The silence grew as all three of them hung on her response.

'I broke up with Mitch years ago.'

'Yes, but—' Callie began.

'I was engaged to Steve.'

Callie rolled her eyes. 'Both bad decisions if you ask me.'

'Both men were bad decisions, yes,' Morgan agreed. 'Men in general, I'd say.' When Margaret cleared her throat, Morgan amended hurriedly, 'With the exception of Jim – and Blue – of course.'

'What's going on with you, Morgan?' Stella asked.

'Oh no! We're not going there. This is about you, not me!'

'I meant,' Callie cut over the pair of them, 'Stella's engagement to Steve was obviously a bad decision, but so was her break up with Mitch.'

Morgan straightened in her chair so fast, she sloshed some of the lemon cordial out of her glass. 'What are you talking about, Callie? Have you forgotten that Mitchell cheated on Stella, for God's sake! You think she should've just forgiven him?' The sound that emerged from her throat was one of pure exasperation. 'He got another woman pregnant! He doesn't deserve forgiveness.'

'I might've been able to have forgiven him under the circumstances,' Stella admitted, 'but, as Steve said—'

'As that bastard you ended up being engaged to said, *"How could you ever forget what he did and trust him again, Stella"*,' Callie supplied in a mocking voice. 'I'm sorry but I never liked Steve when he was your coach, and I liked him even less when he was your fiancé. He was playing you, Stella, making you dwell on the fact that every time you were apart you'd be wondering whether Mitch was in bed with someone else.'

'Well, it was true, wasn't it?' Morgan said. 'I wouldn't have trusted him for a sec—'

'Can't you see that Steve played Stella – had her break up with Mitch – so he could move in on her?' Callie demanded.

'Thank God he did,' Morgan pronounced. 'At least that way she broke up with Mitchell before he made a fool of her and announced he was marrying the mother of his child!'

'Enough, girls,' Margaret intervened.

'Both of you are right.' Stella couldn't swallow down the tears fast enough and they clogged her throat, making her words thick. 'I was stupid. Not once but twice. I was conned by Mitch and then I didn't see the writing on the wall with Steve. Turns out I have lousy instincts when it comes to men.'

Margaret shifted to sit next to her and place a comforting arm around her shoulders.

Callie moved in front of Stella and she took one of Stella's hands in hers. 'I'm sorry, Stell. I didn't mean to upset you. I actually think you should give Mitch another chance.'

'Oh for Pete's sake, Callie!' Morgan all but exploded. 'He broke her heart!'

'That was then. This is now,' Callie insisted quietly. 'I totally believe what Liz told you when we found out Mitch was getting married – that he has no recollection of taking Deanna to bed.'

'Oh please!' Morgan raised both her fists up in front of her face and made a gesture of frustration. 'He was an American college football jock. For all we know he could've been screwing half the cheerleading squad every time Stella went on tour.'

'Morgan!' Margaret admonished sternly. 'I don't like your language and your comments are not helpful.'

Stella bit her lip and looked at the bitterness etched into Morgan's features. It was clear that Morgan was hurting. 'How about you tell us what's going on with you and your boyfriend?'

'I don't have a boyfriend,' came the sharp reply. When they continued to look at her with their eyebrows raised she conceded, 'Don't ask any questions because I'm not prepared to talk about it.'

Heavy silence followed.

All three women knew there was no point in pressing Morgan for details because once she declared a subject was off-limits, that was it. It'd been that way ever since she'd been a kid. Margaret and Jim had always joked they should've known they were in for a stubborn one the moment they'd seen her red hair.

'Those cupcakes should just about be ready to come out of the oven,' Margaret said. 'I'd better go and check on them.'

As their mum bustled away, Callie returned to her swing seat. 'Mitchell made a mistake when he was very young. I don't want both of you to keep paying for it for the rest of your lives.'

'You sound like Liz,' Stella complained.

'A leopard doesn't change its spots,' Morgan emphasised in a warning tone.

'I remember Stella told us that when she let herself into Mitch's room that night, it reeked of stale beer. Think about it,' Callie urged. 'He's been told his parents are unaccounted for in a bomb blast and presumed dead. He goes out drinking, ends up in bed with Deanna and he even did the honourable thing and married her when he found out she was pregnant.'

Morgan's prettiness was marred by her bitter expression. 'Some honour!'

Frowning, Stella tilted her head to one side. 'I've never seen you like this, Morgan. I know you're worried about me, but I'm more worried about you right now.' Sure, Morgan could be prickly sometimes, but never negative and judgemental like this. She barely recognised her sister.

'I'm fine,' Morgan insisted. 'Don't change the subject.'

Callie shot Stella a look that said *Don't go there*, then barrelled on, 'From all reports, Mitchell tried hard to make the marriage work. Deanna had affairs.'

'And our saintly Mitchell didn't?' Morgan asked.

'He did not.' Callie was adamant.

'How would you even know?' Stella asked.

Mitch had been the highest paid quarterback in the history of the National Football League, but that was in America. Australia didn't give gridiron players media coverage. Sure, there were games live-streamed on some of the pay channels but rugby league, rugby union and Aussie rules were the most popular codes nationwide, with soccer also being popular.

'I've googled him from time to time.' She shrugged her shoulders. 'Idle curiosity, that's all. After all, he's famous and we did grow up together.'

'I've seen him splashed over social media – but it's generally been with one or another gorgeous woman on his arm.' Again, there was an unrecognisable harshness to Morgan's tone. 'He wasn't married to his son's mother for long before they were divorced and he's been unable to keep his pants zipped up ever since.'

'I wish *you'd* zip it, Morgan!' Callie told her.

Stella straightened in her chair. As much as they all loved each other, once Callie and Morgan clashed, they could argue heatedly for hours. 'Hey! Please—'

The screen door swung open with a bang. 'Morgan, the

cakes will be another five minutes,' Margaret said as she came back to join them. 'Maybe you could get them out while I put my feet up?'

'Sure.' Morgan took the hint and got up immediately. 'The cool drink is good, but I think I'll put the kettle on as well. Anyone else want one?'

'Yes please,' Callie said with a smile and a side wink to Stella that said she'd be happy to keep Morgan busy in the kitchen for a little while longer.

'That sounds lovely, dear,' Margaret told her.

'Stella?'

'No thanks.'

'Okay. Tea for three.'

When Morgan went inside, Margaret rolled her eyes. 'There's definitely more stormy weather coming from that direction. But for now, let's deal with you,' she said to Stella. 'I don't want to see you heartbroken again, my darling, but it would be nice if you and Mitch became friends again. You were inseparable once and, despite the mistake he made, I've always liked Mitch.'

'Don't listen to Morgan,' Callie said softly. 'She's bitter and twisted at the moment and hating on men in general. We all know that you can't believe everything you read in the newspapers, but I didn't see one picture of Mitchell with another woman in the years he was married to Deanna.'

'He was pictured with many different women after his divorce.' Stella immediately regretted her statement because it was an admission she'd noticed. This did not go unrecognised by Callie if her sister's raised eyebrows were any indication.

Callie didn't pursue Stella's comment directly. 'I don't believe Mitch would've changed so dramatically in character. If he was playing the field – pardon the pun – it was probably because he couldn't find a woman who stacked up against you.'

'He wouldn't have come back to Hope Creek if he was a fast-living playboy type,' Margaret added in his defence.

'Anyway, even if you decide you don't want to move into the caretaker's cottage at the farm, we're neighbours. It'll be difficult if there's any awkwardness.'

Stella rubbed at her eyes. 'Yes, it would be good if we can bury the past.'

But not wanting any awkwardness and being able to interact with Mitch without it were two completely different things. Although she'd only seen him twice, she couldn't look at him without remembering how damned good he looked naked.

On both occasions, there'd been seconds where she'd imagined the way his muscles were rippling under his clothing as he moved and how divine he'd been when he was lying naked on the bed they'd shared. She remembered how her hands had itched as she'd stood next to him as they'd brushed their teeth side by side and his torso had been naked, a white towel wrapped carelessly around his waist. Then, there was the way he'd used his very well endowed body to deliver one climax after another through their nights of endless lovemaking.

Every time he'd glanced her way, she'd needed to quell the desire that rose within her and try to forget the feel of his large, capable hands against her skin.

'Best we all just leave the past in the past and move forward,' Margaret said prosaically.

It would be best, but was it possible?

Stella still felt incredibly vulnerable as she tried to adjust to life off the tennis circuit. Seeing Mitch again had left her feeling confused because, despite all the years they'd been apart – despite having taken Steve as her lover and accepted his proposal of marriage – she had to face the unwelcome truth.

Steve had been a rebound lover. Although she'd relied on him to navigate her way through her professional tennis career – and despite having shared everything related to her tennis career – she'd never felt the close connection with Steve that she had with Mitch.

Had he ever seen her as a woman, rather than a tennis player?

As far as their sexual relationship had gone, she realised now that with Steve she'd been having sex rather than making love. Her ex-fiancé had been a convenient lover and perhaps one she'd used to try to convince herself she was over Mitchell.

It was unfair of her. She owned that now.

Maybe it was also the reason why Steve had turned to Jenny and had an affair with her?

Maybe he'd sensed that Stella had never truly banished Mitchell from her heart?

After seeing Mitch again she knew that somehow, she had to get over her first love.

Given they'd spent so many years apart and she was still carrying a torch for him, distance and time didn't seem to ever be going to help. Logically, then, why not try the reverse? Why not let him back in her life and hope that familiarity bred contempt?

Immediately she discounted the idea. She still liked Mitch. The best she could hope for was that in seeing him frequently, she'd be desensitised to the effect he had on her physical awareness of him and so would not continue to experience this needy response to him.

'Is there any spark of attraction between you two now?' Callie pushed.

Oh, she so didn't want to go there.

Just the mention of a spark and she felt the flames of need fan up like an inferno deep inside her.

Stella shook her head in denial and said firmly, 'Even if I was still attracted to Mitch – which I'm not—' *Liar!* '—I'm hardly the same person now as I was back then so it's not like he'd ever be attracted to me again.'

'Of course he would be,' Callie told her. 'You haven't changed at all and you're now one of the most successful women's tennis players ever. You're a champion in your sport just like he was in his. You have all that in common. It's something few people ever experience.'

'I'm a *former* champion with *one foot*. I doubt any man would see my right stump as being particularly attractive.'

'Stella Simpson!' Margaret admonished. 'Don't you dare put yourself down or start sounding sorry for yourself.' Her mother's features creased with her anguish. 'Don't think for one minute that your amputation makes you any less a woman – any less an attractive woman.'

Stella pushed both feet against the wooden verandah slats to set the swing back into a comforting, rocking motion. Closing her eyes she said, 'I doubt any man would find my stump a turn on.'

'You wouldn't dismiss a man you loved just because of a prosthetic limb,' Margaret said.

'A man with a prosthetic appendage? I think it might actually be a good thing on some men,' Callie quipped wickedly.

'Callie!' their foster mother admonished. 'Keep it clean.'

Stella laughed. The youngest of the three of them, Callie had always had a wicked sense of humour and her comments were often risqué, even though she was completely inexperienced.

'Listen, I'm not even going to ask you what you saw in Steve,' Callie said.

'Please don't bad mouth him, Callie,' Stella pleaded. 'Yes, he cheated on me. But he isn't the outright schemer you make him out to be. What happened… well, it just happened and I was probably just as much to blame as he was.'

'No.' Callie was having none of it. 'You weren't. You were honest and he wasn't.'

No, I wasn't. I never admitted to him that Mitchell was still in my heart.

Then again, she'd never fully admitted it to herself either.

'But let's not talk about him,' Callie continued, 'because I don't even want you to think about him. What was it you saw in Mitchell? His strong, masculine jaw? The breadth of those wide shoulders? His chiselled cheekbones? Or was it his delicious blue eyes or his cute butt?'

'Callie!' Stella stopped the rocking motion of the swing very abruptly, amazed to hear Callie's description. 'Did you have a crush on him?'

'I can't believe you didn't know it!' Callie laughed. 'Truthfully, I did way back before you were going out with him, but I realised very quickly I was definitely just the younger sister and he had eyes for nobody but you. I got over it pretty quickly.'

'I had no idea!'

'Well, hopefully he didn't either,' she grinned. 'Anyway, I want to know. Did your heart flip every time he sent you one of those gorgeous smiles or did you melt in a puddle at his feet every time he looked intently at you and hung off your every word?'

The thought of those killer smiles and those intense blue eyes made Stella pleased she was sitting down, but she wasn't about to reveal her reactions to Callie or anyone else.

'What was the one thing that turned you to mush?' Callie persisted.

One thing?

There wasn't one isolated thing. Everything about Mitchell had made her heartbeat accelerate.

Mitchell had been the classic American poster boy and she loved all the things Callie had mentioned and a whole heap more. She'd once commented to Callie that she could sit and listen to his slight American accent all day.

'Why did you love him?' Callie asked again.

The genie was out of the bottle…

'I fell for him – not just his looks. He always listened to me and took my dreams seriously – encouraged me to pursue them.' She felt her chest hollow out as she remembered all the hours they'd sat by the creek together under the shade of the paperbark trees and talked about their dreams. 'He understood me. He never once mocked me when I said I wanted to win a Grand Slam tournament. He gave me the confidence I could actually do it.'

'And Mitch confided his dreams to you,' Callie said.

She nodded.

'Then, you were both attracted to each other for who you were rather than simply looks – although, frankly, you are gorgeous, Stella.'

Stella looked at her sister. Callie was supermodel-beautiful with her blonde hair, blue eyes and amazing figure.

The Richardsons had always joked that there was no way anyone would ever take them as a biological family when their girls were brunette, blonde and auburn.

'You're all gorgeous girls,' Margaret insisted. 'And you're all very bright girls.' She raised a hand when Callie went to say something. 'Callie's made some good points, Stella. Your attraction to Mitchell wasn't simply based on physical attraction – you two had a real connection. A true friendship. So, why would he care about a prosthetic foot?' Instead of lowering her hand, she used it to point an accusing finger at Stella. 'Don't sell yourself short.'

'You want for us to get back together?' Stella asked the older woman.

'I wouldn't be disappointed to see you two together, but I'm not pushy like Liz. What will be will be. You two will work it out, but at least be friends. You can never have too many of those.'

'I'm not interested in becoming involved in a relationship again right now. I need to sort out my life and find my direction. Tennis was my life and now it's over.'

'You'd told me after the Australian Open this year that you wanted to retire and start a family,' Callie said gently. 'You could do that now.'

Stella shot a look at Margaret.

Marg gave a slight shake of her head.

Picking up a cushion, Stella squeezed it against her chest. She should've known Margaret would respect her privacy and wouldn't have told Callie all the details of her accident. 'I've got to sort myself out before I can even entertain the idea of a relationship.'

'We're all here for you my darling,' Margaret said. 'Whatever you decide, we'll support you.'

'You know, talking this through has helped and I think you're both right. There'll be no harm done in moving into the caretaker's cottage and starting work to make the tennis centre. Mitchell was very reasonable in his proposal that he'd buy me out for all but five acres now and that I'd be able to keep the land I needed for the tennis centre.'

'And you don't want him not to be able to own Hope Farm,' Callie put in. 'That would hardly be fair.'

'Don't you try to make her feel guilty about that, Callie,' Morgan said as she rejoined them. 'If that happens it'll be Liz to blame, not Stella.' She passed cups of tea to Callie and Margaret then sat and nursed her own. 'It's not Mitchell's interests I'm worried about, it's Stella I'm concerned for.'

'No need to be worried about me,' she insisted.

'Well, I am. You were completely devastated about Deanna's pregnancy. How are you going to feel living so close to her child?'

Margaret cut in before Stella had even had time to think of how to answer. 'Whatever you feel, you mustn't show it to Kade,' she said. 'He's not to blame for his parents' actions. He didn't ask for them to sleep together and he certainly didn't ask to be born, so you have to be pleasant to him. I'm sure you'll find he's a really likeable kid.'

'You're a better person than I am even being able to speak to Mitchell Scott again after his betrayal!' Morgan exclaimed heatedly. 'Every time I see him, I'm going to remember how he cheated on you.'

'Behave yourself, Morgan, and let it go,' Margaret chided.

'If Stella can move on, so can we,' Callie wagged her finger at Morgan. 'And, as Margaret says, be especially nice to Kade if you see him. We were all vulnerable kids once.'

'Don't worry, I'm not about to go around ignoring Kade or casting daggers his way,' Morgan said grumpily.

'I'm glad to hear it,' Margaret said. 'We look after each other in this community.'

'What time are we expected to be at the pub tonight for this big announcement?' Morgan asked.

'Five thirty,' Callie replied. 'We'll have the usual BBQ dinner there.'

'I love Saturday nights. I get the night off cooking,' Margaret said, 'and I look forward to gathering with the whole community.'

Mitch and Kade would be part of the community now, too.

'I know it's not what you want to hear, but it was hard for me to see Kade yesterday morning.' Stella probably shouldn't have made the confession, but the words were out before she could filter them.

'It was over a decade ago,' Margaret reminded her. 'You need to let it go.'

'I know,' Stella agreed. 'What Mitch is proposing is a win-win.'

'Sounds like a good plan,' Margaret said. 'But it's your decision.'

It was definitely a plan.

Whether or not it was a good plan remained to be seen.

CHAPTER NINE

The Hope Creek Hotel was packed.

Bill Hickson had spread the word through the small community that they should be there tonight for an important announcement, and the community had answered the call. Mitchell couldn't think of a single family that hadn't shown up.

'Mitchell Scott!' A rather rotund lady in a brightly coloured floral dress called out to him as she cut through the crowd and made her way towards him.

Mitchell grinned. It'd been quite a feat to keep his return to Hope Creek a secret and Mavis Cooper, the community gossip, would be irritated all night realising that she'd only found out at the same time as most of the town.

'Mavis,' he said as she stopped before him, then stood up on her tiptoes and offered her cheek for a kiss. 'You're looking very fetching tonight.'

'Look at you, all grown up and as handsome as sin! I couldn't believe it when they told me outside that you were here. Fancy sneaking into town – and with your son in tow, no less! Where is the lad?'

'I believe Jayden and Patrick Lynch are introducing him to some of the other boys.'

Mavis patted him on the arm. 'Well, welcome back! How long are you in town and—' she lowered her voice conspiratorially, '—does your return have anything to do with our community's most famous daughter?'

He chose to deliberately misunderstand her words. 'Of course. She may be a *New York Times* bestselling author, but she'll always be Aunt Liz to me and I love coming back to see her.'

'Tsk tsk.' She wagged her finger at him. 'I'm sure you know very well who I'm talking about. Your aunt is the second most famous woman Hope Creek has ever produced.' Lowering her voice again she said, 'We're all keeping quiet about Stella's return because we want to protect her from the press. But at least we knew she was arriving. Liz gave us no inkling you'd be back in town! Now—'

'Testing… 1-2-3…'

Screeeech!

Mavis covered her ears as Bill took to the microphone and it produced some high-pitched feedback.

'Turn it down a bit, Bill!' someone yelled. 'I don't want a headache *before* I start drinking!'

There was laughter all round.

Mitchell looked over towards the person who'd made the comment and saw it was Blue from the homestead. Standing with Blue was the whole Richardson clan. They were an attractive family, but it was Stella who made his pulse rate accelerate.

A few inches taller than her sisters, she was flanked protectively by Callie and Morgan, even though she needed no protection in this friendly atmosphere.

She was laughing at Blue's comment along with everyone else, and her smile was the best thing he'd seen all day.

'Can't have that, Blue,' Bill responded. 'You get a headache and there goes the night's profit!'

There was more laughter.

'Seriously though, folks, I've asked you all to be here tonight because I wanted you all together to hear my announcement, but before I do, let's welcome Stella back to town.'

There were cheers and calls of welcome. Mitchell saw Stella give everyone a sunny smile and a big wave.

'Thanks everyone! It's good to be home.'

'It's good to have you back among us, love,' Bill said.

'Hey, Bill! Don't forget Mitchell!' Mavis called.

Bill rolled his eyes and nodded as the community cheered and called out to Mitchell. 'I was getting there, Mavis.'

The publican shuffled on his feet a little and for a moment it seemed as though he was trying to control his emotions. Knowing what was coming, Mitchell guessed the old man was probably in danger of tearing up. 'Now, the welcomes are over... you all know I've been trying to find a buyer for the pub for a while now.'

Everyone stilled.

Bill cleared his throat. 'Hope Creek Hotel has been an important part of this town. It's the place where we all come together on a Saturday night to catch up on family and business news, and the place we've done most of our celebrating. It's also been the venue for some feisty town meetings over the years.'

'Too right!' Bob Lynch yelled. 'The Australian Wool Corporation for one!'

There were some mutterings around the room from the older farmers about the failed Wool Reserve Price Scheme that'd been a disaster for the farmers who'd run sheep.

Bill motioned with his hand for the comments to cease. 'This old hotel has also served as the heart of the community operations in times of bush fires and flooding, and the coordination point of a few rescue missions.' He paused and acknowledged all the head nodding. 'I don't need to go on because you've all been here. You and your families and in most cases, your parents and their parents before them, have gathered here in times of need and in times of celebration – to celebrate love and to support each other in times of loss.'

'Sure have,' the local vet, Tom Ryder, agreed.

There was a murmur of agreement.

'Unlike most of you, I don't have an heir to pass the family business on to and I've reached the point where I'd rather sit with you all on the other side of the bar because my legs are getting tired standing on the opposite side of it.'

'You've done a fine job, Bill,' Jim Richardson said. 'We're all grateful for it.'

There was a round of applause and some 'Here, here' comments.

'I didn't want some city slicker to come in here and take over the reins, and to tell you the truth, I didn't even get a single bite until recently,' Bill continued. 'Then, I was approached by someone I know you'll all respect. Someone who's been part of this community on and off over the years but a man who – no matter how far he's travelled from these parts, and these shores – has always called Australia, and most importantly, Hope Creek, his home.'

Liz interjected with a whoop.

'Tonight, then, it's with a tinge of sadness but a lot of relief, I get to announce that I'm taking up retirement to join you on the other side of the bar and handing the baton over to… drumroll… Mitchell Scott.'

There were some oohs and aahs of surprise and disbelief among the clapping, but there was no mistaking the vibe that Mitchell was welcome here.

'Well done!' someone called out.

Another voice carried over the applause, 'Welcome home, Mitchell.'

'You dark horse,' Mavis said beside him.

Mitchell gave a wave of acknowledgement to all in the room.

'This is where I'd planned to welcome you home too, Mitchell. Now, come up here and say a few words,' Bill encouraged.

He didn't hesitate. He made his way towards Bill receiving many pats on the back as he did so.

'Thank you, all of you. Thanks for welcoming me when I was a kid and accepting me as part of your community. It's your warmth and community spirit that's always drawn me to Hope Creek and from the minute I first arrived, I knew I wanted to return and settle here one day.' He couldn't help it. His gaze fixed on Stella for too many seconds before he made himself look at the rest of the Hope Creek citizens. 'Kade, can you come up here please, son?'

Kade made his way to his side.

'I'm real pleased to be able to bring my son, Kade, with me.'

'Hi Kade!'

'Hey Kade!'

'Welcome to Hope Creek, love!'

There were resounding shouts of welcome and Mitch's chest swelled with happiness. Beside him, he felt as though Kade stood an extra two inches taller. Mitch could've cried with joy because he hoped Kade's confidence would flourish now they'd made the move.

'I know you'll take him under your wing, in the same way you made me part of the community, and I thank you in advance for doing so. Now, the next round of drinks are on the house – and – before you think I'm being too liberal with Bill's money, I'll clarify that I became Hope Creek Hotel's official owner today at midday, so this round is on me!'

A cheer went up.

Marg walked over quickly to Mitch and put out her hand expectantly for the microphone. 'I have one quick announcement to make before those celebratory drinks,' she said. 'Ladies, don't forget our CWA meeting on Monday week. See you all there.'

Clicking off the microphone and handing it back to Mitch, she stood on her tiptoes and planted an unexpected kiss on his cheek. 'I'm really pleased you're back, Mitch.' There was no mistaking her sincerity. 'Now, how about you introduce me to Kade?'

For the next two hours, Mitch was welcomed back into the fold warmly by Hope Creek's citizens, but no matter how enthusiastically he interacted with them, he couldn't switch his attention off completely from Stella.

All night he was aware of where she was and who she was speaking to. It was only natural that she was being greeted every bit as warmly by everyone but it felt wrong, somehow, that she wasn't by his side – that they weren't being welcomed home together.

At one point he found it hard to concentrate on his conversation because Tom Ryder joined the Richardson group. Tom was a great guy and had been the closest of Mitch's friends among the boys he'd been to school with, but he knew Tom was recently separated and his friend was greeting Stella a little too enthusiastically for his liking.

'And we were blown away by the news that you'd had a son,' one of the town matrons was saying.

'He's my pride and joy,' Mitch answered as he tried to drag his gaze away from the warm smile Stella bestowed on Tom. 'Let me introduce you to him.'

Everyone was keen to meet Kade.

Kade had never been on the receiving end of so much genuine warmth and interest, and the transformation in him was heartwarming. Mitch had noticed that where Kade had started off standing fairly close to him and nodding or shaking his head in answer to questions, he'd ended up being comfortable to stand further apart, and had started talking quite excitedly about the goats and all he'd been doing at the farm.

Mitch knew that whatever awkwardness he had to endure with Stella, for his son's sake, he'd made the right decision to return home.

As if the mere thought of her had conjured her up, there she was with her sister, Callie, waiting to speak with him.

Morgan was nowhere in sight, although he knew she was around somewhere. He'd received a rather hostile stare from her earlier.

Checking that Kade was still busy playing a game of darts with the Lynch boys, Mitch turned to the ladies.

Callie just about launched herself at him. Giving him a huge hug, her blue eyes twinkled with genuine delight as she welcomed him home. 'It's so good to have you back. Congratulations on buying the pub.'

Stella was more reserved. 'I'd say your ownership of the pub has been very well received tonight.'

'It's good Bill can enjoy his retirement, now, knowing the hotel is in good hands,' Callie added. 'It would've been awful to have someone from the city – or even Lancaster for that matter – buy it up without understanding how much this hotel means to us here.'

'The nerve centre of the town?' Morgan finally joined her sisters but her words carried a hint of sarcasm. 'I hope you're not planning on making a lot of changes here, Mitchell.'

Oh yep. There was definitely a frosty censure from this one of Stella's sisters.

There was also a flash in Morgan's eyes that made him feel as though he'd just crawled out from under a rock.

'Just a bit of sprucing up,' Mitchell promised.

'What about a bit of sporting memorabilia up around the bar?' Callie suggested. 'You and Stella are town heroes.' She gestured to one of the walls where Bill had already hung a photo of each of them in the gallery of *Hope Creek's Famous Folk*. 'How about each of you donating something from your sporting careers to display in the hotel? It'd be a good draw card for the tourists who pass through, and I'm sure all of us locals would love to see something from you up on display as well.'

'I'm happy to go along with that, but I'd like to keep it something small. As Bill implied, this hotel is the sum of all the community, not just a few,' Mitchell said. 'What do you say, Stella?'

'I guess I could donate the racquet I used in my last match?'

'Perfect!' Callie clapped her hands together.

'Stella, you must be getting very tired. Why don't I drive you home?' Morgan's words weren't delivered as a question. 'I'm rostered on from sunrise tomorrow, so I'd like to get home myself.'

Morgan's dislike of him radiated off her in waves, which was hardly fair, he reasoned, given that her sister had dumped him.

'Thanks for coming tonight,' Mitch told them. 'Hope to see you all again soon.'

'Before we go, can I have a word please, Mitch?' Stella asked.

'Sure.'

'Will you walk us out?'

Morgan shot Stella a look of disapproval, but Callie grabbed Morgan by the elbow and said, 'We'll see you at the car, Stell,' before she propelled Morgan forward and raced ahead.

'Somehow I don't get the impression Morgan's happy to see me back,' he commented wryly.

'She's not a very happy person at the moment.' Stella's tone was apologetic. 'She's got some stuff going on.'

They walked out into the temperate evening.

Stella looked a million dollars in a silky red singlet top and a pair of cream linen trousers, but she had to be the only woman here in long pants.

He guessed it must be because of her foot, but he'd love to see her again in one of those skimpy little summer dresses that she'd used to wear around Hope Creek.

She stopped and turned towards him.

They were far enough away from the pub so as not to be overheard by anyone, and not close enough to her sisters that they'd be overheard by them either.

'I wanted to tell you that I've thought a lot about your offer.'

He held his breath.

'It's very generous of you considering you'd always expected to be able to buy the entire property.'

And? 'Have you made a decision or do you need more time to think about it?'

He waited.

'I'd like to go ahead and sign a separate agreement with you, then move into the cottage.'

He let out the pent-up breath and his spirits soared.

'That's fantastic news, Stella.'

She raised one hand and pushed back a strand of her shiny dark hair behind her right ear, and the gold from the large hooped earring glinted at him in the moonlight.

Hell, but she looked sexy.

Down boy!

Part of him wanted to whoop with joy.

Another part of him wanted to pull her close and kiss her as he'd done years ago – to see the softening of her features in the wake of his kisses and to feel the fullness of those lush lips of hers beneath his own mouth.

Sweet mercy!

He remembered the husky little mewls of pleasure she'd always made when he'd explored her body with his hands and his mouth. And, God help him, he remembered how she'd felt as she'd shuddered beneath him, her inner muscles contracting around him as she'd reached her climax.

'Whatever has been between us in the past, I always valued our friendship,' she told him earnestly. 'We've been reminded tonight just how important friendships are in this community and I hope we can go forward and cement our friendship again.'

It sounded like she'd rehearsed that little speech for hours.

Friendship.

Not relationship.

It was a start, but nowhere near what he really wanted – particularly when he had all those X-rated memories swirling through his brain.

'Sounds good to me,' he said simply. 'When are you planning to move in?'

'I think it's going to take me another week to get myself ready because I'm meeting with the builder a few times this week, so most likely Monday week.'

'Whenever you're ready, give me a yell and I'll come and help you with your gear.'

She took a half step back from him. 'No need. Jim and Blue will help. It's not like I've got a lot of gear and Liz told me tonight it's all fully furnished.'

Mitchell simply couldn't help himself.

He closed the distance between them, leaned forward and kissed her.

It was only a kiss on the cheek.

A brief kiss that was no more than one friend would give to another, but man, the touch of her skin under his lips ignited an inferno of desire that blazed through him.

As he pulled back, the light of the full moon was bright enough for him to see that colour swept from her chest to her cheeks and that her chest was rising and falling more rapidly than it should be.

As though she couldn't help herself, she raised her fingertips and touched them to the spot he'd kissed.

'Goodnight, Stella.'

'Night, Mitch.'

She turned and walked towards her sisters, seeming to pick up her right foot a little more carefully than normal.

As he watched the three sisters drive away from the hotel, he couldn't stop himself from wishing that he was the one who was driving Stella home.

Madness.

Must be the full moon.

CHAPTER TEN

It was just over a week since the night at the pub when Jim and Blue brought in the last boxes from the car.

'And we're done!' Jim told Stella.

'Thanks so much for your help.' There hadn't been very many boxes because Stella had accumulated very little during her lifetime. Living from hotel room to hotel room meant that she'd had no need for domestic items. What she had packed up and moved from Hope Creek Station was mainly tennis memorabilia from her career, and newly acquired household items from a quick and incognito shopping trip she'd made to Lancaster with Margaret.

The two-bedroom caretaker's cottage was already furnished comfortably. Stella loved the renovations Liz had organised. The beautiful timber floors had been repolished, and it now boasted a new kitchen and bathroom, all completed in natural tones.

Liz had asked whether she needed any safety rails installed in the bathroom, but Stella had been coping fine without them at the homestead. Besides, she wanted to live life as normally and independently as possible.

Moving into this light, airy, space of her own was a fantastic way to realise her independence.

'It's very comfortable,' Blue said for the fifth time.

'Oh no! I shouldn't have brought him,' Jim said as he

rolled his eyes. 'He'll be nagging me for a renovation to his quarters now!'

'No need to fear on that count, Boss,' Blue said. 'I haven't any need for fancy digs. I'm only happy that Stella has a nice, comfortable place to live.'

'It's exciting, to finally have a place to call my own,' she admitted.

Home.

Her home.

With the fortune she'd amassed through her tennis earnings, she could've bought a mansion – even a small castle – anywhere in the world, but the caretaker's cottage at Hope Creek Farm was perfect for her.

'If you ever want some company, I'll be happy to accept a dinner invitation,' Blue told her.

'I might have to learn how to cook first!'

'No need for perfection, love. I'll be very happy to be your guinea pig while you practise!'

'I care about you too much to inflict my experimental cooking on you,' Stella told him. She might've been the world's number one woman when it came to hitting tennis balls over the net, but apart from making the odd batch of Anzac slice or chocolate brownies with Morgan and Callie, she'd never had to cook in her life.

'You'll come and join us for dinner most nights, though, won't you?' Jim asked.

'I'd better come most afternoons and help Margaret prepare dinner so she can teach me to be useful in the kitchen.'

'Sounds good,' Jim said as he glanced at his watch. 'Now, do you want any help unpacking, or shall we go and leave you to it? I've got about an hour before I have to check in with the boys to see how the fencing is coming along on the south-eastern border.'

'I'm good from here, thanks.' She hugged them both. 'Thanks for your help.'

'That's what we're here for and don't you forget to holler if you need anything,' Blue said.

'Margy will be over as soon as her meeting's finished,' Jim reminded her.

Margaret had been conflicted when she'd gone to the meeting of the Country Women's Association because she'd thought Stella might need a hand settling everything in, but Stella and the men had persuaded her they could manage.

'Hopefully I'll have myself settled by then,' Stella said. 'I'll be able to welcome her to a well-organised home.'

Blue raised an eyebrow and couldn't resist a dig. 'Well-organised? You? That'll be the day! I still remember you running to catch the school bus with a brush in one hand and a pair of shoes in the other!'

'Yep. Marg and I often joked that we thought you'd appear on centre court one day having forgotten your racquets.'

'Oh, go on. I was never that bad.'

With that last round of teasing and laughter, they left.

As she stood on the small verandah, waving as she watched them drive off, it really sank in that she was alone.

Oh sure, they were only at the neighbouring property, and somewhere Liz, Mitchell and Kade were close by – as were the team of construction workers who'd already made a start to her development – but in driving off, Jim and Blue had left her feeling alone.

Everything was so still and quiet at this time of the day. The machinery from the excavators had gone quiet, telling her the men must be having smoko. Even nature was quiet without a whisper of breeze in the air.

The silence magnified her feeling of solitude.

Her right hand lifted to her abdomen and rested there for a second before she shook off her sadness.

Some things weren't meant to be.

Taking in a deep breath she gave herself a firm talking to and dwelt on how different it would be in the evening and at daybreak. Then, the kookaburras would be laughing and the magpies singing.

With Mitchell having been at the homestead on his holiday visits when he was younger, and living there in his teens, Stella knew both properties like the back of her hand

Ah! An expression about a hand instead of a foot!

She smiled and thought *old hand, lending a hand, handing it to someone, changing hands...*

Yes, there were probably just as many expressions about hands as there were about feet. Anyway, she could hardly stand here all day. She needed to *hop to it* and get unpacked.

Turning back to go into the cottage, she realised she'd never truly had her own space.

While she'd been on tour, she'd initially shared a hotel room with another player to save costs. Then, by the time she'd been earning enough money to have her own room, she'd been engaged to Steve and they'd shared a room or later, a suite.

Even at the rehab facility staff buzzed in and out of her private room. This was hers to do with as she wanted.

'It is what I make it,' she told herself firmly. 'It's what I've always wanted.'

It was what she thought she'd always wanted, but she never thought she'd be putting down roots alone. Crossing over the threshold, she thought how nice it would be if she was setting up house with a lover – being carried over that threshold supported by strong arms and against a solid chest.

Mitchell's image came to mind.

Being held in Mitch's arms had been sheer heaven.

Falling asleep with her head pillowed against his chest and listening to his strong heartbeat had been so comforting.

Making love together...

Oh dear. She had to banish all those thoughts from her mind or she'd blush every time she saw him.

Why were all the intimate memories still so torturously vivid after so long?

Shaking herself mentally, she grabbed a pair of scissors and went to the first box, marked 'Kitchen'. It didn't matter she wasn't sharing this with anyone.

Soon enough, the tennis courts and cabins would be built, there'd be coaches and kids staying and the place would be a hive of activity. In the interim, there'd be a million decisions to make. Margaret had already roped her into helping with the preparations for the CWA fair, so there was plenty to keep her occupied.

Life would fall into a comfortable rhythm eventually and every day when she'd gone to the site and seen the progress, she was happy her immediate plans were coming together.

An hour later, she'd finished unpacking all the new items she'd purchased for her kitchen, and had just put the kettle on when she saw Kade and his puppy at the back screen door.

'Hello!' he greeted easily. 'Can I come in?'

Instantly her heart felt heavy in her chest and her diaphragm seemed to constrict around her lungs, making each breath difficult.

'No. It's not alright,' she wanted to tell him firmly. *'I don't want anything to do with you. Go away and don't come back.'*

'I picked some flowers for you.' He held out a wildly arranged odd assortment of blooms that must've come from Liz's garden. 'I thought you might like them.'

There was warmth in his tone.

Hope in his expression.

Awkwardness in his stance.

Oh hell.

How could she refuse him? He'd done nothing to earn her dislike and he was just a kid.

But he was more than a kid.

He was Mitchell's son.

Deanna's son.

He's a boy who's gone to the trouble of picking you flowers.

He was also a boy who was starting to look uncomfortable – his initial friendly smile turning into self-consciousness.

Jax whined next to him, tilted his scruffy brown head to one side and sent her a pleading look.

What are you doing, Stella?

Don't be mean!

'Hi Kade,' she forced. 'Sure, come in. How lovely of you to have brought me flowers.'

'Er… I'm sorry. I didn't mean to interrupt. Dad told me you were moving in today and Aunt Liz thought you might like some flowers.'

Aunt Liz.

Again.

Stella cursed her neighbour and wished she'd stick to writing her stories and solving her characters' problems.

'Aunt Liz said to tell you she's in the middle of an exciting development for her characters, but she'll pop down later this afternoon to welcome you.'

An exciting development for her characters?

Stella thought of Liz cooking up drama and chaos for the hero and heroine and instantly felt sorry for them. Still, at least if she was busy causing her characters mayhem, Liz wouldn't be focusing any attention on her and Mitch.

When Kade hadn't moved to come inside, she went to the screen door and opened it. 'They're beautiful flowers. Very happy, bright colours and exactly what I need to make the place feel homey.'

Kade shifted from one foot to the other as he handed her the flowers.

When she took them, she knelt down to pat Jax with her other hand. 'Hello, Jax. You're quite an adorable puppy aren't you? I suppose you can come in, too.'

'I love him to bits,' Kade said. 'Aunt Liz bought him for me. I've always wanted a dog but Mom never let me have one and Dad said he couldn't really insist because he wouldn't be the one helping to look after it.'

Stella resisted the urge to cover her ears.

She didn't want to hear about Kade's life and hated that Deanna was mentioned in the same breath as Mitchell.

As much as her self-protective instincts screamed at her to keep the American boy at arm's length, and that she didn't want to have to think about Deanna, she didn't have it in her to upset him. It was fairly obvious he'd become unsure when she was so slow to greet him. She was going to have to work harder at being friendly because it looked as though he might be flattened if she sent him on his way.

'Come on in, both of you, before the flies do!'

He's been through a really tough time.

Mitchell's words echoed through her mind.

When they were both inside and the screen door was shut, she said, 'I've just put the kettle on. I was going to take a break from unpacking and have a cup of tea and some chocolate chip cookies that Margaret – my foster mum who lives at the station next door – makes. I brought some of her homemade cordial with me, too. Would you like some?'

Kade's grin returned. 'Yes, please.'

What on earth am I doing, inviting Mitchell's son to have morning tea with me?

'I met Margaret at the hotel – the pub – the other weekend. She said to go over and visit any time. Did she mean it?'

Stella almost ground her teeth together at the thought that Kade would be in her space at the homestead as well, but she said, 'Marg never says anything she doesn't mean.'

'Dad said she was always busy.'

Yes, Marg was always bustling around doing something, but that didn't mean she wouldn't make time for Kade. 'Well, if you want to learn how to make these biscuits – or her famous scones – I'm sure she'd be happy to teach you, and she always cooks those types of treats after breakfast in the morning.'

'Does she cook them for "smoko"?'

Stella couldn't help but laugh as he tried the word with his American accent. Mitchell's accent had never been as strong – most likely because he'd grown up in so many countries in the world. He'd only been an occasional visitor to the USA before he'd been accepted into Stanford. 'You're learning the lingo fast.'

Kade stood there grinning at her, looking as pleased as punch.

'Oh – I just realised that what we call scones is different from the American version,' she told him.

'Really?'

'Yep. Aussie – well I suppose they might be originally British – scones are lighter. American scones are drier and more brick-like. The American ones I've had have been triangular whereas our scones are round. They're both quite different in texture and taste. I'm told American scones are made with much more butter and have a lot more sugar.'

'Listen to that, Jax!' Kade scratched the dog on the top of the head. 'There's lots of things here to get used to, and I bet you'd like the taste of Aussie scones.'

Stella considered the adorable dog. 'Not sure if I can rustle up anything for you, Jax. Margaret wouldn't be too impressed if I fed you any choc chip cookies.'

'That's okay.' Kade sounded very grown up as he told her, 'Dogs mustn't eat chocolate anyway.'

Stella did know that. She sent the dog and apologetic look. 'Looks like you're going to have to wait for your own snacks.'

The dog sent her a little whine and her heart melted.

Maybe she should get a puppy?

It'd be great company, but might be a little too much for her to handle at the moment. An older, more settled dog would probably be more her speed.

She'd have to give it some thought.

'I don't have a vase, but this will do.' She filled a slender glass with water and did the best she could to arrange the flowers into a presentable display rather than their current shapeless mass. Then, she put them on the breakfast bar.

'I couldn't believe it when Dad said you were moving in here. We used to sit up and watch your grand slam matches on TV.' He pulled a face. 'Well, that's not true, I guess. I was only allowed to stay up and watch if it wasn't a school night.'

They had?

Kade didn't give her any time to comment.

'Dad said you grew up here and both went to Stanford together. My Mom went to Stanford too. Did you know her?'

It was just as well Stella had moved to get the cordial and had her back to Kade at that moment or he might've witnessed her compressed lips at the mention of Deanna.

'No. I didn't know her.'

It was true. She hadn't known Deanna. She had only known of her.

The only time they'd come face to face... well, she'd never forget that moment, when she had opened the door and seen Deanna in bed with Mitch, nor the second when Deanna's momentary flash of guilt had turned to an expression of almost nervous triumph.

'Dad said you're building tennis courts here and you're going to run tennis camps.'

'That's right.'

She was grateful for the boy's constant chatter as she tried to compose herself.

She made the cordial and set out the biscuits as he continued. 'I've had a few lessons and I really love it. Do you think you could teach me to play?'

Stella froze.

What the hell?

Didn't the boy know she'd never pick up a racquet again?

Her gaze was fixed firmly on the glass she held. Each word emerged stiltedly. 'I won't be coaching.'

'Oh. I mean... I read you'd never play tennis again... er... after your accident. But I thought... I thought you might still be able to coach?'

'No.'

Even after all her rehab she still had to concentrate on walking – having to remember to pick up her foot to take a step – especially on uneven ground. She'd lost count of the number of times she'd fallen to the ground while trying to walk with her prosthetic foot. No way was she ready to start running on it.

'Oh.'

When she turned back to Kade he was red-faced and clearly extremely uncomfortable as he realised his gaffe.

Oh geez. She realised she'd spoken harshly. No wonder the boy looked uncomfortable.

Going into damage control mode, she sent him a smile. 'I hope you like choc chip cookies. They're my favourite.'

Instantly, he responded happily. 'Mine too!'

'Shall we eat outside in the sunshine?'

'Sure.'

Life was so simple when you were a child, she supposed.

Despite Mitch having told her Kade had been through a rough patch, he seemed uncomplicated. Sensitive, for certain, the way he'd reacted to her initially less than warm welcome, but quick to accept an olive branch.

'How do you like Hope Creek?' she asked when they'd settled down on the back verandah with Jax at Kade's feet.

'It's really different from home, but I like it so far. I've been exploring and I draw a bit. All the birds you have in Australia are really cool. I love drawing the birds.'

'You must be very talented. I don't have much of a knack for anything artistic.'

'I'm okay. The kids at school used to love my drawings but Mom said it was nothing special and they were just being nice to me.'

Bloody hell! What sort of mother would flatten any child like that, let alone her own son?

'I'd like to see them sometime. You'll have to show them to me.'

Whoa Stella.

Pull back.

Just because his mother's a cow doesn't mean you have to be the one to step up and compensate for her.

'If you like.' He was non-committal and she really did feel sorry for him.

'What does your father think of your sketches?'

Kade grinned. 'Dad says my drawings rival Michaelangelo and should be up on the Cistern Chapel.'

While applauding Mitch's praise for his son, Stella hid a smile as she did a mental correction.

Sistine Chapel.

Kade got the giggles. 'It was really funny. I'd never heard of this dude called Michaelangelo and I thought Dad was talking about one of the characters from the *Teenage Mutant Ninja Turtles*.'

She couldn't help but laugh along – his giggle was so infectious and he was just about doubling up in his merriment.

'I told Dad...' He broke off with more giggles. 'I told him I didn't know any of the turtles could draw and he thought it was hilarious. When he showed me the photo of the paintings in the chapel and told me who Michaelangelo was, we both cracked up.' Finally, his giggling subsided. 'Anyway, I like to draw.' He munched a bit more of his cookie before saying, 'The kookaburras have the weirdest laugh, and I really like the cockatoos. They're funny!'

Stella found herself sitting back, relaxing, and realised she was enjoying Kade's company.

Incredible how he'd bypassed all her defensive shields so quickly.

If it was a case of *Like father, like son*, she'd definitely have to do some serious reinforcing.

'Cockatoos are the best,' he said before imitating the screech of the bird.

'Sometimes people have pet cockatoos and they teach them to say, 'Hello Cocky!''

Kade chuckled. 'Dad said they could be taught to talk.'

Dad.

A bit of melancholy gripped Stella.

She'd love to have had children – to have had her own family.

Her hand went to her abdomen for the second time that morning and she had to make herself pick up her mug and lead the conversation away from family. 'Have you started school here yet?'

'No.' He munched a bit of cookie before saying, 'Dad says I can wait until next year 'cause there aren't many weeks between now and the Christmas school holidays.'

Stella sighed.

With all that had been going on it was easy to lose sight of the rapid approach of Christmas, even though she knew the upcoming CWA fair was always held in the second week of December.

'Sounds like a good idea. We're at the end of November, so there must only be about three weeks of school term left. But wouldn't it be good to meet some of the local kids before the end of the year so you have some friends to spend the summer holidays with?'

'Dad's got that covered. Aunt Liz has already had a few boys over to meet me and I think I met all the kids at the hotel the other night. Dad took us ten pin bowling in Lancaster over the weekend, too.'

'I bet that was fun.' She forced lightness into her tone as sadness gripped her again.

Mitchell sounded like a fantastic father.

What would their children have looked like?

'It was fun.' Kade's eyes lit with remembered pleasure. 'You can come with us next time, if you like.'

She frowned. 'I… that's really nice of you to invite me, but I might have to pass.'

His face fell. 'Is it your foot?'

She nodded.

Strangely, she didn't resent his question. It was asked

with all the directness of a child who didn't understand the boundaries adults knew to respect.

'Does it hurt you?'

'Only if I stand for too long,' she answered.

'It's a real shame.' His features reflected genuine sadness and she was surprised at the level of empathy he had for one so young. 'You could've won heaps more grand slams.'

No.

She'd been ready to retire.

Still, the question made her aware the choice had been taken out of her hands and she had to swallow down on her emotion she answered with pragmatism. 'Well, I've probably won my fair share. Time for someone else to have a turn.' When he opened his mouth to comment, she redirected the conversation. 'As for you being coached, I'm planning on having some of the best tennis coaches in Australia come to coach at my tennis camps. If your dad says it's okay with him, I'll let you have a regular space at the training sessions.'

'Awesome! Thank you so much!'

He demolished another two cookies and downed his cordial while she sipped on her tea.

'How are the baby goats going?'

'They're so cute! Would you like to come and see them?'

Surprisingly she found herself agreeing. 'I'd like that, but not today. Today I'm unpacking and settling into the cottage.'

'Do you need help?'

She smiled. If anyone had told her she'd strike up a friendship of sorts so quickly with Kade, she would've thought they were mad. But Mitch's son was impossible not to like. He was thoughtful. Even if it had been Liz's idea for him to bring her flowers, Liz wasn't here now telling him to offer to help and how many kids his age would've thought to offer?

There was a vulnerability to him, too, that'd pierced her heart.

'Thanks for offering, but I'm good.'

He looked genuinely disappointed. 'It's no trouble. I've got nothing else to do.'

She guessed he must be lonely. All the kids he'd met would be at school.

'Does your dad know you're here?'

'No.' He shook his head as he picked up a few remaining cookie crumbs off the plate. 'He had to go into Lancaster this morning to work out something about the pub, but I said I'd stay with Aunt Liz. Then, she had to do some writing so she said to come and bring you flowers to welcome you to your new house. If Dad comes home, Aunt Liz will tell him where I am.'

And then, Mitchell would come in search of him.

Was she ready to see Mitchell again?

Then again, wouldn't it be better to see him again sooner rather than later and get their first meeting as joint residents of the farm over with?

But did she really want Kade chatting incessantly to her all afternoon?

One look at his hopeful expression and she didn't have the heart to say no. 'I guess you can help me unpack the boxes.'

'Thanks! I promise I won't get in your way.'

Interesting he had to make that assertion.

As well as replaying his mother's nasty comment to him in her head, she remembered Mitch had said Kade had been emotionally neglected. Had Kade been made to feel like he got in his mother's way?

Closing the door firmly on that thought, she finished the rest of her tea. 'Come on then, let's go back in and get started.'

'Should Jax stay outside? I can tie him up to the verandah rail if you want me to.' He produced a lead and rope from the pocket of his shorts.

She thought about it for a moment. 'You know, it might be better if he stays outside.' Feeling a bit mean she explained, 'I'm… still getting used to my artificial foot and if I'm moving a box and he gets underfoot, I might trip.'

'All cool.' A cheeky expression came over his face. 'Sorry. I mean *no worries. She'll be right, mate*!'

Stella grinned. 'You really are learning to speak "Australian"!'

'*Too right*!'

'I'm going to have to introduce you to Blue. If there's anyone who can introduce you to Australian expressions, he can.'

This could be a very interesting afternoon. It certainly wouldn't be boring or lonely.

* * *

Mitch realised his heart was beating a little faster than usual as he made his way to the caretaker's cottage – Stella's cottage. It wasn't nerves. It was anticipation.

The thought of Stella settling into the cottage had him buzzing on all sorts of levels.

Knowing Kade had spent the last few hours with her, thanks to Liz's meddling, made him apprehensive.

What had the two of them talked about all this time?

He'd bet his bottom dollar Kade had let on they'd always watched her matches. Still, did it matter? He'd already told her he'd watched her play, and she'd admitted to seeing some of his games – even if she had implied that it was merely because she'd happened to flick through channels from time to time.

How much had Kade revealed though about Mitchell's non-relationship with Deanna?

Had Stella probed?

Was she even mildly curious about his relationship with Kade's mother?

Had she asked Kade anything about his life in LA?

Jax started barking the moment he saw Mitchell. 'Hello boy! Down!' The puppy was still at the stage where it jumped up on everyone in excitement. 'Hello!' he called out as he reached the front door of the cottage and peered through the fly screen.

'Dad!' Kade appeared from the hallway. 'Shush, Jax!'

'Hi, Mitchell.' Stella wasn't far behind him. 'Come in. Kade's been helping me settle in.'

Her welcome was a positive start. It certainly held more warmth than when he'd seen her at the homestead. Even when he'd taken around the new contracts for them both to sign, she'd been businesslike rather than friendly.

'I got to help Stella unpack her trophies!' Kade said excitedly. 'She had to hand back the real ones from the Grand Slam tournaments, but I actually got to hold all her replica trophies!'

'That's cool,' Mitch replied. 'I hope he's been more help than hindrance.'

'He's been great company.' She sounded sincere, but there was a note he couldn't quite pick.

Had it been hard for her to spend time with Kade?

'Can I show Dad the trophies?' Kade asked.

'Sure.' She looked a bit embarrassed. 'I know he's got a lot of his own trophies, though.'

'They're not as good as yours!' Kade asserted.

Mitchell pulled a face. 'Thanks for the compliment, buddy!'

'It's true, Dad.' He explained to Stella, 'Dad only gets a mini replica of the Lombardi Trophy every time his team wins the SuperBowl, but yours are much bigger.' Turning back to Mitch he said, 'Stella's Wimbledon trophies are three-quarters the original size.'

Mitch grinned. 'Very impressive. I'm clearly outdone.'

'We were just talking about having a break for afternoon tea,' Stella said. 'I'm expecting Margaret to show up soon, too. Would you like a cup of tea and one of Marg's famous chocolate chip cookies?'

'They're delicious!' Kade said.

'You don't need to tell me. I've eaten quite a few of those

cookies in my day and my mouth's watering at the thought of them.' He had so many good memories of life here. He was glad Kade would have them too. 'Yes, please, Stella. I'd love to join you.'

'Come on, Dad.'

'Hang on, son. Do you need a hand, Stella?'

'No, thanks. I'm fine.'

'I helped Stella wash up after lunch,' Kade said proudly.

Mitchell's eyes widened, 'Stella fed you lunch, too?'

'Yep. Ham and salad rolls. I've been here since morning tea!'

Mitchell laughed. 'Sorry, Stella. He's got quite an appetite.'

'Just like his father.' She started to smile, then turned away abruptly as though the memory was unwelcome.

Kade tugged at his hand and led him to where he'd helped Stella put the trophies in a cupboard in the spare room. 'She was going to leave them all in their boxes, but I talked her into unpacking them so I could see them.'

'I hope you weren't too pushy, Kade,' he said quietly when they were out of earshot.

'No, Dad.' He looked momentarily hurt, but bounced back fast enough. 'She said she was going to put them on display at the office she plans to build for her tennis centre, but I said I'd help her pack them all back up and move them again then. I told her she needs to have really good glass display cabinets for them all.'

'That's a good idea.'

'It's a shame they're all just stuck in a cupboard now.'

Maybe. Or maybe Stella didn't want to see the constant reminder of her illustrious career that'd been cut short by her accident?

He only half-listened to Kade as his son handled the precious trophies carefully and told him which event they were from. It certainly wasn't lost on his son what an honour it was for him to be handling the trophies.

Stella called to them from the kitchen. 'Tea's ready.'

Joining her – sitting across the table from her as she poured the tea – created a heavy weight in his chest. He'd imagined sharing this sort of domestic bliss with Stella. He'd thought they'd always be together. Well, not always. He'd known they'd spend time apart when he was in the middle of football season, but he'd envisaged that he'd spend the rest of the year on tour with her, supporting her career. Then, he'd thought, when they'd both reached the pinnacle of their careers, they'd retire and come back to Hope Creek and raise a family together.

They'd talked about it.

At least two kids and definitely two dogs.

She looked up for a moment and their gazes meshed and held.

What emotions could he read in those hazel depths?

Was he deluding himself to think he saw both regret and longing?

'Stella!' Kade cried.

'Oh!'

The connection broke as Stella and Mitchell both became aware that the teacup was overflowing and filling the saucer.

She pulled the teapot up abruptly and managed to tip some of the hot brew over her hand.

Mitch was at her side the instant she gasped in pain.

'Let's get that burn under cold water,' he said as he steered her toward the kitchen sink.

Kade followed them in. 'Are you okay, Stella?'

'I'll be fine,' she reassured Kade. 'Would you mind setting out the cookies from the tin?'

'Sure.'

Mitchell was aware of Stella's jerky gait as she made her way into the kitchen. His arm shot out around her waist to support her and as soon as he turned on the cold tap, he held her burned hand under the cool, running water.

'I'm not normally so clumsy.'

Of course she wasn't. She'd always been incredibly coordinated with fast reflexes.

But when their gazes had locked, everything else had ceased to exist for him and he could only reason that it must've been the same for her.

Reason or hope?

Right now, he was hyperaware of her narrow waist beneath his left hand, and the hard jut of her hip bone beneath his fingertips. The hand he held was soft. Their touch so achingly familiar, it would be the most natural thing in the world to turn her into the circle of his arms and reacquaint his lips with the sensuous feel of hers – to lift the hair back from the nape of her elegant neck and nibble at all those sensitive spots he remembered and which used to have her writhing beneath him.

The curtain of her hair fell forward and masked her expression, but not before he saw the tremble of her lower lip.

'Stella?' he probed quietly.

She could hide her expression from him, but she couldn't hide the slight shiver that ran through her body.

Was it reaction to their physical proximity or was she in shock?

Surely the burn wasn't so bad it was shock?

'I'm okay.' The words were barely a whisper. Then she pulled her hand away from the stream of water and turned in his arms. Her lips pressed together as though she suppressed emotion, but there was vulnerability in her eyes.

A question.

A need.

Dear Lord.

It wasn't just his imagination. Their physical connection was as tangible and strong as it had ever been.

'Do you want me to get a bandage or anything?' Kade asked.

The question broke the trance.

Mitchell stepped back and Stella turned back around and

thrust her hand once again under the running water. After clearing his throat, Mitchell said, 'I think it'll be fine, thanks Kade.'

God, but his lips ached and his arms felt empty.

He'd been wanting to kiss Stella for an eternity.

If it hadn't been for Kade's interruption, Mitchell wouldn't have been able to help himself. He would've kissed Stella – not on the cheek as he had at the hotel, but a proper, passionate kiss that wouldn't hide the depths of his feelings for her.

And he was certain she would've kissed him back.

Holy Hell.

He hoped to God that Liz was right and Steve Carter was definitely out of her life and out of her heart.

She wasn't wearing her engagement ring again today, but did that mean anything?

'Want to go and pour a fresh cup of tea before it all gets stewed?' Stella asked without looking at him in the reflection of the kitchen window that was over the sink. 'And make sure Kade saves a couple of those cookies for us?'

'Good idea.' He took in the breathy quality to her voice and the faint flush staining her cheeks. Part of him wanted to send Kade back to the farmhouse so he and Stella could be alone together.

The other part of him warned he was on dangerous ground.

The palpable attraction between him and Stella had always been strong. It hadn't been enough – their feelings for each other and all the plans they'd made for their future hadn't been enough when she'd decided to focus solely on her tennis career.

Now, her career had ended.

Did she want to resume their relationship because she was on the rebound from a broken engagement and the end of her career?

He didn't want to be a convenient relationship for her.

Knowing the intensity of passion they'd shared, and believing it would still be as strong if they embarked on a relationship again, he might not survive this time if she decided to walk away again. Besides, he'd come back to Hope Creek to provide stability for Kade.

If he and Stella got together again then she decided something else was more important in her life, how could he go on living in Hope Creek with the constant memories of her?

Hell. The only reason he'd managed to hold it together the last time she'd broken up with him was because he'd been sideswiped with Deanna's news that he was going to be a father.

Everything in him had gone into denial.

When he'd been told that his DNA was an absolute match and there was no mistaking the fact that Deanna was pregnant with his child, the hollow ache that'd been inside him since Stella had broken up with him had been filled.

Oh, it'd been nausea that'd filled the void initially. He'd been absolutely gutted that any woman, apart from Stella, could be pregnant with his child. He'd gone into denial before being filled with such rage he'd very uncharacteristically put his fist through a wall in the locker room. But the belief that he'd been responsible for creating a life had at least given him a clear path.

Stella was lost to him.

He'd had to do the right thing and marry Deanna to be his child's father and give his child his name. Everything in him had risen up demanding he provide a stable and loving environment for his child to grow up in – to ensure his child had the kind of upbringing and love that he'd lacked.

Grabbing the tea, Mitch went out to the verandah.

'I wouldn't eat them all. You brought me up with better manners than that,' Kade told him now as he gestured towards the cookies.

Mitchell ruffled his son's hair. 'I sure did.'

He was proud of Kade who was a really good kid. A strong kid.

Deanna had been way too young and immature to be a mother. So needy herself, how could she ever have been expected to know how to love her child when she'd never known love herself? When he'd learned about the childhood she'd experienced, it finally made sense to him that she didn't know how to put Kade's needs first. Deanna had only ever known parental manipulation. She used Kade as a bargaining chip to get whatever she wanted in life – just as her manipulative father had used her.

Mitch was determined to break that pattern.

Nobody would use or abuse Kade and, whilst he knew he couldn't wrap his son in cotton wool, he wanted to do everything he could to prevent him from being hurt.

It would hardly be fair to Kade if Mitch embarked on a relationship with Stella – whom he clearly already idolised – only to have his son shattered if Stella walked away from them.

No. He couldn't do that to Kade.

His gut rolled with a mass of seething emotions that pulled him in different directions.

Would it ever be possible for him and Stella to have a solely platonic relationship with all this sexual tension between them? He believed that at some point it was inevitable the dam of pent up sexual desire would burst. Where would that leave them?

Jax started barking and wagging his tail.

'Oh look, a visitor. Is that Stella's foster mom, Margaret?' Kade asked.

'Mrs Richardson to you, son,' Mitchell corrected.

'Sorry.' Kade looked abashed for three seconds before he yelled inside to Stella, 'Your mom's here, Stella!' Then he added, 'Aunt Liz will be here soon, too.'

With a son, a dog, arrival of a foster mum, and soon his aunt, any further hope of kissing Stella today had totally flown out the window.

CHAPTER ELEVEN

'It's so good to have you home, Stella,' Callie told her when she came up to visit again about ten days after Stella's move into Hope Farm Cottage. 'And it's fantastic to see the progress that's already been made for your tennis centre.'

Stella touched her sister's arm. 'I'm so pleased you've come back to see me again so soon.'

'It's hard to get time off work on the weekends, but at least the traffic isn't as bad getting in and out of Melbourne when I come up mid-week. Besides, I wanted to see you and check in on Morgan. How's she been?'

'She's working long hours, so I've hardly seen her. If she's home for dinner, she only talks about her work day or updates on her apartment renovations. There hasn't been the chance to sit her down and work out what's going on with her, but I'm presuming she's nursing a broken heart over the surgeon who's left town?'

'That's a safe bet, but she's always been slow to confide when she's hurting and I don't know much more than you do except that Dean didn't leave lightly.'

'She said he'd taken up a post at North Shore Hospital. It's understandable if he wants to get more training. He's not going to receive that sort of training while he's with the RFDS, is he?'

'No. When I met him he spoke about getting lots of general

emergency experience as an RFDS doctor, but not specialist experience.'

'It's a shame. Whenever she spoke about him, she seemed pretty wrapped up in him.'

Callie tilted her head to one side. 'I'm not convinced he was the one for her, but who knows? He asked her to move to Sydney and apply for a job with one of the major airlines, but she's determined she'll spend her entire career with the RFDS.'

'I understand that. RFDS is a calling for her.'

'Yes. Anyway, I'll try to get some one-on-one time with her over the next couple of days. It's why I decided to stay up at the homestead this visit rather than bunking down in your spare room.'

'If anyone can get her to confide in them, it'll be you.' Stella stopped looking at where she was placing her feet on the uneven terrain as they walked from the development site back to the cottage, and turned to Callie. 'You know, you're special. When you came to visit me at the rehab centre in Switzerland, you were your typical upbeat, positive self and you kept talking about all the various things I could do with my life.' Callie had been a regular Pollyanna, reeling off a whole list of things that Stella could still do.

'And it turned out I didn't need to make any suggestions because Liz offered you the share in Hope Farm to develop your tennis centre. *Ét voila*! Here it is!'

'Yeah.'

Callie sent her a long look. 'That doesn't sound very enthusiastic?'

'It's… I'm sure I'll enjoy it and I'm happy to be providing the opportunity for kids to come to a camp and have expert coaching.'

'But it's not the same as competitive tennis,' Callie surmised. 'I know you told me quite some time ago that you'd had enough of the circuit but I guess now you're actually away from it, you're really missing it and life must seem pretty slow and unglamorous here?'

'No!' Stella realised she made the denial so sharply, Callie's drew her head back in surprise. Drawing a breath, she said in a more measured tone. 'No, I'm not missing it.'

'Not even a little bit?'

Incredibly, Stella knew she would be completely honest in saying she really didn't miss it at all. 'Not one iota.'

'But—'

'Callie, this going to sound... well...'

'Go on.'

'I don't know how to say this.'

Callie frowned in concern.

Rubbing her hand across her own brow, Stella said, 'The tennis camp sounds great – at least it did sound great when I was in Switzerland, but now – even in the midst of having it constructed around me and being excited about it – I'm not so sure.'

'Mitch's not making things difficult is he?'

'No. Far from it. He's been fine.' She shook her head, unsure how to express her innermost feelings.

'You're getting cold feet.' Callie groaned. 'Oops! Those foot expressions keep coming, don't they?'

Stella let that one wash over her because she was concentrating on trying to put her finger on her inner restlessness and how to express it to Callie.

'You know, we're living in a world where there's an expectation on women to succeed – to break through the glass ceiling and be forces to be reckoned with, but...'

'But?'

'I don't want to be out there in the world proving myself – proving how strong a woman I am to come back from this injury. I don't want to be held up as an example and I don't want people to think that if I'm not achieving something, I'm not happy.' She tilted her head back for a few moments so her face turned up to the sky. 'I just want to settle back here out of the spotlight and enjoy all this around me,' she told her sister and the universe.

It was a beautiful part of Australia.

'I'm not sure Marg would approve,' Callie said. 'You know what she's always said…'

'Hope Creek is a place to heal not to hide,' they both said in unison.

'Except that isn't what I'd be doing,' Stella denied as they continued walking. 'I haven't limped back to Hope Creek because I want to hide away and lick my wounds.'

Callie's raised eyebrow revealed her doubt.

'I'm here because this is where I belong. This is my community and I've missed it. I even wonder whether I'm doing the community any favours by going ahead with the tennis centre. I don't want to be responsible for changing the feel of the place.'

'In case you haven't noticed, Hope Creek is already busier than when you left thanks to some tourism and the vineyards. As sleepy as you might like to think it is, we're moving with the times here. Besides, what are you going to do here if you don't have the tennis centre?'

'That's just it! There's this expectation that I'll do something when all I really want to do is lead a quiet existence and raise a family.' She slapped the heel of her palm against her forehead. 'I'm thirty for heaven's sake. I've been traipsing all over the world and I want to settle down. I want the old-fashioned dream – marriage, kids, the picket fence. God, I feel like I should belong to another time. I feel as though voicing those needs in this day and age will bring a whole lot of women rushing towards me telling me I'm letting the sisterhood down.'

Callie looked at her as though she was weighing every word and not making sense of it. 'You're allowed to want those things. I'm sure wanting a family is still pretty acceptable. I don't understand where you're coming from.'

'Is it? Is it acceptable? Maybe I just don't know what

"acceptable" is anymore. All my life it feels like I've lived with these huge expectations. Is it okay these days for a woman to want to stay at home and look after the family? Aren't we expected to be superwomen who juggle work and family and everything else in between?'

'You're overthinking this. Besides,' she reached out and patted Stella's arm, 'even if we lived in the type of world you're describing, you've already made your mark on the world – far more than most people. You got to the top of your chosen career path.'

'I know darned well that when I finally give a press conference, the first question that's going to be asked is, 'What are your plans for the future?''

'Mm, yes. Probably. It's probably a pretty standard question and people will be interested in what you'll be doing with your life.'

'I thought that it was a good idea to start a tennis centre to give back and to give kids more opportunities. It seemed like such a good idea at the time, and I guess it still is.'

'But?'

'But I don't know whether I want to be the businesswoman who runs it.' She let her head drop forward. 'What I want most of all is to have a family of my own.'

'Stella, there's nothing wrong with that. I want it too one day when I meet the right guy.'

Loving Callie and feeling so close to her she confided, 'I'm afraid that'll never happen now for me.'

'Why wouldn't it?'

'First – I have a disability and that might make it harder for me to run around and look after little kids.'

'Oh, Stella—'

'Second,' Stella cut her off, 'now I'm back in Hope Creek, who am I going to meet?'

'Stella…' Callie began impatiently before stopping abruptly. The twist of her lips indicated she'd thought better of continuing with her thoughts. 'You can always come to Melbourne and go out on the town with me.'

'Also…' Unable to take another step, Stella confessed, 'I had seat belt injuries from the crash and they caused some internal damage. It could be harder for me to conceive.'

Callie's forehead wreathed in lines as she frowned. 'Oh darling! I had no idea!' Stepping forward, she held out her arms and they had a long hug. 'Do Jim and Margaret know?'

Stella nodded.

'You poor thing!'

Callie hugged her again. 'You've been through so much. Why didn't you tell me earlier?'

'I actually thought I might be pregnant during the French Open final, but I hadn't had time to get to a pharmacy to buy a test.'

'But you weren't pregnant?'

'No. But I was really sick during the finals and I thought it might be a slim possibility – even though my sex life with Steve had become almost non-existent.'

'Oh shit! Did Steve know you suspected you were pregnant?'

'Yes,' she admitted.

'What was his reaction?'

Stella closed her eyes for a moment. 'He was panicked. Horrified. Angry.'

Callie pressed her lips together thoughtfully but remained silent.

'He knew I wanted to start a family, but he said he wasn't ready. I thought that if he knew my suspicions he'd change his mind.'

'He didn't.'

She shook her head. 'I was so excited thinking I might be able to quit the circuit. I wanted to dash out to the pharmacy and get a test before the presentation dinner. I thought if the test came back positive, I could convince him to let me leave the circuit and to persuade him to announce my retirement that night at Roland Garros.'

Callie swore, then her gaze sharpened as she looked at Stella. 'Stell! Listen to yourself. Did you hear what you said?'

'What do you mean?'

'You didn't say you were excited about the possibility of being pregnant. You said you were excited about being able to leave tennis.'

Stella's eyes widened slightly. 'You're right. I was more excited about leaving tennis at that stage.' Callie's observation hit her hard. Stella reasoned she was more excited about quitting her career than being pregnant because she didn't even know for sure she was going to have a baby at that point.

'And you said you wanted to convince Steve to *let you* leave tennis!' She moved her arms up in a gesture that spoke of her disbelief. 'It should never have been *Steve's* decision. If you wanted to retire from the circuit, that was *your decision* to make, not his. Geez, Stella! You were in an abusive relationship.'

Stella opened her mouth to deny it, but the words died in her throat because she knew Callie was right.

'You had a lucky escape not having a child with that man,' Callie said emphatically. 'Imagine if you had been pregnant. Even if Steve decided to stay with you for the child's sake, it would've been an unhealthy decision for all three of you.'

'He wouldn't have stayed,' Stella said adamantly, remembering her conversation with Steve about when she'd suspected she might be pregnant.

'I think I might be pregnant,' she'd said tentatively.

'You can't be,' he'd replied. 'You're on the pill.'

But she'd had a stomach virus a few weeks before and been physically ill, and although Steve rarely seemed in the mood for sex these days and insisted on her sleeping alone the nights before she played any matches, they had shared a bed after she was ill with the virus.

'If there's been an accident and you are pregnant, you can have a termination.'

'What are you saying? We've talked about having kids.'

'No. You talked about having kids.'

'Steve—'

'I can't be a father. I didn't sign up for that.' He pointed an accusing finger at her. 'You can't be a mother, either. It would ruin your career.'

'My career? But you know I don't want to keep playing tennis. I would've retired last year if you'd let me.'

'You've still got years of tennis left in you, Stella. I don't even think you're at the top of your game yet. You can set records that no other woman will even come close to beating for decades to come.'

'There's more to life than tennis.'

'No. There isn't. Tennis is our lives. You're exceptionally talented. Nobody throws a gift like yours away.'

'I haven't thrown it away. I've worked damned hard, made a lot of sacrifices and I've accomplished so much, but I don't want to compete anymore.'

'No more.' He held up his hand. 'I'm not listening to anymore of this. You're not thinking straight.'

'We've talked about this.' She heard the pleading note in her own voice.

'No children.'

Each word stabbed at her.

'As soon as you've another clay court championship under your belt, we have to start our preparation for Queens' and Wimbledon.'

'No.'

'Stella.' The two syllables held a steely warning she'd never heard before in his voice.

'How could you even suggest it? I'm thirty. I want to start a family.'

'You want... what about what I want? I never saw children

in our future. Hell! If I'm completely honest, I didn't see any future between us beyond the life we're living now.'

Stella reeled. Every word he uttered was like a stallion's kick to her guts and she stood there gaping at him.

'Our lives are bound by tennis. I don't even know who you are off-circuit. We've never even had a proper holiday together except to fly back to your foster family in Australia and that was as boring as bat shit.'

What was he saying?

All this time, she thought they had an understanding... thought they were on the same track.

'But that's where we're going to live.'

'No. Don't even think about it. Your job is to keep playing and keep winning tournaments. That's all you should be thinking about. You owe it to the tennis world, Stella.' He paced back and forth as he ranted, then he stopped and pivoted on his heel to face her as he delivered the lowest blow of all, 'You owe it to your parents. They died so you could live this life.'

She recounted the gist of the conversation to Callie and noticed a white ring appear around her sister's lips as she pressed them together tightly. 'What an absolute, utter bastard!' She raised her fists and made an action in front of her as though she had Steve by the collar and was shaking him. 'Don't ever tell Morgan those details,' she warned, 'or I think we'd be visiting her in prison where she'd be serving a life sentence for murder. Shit! I'm tempted to visit my parents in jail, delve into their murky past and ask them if they can use their connections and have a pair of concrete boots made for Steve Carter.'

'Callie!'

'Oh, of course I wouldn't – even though he deserves it.' The rage left her face as she looked more kindly at Stella. 'Listen to me. You're young, and you're a beautiful person inside and out. You said there was only a possibility you wouldn't be able to have children but you didn't say it was a certainty.'

'I lost an ovary.'

'Well you've got another one!' Then she looked awkward. 'Or, was it damaged, too?'

'They think it's okay.'

'Then, Stell, you're dwelling on negatives instead of positives. Besides, even if you can't have children, look at Marg and Jim. They've been the best parents and we love them as though they're our parents.'

'You're right, but I... I feel a bit useless and... okay, I feel unattractive.' She looked down at the trousers covering her prosthetic limb. 'Don't think I'm not happy that I'm alive. But it's not very nice, is it?'

Callie had seen her stump in Switzerland. She'd been there with Stella when she'd had her first fittings.

'And it limits me.'

'It's still early days,' Callie's voice was laden with concern. 'Do you need to have some more counselling?' she asked.

'I don't know,' Stella admitted. 'If I decide I do, I can always do a video call with Dr Meyer, the counsellor I saw in Switzerland. I was comfortable with her.'

'Good. I'm always ready to listen, but sometimes it's a professional who can really get to the heart of the issue. Your confidence has had a battering and given all you've been through – both before and after the accident, that's not surprising. Yet,' she gave Stella cheeky smile, 'you can't say you wouldn't meet anyone here. If I'm any judge, you had more than one admirer when we went to the pub the other night.'

'No!'

'Yes. Tom Ryder was more than interested in you. Don't deny it because I heard him asking you if you'd meet up for drinks.' Callie drew her head back and sent Stella a searching look as Stella felt heat scorching her cheeks. 'Have you had drinks with him already?'

'I'm not interested in Tom. He has called me but I turned him down. As far as he knows I'm still engaged to Steve, and

I wouldn't want to let him think I was interested in him by accepting an invitation.'

'Okay,' she said slowly before she asked, 'Stella... how do you feel about Mitch?' She put her hand up the second Stella opened her mouth to reply. 'Hang on. Before you answer that... I know you denied having any feelings for him when we were sitting out on the verandah together not so long ago, but now it's just the two of us... how do you really feel?'

Stella sighed. 'Like he's the sexiest man on the planet and he's still got all the same qualities I fell in love with.'

'But?'

'But he hurt me, and I don't want to have my heart broken again.'

They'd reached the cottage and both sat down on the stairs, enjoying the cool of the evening. In the distance a magpie sang and kookaburras laughed. Stella loved this part of the day.

'How do you think Mitch feels about you?'

'I'm not sure.' She raised one hand and held it palm up in a gesture of frustration. 'At times I think there's attraction between us.'

'What do you do at those times?'

'Pull away. Go into defensive mode.'

'You're the one who pulls away before anything further can happen?'

Stella thought about it. 'I guess so.'

'Then,' Callie said thoughtfully, 'if I were you, I'd have a really hard think about how you feel about Mitch. If you're still attracted to him and still find a lot about him to love, then you need to give the two of you a second chance. If and when you decide to do so, just go for it.'

'You make it sound so easy.'

'I think it could be if you don't make it complicated. You know each other so well and were very close once – best friends as well as lovers, right?'

'We were.' It'd made their breakup all the harder because

there'd been so many times when she'd wanted to phone him and talk to him.

She mulled over her sister's words. 'Thanks for the sisterly advice.'

'Any time.' Callie put her arm around Stella's shoulders and gave her a hug. 'Just one thing though…'

'Go on.'

'I truly believe Mitch is a great guy so be sure you know what you want before you go for it. Don't go giving him any mixed signals because that wouldn't be fair to either of you.'

'When did you get to be so wise about relationships?' Stella asked. 'You should've been a psychologist.'

'Ha! Am I wise?' She pulled a face. 'If I was wise about relationships I'd be in one!'

'You've given me a lot to think about, Sis!'

Lots to consider and lots of emotions to untangle.

Ultimately, Stella realised she couldn't expect to navigate a course to a happy, fulfilled destination if she couldn't figure out exactly what it was – or maybe in her case, who it was – she wanted.

CHAPTER TWELVE

Mitchell was over at a round table in the corner of the main bar area filling out some paperwork when a stranger walked in and approached the young bartender he'd employed.

'G'day!'

'G'day,' Simon replied. 'Can I get you something?'

The conversation between the two followed the normal course for a couple of minutes while Simon poured the guy a beer, yet something about the newcomer had Mitchell's radar pinging.

Kitted out in what looked like brand new blue jeans, a checked shirt and a new-looking Akubra hat, it was as though the guy was dressed to fit in – as though he'd expressly bought the outfit to look like he belonged. Hell! His R.M. Williams boots weren't scuffed at all. Something was definitely off.

Mitchell couldn't redirect his focus to the supply order he'd been working on.

The guy settled into the bar and nursed his beer. At first he chatted about the weather and the growth of Lancaster. Then he said casually – too casually – 'I've heard Hope Creek is home to Stella Simpson.'

Mitchell's grip tightened on his pen as it hovered over the paperwork. Every one of his muscles tensed as his protective instincts kicked in.

'Sure is,' Simon replied.

'Is she around these days?' the guy asked.

Mitchell would've shot Simon a warning look, but his employee wasn't looking his way.

Reporter.

He has to be a reporter.

Willing Simon to guard Stella's privacy, he was relieved when the young local delivered the perfect response. 'Last I read about her, she was in Switzerland somewhere recovering from her accident.' Simon's tone was matter-of-fact as he wiped down the bar. 'Are you a tennis player yourself, then?'

'Mad keen. Was hoping if she was back home here, I might be able to get her autograph while I'm in town.'

Mitchell didn't buy it for a second.

'I suspect there'll be a few autograph hunters around when she does come back for a visit, but as far as I know she's not planning a visit anytime soon.'

Correct again. Stella was hardly planning a visit to Hope Creek when she lived here.

The sandy-haired newcomer nodded then looked over his shoulder, making direct eye contact with Mitchell. 'Hey! Aren't you Mitchell Scott?'

Excitement lit up his eyes and Mitchell likened him to a bloodhound on the scent of a story.

'I am,' Mitchell responded. 'Are you a fan of American football as well as tennis?'

'Not really, but you're pretty famous. I hadn't heard you were in the country let alone back in Hope Creek.' The guy, who looked to be in his mid-twenties, got off the bar stool and approached Mitch with his beer still in one hand. 'I sure am a fan of what you've achieved in your career.' He extended his hand. 'Jason Mannering from the Melbourne Daily Chronicles.'

Mitchell stood and shook the proffered hand. 'What brings you to town, Jason?'

'I'm following a lead on Stella Simpson. She's left the

medical centre in Switzerland and my bet is that she's come back home to finish her recovery.'

It was hard work not to grab the guy by the collar, march him out of the pub and suggest very firmly that he leave town.

Although this guy was a reporter, rather than the paparazzi who'd contributed to Stella's accident, Mitchell knew Stella wished they'd all leave her alone.

'Stella grew up around here,' Mitch said in a friendly voice, realising he wasn't telling the reporter anything he didn't know. 'We'd sure love it if she returned for a visit but, as far as I know, that's not her intention.'

'I don't think she'll come back for a visit. I think she'll move back – if she hasn't already.'

Mitchell managed a short laugh. He could hardly say that Hope Creek was too small a place for an international sports star to settle, considering he was settling here himself. Instead he opted for, 'Maybe, if she was single. I doubt her fiancé would want to move too far away from the international tennis scene. You'll probably find he's even signed up by now to coach someone else.'

Jason put his beer on Mitch's table before reaching into his trouser pocket and pulling out a piece of paper.

Mitchell's first thought was that Jason had managed to get his hands on a copy of the development application Stella had made for her tennis centre. Once the paper was unfolded and Jason thrust it towards him, he realised that a copy of the DA would've been a better option.

'This photo appeared in all the British tabloids yesterday,' Jason told him.

'This' was a series of photos of Steve Carter in open displays of public affection with the woman who Mitch recognised as having been Stella's physiotherapist.

Liz was right. The engagement was off.

Part of him was relieved, the other was angry at Carter's behaviour. Allowing himself to be photographed like this was serving Stella up a big slice of public humiliation.

'Looks like Steve Carter has dumped Stella personally now she's no longer any good to him professionally.'

'If that's true, he's a bastard,' Mitchell vented.

Had Carter been having an affair with the physio before the accident?

Was that the reason they'd broken up?

Liz had said Stella had realised Carter's true colour so…

'The reporters from London found she was no longer in Switzerland at the rehab centre. I assumed she'd come back here.'

'Who knows where she'd go?' Mitchell shrugged. 'If she's not wanting to be found I don't suppose she'd come back here considering this would be the first place you'd look for her. I'm sorry you've made the trip up from Melbourne on a wild goose chase.'

'Not such a wild goose chase,' Jason disagreed. 'I've got the scoop on you being back in town. What's brought you back here?'

While Mitchell didn't want his personal life splashed all over the newspapers, at least the reporter might go away if he gave him a story. 'I've moved back to Australia permanently with my son.'

Jason folded the newspaper article away and shoved it back in one trouser pocket as he asked, 'Would you consent to an interview?'

Mitchell shook his head. 'There's no story here. Just spent a lot of my formative years in Hope Creek, loved it and want my son to experience the same.'

'Your aunt's Liz Burton and she lives here, doesn't she?'

'Yes.'

'What about your son's mother?'

'She's in America but she's happy with the arrangement.' At least she had been. Deanna had always been unpredictable. Whilst she had, in the end, acknowledged that she didn't know how to be the mother Kade needed and was relieved not to have responsibility for Kade any longer, Mitch wouldn't be surprised if she decided at some point in the future that she wanted occasional contact with Kade despite their firm agreement. 'We've been divorced for years.'

'How do your parents feel about your move to Australia? Your father's such an influential man in American politics and such a patriot, won't he see this as a defection of sorts?'

The mere mention of his father was enough to make Mitchell's blood pressure rise, but he reminded himself sternly that he had to keep his cool. This was a journalist he was talking to and he didn't want there to be any whiff of a story. 'My mother was born in Hope Creek. I think they both understand why I want to call Australia home.'

They understood alright.

He wanted to get as far away as possible from his parents and their political ambitions.

He didn't care if he never saw either of them again.

'Didn't you used to date Stella Simpson?'

There was no point in denying it. 'For a short time in college. I guess it was natural drifting together seeing we were both essentially kids from this small community who'd ended up at Stanford. We both moved on.'

'Any chance of reigniting that relationship?'

Mitchell gave a short, dismissive laugh. 'Listen, James. I know you're angling for a story, but unless you're writing a sports history column, I wouldn't go linking my name romantically with Stella's. That's ancient history.'

The newspaperman gave him a speculative look. 'Can't blame a guy for trying, and I'm looking for a personal angle here. Most of my readers have no understanding of American football so your career highlights wouldn't be of interest to them. Now... something along the lines of American football hero rekindles his romance with Queen of the Court in their home town... that would capture their attention, especially now it's obvious Carter's moved on.'

Mitch made himself laugh out loud. 'Are you writing for a

newspaper or are you here to try to push my Aunt Liz off her throne as Australia's best-selling romance author?'

The young man looked sincere when he added, 'Stella's a tennis legend who's had the whole country rooting for her. I think everyone would want to know she's recovering well and that she's found happiness.'

Jason produced a business card from his wallet. 'Can I call you if I have any more questions?'

'Sure. I've just bought this hotel, so you can contact me through here.'

'In that case, can I take a picture of you over near the bar?'

'I guess so.'

'Great. We journos have to do our own photography these days, too.'

'I'd heard.'

Mitchell maintained his outwardly cooperative stance but itched to see the last of the young journalist. Finally, pictures taken, he was able to say, 'Have a safe drive back to Melbourne.' Mentally, he added, *And please stay there.*

'I've booked into a motel in Lancaster for the next couple of days.'

Shit.

He'd have to warn Stella to keep a low profile.

'Enjoy Lancaster.'

When Jason had left, Mitch thanked Simon. 'You did well, Simon.'

The bartender grinned. 'Stella's one of ours and she knows it. Mavis organised for everyone in the town to sign a *Get Well* card and we all agreed to protect her privacy when she returned.'

'Hopefully Jason will spread the word he's made a wasted trip up here, but I doubt he's the last reporter we'll see.'

'Would you like me to call her and let her know there's been a reporter here, or will you?'

Mitch would do better. 'I'll give it a few minutes in case our friend is lurking, then I'll go back to the farm and tell her in person.' He'd also find the article on the internet and see exactly what had been printed before he made Stella aware of it.

* * *

Stella was finishing her conversation with an excavator driver when she saw Mitch striding over to them. It seemed there was no way she could Mitch-proof her body's reaction to him – no way she could slow her heart rate, or prevent the thrill of recognition that speared right through her every time she caught a glimpse of him.

'Hey Mitch.'

'Hi Stella.' He nodded at the driver. 'G'day Pete. Are you two at a point where I can steal Stella away from you for a few moments?'

'Yep. We were just finished,' Pete said. 'I've got all that, Stella, so I'll get on with it.'

'Fantastic. Thanks.' She looked questioningly into Mitch's blue eyes as Pete walked back to his machine and climbed up into the cabin. Dear Lord, her former lover seemed to get better looking every time she saw him. With a slight clearing of her throat she asked, 'What's up?'

'Let's go back to the cottage and talk.'

'Sounds serious.'

'Best discussed over a cuppa, anyway.'

A lump of unease settled in her chest. 'I don't like the sound of that.'

'Looks like they're setting a cracking pace here.'

Did his change in topic mean their upcoming chat was serious or not so serious?

'The concreters will be here by the end of the week to form up, then, if the weather holds, they're looking at pouring the slabs mid next week.'

They'd almost reached the cottage when he asked, 'You realise what you're doing here is likely to attract attention?'

'Sooner or later,' she agreed.

'Have you thought it might be better for you to make an announcement to the media about what the tennis centre before they break the story as a big scoop?'

'I've thought about it, yes, but I'm not certain I want the world to know what I'm doing yet.' She walked carefully up the few stairs and on to the cottage verandah before wiping her feet awkwardly on the outdoor mat. 'Why do you ask?'

'Let's sit out here.' He indicated the chairs.

'Don't you want a cuppa?'

'Later.'

That was fine with her. 'What's going on, Mitch?'

'There was a reporter at the pub today,' he told her as she settled onto one of the chairs and he sat on the one next to her.

'Oh.'

Mitch reached for her left hand and took it in the strength of his, before he used his other hand to rub along her bare left ring finger. 'You no longer wear his ring. Are you still engaged to Carter?'

Between the surprise question and the all the sensations rocking her body from his mere touch, Stella felt disorientated.

'Stella? Please tell me the truth.'

'I... no. We're not together anymore.'

His exhaled breath was audible.

The loss of his touch as he reached into his hip pocket to pull out his phone made her feel bereft.

'Are you aware he's involved with your former physiotherapist?'

Stella stared at the image on the screen as he extended the phone to her.

'Stella?'

She closed her eyes, unable to look at the images.

'Stella, I'm sorry. Has this come as a complete shock to you?'

Forcing her eyes open, she took a deep breath and steeled herself against the empathy she saw in his expression. 'It's not a shock, no. I found out Steve was having an affair on… on the night… at the celebration dinner for my last tournament.'

'The night of your accident.' Mitchell cursed and she watched as his hands curled into fists. 'How long had it been going on?'

She looked back at the screen of the phone which had now gone dark. 'I think maybe for a year or so.'

'Geez.'

'With the benefit of hindsight, I admit I was stupid and naïve.' She passed the phone back to him.

'I'm sorry, Stella. He didn't deserve you.'

Her lips thinned and she gritted her teeth together as she realised the irony of her situation. Mitchell Scott – the man she'd loved – the man she was still damned well attracted to, was sitting next to her commiserating on Steve's lack of fidelity when Mitchell had done the same bloody thing!

Okay, his affair with Deanna probably hadn't gone on for such a long time right under her nose, but he'd still cheated on her.

'It seems I don't have very good judgement where men are concerned.'

The jerk of his body revealed her words had hit their target. Good.

When she'd learned of Steve's deceit she'd felt so foolish. She'd run rather than facing him – the same way she'd run when she'd learned of Mitchell's betrayal.

She'd thought a lot about the wisdom of Callie's words and she'd had a late-night call to the counsellor in Switzerland who'd told her it was time to stop running. When Stella had confessed that she'd lost her foot after running away from a confrontation with Steve, but that no amount of pain had come close to her breakup with Mitchell – who'd ripped out her heart – the psychologist had encouraged her to speak to Mitchell about the hurt he'd inflicted.

Stella had been working up the courage to do it.

Was now a good time to address it?

The truth was Mitchell *had* been cheating on her, and he never owned that when he flew to Japan to try to talk things through and to beg her not to throw their relationship away.

Pride had dictated that she end the relationship without acknowledging he'd been unfaithful.

Pride, and Steve had told her to treat him as though he didn't matter rather than let him witness her heart smashed to pieces and lying in dangerously sharp, splintered shards at her feet.

The counsellor had told her that her pride had allowed Mitchell to get off the hook instead of facing up to what he'd done.

Stella had been told that even though Mitchell had been young, he'd still been old enough to know what he was doing and he'd abused her trust.

The counsellor was right.

Even if Mitchell had matured and might never cheat on a partner again, he hardly had any right to judge Steve.

And as for Steve… she should've told him what she thought of him instead of leaving it to Jim.

Steve had abused her trust even more than Mitchell, and he'd been doing it deliberately – for a longer time.

Hurt and anger bubbled through her veins and she felt the heat rise from her chest, up her neck and right to her ears.

So much anger and emotion. How she wished she could go out on a court and let all the hurt out by whacking the begeebers out of a tennis ball.

'Steve used me.' Every word held bitterness. 'With my number one ranking, the prize money and sponsorships kept rolling in. My success bankrolled him and Jenny. Steve absolutely had me conned. He told me it was advantageous for taxation reasons to pay my staff more money – a tax deduction. He said that whatever either of us earned was for both our benefits anyway, and so I signed the contract and he became the highest paid coach on the circuit while his lover became the highest paid physiotherapist.'

Mitch's jaw was clamped together so tightly she thought she might hear his teeth grinding together any second. In fact, he appeared to be trying to get his anger under control.

You're still hiding your hurt from Mitchell behind your anger for Steve, her inner voice warned.

Yet, it warmed her – that Mitchell would feel so outraged on her behalf.

It felt good to know he still cared – even if it was hypocritical of him in the extreme.

'How did you find out about the affair?'

As he looked into her eyes and asked the question, the sheer profundity of his caring was in every one of his handsome facial features.

Crossing her arms over her chest, she tried to stay strong.

She shouldn't tell him.

Even if he cared now, he didn't have the right to bear witness to the heartache Steve had caused her and be angry about it when he'd caused her more grief.

Maybe it was their familiar surroundings reinvoking the trust that used to be between them and the deep confidences they'd shared as friends. Maybe she was enjoying his caring and his outrage too much. Maybe she just needed to vent again in the wake of this newspaper article.

Tears scalded her eyes and the back of her throat.

She wasn't even certain whether she was miserable because she was reliving the discovery of Steve's betrayal. She suspected all the grief was resurfacing because she was here with Mitch, feeling his caring, and mourning the loss of his care for all these years.

Because there was so much of her that ached – so much of her that wanted that caring from him – she found herself telling him the story with a voice that was thick and sluggish with emotion.

'Jenny had excused herself to go to the ladies, and Steve had already wandered off.' She couldn't look him directly in the eye as she recounted the details, so she stared at the tanned, flesh exposed in the vee of his shirt. 'Jim and Marg were there too, and Jim told me he thought he'd seen Steve going outside.'

She caught her breath as she remembered she'd sought Steve out to confront him again about her suspected pregnancy, but that wasn't something she was prepared to share with Mitchell.

'I went to go outside, but the lifts were slow. I decided to take the stairwell.' For a moment she thought about how she'd taken it for granted that she could run down the stairs – and in heels! She paused as she retrieved a tissue from the pocket of her light-weight trousers and blew her nose. 'When I cracked the door open to go outside, I saw Steve and Jenny kissing. Passionately. I was rooted to the spot. I couldn't even retreat.' She'd had a flashback to when she'd caught Deanna in Mitchell's bed, but she wasn't about to admit that. 'I couldn't believe it. I heard Jenny pleading with Steve to come clean with me about their affair. She said they had enough money – they didn't have to keep up the pretence and wait until the end of the year. She said it'd been twelve months and she was sick of the pretence.' Now, Stella rested her hand on her abdomen, feeling physically ill when she remembered learning about their deception. 'Jenny said Steve had been well and truly cemented as the top coach in women's tennis and didn't need me anymore.'

'I made Stella number one, Jenny.'

'And you can take any other player with raw talent and make them number one,' she gushed. 'She needs you more than you need her. I need you, Steve. I want to be open about our relationship.'

'She thinks she might be pregnant.'

Jenny pulled back away from him. 'No! How could that happen? You told me you weren't having sex with her anymore!'

'I'm sorry. I… I cared for her a great deal once. You know I did.'

'You cared for her, yes, but you said you never loved her

the way you love me.' Jenny's voice was rising and Steven told her to be quiet. 'You said the relationship just happened – that it was convenient.'

'It did and it was. You're right. I didn't realise I didn't love her until I fell in love with you, but I never meant to hurt her, Jenny.'

'What if she is pregnant?'

'I've told her she has to have a termination, but she doesn't know for sure yet whether she is.'

'Either way, I'm not prepared to keep our relationship in the dark anymore, Steve. You have to break up with her. Tonight.'

'I will. I promise. I'll tell her about us as soon as we leave here and get back to the hotel.'

Mitch leaned towards her and the magnetism between them pulled her away from her painful memories.

'Stella, I'm so sorry.'

Gaze flicking over the breadth of his shoulders and chest, she ached to take comfort in his arms and to be held against him. Instead she ploughed on. 'I ran back up the stairs and grabbed my bag. I managed to hold it together until I got to the entrance way, then the tears came… I jumped into the nearest cab and asked him to take me back to my hotel.'

'The photographers saw you leave – saw that you were upset.'

She nodded. 'They chased the cab. What happened after that you know – everyone else in the world knows.'

Mitch was up, out of his chair and hauling her into the comfort of his arms before she could even react. She didn't resist. Couldn't resist. Why would she resist when this was the place she most wanted to be.

She hadn't realised she was shaking like a leaf until she was pressed against him.

Breathing in the faint scent of his aftershave, she realised he still used the same product. Masculine sandalwood with hints of citrus.

So divine…

The security of his strong arms around her made her feel as though she was in the safest place in the world – that he'd protect her from anything and deflect whatever blows came her way.

His chin had been resting against the top of her head as he stroked one hand soothingly down her back. He raised his head now as he asked, 'Do Steve and Jenny know you saw them – overheard them?'

'I haven't spoken to either of them since I was at the function, but they know because Jim told Steve I'd found them out.' Despite herself, she snuggled closer against him as she spoke. 'When I regained consciousness at the hospital the morning after my surgery, it was Marg and Jim who were at my bedside. I told them what I'd seen and heard.'

One of Mitchell's hands continued to stroke over her reassuringly and she revelled in it – never wanting to lose this connection with him again.

'*Stella!*' she imagined the admonishing voice of her counsellor. Oh, Dr Meyer would definitely not approve of her behaviour. '*Stop the hugging and start talking about how he let you down.*'

'*I will. I promise I will, but not now.*'

Stubbornly, she blanked out her hurt from Mitchell and focusing instead on what Steve had done.

'Marg and Jim told me Steve and Jenny had come to the hospital with them that night. I was already in surgery and hadn't had a chance to speak to Marg and Jim. When Steve learned my lower leg and foot were to be amputated, he left. He told my parents that Jenny was distraught and he thought he should take her back to the hotel and comfort her – that he'd be back to see me in the morning to know how the operation went.' She smiled a little as she confided, 'After I'd told Marg and Jim the truth, I'm told Jim did a surveillance walk around the hospital that same morning, prior to Steve's arrival. Margaret said Jim took Steve to one side and said he wanted somewhere private to update him on my health. Apparently, Jim made sure the spot was quite private, with no security cameras. He told Steve what he thought of him and gave him a good uppercut to the jaw, then came back and said that I wouldn't be hearing from Steve or Jenny again.'

Mitchell's arms tightened around her and he planted a kiss against her hair. 'I've always liked your foster father. I'll be sure to take him a case of beer next time I visit.'

Except that Stella now acknowledged that Dr Meyer had been right when she'd said that it should've been Stella who'd had the confrontation with Steve and that Jim had unwittingly disempowered Stella by taking that opportunity from her.

And, thinking of Dr Meyer again, Stella knew it was time to pull away from Mitch's embrace.

Any longer in his arms and she'd never be able to pull away.

His arms fell to his sides and he took a step back away from her the instant he felt her moving. Trying not to dwell on how much she wanted to step right back against him, Stella said, 'Through their lawyer, Steve and Jenny asked me to wait until the new year before either of us let the world know we were no longer together.'

'I'm guessing Carter wanted to make certain he didn't look like a complete bastard for deserting you when you needed him most, not to mention abandoning you the minute he couldn't profit from you anymore.'

Mitch's harsh words stung, but they were true. 'I'm certain you're right. I agreed because I had enough to contend with as I embarked on my rehab. I didn't want a media circus delving into an extra layer of personal pain.'

'Carter hasn't held up his end of the bargain.' Mitch followed her lead and they both sat. 'I did an internet search and these photos are being run across all the major tabloids in the UK and in Europe. I'd say our reporter today was the first of many to come.'

'Ah great! The two of you together!'

Both Mitch and Stella looked up and saw Liz walking toward them quickly.

'What's up, Liz?' Mitch queried.

Stella said hello and sent a prayer heavenward that Liz hadn't arrived a few minutes earlier and found them locked in an embrace.

'Perfect!' In a couple more paces, she was on the verandah with them, brandishing her iPad. 'I set a google alert for your name some time ago, Stella. These articles flashed up at me just now as I turned it on.'

The iPad screen showed one of the images of Steve and Jenny.

'This is a disaster!' Liz declared dramatically. 'How dare he carry on like this in public, knowing full well there was likely to be someone close by with a camera.' She sank into another chair and smacked the heel of her hand against her forehead. 'We're going to be besieged by reporters tomorrow if not later today. We need to swing into damage control mode.'

'We've just been discussing this, Liz,' Mitch told his aunt. 'There was a reporter at the pub this morning who'd driven up from Melbourne.'

Liz groaned. 'I could skin that damned Steve Carter alive!'

Although skinning him alive was a bit drastic, Stella agreed with Liz's low opinion of him.

'Well, he's dropped you right in it, Stella,' she raged. 'But, instead of having you coming off as the victim here, I have the perfect solution.'

Mitch wore a doubtful expression. 'I'm not sure I want to know.'

Liz was determined to tell them both whether they wanted to hear it or not. 'There he is basically telling the word you're not good enough for him anymore, when clearly it's the other way around.'

Stella frowned, not understanding what Liz was driving at.

'You don't have to be the object of the world's pity, Stella!'

Her hands cut through the air in emphatic movements as she spoke. 'You call a press conference and tell the world it was a mutual parting – then you present the world with your new fiancé. Mitchell!'

Liz's expression was jubilant.

Mitchell's facial expression revealed his horror at the suggestion. 'That's it, Liz! I'm calling the men in white suits.'

'No, no! It's the perfect solution. Just ride with it.'

'Liz!' Stella finally found her voice. 'Nobody is pretending anything. Lies just land people in more hot water.'

'Then, don't pretend. Get engaged for real.' She looked from one to the other of them. The light in her eyes challenged them without words. *You know you want to!*

'Is this the ludicrous plot line from another one of your romance novels, Liz?' Mitchell demanded.

'I think it is,' Stella confirmed. She was sure Liz had written a couple of stories where characters had pretended to be engaged for one reason or another and then had ended up falling in love with each other for real.

'Mitchell,' Liz stood. 'Time for you to step up to the mark and be chivalrous so Stella doesn't lose face here.'

Mitchell stood and stared her down. 'This is the most preposterous load of bunkum I've ever heard!'

'I don't need a pretend fiancé,' Stella told them both as she stood. 'I will call a press conference, and I'll be honest. I don't care less whether the world knows that Steve and Jenny have been having an affair since before my accident, and I certainly won't have anyone feeling sorry for me. When people know my tennis development is already started and, if I'm moving on with my life, hopefully they'll be happy for me and lose interest in me altogether.' She shook her head. 'I knew I was going to have to face the world sooner or later and – with the CWA Fair about to happen – I had thought I probably should let the world know I'm home.'

'That's true,' Liz said. 'There are always so many out-of-towners who come to the fair and any one of them could whip out their mobile phones and take a photo to put on social media.'

Liz's thoughts had mirrored her own. 'Maybe it's better to get the whole thing over and done with.'

Nodding his approval, Mitchell said, 'Up to you but would you prefer to have a press conference, or a less frenetic sit-down interview with this young journalist who was up here this morning? I have his card and he told me he'd be staying in Lancaster for a couple of days.'

Which would be better?

'What was he like?'

'Seemed okay. Seemed as though he thought people genuinely wanted to know you're okay.'

'I think I'll give him an interview, then.'

Reaching into his wallet, Mitchell retrieved the card Jason Mannering had given him and passed it over. 'You might like to think it over before you make a firm decision, but here are his contact details.'

'Thanks.' She'd discuss it with Jim, Margaret and her sisters tonight before she rushed into anything.

'Hey!' Kade's voice startled her as she hadn't seen him approaching. There he was with Jax hot on his heels looking as though he didn't have a care in the world. His easy smile and manner told them all he'd just arrived and had no idea what they'd been discussing. 'Want to come and see the kids with me now, Stella? They're growing up fast and I want you to see them while they're still so cute.'

'They are ultra cute,' Mitchell agreed.

'I'd love to, Kade.' Mitchell's son had perfect timing.

Kade had shown up at exactly the right moments, rescuing her now on more than one occasion from a sticky situation.

'Cool! You want to come too, Dad? Aunt Liz?'

Liz looked at her watch and appeared to feign surprise. 'My goodness! Is that the time?' She ruffled Kade's hair. 'I'd love to go but I'm expecting a call from my editor soon to check on the development of my story, so I'd better get back to the main house and get ready.' Before she left she said, 'Do what you will, but I think my suggestion was a better one.'

Mitchell shot Liz a sharp look of disapproval before turning to Kade. 'Count me in, buddy. I'd love to come and see them again and see how they're growing.'

Kade's constant chatter lightened the vibe between her and Mitchell but it was impossible to completely ignore the constant thrum of awareness.

Did Mitchell feel it too?

At times she'd swear he did.

Other times she thought she might be reading too much into the situation – might be imagining she saw things in his eyes and in his expression because she wanted to see them there.

He'd looked appalled at Liz's suggestion they become engaged.

Maybe he really was only offering friendship.

And, if he was, wasn't that for the best?

She knew he could be a good friend.

As embarrassing as it'd been to reveal what a naïve idiot she'd been with Steve, she hadn't been afraid of Mitch's judgement. He'd shown her caring and respect – something that should be the basis for friendship.

But if he wasn't just wanting friendship...

Oh gosh. If he wanted more, she wasn't certain she could resist falling back into his bed?

'Stella!' She heard Dr Meyer's voice rise slightly in exasperation. *'We've talked about this. You need to hold him to account. You need him to respect your feelings and he needs to understand what he did to you. You didn't deserve what he did to you and you need to believe in your own worth and hold others to account for how they treat you.'*

The voice might simply be in her head, but she couldn't dismiss it.

Couldn't stop the image she had of Dr Meyer looking at

her over her steel-rimmed glasses and pinning her with her kind but confronting gaze until she acknowledged the truth.

'You, Stella Simpson have to find the courage to be strong and to articulate your feelings.'

'I will,' she promised.

'When?'

'Soon.'

The conversation would rip open old hurts, but Marg had always said that you couldn't just put a Band-aid over an infection. She'd maintained that the only way to heal properly was to open up the wound, let all the toxic muck out, and then – and only then – could the process of healing truly begin.

Stella was surrounded by wise women and she knew she had to take the next opportunity she had with Mitch and have the conversation she'd put off.

He hadn't been honest with her, but she hadn't been honest with him, either.

CHAPTER THIRTEEN

Stella woke up extra early and went next door to the homestead for breakfast so she could read the *Melbourne Daily Chronicles* which Jim always had delivered.

Sitting in a comfortable wicker chair in the sunny conservatory, munching on a piece of toast and Marg's fabulous homemade strawberry jam, she reflected that the interview she'd given a couple of days before turned out to have been the best move.

The reporter, Jason, had met her at the hotel.

Mitchell had set them up in his office, letting them know he'd be close by if he was needed.

If it'd been a warning to Jason, it hadn't been necessary. The young reporter put her at ease and Mitchell had been right in judging that – as well as scoring the scoop – Jason genuinely seemed to want to let his readers know how she was doing.

He'd been quite astute, too at reading between the lines.

Stella thought back to their interview.

'Had your coach and physiotherapist been involved prior to your accident?'

She nodded. 'I feel stupid not knowing.' She took a sip of some orange juice then said, 'I had no idea until after the French Open final.'

There was only once she'd felt uncomfortable and that was when he'd asked about Mitchell.

'Your coaching centre is on land belonging to Liz Burton rather than to your foster family. Why is that?'

The fine hairs on the back of her neck stood up in alarm and she tried not to sound defensive as she replied, 'Liz wanted to sell.' Even before he asked his next question, she thought she knew exactly where he was going with this.

'Does this have anything to do with Mitchell Scott?'

She knew it. He was trying to connect them together.

Frowning, she tilted her head in question and hoped she'd be able to feign a lack of comprehension. 'What do you mean?'

'I know he's moved back to Hope Creek permanently and has bought the hotel, but he's living at Hope Farm, isn't he? Not at the hotel?'

'I'm still not sure how Mitchell has anything to do with me buying into the farm but yes, Mitch and his son live with Liz up in the main house. I live in a separate cottage – but please don't write in your article that I live alone. Even in a place as safe as Hope Creek, it would make me feel... vulnerable, I guess for people to know where I live and that I live alone.'

'Fair enough. No worries.' He drew a line through something on his notepad before saying, 'I asked Mitchell whether there was any chance you'd both rekindle the romance you had in your high school and college years.' He'd sent her a questioning look.

'Ha!' The second she heard it, she knew her laugh sounded false. 'That's why you asked about him.' She hoped she conveyed that it was so off-base she hadn't even connected the dots. 'Have you been reading Liz Burton's romance novels?'

Jason laughed. 'Mitchell asked me the same thing.'

'Well, there you go,' Stella said hastily. 'I think what we're both saying is that you shouldn't confuse fact with fiction.' She sent him what she hoped was an easy smile. 'It's been great to come home, and lovely to see Mitch again and to meet his son. We were friends for years and I think when you've been

close to someone, it's nice to re-establish that connection. But no romance. No. It's been wonderful to see all my neighbours again.'

What she'd said to Jason and how her body reacted to Mitch were two different things entirely.

Jason had asked her some probing questions about her career and the loss of it, how she was coping with her prosthesis, and whether she thought she might still be associated with women's tennis as an advocate or commentator. Truthfully, when Callie had suggested the same types of roles, she'd been quick to dismiss them. She couldn't see herself in those roles now, but she guessed she should never say never.

He'd also asked a lot of questions about her plans for her tennis centre, and she'd been glad to focus on those plans because these questions enabled her to get her a lot of free publicity for the centre.

'Fantastic article, Stella,' Jim told her as he came in from outside and flung his Akubra down on a nearby chair.

'I'm happy with it,' she said. 'Thanks for listening to me try to figure out whether or not I should go ahead with it.'

'For as long as Marg and I are on this earth, we'll be there to guide and support you girls if and when you need us to.'

She got up out of her chair and went to fling her arms around him. 'You've been fabulous parents. The three of us love you both so much.'

'Oi! Do I get one of those?' Blue asked as he came in.

'Of course you do! Marg and Jim have been my second parents, but you've definitely been an honorary uncle, Blue.'

He treated her to his crooked smile and a firm hug. 'Aw, you three grew up way too fast. I wish you were young ones again, running around the place and laughing your heads off.'

'Not to mention Callie and Morgan filling the place with their arguments,' Marg said as she joined them. 'Morning Blue! You here for a second breakfast?'

'If there's one going and you're offering, have you ever known me to say no?'

'Let me think about that for a moment,' Marg joked as she raised her forefinger to her chin.

Blue's appetite was legendary, but given the hard physical work he did around the station, it wasn't surprising.

'I wouldn't want you to be offended if I turned you down,' Blue told her.

'Well, you pull more than your weight in a day, Blue, so it's only fair you should eat your weight, too!' Marg teased.

'Blue and I have just been along the boundary fence and seen all the earth-moving work they're doing for you. They're setting a cracking pace,' Jim said as he settled himself down and Marg poured him a cup of tea.

'I'm really happy with what they're achieving in a day,' Stella agreed. 'At this rate, I'll be opening ahead of schedule mid-next year.' She indicated the newspaper. 'This story was a nice piece of publicity for the place.'

'Are you busy today, Stella?' Marg asked.

'I promised Kade we'd have a picnic by the creek, but after that I'm free. Would you like a hand with something?'

'Some of the cuttings I propagated to sell at the plant store for the fair need to be potted up into larger pots. I wondered whether you'd be free to help me?'

'Sure. I arranged to meet with him at twelve, so would you like a hand now or this afternoon? I imagine we'll only be an hour and a half or so.'

'This afternoon would work better. You're getting along well with him, then?' the older woman asked.

'He's impossible not to like. He's so open and friendly.'

'Good.'

'I seem to remember his father was that way too when he was a boy,' Jim commented. 'Sounds like a chip off the old block.'

'Funny though,' Blue mused. 'Kade must be the spitting image of his mother because I can't see a single physical feature of Mitchell in him.'

Stella tilted her head thoughtfully as she summoned

up Kade's face in her mind's eye and then compared it to Mitchell's. 'Mm. I'll have to look at them side by side I think before I make a comment.'

'You knew his mother, didn't you?' Blue asked.

'I knew who she was.' Instantly seeing Deanna in her mind's eye, the pull of muscles across Stella's forehead tightened as she tried to make comparisons. She shook her head. 'It was so long ago, I don't think I could make the comparison there either unless they were standing side by side.'

Morgan breezed into the room looking very smart in her RFDS pilot's uniform, her auburn hair tied back in a sleek ponytail. 'Morning all! How was the article, Stell?'

'Good. I'm happy with it.'

'Great! I'll read it at work when I get a chance.' She buttered some bread quickly then lathered the strawberry jam over it. 'Got to run! I'll have this in the car on the way, Marg.'

'Don't get it all over your uniform,' Margaret called.

'I'll try not to.' Morgan planted a kiss on Margaret's cheek. 'Thanks for breakfast. See you tonight.'

'And she's off,' Jim said with a smile as Morgan raced out through the doorway. 'Whirlwind Morgan. Always in a rush.'

'Always been the same, hasn't it?' Blue agreed.

'You have to agree she's predictable,' Margaret added.

But Stella wasn't so sure.

She was glad she was home.

Hopefully Morgan would open up to her soon about the breakup she'd had with the doctor she'd been dating. Stella was pretty certain her sister needed a shoulder to cry on.

* * *

Stella looked at the clock and gathered her wide-brimmed straw hat. The picnic basket and rug were on loan from Margaret, but she'd made a mental note to buy her own when she was feeling up to driving into Lancaster.

With no sign of Kade, she decided she'd start walking up to the farmhouse and meet him on the way.

About to go through the door, she was surprised when she saw Mitchell, not Kade, at the bottom step of her verandah.

Whoosh!

The sight of well over six feet of sheer masculine virility sucked the air out of her lungs – again. Was it ever going to be possible to look at him without reacting to him?

'Hey, Stella.'

'Hi, Mitch. Where's Kade? He's not standing me up, is he?'

His lips twisted a little. 'He's not feeling too well, I'm afraid, so he's sent me as his proxy. You okay with that? We did agree to have a picnic together at some point.'

Looking at him, she felt some weight move off her shoulders and imagined that something monumental shifted in her brain.

Was that the toppling down of a wall of mental resistance she felt?

Callie had advised her not to pull away.

'I'm very happy to have a picnic with you but it's not good Kade's unwell. What's wrong?'

'Hm. Well, he says he's got a bit of a sore tummy.'

'You don't believe him?'

He rubbed his fingertips across his brow. 'As far as I know, he's never lied to me before.'

'But?'

'I'm wondering whether Liz has got into his ear and suggested he might opt out and send me in his place.'

'Surely not?' But as soon as the words had left her mouth she rolled her eyes and looked heavenward. 'I forgot. This is Liz we're talking about.'

'Yep.' He grinned at her. 'Beautiful day for a picnic though. I can't say I object too much in this instance if she's manipulating us.'

His smile was enough to make her knees weak. 'I'd forgive her just this once for a bit of manipulation.'

They both stood grinning at each other for a moment, then Mitch extended his hand. 'Here, let me take those from you.'

Even as she handed the picnic basket and rug to him, the fragments of an inner voice whispered to her she was treading on dangerous ground. It warned her that she was deluding herself if she really thought she could ever comfortably be friends with Mitchell while she nursed this remembered passion for him.

I need more than friendship.

Oh goodness. Something had definitely let the tiger out of the cage.

'Remember what we talked about,' Dr Meyer's voice nagged at her.

Yes, she remembered.

She had been rehearsing the discussion she had to have.

Today's picnic seemed like the perfect opportunity so she had to find the strength to open herself up and reveal her hurt.

'I read your interview online this morning. Were you happy with the article?'

'Yes. I'm glad I did it.'

'How's the walking going?' he asked as they started toward what used to be their favourite picnic spot. 'Will you need a hand over the rough ground?'

'I should be fine, but I'll let you know if I do. Certainly, a bit of support as we go down the slope of the creek bed would be a good idea.'

He nodded before saying gently, 'To someone who knows absolutely nothing about it, you look like you're coping well with your new foot.'

'It's been a process.'

'I can't begin to imagine.' They walked a little further, around the goat shed and the chicken coop before he said, 'I admire the way you've coped and kept yourself going with your project.'

She smiled ruefully at him before she quipped, 'It's a matter of having to keep putting one foot in front of the other.'

'Or your best foot forward?'

It was so nice to be able to laugh with him about this – to have him shoot something straight back at her instead of him being uncomfortable about it.

It was easy yet it defied logic.

Every cell of her being was aware of him as a woman is aware of a man.

As a woman responding to a man, logic told her she shouldn't dwell on what she believed was – and what she thought others would regard as – her very unattractive disability.

If she wanted him to find her attractive, she shouldn't be drawing attention to it at all, right?

Yet, she found she felt okay being frank with him about what'd happened. 'It was a hell of a shock finding out I'd had my leg sawn off below the knee. As Marg and Jim will testify, I didn't take it well. I was a mass of denial, tears, and anger as I tried to come to terms with my loss. But I had a fantastic team with me every step of the way.' She pulled a face because she hadn't intended that play on words. 'The rehab doctor, physios and occupational therapists worked with the prosthetist to get me back on my feet again physically, but the rehab psychologist was just as important in helping me deal with the grief and loss. She explained that what I was experiencing was akin to a post-traumatic stress disorder.'

'I don't know how I would've coped if I'd been in…' He pulled himself up. 'God, it doesn't end does it? I was about to say, if I'd been in your shoes!'

'It is funny when you stop and think about it. I remember feeling really bad when I was a kid – must've been about ten I guess. Mum and Dad were still alive and we'd just been to see Mum's very aged aunt who was blind. I remember saying, '*See you soon*', as we left and then I realised I'd… oh golly! I'd put my foot in my mouth!'

Stella couldn't help it, she stopped and had to hold her sides, laughing so hard she had to wipe away the tears at the continued foot references. 'Oh dear!

When she looked up at Mitch, he wasn't laughing anymore but there was a depth of admiration in his regard that she thought she'd remember forever.

Before she could blink more tears away, she realised he'd put the basket and blanket down. One firm hand was under her chin, tilting her head up towards him, and with the fingertips of his other hand, he wiped away some of the happy tears that had trailed down her cheeks.

Stella's breath stalled in her chest.

She was too scared to breathe. Too scared to move in case she spoiled this moment.

There was a question in Mitchell's regard.

She couldn't enunciate a response so she answered his question by leaning closer into him and angling her head so she offered him her lips.

The warm, seductive whisper of his breath fanned across her lips and she closed her eyes, wanting to block out every other sense so she could feel more acutely.

'Mitchell,' she said huskily.

'Stella.'

Yes.

Exultation bloomed inside her as their lips met – his lips brushing ever so softly over hers in a barely-there kiss. Clinging, savouring, coming back for more. Exerting a slightly harder pressure. Lingering a little longer, with every touch sweeter and more sensationally erotic than the last.

'Beautiful Stella,' he whispered as his hands dropped to her waist.

She longed for the never-forgotten feel of his hard, muscular body against her, yet he maintained a gap between them; settling instead for deepening their kisses, his tongue tip beginning its sensuous sipping, tantalising her until she was the one who wrapped her arms more firmly around him and pulled him against her.

She was caught up in a maelstrom of pleasure even as her body pulsed and clamoured for the more intimate satisfaction she knew Mitchell could deliver.

With a tortured groan, Mitchell ended the kiss.

Still wrapped in each other's embrace, he was bent so his forehead rested against hers for a moment. Then, he straightened and pulled her against his chest.

There were no words.

Everything they'd needed to say was in their kisses and in their bodies' responses to each other.

A few minutes later, Mitchell took one of her hands in his, picked up the basket and blanket with his other hand and led her towards the creek.

They walked in silence until they reached what had always been their favourite spot – a shady and fairly flat area beneath a copse of paperbark gums.

He spread out the blanket and helped her as she sat down.

Sitting opposite her, he reached out and cupped her face in one hand. 'There's still something special between us, Stella.'

Throat dry with longing, she could only nod as she swallowed.

'I don't think it's going to go away,' he said softly as he stroked her cheek with his thumb.

'I don't know that I want it to,' she admitted, 'but it's complicated now.'

They had to talk about the past.

Mitchell let out a long breath. 'Keeping our relationship to friendship is… well, it's unrealistic considering I'd like nothing more than to make love to you right now… I've been fighting this attraction ever since I saw you again.'

He wasn't the only one. She hadn't felt this turned on in… her hands went to her cheeks and she felt them grow warm under her palms. She hadn't felt like this since she and Mitchell had been lovers.

'Let's take it slow,' he suggested. 'Let's give ourselves time to get to know each other again.'

She both loved and hated that he wanted to take it slowly.

And they still needed to talk about the reason for their breakup.

'I have Kade to consider, and… Stella, if we get together, I want us to have a chance. I can't help imagining us being lovers again, but, unless you've changed, something short-term wouldn't be right for either of us.'

'I haven't changed. I couldn't go into a relationship without hoping there would be a future in it,' she told him honestly.

'We have to rebuild emotional trust too,' he said gravely. 'There's been a lot of hurt.'

Was that his way of acknowledging how he'd hurt her?

Nerves and emotion made it impossible to say all she wanted and needed to say.

Talk to him about Deanna, her inner voice pleaded. *This is the perfect time to bring it up.*

Trying to summon courage, she looked around them at what had been their special place.

Did he remember he'd kissed her for the first time right at this spot?

'I didn't bring a single thing because I wasn't expecting to be on a picnic today,' he said.

The deep and meaningful conversation was over.

The opening words she'd been preparing were gone.

Maybe now wasn't the best time?

It might be better if they had a bit more time to establish a status quo?

'Don't worry.' She followed his matter-of-fact tone. 'I catered enough for Kade, so there should be enough there for you.'

'Thanks.' He sent her a wry smile. 'It's a wonder Liz didn't have a basket ready to go – complete with a bottle of champagne.'

'That might've made any manipulation on her part a bit too obvious.'

'Just a bit,' he conceded. 'Are you hungry?'

Boy was she hungry. Mitchell had stoked her appetite but it wasn't food she wanted.

She cleared her throat. 'Yes. Let's eat.' The ham and salad rolls would be better eaten sooner rather than later in this heat.

'This is good,' Mitch said as he tucked into the one she passed him.

Same Mitch.

He'd always had a healthy appetite.

Healthy appetites.

Oh dear. If she kept her thoughts going in this direction she'd end up needing to jump into the creek to cool down her body temperature.

'I've missed you, Stella,' Mitchell told her. 'It's... amazing to be here together again.'

Stella had to swallow down on the lump of emotion that blocked her throat. She'd missed Mitch, too. Being with him here, now, she thought about all the times they'd shared and wondered how it'd all gone so horribly wrong.

Once she was certain she was composed, she answered. 'We had some good times here in Hope Creek.'

'Did you love him, Stella?'

The straight-to-the point question startled her and she turned her head to face him.

She thought she saw his inner battle – his need to know versus a preference not to?

Had she loved Steve?

She strove for honesty. 'No. Now that it's over and I look back at what was between us, I don't believe I did.' That sounded harsh, but as she said it, she knew it was true. If she'd loved him, their breakup would've hurt more. 'I relied on him. He was my coach and my business manager.'

No. She couldn't have loved Steve because she'd been shocked by his betrayal and angry to know how he'd used her and lied to her, but she hadn't been heartbroken. Sure, she'd been going through a lot of other losses at the time, but still, in the end, it'd been a relief to know she'd never have to see Steve again and she hadn't missed him for a single second. She'd thought about him and his deception and castigated herself for her lack of awareness of the true state of their relationship, but she hadn't missed him.

If she'd loved Steve, surely it wouldn't have been so easy to rekindle all she'd ever felt for Mitch?

Still, she had to acknowledge that her time with her coach hadn't been all bad. 'Steve pushed me and I was grateful to him because he got me to the top.'

'Rubbish!'

Her eyes widened at the vehemence of Mitch's tone.

'Any one of a thousand coaches could've supported you on your journey to the number one ranking, Stella. You were the one with the talent, not your coach.'

Her gaze fixed on the slow flowing current of the creek. 'I was on the court but Steve knew exactly which buttons to push – what to say to fire me up. Exactly what to do to re-energise me when I was starting to flag or lose concentration in a match.'

'All coaches study psychology. My football coaches were the same. All the good ones know how to get into an athlete's head to bring out the best performance.'

'I guess you're right.'

'I know I am.'

Stella laughed. 'You were always so confident.'

'And you weren't as confident as you should've been.'

She'd been super confident on the court. That had been her arena. The one place she usually felt invincible, but off the court... not so much.

'How's the pub going?'

You're a coward, Stella!

It was true, she'd missed another perfect opportunity to

discuss how her lack of personal confidence had made her hide away from Mitchell's betrayal.

'Business wise, it's turning a profit – not making a fortune, but I don't need it to. I'd be happy for it to kick along to cover expenditure. That's the only aim I have. I'm not wanting to make money out of the people at Hope Creek.'

'We're both fortunate not to have to worry about money.'

'I've been thinking of how best to spend some of mine to help the community.'

'Hm.' She thought on it for a few moments. 'This CWA Christmas Fair is raising funds for the local Bush Fire Brigade. Marg's told me they have a whole heap of equipment on their wish list.'

'Great. I'll look into it.'

'I was wondering about funding a community bus that could pick up some of the more elderly and take them out and about on excursions.'

They exchanged ideas for the next half hour.

'This feels really good,' Mitch said. 'We used to sit under this tree and dream about success in our sports. Now, we're talking about how our success can help others.'

It did feel good.

Mitchell moved down the blanket a little so he could face her more easily. 'Was winning Wimbledon and being number one for so long it everything you'd hoped it would be?'

She sighed as she remembered the triumph of her first Wimbledon title. 'Holding the Wimbledon plate for the first time was surreal. It was an incredibly emotional experience not just because I'd trained for it and dreamed about it. I held it high for them, Mitch, for my parents. They made the ultimate sacrifice for me. If they hadn't taken me to that tournament to get national rankings points, they'd still be alive.'

She'd talked to Mitch many times about the guilt she felt about her parents' deaths.

Her parents' car crash had been on the way home from a tennis tournament. Stella had only been saved because she'd asked them if she could travel home with her doubles partner, Susie Lee. The Lee family had been following her parents down the highway.

She shuddered now at the memory of it.

She hadn't seen the actual impact of the collision as the oncoming driver had swerved across the highway and run head-on into her parents, because she and Susie had been entertaining themselves in the back of the car by playing Rock, Paper, Scissors.

The sound of the crash coinciding with Mr Lee ramming on his brakes, and the vision she had of her parents' car wreck, was one she'd never banish from her brain.

Mitchell took his hand in hers. 'They were doing what they wanted to be doing, charting your future in tennis. It never struck me as a teenager but I've thought about it a lot over the intervening years. I've wondered whether winning Wimbledon was really your dream or was it their dream for you?'

Before she answered him, she looked up to where a magpie sat on a branch overhead and began singing its beautiful song.

'Oh, I love to hear the magpies singing. It's so good to be home.'

'Kade has been blown away by all the different birds here. He's begging me for a pet cockatoo.'

'Are you going to get him one?'

'No. I don't like the thought of having birds in cages.'

'I'm with you there. Although, Blue rescued a cockatoo with a broken wing years ago and he ended up keeping it because he couldn't return it to the wild.'

'Did he teach it to say "Hello Cocky?"'

'No.' She chuckled as she recalled, 'It said, "Time for Smoko. Put the kettle on, love!"'

Mitch threw his head back and laughed. 'Only Blue!'

Yes. Only Blue.

Going back to respond to Mitch's question she said, 'You know, it's impossible for me to answer your question. One of my earliest memories is of getting a tennis racquet for my fourth birthday and thinking it was some sort of stringed instrument.' She rolled her eyes as she laughed a little. 'I remember holding it in front of me and trying to strum the strings as though it were a guitar.'

He nodded. 'I remember you told me that it wasn't a present you'd asked for.'

'Right. Dad had to explain what it was. He took me out into the back yard and threw a ball until I managed to hit it. I remember Mum looking on and saying, 'And so the road to Wimbledon begins.' Dad had to explain what Wimbledon was.'

'I can't remember whether you ever said. Had they been tennis players?'

'In mixed doubles they'd been the state champions two years in a row before Mum fell pregnant with me.'

'They wanted you to succeed in their dream then – to live vicariously through your achievements?'

'Maybe.' She reached for the picnic basket. 'I helped Marg make this chocolate slice yesterday. Would you like a piece?'

'Ha! That'll teach Kade to go along with Liz's machinations. I'll make sure he hears about this chocolate slice and then he'll be sorry if he's been playing possum.'

'Oh! Go you! Listen to you and your Australian phrases! Kade's been spouting them too.'

The wink he sent her made her insides go all mushy.

'The first time I was back here with Aunt Liz after you'd move in with the Richardsons, I remember Jim had taken you to Melbourne and you'd won your age group in the state tennis championships.'

'All the running around they did with me was amazing.' She passed him some slice. As if fostering kids hadn't been a big enough task, they asked each of the girls whether they had any dreams for the future.

It'd helped that the Richardsons had never had to do it tough financially. Nobody would ever know it from the way they lived their lives, but both Marg and Jim had come from old money with their forebears all having been on the land and having amassed a fortune.

Stella hadn't realised how wealthy they were until she started earning well enough that she wanted to send her cheques home to help the Richardsons with their expenses of running the farm. It was then they'd sat her down and told her they were multi-millionaires. She still remembered how strained her eyes had been as they'd widened at the figure. They hadn't needed any of her winnings, that was for sure.

Mitchell's voice broke into her reminiscences. 'Did Liz push you into applying for the Stanford scholarship?'

'No.' Her denial was immediate. 'She suggested it might be possible for me to get one, but she didn't coerce me into applying.' She smiled. 'I think she's become a lot pushier as she's aged.'

'Ain't that the truth!'

'That Stanford scholarship was the making of my career and I have you to thank for it. If you hadn't been awarded the football scholarship to Stanford, I wouldn't have even known to apply. Liz encouraged me to do it. I think she knew I was more interested at that point in following you to America than I was in the tennis. The scholarship was a means of being with you again.'

He ran his hands down over his face. 'Yet, tennis became more important than me.'

'Mitch—'

'I never understood why you threw away your scholarship,' he said.

Here goes.

Time for some honesty and some home truths.

It would either make them or break them from here, she guessed, but the truth needed to come out and it was better to come out now than once they'd re-established a relationship.

'I couldn't stay at Stanford after we broke up. When I found out about you and Deanna… it was too painful.'

Mitch sat straighter, frowning as he said, 'But you'd already broken up with me.'

'You slept with her while I was away at a tournament!'

He sent her a piercing look and opened his mouth as if he was about to deny her accusation. Then, she saw him close his eyes for a moment before he looked away from her. 'Recriminations are useless at this point.'

Stella looked at him, taking in the tension in his posture and noting the tightness of his features before he'd turned away. He might not want to talk about it, but she couldn't let it go now he'd broached the subject. 'Tell me, if I hadn't broken up with you, what would you have done a month later when you found out Deanna was pregnant with Kade?'

He was quiet for a while. 'I married Deanna because she was pregnant. I didn't have any feelings for her.'

Which made his betrayal even worse.

He'd gone to bed with the promiscuous cheerleader without feeling anything for her. He'd used Deanna for sex and while he'd used her, he hadn't considered how crushed Stella would be.

Tell him how crushed you were.

Make him understand.

Before she could make the confession, he confessed, 'Knowing my relationship with you was over made it easier for me to marry Deanna, but even though I convinced myself I was doing the right thing by her, I wasn't. I didn't love her. I loved you.' He buried his face in his hands for a moment. 'Hell! I didn't even like her and I certainly didn't have a shred of respect for her.'

'You slept with her and you married her. You must've at least been attracted to her.'

'No. When we were married, we didn't even share a bed.' He stood up and frustration beat off him in waves. 'I know you moved on with Carter. But, even knowing that, I... well, you... you were a hard act to follow and I couldn't...'

Her eyes widened as she understood what he was telling her. 'You couldn't…?'

He shook his head. 'I was miserable and trapped in a marriage I'd never wanted. I only stayed because of Kade, so it was a relief when she ended up finding a wealthier man who wanted to marry her. She didn't object when I finally demanded a divorce.'

Oh. She felt winded by his admission, realising that his betrayal had cost them both dearly.

'I missed you every second of every day the first six months after we broke up. A year after our split I was still crying myself to sleep at night, Mitchell.'

His regard was intense. 'But you broke up with me, Stella.'

'It… I…' Despite Dr Meyer's advice she found she couldn't tell him what had happened. 'We were on two different tracks, hardly ever seeing each other because of our sporting commitments. I believed it was for the best, but that didn't mean I didn't miss you.'

'We could've worked around it, Stella. Hell! I wanted to work around it but you said your feelings for me had changed.'

Her feelings had changed when she'd realised he'd taken Deanna to bed.

Tell him.

'I guess we were young and we both made mistakes.'

His cheeks hollowed and he looked haunted. 'I'm sorry, Stella.'

She knew he meant it.

They'd both suffered as a result of him taking Deanna to bed and it was ironic to think that he'd managed to have sex with Deanna when he'd been roaring drunk but hadn't been able to have sex with her again during their marriage.

No wonder he and Deanna had finally divorced.

'I didn't miss Steve when we broke up.' She needed to set the record straight. 'Our relationship had evolved through convenience.'

'Maybe it did for you, but I think he was keen on you right from the start.'

'No, I don't think so.'

'Have it your way, but the guy left his position at Stanford so he could coach you privately the second you quit the scholarship program.'

She wasn't certain Steve hadn't simply cultivated her trust and proposed to her because he was keen on all the kudos and financial benefits she'd bring him. He'd told Jenny he'd never meant to hurt Stella but…

'He was a good coach and my mentor. I'd come to rely on him heavily. With nobody else around, it was probably inevitable I eventually fell into a relationship with him.'

Mitchell was quiet.

'If I hadn't come to the Stanford program, I certainly wouldn't have been able to compete in the tournaments leading up to the US Open and I wouldn't have been granted a wild card entry.'

There was a soft note of pride in his voice as he remembered, 'The Aussie wild card who reached the semi-finals that year!'

The prize money and sponsorship deals after her success in that tournament had made it possible for her to go on from there and for Steve to have become her full-time coach.

In some ways, Mitchell's betrayal had helped her. When their relationship was over, tennis had been all she'd had and she'd focused on it with more single-minded determination than ever. She'd vented her heart ache, anger and emptiness on every single ball she'd hit for at least two years after she left Stanford. Nothing else mattered except winning points, sets, games, championships, and attaining and keeping the number one world ranking.

'Back to my original question, was it all you expected it to be? Was it worth it?'

Had it been worth it?

She'd left behind her family in Hope Creek and all the stability both they and the rural community in general had provided for her. The comfortable and wonderful familiarity of waking up to kookaburras singing, or the smell of bacon and eggs cooking as Marg cooked breakfast for Jim, Blue and any of the other ringers that'd come and gone over the years had been traded for a never-ending stream of different hotel rooms.

Instead of bird song, the strident sound of an alarm clock would wake her each morning and sometimes when she opened her eyes it'd been hard to remember which city she was in. Unsurprising really considering she hardly saw any of the cities she travelled to.

Far from being glamorous, life had consisted of hotel rooms, car trips to the tournament centres, locker rooms, and different courts with different crowds calling out between points in different languages.

The consistency in her life had been the feel of the racquet grip in her hand, the knowledge of the space she ran around in and those white lines that she had to keep her shots within to make every point a winner. While she'd been on tour, her world had shrunk to the game, her coach and later her trainer and physiotherapist.

Four times a year, Marg and Jim had travelled to her grand slam events and a few times her sisters had managed to come as well, but her life had been narrow in the extreme.

Aware Mitchell was waiting for an answer she said, 'There's satisfaction in having achieved my goal. It's set me up financially for the rest of my life.' She shrugged. 'A lot of people who have serious accidents don't have financial security.'

His look was considering and his tone gentle as he probed, 'How are you coping now it's over?'

Her laugh was slightly bitter. 'Honestly? I was ready for it to be over. I just didn't expect for the universe to take that decision out of my hands.'

'Really? But you were still at the top of your game.'

'So were you, yet you retired.'

'I was still enjoying football – the competition and the teamwork – but not so much the travelling.' He sat down next to her again.

'So, why did you quit?'

'I became aware that Deanna was neglecting Kade. I knew I needed to assume full responsibility for him and once I did that, my focus was split. I became less invested in the game.' He moved his hands expressively as he spoke. 'I wanted to get the games over with and get back home to him.'

'You said you had full responsibility for him, but who looked after him while you were away?'

'I hired a middle-aged couple as my housekeeper and gardener but they were great with Kade and I knew he was being looked after by them.' Those broad shoulders of his lifted in another shrug. 'I saw out the end of my contract and that was it for me.'

'I guess parents make those sacrifices for their kids.'

'It was no great sacrifice.' His lips twisted. 'Even though I still enjoyed football, I was probably past ready. Kade gave me a reason to retire. Without the responsibility of caring for him full-time, there was nothing else I wanted to do with my life. Football was all I knew, and without him maybe I would've been like Tom Brady and still been playing quarterback in my mid-forties.'

Stella had heard Mitch compared favourably to the legendary quarterback on many occasions when she'd tuned into games. 'You had your night clubs. From what I've heard, they've been highly successful. You didn't contemplate leaving football to run those?'

'I've had very little to do with the running of those. I just put up the money and hired some brilliant managers. They've been on very lucrative bonuses for keeping the clubs going well so they've had a lot of incentive to manage them well. I won't be sorry when the last two sell.' He pinned her with her gaze. 'Nice sidestep there, by the way, but why did you want to retire?'

'Because I came to the conclusion that life was about more than hitting balls back across a net.'

He nodded. 'There are a lot of sacrifices in professional sport. Sacrifices that only another pro can understand.'

'Look at us, all these years later.' She sighed. 'Last time we sat on this creek bank, we were just dreaming. Now, both of us have accomplished those dreams.'

'Some of them,' he said. 'But maybe we were wrong about which dreams were the most important?'

'Easy to say when you've achieved a career most people can only dream about.'

'What do you dream about now, Stella? What do you want most in life?'

'What I've got now. A home of my own.'

A loving relationship and a family.

He was quiet for several minutes. 'Funny, isn't it? All that time travelling over the world and living out of suitcases, going from court to court – or in my case one locker room and field to another all over the country – and both of us are yearning for something simple.'

He was right. It was important to have dreams, but having turned such a huge dream into reality, she now understood the value of simple dreams that were in most peoples' grasps.

'You decided Hope Creek Farm would be that home.'

'When Liz came to visit me in Switzerland at the rehabilitation centre, her proposal was ideal. A home next to my former home. Enough space to develop my tennis centre.'

'Do you just want a home to call your own, or do you want a family to share that home with?'

Mitch could still read her heart.

'Maybe.' Changing the subject she said, 'You own the hotel but what are you going to do with the farm?'

He stretched his long legs out in front of him. 'I enjoy the idea of a hobby farm but I'm not up to running it as a dairy farm again – unless I hire an overseer-manager for that. What I am going to do is tidy up the vegetable garden, re-net the orchard which is still producing fruit for market, and I'm thinking of getting a couple of horses for Kade and me to ride around on. Like you, I don't have to think about turning a property into a commercial venture. It's the lifestyle here that appeals to me more than anything.'

'Was your football career everything you hoped it would be?'

'It was better.'

'In what way?'

'Most quarterbacks retire in their twenties after just a few seasons. I was lucky enough to be injury free and I didn't still expect to be playing at thirty-one.'

'Someone once told me that NFL stands for not for long.'

He laughed. 'That's about right. I just got lucky.'

She knew luck had nothing to do with it. The position of quarterback was the most glamorous position on the field because it was the one that carried the most pressure and expectation. All the commentators had said Mitch had one of the highest game IQs they'd ever seen. Quarterbacks were not only required to handle the ball, but had to make decisions every single play, being an on-field coach and leading the team to run the offensive moves to win the game. She'd read that Mitch had remained injury free because he read the game so well and seemed to stay one step ahead of his opponents.

His communication on field, mental acuity, strong arm and consistency in passing touchdowns and rushing touchdowns had made him one of the most sought-after quarterbacks in the league and earned him over fifty million dollars a year.

'By all reports you were incredibly skilled.'

He shrugged it off. 'It's team work. I had good players around me.'

'Do you miss it?'

'I miss some elements of it.'

'What elements?'

'This is going to sound contradictory but at times I miss the intensity. The pressure. The camaraderie and the challenge. Mind you, raising a child is not without its challenges.'

'How's Kade doing?'

'He loves it here. I was in two minds as to whether or not it'd be a good thing to uproot him from his friends and move to Australia, but it turned out he wasn't particularly happy at his school anyway.'

'So he's happy to be here? He's not missing the States?'

'It's the best thing I could've done for him. Apparently being known as Mitch Scott's son was something of a burden to him at school. He's not particularly athletic and he was being bullied for his non-prowess on the football field.'

Stella turned those words over in her head, wondering how any son of Mitchell's could fail to be athletic. Every inch of Mitch was like a finely tuned human machine. And, okay, he worked out to build up those impressive muscles he had, but surely the reflexes weren't a product of training but were simply in his genes?

Deanna must've been completely unathletic and Kade must've inherited her genes.

'Apparently, he'd begged Deanna to move him to a different school and she'd ignored him. He never raised the issue with me because he assumed we'd talked and made the decision to leave him there.'

'Why didn't she let him change schools?'

'I don't know for certain. We never discussed it because I thought Kade was happy there.' He shrugged. 'It was a prestigious school and a lot of the kids there had parents who were quite famous in Hollywood. Deanna liked rubbing shoulders with the uber-wealthy and famous so I'm assuming she kept Kade there because it allowed her to mix socially with the parents. She'd always been a party girl and she'd lived for the bright lights and the social life.'

Party girl was putting it kindly.

A mutual friend at Stanford had told Stella how Mitch had insisted on having a DNA test to determine Kade's paternity. There'd been a reason Mitch had insisted on the test. Once Deanna's pregnancy had become general knowledge, everyone said Kade could've easily been the son of quite a number of the players on the football team.

'Deanna craved attention,' Mitch said slowly. 'It took me a long time to understand that she craved it because she'd never had it as a kid.'

Stella heard the note of pity in Mitch's voice and wanted to know more. But before she could ask, her mobile phone rang and she looked at the screen.

'Oh no! I'm late!' she told Mitch. 'Hi Marg, I'm so sorry. I lost track of the time. I'll come over right away.'

'No hurry, love,' Margaret said. 'I just wanted to make sure you were okay.'

'I'll see you soon.'

'Okay.'

'Sorry,' she told Mitchell. 'I'd forgotten I promised Marg I'd go over and give her a hand with a few things she's preparing for the fair.'

He looked at his wristwatch. 'I didn't realise how late it was getting. I said I'd call in at the hotel this afternoon and I want to check in on Kade before I leave.'

Mitch stood up and reached down a hand to help Stella.

The spark of attraction flared through Stella again the second she placed her hand in his.

The darkening of his blue eyes suggested he felt the same way. And, if there was any doubt I her mind, it was soon proved wrong as Mitch claimed her lips again with his.

Heaven.

Her arms went up around his neck as he deepened the kiss and their lips clung and moved in sweet promise.

All too soon, Mitch was lifting his head away from hers, but his hands remained at her waist as he said. 'Slowly.'

She took a deep breath as she smiled. 'Slowly but surely.'

CHAPTER FOURTEEN

'Now, your job is to put the little milk chocolate chips down Santa's coat, to be his buttons,' Marg told Kade.

The Richardsons' kitchen was a hive of activity two days before the Christmas fair.

Marg had been up baking cupcakes, shortbread and gingerbread biscuits since the break of dawn, and Stella, Morgan and Kade had been roped into helping her. Kade was with them for the day while Mitch took care of some things at the hotel and Liz made a quick trip to Melbourne for a meeting with her publisher.

As each new batch of the gingerbread cookies had cooled, Stella and Morgan had been responsible for icing them before Kade put on the final decorating touches.

Blue had popped his head into the kitchen at one stage. 'Any of those need taste testing?'

Marg had put a couple on a saucer for him then shooed him out of the kitchen with a firm, 'Don't come back until lunch time!'

'It's pretty cool that you're a pilot,' Kade told Morgan as he looked up from his decorating. 'Do you reckon you could take me up with you one day?'

'Sorry, Kade. That wouldn't be allowed.' Her tone was sincere and Stella was relieved Morgan had put away her icy feeling towards Mitchell away and was able to be friendly towards Kade.

'You're doing really well there, Kade,' Marg told him.

'This is so much fun!' Kade said enthusiastically. 'Last weekend I was over with Jayden and Patrick and their mom and Aunt Liz had us helping to make Christmas cards and some other crafty things for their Christmas craft stall.'

'Ooh, I'll have to stop by and buy some,' Morgan said. 'How did you decorate the cards?'

'I did some sketching on some and then Patrick and Jayden coloured them in. We also cut out some pictures from old Christmas cards and stuck them on the front of others. Mrs Lynch had heaps of craft stuff to use.'

'Did you have a favourite?' Stella asked.

His cheeks reddened for a moment. 'I do, but that one isn't for sale. I'm saving that for you for Christmas, Stella.'

'Aw. That's so sweet of you,' Morgan said.

Stella was touched. 'I'll look forward to it.'

'What about the crafts?' Marg asked. 'What did you make?'

'We made really cool Christmas wreaths using pine cones and gum nuts. We spray painted them and some gum leaves with all the Christmas colours – red, green, gold and silver – and then we used a hot glue gun to stick them to the wreaths.'

'They sound beautiful,' Morgan told him as she mixed up another batch of icing.

'Mrs Lynch had some Christmas ribbon too, so we used that in a loop so the wreaths can be hung up. We all reckon they look pretty good.' Every word was full of pride but then his little face fell. 'I never got to do things like that at home. I asked Mom once if I could do some painting and she didn't want a mess. She said I should be happy playing computer games.'

'Oh well,' Marg rushed in an upbeat tone, 'you're making up for it now.'

Kade didn't look any happier. 'I don't think my mother likes me very much.'

Seeing he looked as though he was about to burst into tears, Stella put down her icing bag and said, 'I've been standing up for too long and I need a break. Want to come for a walk with me, Kade? I could use a hand so I don't trip down the stairs.'

'Is that okay with you, Mrs Richardson?'

'Absolutely. You've been working like a Trojan.'

He cocked his head at her. 'Is that another Aussie expression?'

Marg laughed. 'No, I think that one is an international saying. An Aussie expression for hard work would be, *"Flat out like a lizard drinking"*.'

As Kade repeated the phrase and giggled, Stella realised she probably needn't have dragged him away from their endeavours because he seemed to have recovered from his melancholy. Still, the walk outside would do them both good and it probably was time for her to move around.

'Flat out like a lizard drinking,' he said again and dissolved into more giggles. 'I've never seen a lizard drinking!'

'Come on, you!' She gave his bicep a playful punch. 'Let's go.'

He laughed almost all the way out of the house, but sobered at the top of the steps.

'Can I ask you about your foot?' he asked as she placed one hand in his and held on to the rail with the other.

She understood he was curious and didn't feel uncomfortable about it. 'What do you want to know?'

'How does it attach?'

'Well, we talk about my foot amputation, but in fact they amputated just below my knee.'

'Oh! I thought it was just your foot.'

'No. What I had done was called a below-knee amputation which removed my lower leg, foot and toes. And, to answer your question, the prosthesis uses suction to fit to what's left of my lower leg.'

'I read that your foot and ankle were mangled.'

'That's right.' They'd reached the pathway now and she let go of Kade's hand, but placed her arm around his shoulders as they continued – not because she needed the support but more because she was feeling increasingly close to Mitchell's son and it seemed right.

'Does it feel like walking on a numb foot or a leg that you've sat on for too long?'

She nodded. 'That's exactly what it feels like for me, although I don't know whether other amputees would describe it that way.'

'Do you need to do special exercises?'

'Yes, I have a routine I do every morning so that I can work on my muscle strength and prevent contractures – that is what they call it when muscles and tendons, or even skin and soft tissues, shorten. If that happens it prevents normal movement because the joints get stiff.'

'Do you ever take your foot off?'

'Yes.' Gosh, he had so many questions. 'I have to take it off to clean it and my stump – that's what we call what's left of my leg. It's important that I check it to make sure there's no swelling or irritation.'

He looked a little discomforted. 'I've been reading about it, online and I was wondering – do you ever get any phantom pain?'

Goodness. He had been doing his homework.

'No. I've been fortunate. These days phantom pain isn't as common because they have a procedure that decreases the chances of it happening.' There was genuine interest in his expression and she knew he was a smart kid, so she found herself explaining, 'Amputees used to get sensations – those phantom sensations as you called them – that their brains thought were coming from the part of their body that'd been removed. The way it was explained to me is that nerves try to regenerate – regrow – and because there was nothing to grow on to, they became a disorganised mess sending confusing signals to the brain.' He nodded, following her keenly. 'In my case, the surgeons rerouted the nerves that were cut and they redirected them to other nerves. That's supposed to stop the 'phantom' sensations like itching and pain. So far, it's working very well in my case.'

'Do you have to take medicine?'

'Not so much these days. I did have medicine for the pain and to reduce the swelling, but I've healed pretty well.'

'That's awesome.' He looked super impressed. 'I might become a surgeon one day.'

'That's a good goal to have.' A lot of study, but he seemed bright enough and she and his father were proof that if you wanted something badly enough, you could achieve it. 'I had help from exercise physiologists and occupational and physiotherapists, too. Acupuncture – which is where they put fine needles into the body to help treat it – and massage were also really helpful as I was recovering.'

'Your recovery was team work then? Everybody has a different thing to do then, just like on a football team?' he asked.

She smiled at the analogy. 'Exactly like that.'

A shadow seemed to reach over him again and darken his mood. 'I'm useless at sport.'

Her heart cramped. 'I'm sure that's not true.'

'It is,' he insisted sadly. 'I can hardly catch a ball and I was the slowest runner in my class at school.'

Stella stopped and encouraged him to turn around and face her. 'Some people are good at sport and some people are musical. Some are good at English and others at maths.' She made a dismissive movement with her hand. 'What's the most important thing is what's in here.' She placed her palm over her heart. 'You're kind and caring and funny and smart. It doesn't matter if you're not as sporty as your dad. If you still decide you want to be a doctor when you grow up, I think you'll be a good one because you care about people.'

A second later it was just as well Stella had her balance,

because Kade was right up against her with his arms wrapped around her waist giving her an enormous hug. 'You're the best, Stella.'

Recovering quickly from the shock of him launching himself at her, Stella hugged him right back.

He pulled away from her and looked her straight in the eye as he said, 'Aunt Liz thinks you and Dad might start dating?'

'I…' Stella put her hand up to her mouth and coughed. 'I don't know about—'

'I hope you do, Stella. Dad's a really good guy – I mean *bloke* – and I think if you got together it'd be fantas – I mean, *Bonza* – because I think you'd be a great mom!'

'Well—'

'There you are!' Blue said. 'Are you two shirking out here while Mrs R and Morgan slave away inside?'

'No!' Kade denied immediately. 'We—'

'It's okay, Kade. I was just pulling your leg. I wasn't being fair dinkum.'

Stella smiled, 'I told you Blue could teach you an expression or two!'

'Anyway, you run inside now and get back to it,' Blue said. 'I need to have a quick yarn to Stella.'

'Righto, Blue,' Kade said with a terrible impersonation of an Aussie accent before he took off laughing.

'What did you want to chat about?' Stella asked, intrigued.

'Nothing,' Blue admitted. 'I was within earshot and heard your conversation. Thought it was getting a bit awkward for you so I thought I'd come to your rescue.'

Stella kissed him on the cheek. 'Thank you.'

'Any truth in it?'

She looked at him blankly for a moment. 'Oh, you mean Mitch and me?'

'Duh!' He pulled a face.

'I don't know, Blue. We'll see.'

'I like the sound of that,' he told her. 'I know he let you down badly and to this day I can't get my head around it. But the young lad was right when he said that Mitch is a good bloke, and I'd like to see all my girls happy.'

She loved Blue.

He'd always thought of Callie, Morgan and her as his girls.

'Well, I think Morgan's the one we need to be worried about at the moment.'

'Yeah,' he agreed. 'She puts on an exterior as though she's tough as old boots, but really she's a marshmallow inside.'

'She won't talk about it, either.'

'She will when the time's right,' he said wisely.

Stella knew he was right. 'I'd better get in or our marshmallow-soft Morgan will be showing her razor sharp– tongued side!'

* * *

Later that afternoon, when Mitch called in to the homestead to pick up Kade, he found his son hard at work with Marg and Stella. They were busy packing cupcakes and biscuits into Christmas boxes and tins.

'Wow! You guys have been busy.'

'Dad!' Kade ran to give his father a hug. 'It's been the best time. We've hardly stopped all day and I've been helping out *and* having fun.' He only just paused for breath before he said, 'Morgan was here too until she had to go to work. Callie's driving up later tonight from Melbourne so she can help tomorrow and then be here for the whole weekend.'

Mitch felt his heart swell, loving every second of his son's excitement.

'Thanks for having Kade today,' Mitchell said to the ladies.

'He was a huge help and a delight to have,' Marg said. 'He's welcome any time.'

'How are the preparations coming along in town?' Stella asked.

'Everything is on schedule and we're awaiting inspection tomorrow from our wonderful CWA president extraordinaire.'

Marg rolled her eyes at him. 'Flattery will get you nowhere, Mitchell Scott.'

'I was rather hoping it might get me a cookie or two!'

'You're as bad as Blue,' Stella laughed.

'Here you go.' Marg offered Mitchell one. 'You'd better have another one, too, Kade – as long as it won't ruin your appetite for dinner.'

'Yum! These are delicious,' Mitch exclaimed.

'We have to buy a tin of biscuits and a box of cupcakes, Dad.'

'We sure do. These are so good, I think we'd better buy two of each.'

'Seriously, Mitch,' Marg said, 'How's it all looking?'

Jim had spent the day supervising about thirty men who'd volunteered to set up stalls in the park across from the hotel. 'It's looking great. Jim said to tell you he'd be home in another hour and a half. The carnival people have just arrived up from Melbourne and he's finalising arrangements with them about where to set up the rides, and the side show attractions, then he'll be home.'

'Jayden said there'd be rides but he wasn't sure what sort of rides,' Kade said excitedly.

'I believe,' Mitch said with a questioning look at Marg, 'There'll be dodgem cars, a carousel and…?'

'We've organised a tea-cup ride for the younger kids and some sort of spinning nausea-inducing ride for the older kids.'

'Alright!' Kade slapped one hand against his thigh.

'The carnival people are staying at the hotel tonight, right?' Marg asked.

'All booked in,' Mitch agreed. 'This fair is bringing a lot of business to the town. Mavis told me today that all the B&Bs in the area are fully booked and that motels in Lancaster are also saying there's no vacancy.'

'It's a lot to organise but it certainly pays off.' Marg nodded her satisfaction. 'Jim and I are thinking that there might be a bit more interest in the fair this year from out-of-towners because the interviews you both did have put Hope Creek on the map recently.'

'Main thing is that we have fun and turn a profit for the rural bush fire brigade,' Mitchell said.

'I'm pleased I had the interview with Jason Mannering but I hope people aren't coming to Hope Creek to try to gawk at me,' Stella said sharply.

'I guess some die-hard tennis fans would realise you're going to be at the fair,' Marg said. 'I'm sure people will respect your privacy.'

'It's not as if you haven't given a few interviews now,' Mitch said. Stella had told him that many national and international news outlets and magazines had contacted her since Jason's article. She'd answered a few questions over the phone for the newspapers and said she'd think about the magazine interviews once her tennis centre was up and running.

'I'm so excited,' Kade told them. 'I'm not going to sleep for the next two nights!'

'It's a pretty big fair,' Mitch agreed. 'I was usually staying with Aunt Liz every year when it was on because I was on school break. Do you remember when I won you those God-awful fluffy dice on one of the side show stalls, Stella?'

'Oh yes,' Stella agreed. 'I think I've probably still got them somewhere. I'll have to dig them out and give them to Kade.'

'Please don't,' Mitch groaned. 'He'd probably insist on having them hang from my rearview mirror.'

The adults laughed but Kade was intrigued. 'What are fluffy dice?'

Mitch shook his head. 'They're exactly what they're called.'

His interest in the dice was forgotten as Kade came to stand beside him. The next thing he knew, his son's elbow was digging into his side. Raising his eyebrows he asked, 'What's up, son?'

'Ask her,' came the reply through clenched teeth and in a real stage whisper that wasn't missed by anyone in the room.

Mitch knew exactly what he was talking about but feigned ignorance.

'Ask Stella,' Kade implored.

'Oh! Right!' Mitch sent Stella a wink. 'Stella, would you do Kade and me the honour of allowing us to accompany you to the fair?'

'She'd love to go with you,' Margaret said before slapping her hand over her mouth. 'Oh my. Sorry. I must've spent too much time this last week in your aunt's company. This is my cue to leave.'

Stella giggled as Marg walked away with cheeks so red they'd light her way down the hall.

'Stella?' asked Kade.

'I would love to go to the fair with you. Thank you.'

'Yes!' Kade pumped the air with his fist. 'See, Dad. I told you she'd say yes.'

Oh good one.

Thanks, Kade.

'I'm glad you had so much confidence in me, Kade,' he said.

'I knew Stella would want to come with me,' Kade clarified.

Stella sent Mitch a smirk. 'I do have to man the Christmas cooking stall for a couple of hours but Marg's only got everyone who's not an actual stall organiser rostered on for a maximum of two hours because she wants us all to enjoy the fair.'

'I'm rostered on the BBQ from ten to twelve,' Mitch told her.

'Well, fancy that!' Stella declared. 'Marg must be psychic because those are the same hours I'm working.'

'Aunt Liz has already told me she needs my help from ten to twelve,' Kade said.

Stella exchanged a glance with Mitch. 'Looks like the stars are aligned.'

'Hm. What are the chances?' he asked drolly, knowing he and Stella were both fully aware who'd aligned them. 'Go on out to the car, Kade, and say hi to Jax.' He'd had the pup with him all day rather than leaving him at home by himself or underfoot at the Richardsons'. 'I'll be out in a sec.'

'Okay, Dad.'

'I can't tell you how wonderful it is to see him so carefree,' Mitch told her. 'Thanks to all of you for being there for him today.'

'We loved having him with us,' she said.

'Even Morgan?'

'I've noticed she's prickly towards you, Mitch, but I don't think she's kindly disposed to any adult male on the planet now who's not Jim or Blue,' Stella said. 'Funnily enough, I think Morgan enjoyed Kade's company even more than Marg and I did. Some of the comments he made had her cracking up with laughter and it was great to hear her laugh.'

'Are you still staying here tonight?'

'Yes. Marg's been up cooking since dawn and I know she's got a whole long list to work through again tomorrow so I want to be here right from the start.'

Mitchell moved closer to her and took her in his arms, loving the way she stepped into them so willingly. 'I can't stay but I can't leave without holding you and kissing you.'

He didn't have to kiss her.

Stella was on her tiptoes and reaching up to press the sweet lushness of her lips against his.

Oh Lord.

Mitch had to stop himself from groaning, and, as his hands explored the contours of her waist and hips, then moved around to the tautness of her backside, he had to resist the urge to pull her firmly against the hardness of his arousal.

'Going slow is hell,' he rasped against her lips.

'It is,' she agreed.

'We need some alone time.'

'As soon as this fair is over,' she promised.

'It won't be soon enough.' With supreme effort he stepped away from her. 'I have to go.'

'I know.'

'Will we leave at eight thirty on Saturday?' he asked.

'I'll make sure I'm at the farmhouse and ready to go, or, if I stay here again tomorrow night, I'll let you know so you can swing by and pick me up.'

'Going to the fair together will be just like old times,' he said.

'Kade's not the only one who's excited.'

He couldn't help himself. He claimed one more long, hot, searing kiss before he left.

He hadn't exaggerated. Going slow really was hell.

CHAPTER FIFTEEN

Mitch let out a low whistle as he and Kade left the house on Saturday morning and saw Stella leaning against the door of the four-wheel drive.

'Hi Stella!' Kade waved.

'Hi.'

Mitchell reached her side in a few easy strides.

Kade was already opening the rear door of the vehicle and throwing in a few things that Liz had forgotten and texted them to ask if they could bring them along.

A quick glance at his son told him it was safe to give Stella a quick kiss, but as his hormones surged, he realised it hadn't been a good idea.

'You look gorgeous,' he told her with a soft growl. 'You smell delicious and,' he stole another quick kiss, 'you taste divine.'

And, now that he'd kissed her, her hazel eyes were filled with desire and turned him on even more.

'Kade,' she warned quietly.

Mitch cleared his throat, then opened the car door for her. 'Your chariot awaits.'

'Hey, Dad! Did you remember to freshen up the goats' water today? I forgot.'

'All taken care of.' Thank God he'd remembered, or Kade would've scampered away to do it and goodness knows what he would've found when he returned. Mitch definitely needed his son to play chaperone today.

Once Stella was safely in, he closed the door then watched to make sure Kade was strapped in.

As he drove down the long drive and through the gates of the property, he looked in the rear vision mirror and gave Kade a wink before his gaze darted sideways to Stella.

They felt like a family.

In another lifetime they would be a family and Kade would've been their son.

There was no question that Kade loved Stella and had formed a really close bond with her in a very short time.

Initially, he'd sensed Stella's eagerness to keep some distance between herself and Kade – and he thought he could understand how she was feeling. But, in no time flat, that bump had ironed itself out and he knew Stella reciprocated Kade's genuine affection.

Instead of making things easier to push on in renewing his relationship with Stella, it made him hesitate more.

If Kade hadn't liked Stella, he wouldn't be affected if Mitch had got together with her and then it hadn't worked out.

Now, however, Kade was making little comments every day about how much he loved Stella and how kind she was. He'd told Mitch that Stella had really cheered him up two days ago when she'd said it didn't matter that he wasn't sporty. Mitch had been thrilled that some of Stella's positivity was rubbing off on his son and that Kade was developing a lot more self-esteem. Then, Kade had broken down and said how much better he liked Stella than his mum and how he was sure Deanna hated him. Kade confessed that Deanna had told him on more than one occasion that she shouldn't be a mother.

It had been devastating to hear because while Mitch was pretty certain Deanna had uttered the words because she'd felt out of her depth. Kade had taken it to mean that she wished he'd never been born.

And, while Mitch knew Stella would never say anything

to destroy Kade's confidence and self-esteem, he knew that if Kade thought she was a fixture in his life and then she walked away, his young heart would shatter.

Kade's wouldn't be the only heart shattering.

'Your dad and I always went to the fair together,' Stella told Kade now.

'Except that we'd have to go when the sun was rising,' Mitch put in. 'There was no sleeping in because Marg and Jim always had key roles to play in organising things, and neither Stella nor I were old enough to drive, so we had to get up and be ready when they were ready to leave.'

'Couldn't you have gone in with Aunt Liz?'

'Yes, but Stella was my best friend and I wanted to go in with her.'

'I heard Aunt Liz talking to Mrs Lynch. Did you two really date back in high school and college?'

After a slight pause, Stella said, 'We did.'

'But didn't Mom have me when you and she were both still in college, Dad?'

Mitch swallowed. 'Stella and I had broken up by then, and no, I wasn't in college when you were born. I'd been drafted into the NFL.'

'Oh! Look at the traffic!' Stella commented in an obvious attempt to change the subject. 'I think the whole of Lancaster must've decided to turn up to the fair.'

It was true. The traffic was ridiculous. He'd never seen the like in Hope Creek.

'It's not as bad as LA.' Kade was completely unfazed.

'Just as well we left when we did,' Mitch said as they joined the queue which was stretched back a couple of kilometres from the fairground. 'Where have all these people come from? I don't remember ever seeing this many people at the fair.'

'Are we going to be able to cope with so many visitors?' she asked.

'We'll cope.'

'How many visitors do you usually get?' Kade asked.

'I haven't been home at this time of year for a long time,' Stella said, 'but I certainly don't remember there ever having been this many visitors. I don't remember ever being told that the fair had grown so popular, either.'

'Maybe Marg was right and this is a result of your interview.' Mitch wished he hadn't voiced his thoughts aloud when he saw Stella shrink back against her seat in an obvious attempt to make herself small.

He reached out and took her hand in his for a few seconds to give her a comforting squeeze.

Oblivious of the adult interaction, Kade chatted on and asked questions about all the different stalls.

When they got about eight hundred metres from the parking, the traffic became stop-start.

'I think we could've handled another few rides,' he said. 'The queues are probably going to be horrendous.'

Kade grumbled.

'At least you can park at your spot at the hotel and we don't have to line up for entry,' Stella said brightly.

Always positive.

It was one of the many things he loved about Stella.

Mitch pulled himself up sharply as he realised he still loved Stella.

He didn't only desire her.

He loved her.

All well and good, you loving her, he told himself. *The real question is does she love you?*

He amended that question. *Does she love you enough that she won't want to walk away again?*

As frustrating as it was, he knew it was the right thing to go slowly rather than jumping straight back into a relationship. They weren't teenagers in a hurry now.

When they were finally parked, Stella said to Mitch in front of Kade, 'There are so many people here and could be a bit of jostling. Would you mind holding my hand as we walk around?'

'Of course.' Had she phrased it like that so Kade wouldn't read anything more into it, or did she genuinely want the security of knowing she was supported?

He had his answer soon enough because once they'd dropped off the bits and pieces to Liz and begun to explore, Stella put her arm around his waist. 'This is more comfortable,' she said.

He put his arm around her shoulders so they walked hip to hip. 'You know we're making a statement?' he asked.

She nodded. 'It's a statement I'm happy to make, if you are?'

He turned for a second so he could brush his lips over hers. 'May as well underline the statement, then.'

'That's Stella Simpson and Mitchell Scott!'

When Mitch raised his head away from Stella's lips, he saw a few people pointing and looking their way. None of them were locals.

Shit.

Liz had told them moments ago that the organisers were surprised at the turnout because they'd never drawn such an enormous crowd. She'd pointed out that Mitch and Stella's interviews had put Hope Creek in the spotlight, but now Mitch wondered whether it was Hope Creek Fair that was drawing the crowd or the chance of seeing Stella.

With his spare hand, he reached out to where Kade was walking slightly ahead of them. 'Stick close, Kade, and if we lose you, meet us back at Aunt Liz's stall.'

'Okay, Dad.'

People were polite but still intrusive.

Unlike what he'd experienced in some other places during his football career, people here actually asked permission to take a photo rather than simply thrusting the camera in their faces. Still…

'Hi Stella. Would you mind us having our photo taken with you?'

Stella was polite back. 'Hi. Just a quick one.'

'Would you mind being in the picture too, please Mitchell?'

Kade could only stand so much and Mitch understood his impatience. They were here to see the fair.

'Looks like we should've had our own stall,' Mitch said to Stella in exasperation as a small line formed.

'You're a genius,' she said before announcing. 'Hey guys, I'm happy to have photos taken but I'm keen to enjoy the fun of the fair right now. I'll be at the cookie and cupcake stall between ten and twelve so, I'll serve you there and have a photo taken at the same time I pass you over your baked goodies.'

'I predict the baked goodies will sell out by the end of your shift,' Mitch told her quietly.

'Thank goodness!' Kade said when they were finally moving again.

'Hey son, remember how excited you were to meet Stella?'

'Yeah,' he agreed grudgingly before he said to Stella, 'When we lived in the States, I couldn't go anywhere without people wanting to take photos with Dad. Now, we're in Australia and everyone wants a photo with you and Dad.'

'It won't be forever,' Stella said. 'One day people will forget who I am or they won't recognise me.'

Mitch wasn't sure that would be true. Changing the subject, he said, 'Hey look! There are the dodgem cars. How about I buy all three of us some tickets?'

'Er…' Stella hesitated. 'You two go ahead and I'll watch.'

Mitch tilted his head at her. 'Are you worried about your foot?'

She nodded. 'Everyone runs to grab a car and… I'd rather sit this one out.'

'Let's sit it out, too, Dad. I'm going to meet up with Jayden and Patrick because we're all helping out at the stall at the same time. Then, we thought the three of us might go around together. We could go on the dodgems then.'

Mitch hesitated. If they'd been in the States at a big fun park, he wouldn't have let Kade out of his sight.

'This is Hope Creek,' Stella nudged, clearly reading his indecision. 'Yes, there are a lot of people here today that we don't know, but as long as the boys are all stranger aware and promise to do their best to stick together, they'll be fine.' When he continued to hesitate, she said, 'Besides, look around you – despite all the people we don't know, you don't have to look too far to see a local.'

She was right. 'You heard Stella, Kade. If you feel uncomfortable at all, just head to the nearest stall because all the locals know you.'

'We'll be okay, Dad.'

His boy was growing up.

'How about we go to the ring where they're showing how the border collies round up the sheep?' Mitch suggested, knowing that it would be unlike anything Kade had seen before.

'Oh, cool! Are Ned and Ben going to be working?'

'No,' Stella told him. 'Ned and Ben are family dogs. Farmers usually keep the working dogs and the family dogs very separate.'

The fair was more like a mini-scaled agricultural show.

As they approached the stands that'd been hired and set up especially for the occasion, Stella frowned. 'I can't make it to the higher stands. You two go up, but I'll have to squeeze in next to someone.'

The Williams family were sitting on the first row of seats and must've seen Stella's hesitation. Instantly, the locals stood.

'Morning all!' Darryl Williams waved the over. 'Here, you take our seats and we'll grab a better view up higher.'

Stella smiled. 'Thank you so much for your thoughtfulness. I can't manage stairs very confidently yet.'

'No problems at all,' Denise Williams told her as she rounded up their three children. 'Come on munchkins, let's move go up to the back row. You'll see better from there.'

Mitch shook Darryl's hand and added his thanks only to be told, 'No worries, mate!'

It struck Mitch as a typically kind action from the people of Hope Creek who continued to be aware of others.

Settling in, they watched the border collies at work followed by some of the local kids doing some fancy dressage moves with their horses.

Kade sat between Mitch and Stella totally absorbed in the activity in the show ring, and Mitch felt a sense of completeness. It was easy to imagine they were here as a family as they sat together and enjoyed themselves.

'I could've entered the goats!' Kade was clearly disappointed when there was a contest in the ring for children and their pets with prizes being given out for all sorts of categories including the pet that was the shaggiest, best behaved, and the one that had the biggest smile.

'I thought about it,' Mitch said. 'Aunt Liz and I both thought they'd be too distressed if we took one of the kids away from its mother.'

'Yeah,' Kade said immediately. 'I guess.'

'Next year, Liz said you can enter your sketches in a contest as well.'

'Oh! Did they have a contest for that too?' He sounded a little miffed he'd missed out on that as well.

'They don't presently,' Mitch told him, 'but Liz said she was going to suggest it to the committee for next year.' He sent Kade a wink. 'You'll be a shoe-in?'

'A shoe-in?'

'Absolutely certain to win.'

'How about we go and get something to eat?' Stella suggested. 'We've only got a little time before we all have to go and man our stalls.'

The air was thick with the tantalizing smell of a BBQ, but Kade said, 'How about some cotton candy? Do they have that at Aussie fairs?'

'We call it fairy floss,' Stella answered. 'I'm sure I saw that stall on Marg's list. Let's go and find it.'

Mitch put out his hand and helped Stella to her feet, then they meandered through the crowd, searching the colourful booths and attractions for the cotton candy.

Laughter and chatter blended with cries of delight from children and adults alike as they saw something they liked, and the atmosphere was buoyant.

'Mitchell! Stella! Can you look this way and smile for me, please?'

Mitchell looked towards the guy who'd called out to them, but doubted his expression could be construed as a smile.

'Goodness!' Stella exclaimed to Mitchell.

He was so used to it in America but found it jarring here in Hope Creek. 'Knowing our photos might end up making the news, are you still happy for us to be seen this way?'

Her hazel eyes were as clear as her response. 'I am.'

Mitch just refrained from kissing her again as Kade said, 'Oh yum! There's the cotton candy.'

'And look!' Stella told him as she pointed to a stall that had colourful cans set up in pyramids. 'The knock-em-downs are right in the next booth. You'll have to try them out.'

Kade's face fell. 'I don't think so. I'm not very good at those. I don't have a good throwing arm like Dad.'

'I bet you're better than I am!' Stella told him. 'I challenge you, Kade Scott.'

Mitch could see that Kade was still a little uncertain, but Stella's eyes were alight with fun and challenge and his son responded to it. 'Oh, okay.'

'No fathers with professional football throwing arms allowed,' she told Mitch with mock sternness.

He put his hands up in defeat. 'I get it!'

Although Mitch was certain Stella had purposefully thrown the bean bags way off target more than once, Kade did manage to knock the cans down with one of his throws and he was jubilant.

Kade and Stella hi-fived each other as the stall holder gave Kade a yo-yo as a prize and set up the cans again.

'Oh Dad! Stella!' Kade was jumping up and down on the spot as he held on to the cheap plastic toy. 'I won something! I actually won something!'

'Well done, buddy.' Mitch loved Kade's excitement and, as he caught Stella's eye, he could see she was thrilled, too.

'Brilliant stuff, Kade. What were you saying about your throwing arm?' Stella teased. 'Hey, guys, we can come back here after our shift but we've got to get going now.'

'We'll walk with you to the cake store, then I'll drop Kade off with Liz before I report in for BBQ duties,' Mitch said as he put his arm around her waist once again. It felt so right and so natural, the three of them together.

As they made their way to the cake stall, Mitch came to a realisation and made a decision.

The future was uncertain.

What was certain was this feeling that the three of them fit well together.

No more holding back.

Mitch wanted Stella and he was through taking things slowly.

Whatever the future held for them, he'd do everything he could to show Stella that they belonged together.

CHAPTER SIXTEEN

'That was the best day ever, Dad!' Kade told Mitchell as they arrived home from the fair and got out of the car. 'I love living in Hope Creek.'

Stella's heart warmed knowing Kade had felt the love she'd felt when she'd become part of the community.

Car lights lit up the driveway behind them as Liz arrived home.

'It was a fantastic day,' Mitch agreed. 'I always loved the fair as a kid. I'm really glad you've been able to enjoy it too, Kade.'

'What did you enjoy best, Stella?' Kade asked.

Stella thought on it. 'I think I enjoyed your huge smile when you won the yo-yo.'

Kade's smile wasn't quite as huge now, but most likely that was because he was tired.

'Phew! What a day!' Liz greeted them.

They chatted for a short time about the success of the day then Liz said, 'Mitch, why don't you walk Stella safely to the cottage and let me have some time with Kade to hear about his day before he goes to bed?'

Mitch leaned forward to give Liz a kiss on the cheek. 'That'd be great, thanks Liz. I'm sure Kade would enjoy telling you all about it.' He gave Kade a hug. 'If I'm not back to tuck you in, sleep tight and I'll see you in the morning.'

Kade hugged him back then moved to give Stella a huge hug. 'Thanks for coming with us today, Stella.'

'I had a lot of fun. Thank you for inviting me.'

As Liz ushered Kade away, anticipation made Stella's pulse beat more rapidly when Mitch captured her hand in his.

'Let's go.' His voice was deeper and she thought it was slightly rougher with desire.

She hardly dared to look at him because she was certain she'd see her own need mirrored in his eyes.

I'm ready for this.

It'd been a fantastic day. A fantasy day where it'd been easy to forget that they weren't a married couple and Kade wasn't their child.

Could Mitch hear her heart pounding harder the closer they got to the cottage?

The second they were inside and the door was shut behind them, Mitch drew her close and she melted against him, relishing the sensual onslaught of his kisses and the feel of his hands as they slipped under her blouse and caressed the skin of her back.

Stella shivered with delight even as she longed for more.

Needing to touch him, she tugged his shirt out from his waist band and reacquainted herself with the feel of his muscular back.

'I want you so bad,' he told her between kisses. 'All day, it's been driving me crazy to hold you against me when I want you naked beneath me.'

Whoa!

Oh Lord.

Handbrake. Now.

'Mitch.' Stella groaned as she realised she couldn't let this go any further without talking about the past. 'We have to talk.'

'Now?' he asked her as he dipped his head and began kissing the supremely sensitive flesh of her neck.

'Not now. Later,' lust demanded.

'Now.' Sense prevailed.

'Okay.' There was reluctance in each syllable, but Mitch pulled away from her and regarded her steadily.

Now, what did she say?

'I...' What was it she'd rehearsed? 'Today was wonderful.' She turned away from him and took a couple of paces before she turned back to him. 'You have a fantastic bond with Kade. You're a terrific father.'

No. that wasn't what she wanted to say.

'I...' She felt hopelessly, helplessly emotional and couldn't remember a darned thing she'd played over and over in her mind as she'd tried to work out how to talk about how hurt she'd been by his betrayal with Deanna. Now, she felt the skin prick across under her eyes and across the bridge of her nose and knew tears were close. 'I... I wish I was his mother,' she cried. 'Damn it all, Mitch, I should've been his mother. He should have been our child. Why did you cheat on me?'

The dam broke.

A huge torrent of grief – over a decade of bottled-up sadness and confusion and anger at his betrayal – washed right over the wall and she was unable to stem the flood of tears.

She saw his deep frown of confusion before his features blurred completely.

And, as much as she wanted the comfort of his embrace, when he drew her against his solid chest and wrapped his arms around her, she wrestled out of them then started to thump her fists against his chest as she howled, 'You broke my heart! I never recovered, Mitch. How could you have betrayed my trust and been sleeping with Deanna when you told me you loved me?'

For a moment, he stood motionless, not reacting at all to the ineffective thumping of her fists against him. Then, he swept her up into his arms and carried her to the couch where he sat with her, cradling her against him on his lap.

'Stella, I—'

'No. Don't say anything yet. I have to tell you how much

you hurt me. You have to know how devastated I was when you and Deanna… I loved you, Mitch. I loved you with every cell of my body and I still love you, damn it all. And I know I can't. I know I mustn't because I couldn't stand it if we became lovers again and then you cheated on me with someone else.'

'Stella.' He shifted her a little on his lap. 'Look at me, Stella.'

Feeling shattered all over again, as though the events of over a decade ago had just happened, it was hard for her to meet his gaze.

'I had no idea you felt this way,' he told her. 'You… we weren't dating. You—'

'We were dating,' she accused. 'Kade's birthdate proves you slept with Deanna before I broke up with you.'

He let out a long breath. 'Oh, hell! You're right. We need to talk. If we're to go forward, I owe you the truth.'

The truth?

She knew the truth.

Now she had to hear him admit it.

Dr Meyer had a point because if Stella and Mitch renewed their relationship, not only did he need to be honest, but they also needed to figure out what had been so lacking the first time around that caused him to be unfaithful.

'Let me up.' Stella scrubbed the tears from her cheeks with the backs of her hands as she got off Mitch's lap and sat on the couch next to him. 'Even if we weren't going forward, you still owe me the truth.'

Now she'd opened Pandora's box, she wasn't certain she really wanted to look inside it, but she knew she had to.

Mitch ran a hand through his hair and she watched his broad shoulders rise and fall on a deep breath. 'The morning after the US embassy had been bombed and I thought my parents had died, I woke up and found Deanna lying naked in the bed beside me.' His voice was quiet and his expression was distant but there was a trace of horror in the lines that bracketed his mouth. 'I couldn't believe it. It was a total nightmare. She was acting all loverlike and climbing on top of me. Telling me how fabulous I'd been the night before and how she wanted to do it all over again.'

'Please don't go there.' That wasn't something Stella needed to hear and she wanted to put her hands over her ears rather than listen to all the painful details.

'I've got to start at the beginning and tell you what happened. All of it,' he said earnestly. 'You have to know I never liked Deanna. I couldn't credit I'd taken her to bed because I neither liked her nor had I ever been attracted to her. I told her to get out – I wasn't too kind about it, either. Whether it was finding her in my bed, the hangover, or a combination of both, I had to bolt to the bathroom where I spilled my guts.'

'You're telling me you had sex with her because you were drunk.' Her words were flat and Stella felt a dull ache in her chest now rather than a sharp pain.

'No! Hear me out, Stella!' he implored.

When she nodded, he continued, 'I spoke to the guys later that day and they were teasing me about having put me to bed and how I'd been telling them over and over that I just wanted you. You remember Reevy?'

'Of course.' Reevy had been his best mate at Stanford.

'He told me Deanna had tried to come on to me when I'd been at the club drinking. He confirmed to me that I hadn't had any interest in her and apparently I'd told her so. He insisted that when the boys had put me to bed, I was quite alone and that they'd locked the door as they'd left.'

'Then how…?'

'Deanna spilled the truth right before I filed for divorce. She talked her roommate into getting my roommate, Chad, into bed. When Chad was undressed, Deanna's roommate excused herself to go to the bathroom, but she took Chad's keys and gave them to Deanna.' Mitch got up and paced away and then back again as he rubbed the back of his neck.

212

'Deanna let herself into my room but I was out cold. We never had sex, Stella. She lied about everything.'

She frowned at him and shook her head in total disbelief. 'But Kade?'

'In every way that counts, Kade is my son.' His jaw clamped for a moment before he added, 'He's just not my *biological* son.'

Stella's head spun. The room seemed to close in on her and it was impossible to take a breath. None of what he was saying made any sense. On a series of shallow breaths she said, 'If you… were so sure you… hadn't had sex with her, how… come… you accepted her story?' She paused and forced in a huge breath to finish, 'How come you accepted you were Kade's father when she told you she was pregnant?'

'I didn't!' His denial was vehement. 'Knowing her reputation, and being certain I couldn't have been her baby's father, I insisted on a paternity test.'

She remembered being told he'd forced the paternity test. Now, she raised her arms in front of her and turned her palms up in incomprehension. 'And?'

'It's a really tangled mess – one of those situations that's… unbelievable – unless you really know the people involved.'

'Tell me, Mitch.' She was listening. 'Untangle this for me because I can't move forward with the load of hurt I'm carrying in my heart.'

Mitch wiped his palms down his face and resumed his pacing for a few moments, looking as though he steeled himself to continue. Finally he said, 'When my parents were found alive in the rubble from the blast in Iraq, their pictures were all over the press.'

'I remember seeing the images.' She remembered Mitchell's parents had become American heroes. All the major news channels had been covering the bombing and she knew Mitchell's father had been hailed as a patriot who'd served his country in diplomacy for years and had almost paid the ultimate price of his life for his loyalty to the American nation. 'It was how he got his nomination for the senate, wasn't it?'

Bitter lines etched around the tightness of his lips. Bitterness she'd never seen before in his expression 'Oh yeah, that's what he'd have you believe. My father the American hero and my mother his saintly supporter.' Sarcasm dripped from every word.

His reaction baffled her.

Why was he talking about his parents and the bomb blast now?

She'd figured he'd taken Deanna to bed when he'd been drunk and at a personal low, but what she wanted to know was why he was still denying having taken her to bed and why he was denying he was Kade's father.

Yet, she also wanted to know when and how the lack of closeness he'd had with his parents had turned to this deeper dislike? Gosh, his tone and expression conveyed hatred. And, as strong a word as hatred was, she sensed hatred and disdain were the emotions he felt for them now.

'I know you didn't have a close relationship with your parents when you were a kid, but… you almost lost them. Hasn't it got any better now you're older? Now you're a parent yourself?' She didn't understand it. As much as she loved the Richardsons she'd do anything to have her parents back as well.

Each word was clipped as he told her, 'My *relationship* with my parents is non-existent.'

'Is that because they're upset with you because you've moved to Australia?'

'That's putting it mildly. It's not good optics for a senator's son to abandon his home country and it'll cause a huge stink when I actually live in Australia long enough to apply for citizenship here.' The muscles in his cheek worked as though he was clenching his teeth together. 'It's all about optics for dear old Dad as he tries to work – or rather, grease palms – all the way up to the Oval Office.'

Every muscle in his body had tightened. She'd never seen him so worked up and she frowned at him, sensing his deep pain beneath the anger. 'Tell me, Mitch, what's happened between you that you despise him so much?'

He let out a long, audible breath. 'He'd always wanted to enter politics but he didn't have a service record in any of the forces and believed that would count against him. That bomb literally blasted him into the American political arena. Suddenly, everyone in the nation knew who he was – knew of his diplomatic service and knew he'd almost been killed. My mother was adored because she was an Australian who'd given up her citizenship to marry the man she loved and stand by his side as he was transferred from country to country in service of the American nation.

'Dad was noticed by the political heavyweights too. More emerged about him. Not only was he the son of a quarterback legend but I was fast making a name for myself in the game and everyone was saying I'd be a top pick in the upcoming draft. All those things went in his favour.'

Stella sat on the edge of the chair and hung on his every word, wondering where this was leading, but not prepared to interrupt.

'Turned out that Deanna's father is a heavyweight in my parents' political party. After all the publicity my parents received, there'd been some discussion about putting my father forth as a candidate at the next election.' He ran one hand through his hair in what she recognised as his classic sign of frustration. 'Knowing I was at Stanford, Deanna's father asked her if she and I were friends. By then, Deanna knew she was pregnant. She was scared shitless, knowing that if her parents found out, they'd probably disown her. When her father asked about me, she saw his interest in me as an opportunity to turn the situation around. She told her parents we were in a relationship and that I was the father of her child.'

Stella was certain the furrows across her forehead

deepened as she tried to understand where Mitch was going with this.

'It had the desired effect.' He shook his head. 'Rather than disowning Deanna, her parents fawned all over her, thrilled to bits that there'd be a connection between the two families.'

'That's—'

'Outrageous,' he finished for her. 'Our fathers struck a deal, Stella. My father had to convince me to marry Deanna and, in exchange, he'd be given party backing for his first run at a position in the senate – in a seat that was basically a shoe-in.'

'Your father talked you out of insisting on a paternity test so that he could become a senator?'

'Worse. He tried to talk me out of it, but I wouldn't budge. I insisted that I knew Deanna had slept with others and there's no way I'd marry her without knowing for certain the baby was mine.'

Stella blinked a couple of times and shook her head because Kade's mother's promiscuity didn't change Mitchell's actions. 'So, when the test came back and you realised Kade was your child, you did the right thing and married her.'

She was confused.

Had she heard him properly when he'd denied Kade was his child?

'You don't see at all.' His hand made an emphatic slashing gesture before he moved to sit beside her. As he shook his head, he looked pained. His words were soft and laced with defeat as he vented, 'Neither did I. Even though there were clues hidden in plain sight, I didn't see until Kade had an accident and I found out that his blood type is B.' The pause was lengthy before he explained. 'My blood type is A and Deanna also has type A. Any child we had together would have to have type A or type O blood – not type B. At that moment, I knew there was no possibility he was my son. Whoever fathered Kade had to have had B or AB blood group.'

What?

She had to replay his words to make sense of them.

'My God! How on earth did they get the DNA test wrong?'

'They didn't.'

'But…? I don't understand.'

He sat forward. 'Not only did Deanna confess to me that we didn't have sex at Stanford – not for want of trying on her part either she said – but she also said I'd been set up by her father and mine.'

Stella sucked in a shocked breath. 'How?'

'My father and Deanna's made sure the DNA test results were sent to Deanna, not to me. When they found out I wasn't the father, they confronted Deanna and she confessed she'd never had sex with me.'

Stella ran her hands down over her face. 'She'd lied all along?'

'She was scared.'

He was making excuses for her.

Anger beat through Stella's veins. She couldn't credit the empathy she heard in Mitch's voice. 'Deanna's lie ripped us apart, Mitch!'

'I know.' He hung his head for a moment. 'I hated her for it. Part of me still does. Yet, she was just as much manipulated by two politically ambitious, powerful men… and she was as trapped as I was in a loveless marriage. Worse, she was pressured to give birth to a child who'd seal the political alliance rather than being supported to have the termination she would've opted for.'

'She would've terminated Kade?' Wishing she could have a family, Stella knew she was being very judgemental but ignored the voice in her head that acknowledged Deanna had been so young.

'Deanna grew up in a totally patriarchal household. Her father ruled. Her mother obeyed. Both were politically ambitious creatures and they ticked the family box by having one child that they only ever brought out when they waved the all-American family banner. What she did was wrong, but her life's been a bed of thorns, not of roses.'

'I can't believe they were so deceitful.'

'Here these two men had been congratulating each other and sealing political deals assuming I was the father. Their deals were too far down the pipeline so they agreed they'd lie to me.' His cheeks hollowed out again for a second as he clenched his teeth again before he ground out, 'My father wanted to be in office. Her father had supported his candidacy and wanted his daughter married to the son of a senator – wanted his grandchildren to be born into a politically powerful family. They doctored the paperwork.'

'Mitch!' It was extraordinary. Incredible. Unbelievable. 'Are you certain Deanna wasn't lying to you about their involvement in the deception to cover herself?'

'I'm certain.' She could see the anger pulsing in a vein at the base of his neck and knew, when he stood again, that he was too furious to sit still. 'Both claimed they'd been there when the results had come through – that they'd both watched as she'd opened the envelope – and that the DNA test had been irrefutable. That I was the father.'

'That's… diabolical!' she exclaimed.

'Oh yeah.' He laughed bitterly. 'My parents had then been as insistent as Deanna's that we were married immediately. I went through shock, denial and anger. I can't tell you how many times I read and re-read the DNA results trying to make sense of them. I couldn't argue with what I thought were irrefutable results and I felt trapped. I might've fought harder – resisted the pressure of marriage – but you'd made it clear we had no future. Ultimately, I believed I had an obligation to my unborn child to marry Deanna and to try to parent as a team – especially because I'd been an unwanted child and I didn't ever want any child of mine to feel as I'd felt.'

'Oh my God! Mitchell! That was…' Fresh tears streamed down her cheeks as she understood the conflict Mitchell must've felt – and how terribly let down he'd been by his parents. 'It was positively evil of both men,' she condemned angrily. And despite Mitch telling her Deanna was just as used, she couldn't bring herself to forgive Deanna right now. Deanna's lie to her father had set the whole chain of events into motion.

'Now you know why I don't see him. He was never a good father and my mother was just as complicit because she knew the truth and didn't try to stop the lie. She's every bit as power-hungry as my father and she basks in the attention she receives as his wife.'

'I can't imagine—'

'Neither of my parents really wanted a child because they believed a child would be a hindrance to their careers. Ironically, I proved to be a major key to my father's political career. The embassy bombing opened the door for him but the second Deanna pointed to me as the father of her child, the political door opened wider.'

'Everyone always talks about deals done behind doors,' she commented.

'I hate to think,' he said bitterly. 'With my father's situation, it was a win for him and for his party. He was an American diplomat hero, son of NFL Hall of Fame quarterback and then, the icing on the cake, he had a son who was a rising star in the league. I even damned well campaigned on his behalf and helped get him win his seat!'

'I can't understand any parent using their child that way – lying to you at all let alone about something that changed your life completely and unfairly.'

He cupped his hand over the back of his neck and squeezed as if relieving some muscular tension.

'I'm sorry,' she said simply.

'The true irony is that while I was campaigning for him, I felt we were closer. I felt like he needed and appreciated me, and we spent time together. But all the time he was using me.' His fists clenched and unclenched at his sides. 'I would never have campaigned for him if I'd known the truth of what he did. If he can lie to me, what the hell is he capable of doing to the American people? Although he was being considered for candidacy, he was only ever bloody well firmly endorsed because Deanna's father wanted to secure a marriage for her and I happened to be a good stooge.'

Unable to fathom the betrayal he must've felt, she was about to stand up, wanting to reach out and comfort him, but before she could move he sat next to her.

'It's part of the reason I came back to Australia. I needed to get Kade out of that environment. I didn't want him to be touched by my father's politics or influenced in any way by his natural grandfather.'

Placing her hand on his arm she said, 'I'm surprised they didn't do something to stop you.'

'They probably would've if they'd known.' She watched as his throat worked up and down. 'Deanna agreed not to tell them until we were in Australia.'

He looked away from her.

'There's something more, isn't there? Something you're not telling me?'

'Deanna and I argued a lot about Kade.' She heard the strain in each of his words. 'She couldn't cope with the responsibility of parenting him, but the way she'd been brought up... she continued to use him as a bargaining chip. Deep down she realised she wasn't a good mother to him but in a way that only made her more desperate to hold onto him, because she didn't want parenting to be one more thing she'd failed at. She didn't want her parents to have one more thing they could call her out on because she hadn't lived up to their expectations.'

'She was still striving for their approval?' It was incredible to think that anyone could want the favour of people who were so awful.

'And, I think she desperately wanted Kade to love her too, but she blew so hot and cold with him, their relationship was getting worse. It's tragic because under her brash exterior, she's deeply unhappy. I believe she's still a lost little girl wanting the love she's never found but she's refused all my suggestions to get counselling.'

Stella sat back and closed her eyes. Mitch's pity was obvious and she guessed that if he could find some shred of compassion for a woman who'd wronged him so badly, she should be able to as well, but right now she went from feeling angry to numb.

'Even though I'd only ever had Kade with me part time, eventually Deanna and I signed an agreement and she gave me full custody of Kade.'

'An agreement?' When he didn't respond, her shoulders sagged and she let out another breath of disbelief. 'You paid her.'

'It was the only way to get Kade out of that toxic environment.'

Stella's heart ached for the young boy she'd come to know and… yes… to love.

How could any mother sell her child?

'Thank God he's got you.'

'He'll always have me,' Mitchell vowed. 'I'll never turn my back on him and I'm intent on giving him a happy and secure upbringing away from all the instability of his mother and the poison of her father.'

Stella slipped her hand into his and squeezed it.

Then, she blinked a few times as she finally absorbed the information.

Everything she'd believed had been a lie.

Mitchell had been passed out drunk in bed.

Hence the room smelling like a brewery!

He hadn't had sex with Deanna.

All this time – all these years – she'd thought Mitch had betrayed her.

If only she'd had the confidence in herself, she wouldn't have turned tail and run that night when she'd walked in on them.

Oh, dear Lord! Things would've been so different.

Her cowardice had contributed to the nightmare his life had become.

Shock rolled through her brain like thick tendrils of fog, making it impossible to think or to speak coherently.

'I'm telling you the truth, Stella.'

She believed him.

As far-fetched as it seemed, it made sense.

Hadn't Liz made several comments to her over the years about how Kade didn't look like either Deanna or Mitchell particularly – that the only feature that possessed any likeness to either of them was his mother's shaped eyes?

Geez. Blue had made a similar comment about Kade looking nothing like Mitchell.

Then there was the other clue that'd her subconscious had been trying to accept. Kade wasn't athletic.

Oh, God.

'I believe you, Mitch.' She'd been such a fool. 'Do you know who Kade's real father is?'

'I'm his father,' Mitch bit out.

'I'm sorry.' Less bluntly she explained, 'I mean his bio—'

'Sorry. I know what you mean, but for years I thought that little guy was my own flesh and blood.' He disengaged his hand from hers before burying his face in his hands as though he was trying to collect himself. 'Hell, Stella!' he cursed as he looked back at her and explained, 'I've walked the floors with him at night when he wouldn't settle, changed his diapers, patched up his cuts and scrapes and taught him to tie his shoelaces…' His voice broke. 'He's my son in every way that counts and if ever his biological father crawled out of the woodwork, I'd fight with everything I have to keep custody.'

The love and passion in his voice made her proud of him. 'I'd expect you to. It wouldn't be fair on you or Kade for you to do anything but fight for him.'

All this time she'd felt betrayed by Mitch but it'd been Mitch who'd been betrayed – not only by Deanna, but by the people he should've been able to trust above all others in the world. His parents had betrayed him, yet hadn't she betrayed him too by not having had faith in him?

'You're an amazing father to Kade.'

Kade's biological father probably had no idea he'd fathered a child with Deanna.

It was possible Deanna didn't even know who the father was.

'Does Kade know the truth?' she posed tentatively.

'No.' The word was immediate and vehement. 'One day… one day I'll tell him, when the time is right.' There was vulnerability in his voice as he shared, 'I'm hoping it won't make any difference to him.'

Her heart ached for both of them, but particularly for Mitchell.

Not only had his life been thrown off course by the lie he'd been told, but now that he'd loved Deanna's son as his own, he was afraid that the truth would come between them.

'It won't come between you,' she assured him. 'Kade loves you.'

'I asked him if he wanted to stay with his mum or move to Australia to be with me. I gave him that choice and he chose me over her.'

'Wise boy. Smart boy.' She took Mitchell's hand again. 'I love Margaret and Jim and although I'll never forget my biological parents and wish they were still with me, I consider the Richardsons every bit my parents. It doesn't make any difference that we're not blood relatives. It doesn't matter that Callie and Morgan aren't my blood sisters. We're family in every way that matters just the same way you're Kade's father and he's your son.'

He raised one hand to wipe at his eyes. 'I worry he might resent me for not trying to find his father.'

'Where would you even start?'

'She was promiscuous – even during our marriage.'

'Do you think...?' Stella frowned. 'I'm no psychologist, but do you think Deanna confused sex for love?'

'Yes. It's what I've always suspected. Her parents are such cold people. I...' His voice cracked. 'Once she tried to cuddle up to me and I pushed her away. Her reaction was... God, Stella, she curled up into a ball and sobbed her heart out because I'd pushed her away. At first I thought she was trying to play me, but she told me how her parents never cuddled her... how she'd seen other children being cuddled by their parents and she'd tried to get close to her parents and they'd pushed her away. My action that night triggered a deep pain I hope never to see again in anyone.'

Mitch's recollection broke Stella's heart as she gained an insight into Deanna's painful past. 'She sounds deeply troubled. Thank God Kade is away from her.'

'Although I won't ever reveal his mother's promiscuity, he did mention one day to me that sometimes he'd come down for breakfast and that his mom would have a friend visiting – a male friend. As he gets older he'll no doubt realise the significance.'

'Mitch...?'

'Yes?'

'You never had sex with her even when you felt sorry for her?'

'Not once.'

She found it difficult to believe because Mitch had always seemed perpetually ready to make love when they'd been together. 'You were married for two years!'

'I was celibate for all that time. Initially I resented her because up until she'd told me I was her child's father, I'd been hoping to get back together with you. How could I share a bed with her when I was still in love with you?' He shook his head. 'I was divorced and you were engaged before I had some casual affairs.'

She reached out and took his hands in hers. 'Did you divorce her as soon as you learned the truth about Kade?'

'No. After I found out about Kade's blood type and realised the truth, I was concerned if I divorced her, she'd end up denying me access to him on the grounds that I wasn't his true father.'

'How did you get around that?'

'The tipping point was when I came home and found her in bed with a lover while Kade was parked in front of the television watching kids' cartoons in the next room. There was enough intimacy caught on home security footage on the way to the bedroom, so I used that as leverage in the divorce. It was kept private, with only our lawyers being savvy to it, but she agreed both to the divorce and to joint custody.'

'How did your fathers cope with the divorce?'

'I told them if they tried to interfere, I'd tell the world what they'd done – how they'd doctored the DNA test.'

She nodded. 'That would've worried them.'

'My mother phoned and begged me not to say anything. She tried to use all sorts of emotional blackmail – even telling me I might push my father into a heart attack.' Disdain etched into his mouth and Stella yearned to kiss it away. 'I told her I didn't care and it was the truth. I was long past the point of caring about either of them.'

'I'm not surprised, Mitch. Love has to be earned and they've let you down terribly. Do you have any contact with them now?'

'No. Regardless of the circumstances, I won't ever speak with them again.'

She bit down on her lip and tried to keep the tears at bay as she felt his pain on top of her own at the needlessness of all her years apart from Mitch. 'I have... I need to tell you something.'

She took her hands away from his and held them together tightly in her lap.

He tilted his head slightly and his brows drew together at her hesitation and clear discomfort. 'Go on.'

'I saw you in bed with Deanna.' The words tumbled out in a rush. 'That's why I ended our relationship.'

He jerked up straight. 'What?'

'The minute I saw the news about the bombing of the American embassy in Iraq, I dropped everything and headed for the airport. Steve was furious with me but I told him that nothing was more important than supporting you while you waited for news of your parents.'

He paled. 'But I phoned you and couldn't get hold of you.'

'I didn't call you because I wasn't sure you'd even heard from the officials or seen anything on the television and I didn't want to have that conversation with you over the phone. As soon as I heard the news I made the decision. I went straight to the airport, made a flight just as it was closing, and headed back to Stanford.'

'Your phone was turned off. I called—'

'It would've been off because I was on the flight.'

'I called Carter when I couldn't reach you, and all he did was rant at me and tell me how selfish I was to expect you to drop out of the semi-finals of the event. He didn't tell me you were on your way back.'

'Oh God! What a mess!' She couldn't believe how events and people had conspired against them. 'When I saw you in bed with Deanna, I felt physically ill. I was… my whole world was torn apart. I'll never forget opening the door and her lying there in bed looking at me.' Mitch groaned.

'I was heartbroken. Embarrassed. I… couldn't take it. I turned tail, fled, and I was in a taxi on my way back to the airport then boarding a plane to return to the tournament before I even registered what I was doing.'

There was anguish in each syllable as he reached out, took her hands in his and said, 'All this time and I had no idea you'd even been there.'

She sent him a sad smile. 'I realise now that I shouldn't have run away. I should've stayed and confronted you both. But to say I was devastated doesn't even cut it.'

'I'm to blame. If I'd told you I'd woken up to find her in my bed, we might've talked through it.'

So many ways to say *if only…*

'Steve ranted and raved at me when I got back and I ended up breaking down in tears and telling him what I'd walked in on. I didn't know it at the time but I know now, in retrospect, that he played right into my fears and vulnerabilities. He told me he'd suspected your infidelity for some time and that he'd heard things that he hadn't wanted to share with me because he had hoped I'd see the light for myself.'

'Lying bastard!' he said savagely. 'I was never unfaithful to you.'

She believed it now but she'd been so devastated, Steve had played her like a virtuoso plays a violin.

'He convinced me you'd never be able to stay faithful to me and said I'd never be able to focus on my tennis career worrying that every time I was away, you were taking someone else to bed.'

Mitchell swore.

She gave a self-deprecating laugh. 'You have no idea how well he played me over the years. But, back then, he played on my guilt – telling me that if I didn't break up with you, I would never be able to honour my parents' memories and make it to number one. He always played on my guilt about my parents.'

'They died for you Stella. You told me so yourself. They sacrificed their lives because they were trying to give you every opportunity to make it in tennis. You don't want their sacrifice to be meaningless do you? You have the talent to make it all the way to the top, but not if you're pining over Mitchell Scott. Tell me, who is more worthy of your emotion – loving parents who died on their way back from taking you to a tennis tournament or an unfaithful, lying low-life of a boyfriend?'

'Steve knew I'd found you in bed with Deanna. He put every word in my mouth the day I finally spoke to you over the phone.' She remembered it all so clearly. Steve had insisted she say she was upset for Mitch but that the tournament was her first priority and she wasn't going to simply jump on a plane to wait by his side for news of his parents to emerge.

'He told me it was important for me to save face – that I needed to tell you tennis was more important than supporting you.' She closed her eyes tightly, ashamed at how quick she'd been to follow her coach's advice when she should've been honest and demanded an explanation from Mitchell.

'All these years we've been apart…' Mitch's pain was etched into each word as they squeezed through tightened vocal cords.

Stella felt his pain.

Shared his pain.

Then, she was in his arms, pressing herself against him and telling him, 'I'm so sorry. I should've had more faith in you.'

'No. Well, maybe,' he said as he hauled her onto his lap. 'But I should've fought harder for you, too, and told you what happened. I'm just as much to blame.'

Stella wasn't certain how long they sat together, holding each other and just savouring the physical contact.

Who angled their head first to invite the kisses they shared, Stella couldn't say. All she knew is that their kisses were bittersweet to begin with and mingled with salty tears. Both of them felt the sorrow and regret for all the time they'd lost and all the pain they'd suffered.

Then, they were needy kisses – lips clinging greedily, wanting each kiss to last forever, with hardly a pause for breath in case the moment vanished.

And finally, they both gave into their passion by mutual consent, with fingertips raking through each other's hair and hungry hands seeking to reacquaint themselves with every firm contour of the other's body.

Stella moaned into his mouth. Her heart was lighter and everything about being with Mitch was so natural. So right.

Mitch ended their kisses and pulled back a little from her

so he could look down into her eyes. 'Did you mean what you said before?'

'About?'

'Do you really still love me?'

'Oh, Mitch.' Tears made his features blur once again. 'I've spent all these years trying to deny it – all my time with Steve trying to forget you, but I think I always knew deep down that I never stopped loving you.'

He pressed a kiss to her forehead then used his fingertips to wipe gently at her tears. 'You're the only woman I've ever loved, Stella.'

She tilted her head at him. 'Am I imagining things or is there a hint of hesitation now?'

'Not on my behalf, but I've got Kade to consider.' He caressed her cheeks again with his fingertips, then framed her face with his hands. 'He adores you. How do you feel about him?'

His hands prevented her from hanging her head in shame, which is exactly what she felt when she thought of her initial reaction to Kade. 'Honestly, I was upset when I knew you'd brought him here to live, but—'

'I can understand that.' He nodded. 'It must've been confronting for you, especially thinking I'd been sleeping with Deanna while we'd been together.'

'When Kade first turned up at the cottage, I wanted to scream at him to go away.' She shook her head a little in regret. 'I couldn't not like him, Mitch. He's a great boy.'

'I want you in my future, sweetheart, and that means you'd be in Kade's too.' He moved his hands to run them through his hair. 'It struck me today how right it felt, the three of us being together, but I need to know you feel that way too.'

'I did.' It was the absolute truth. 'Even before I knew you weren't his biological father, Mitch, I loved being with both of you today. I was really happy.'

'I know we've talked now about what happened and why you broke off our relationship but there's a part of me that's…

it sounds unmanly to admit, but I guess there's a part of me that's insecure – that you might walk away from me again. And I've got Kade to consider, too, now.'

'I'd say it's human of you – not unmanly. But I've grown in myself now, Mitch. I can see how wrong I was not to face what I thought was a problem – not to stay and talk.'

'You're prepared to take me on knowing Kade is part of the deal?'

'One hundred per cent.'

'Then,' he began as he lowered his head towards hers, 'I think we're done talking for now.'

Her heart caught with sudden realisation. 'Mitch... I'm... what about my leg – my foot?'

'What about it?' He both frowned and smiled at the same time. 'Do you really think that you losing part of your body makes the slightest bit of difference to me?'

'I...' She shook her head. 'It's not very attractive.'

He got down on his knees. 'Stella, I've loved you as a friend since childhood and as my love since our teens. The loss you've suffered makes no difference.' He place his hands on each of her thighs and ran them down her legs, ignoring her as she stiffened when he reached her prosthesis. 'I promise you, I will love you forever.' He placed a kiss through the light fabric of her trousers and against her knee, above her prosthesis. 'My love won't falter. Your loss of limb doesn't matter to me. I'll still love you even if, when we both grow old, you lose your memory.' He leant his head against her thigh and she heard his voice thicken as he said, 'No matter what loss either of us suffers, the only thing I couldn't bear would be the loss of having you in my life again.'

The sincerity of his pledge and the emotion with which it was delivered had Stella placing her hands on his head to urge him away from her. 'I need a tissue!'

Mitchell laughed. 'Make that two!'

Stella sat on the couch, blew her nose and then took a deep breath before she bent forward and started rolling up her trouser leg to reveal her prosthesis to him. Holding her breath, she watched him look as the carbon-fibre and titanium alloy gleaned in the soft light.

'It's true engineering artistry, isn't it?' he marvelled.

It was, but it was also a reminder of the accident that had changed her life.

She smiled when he told her matter-of-factly, 'Definitely not as sexy as your left leg, but amazing what the doctors and technicians have been able to achieve.'

'It's not a turn off for you?' He hadn't recoiled or shown any revulsion but she still had to be sure.

'You, my darling Stella, are a total turn-on.' He sat down on the couch next to her and brushed his lips over hers. 'I'm in awe of your strength and your courage.'

'You know how to melt my heart, Mitch. You've always known the right things to say.'

'I hope I can convince you to stop wearing these trousers all the time and start wearing those sexy little summer dresses you always looked so hot in.'

'I might need a bit more time for that.'

Mitch gave her a steely look. 'No, Babe. Be brave. Won't it be more comfortable to be in a dress in this summer heat than in a pair of trousers, no matter how lightweight they are?'

He was right.

'I'll consider it.'

'Know that you will always have my unwavering support no matter what decision you make.' His fingertips trailed along her jaw, soothed the skin of her neck then dipped tantalisingly into the vee of her blouse. 'But how about I show you just how sexy I find you?'

She was smiling and nodding her consent when her mobile phone went off in her handbag. 'Oh. Hang on! That's Marg. If I don't answer, she'll drive over to make sure I'm okay.'

Mitch was off the couch straight away and retrieving Stella's handbag from the bench.

'Hi Marg,' was all Stella managed to say when Morgan cut in.

'It's not Marg, Stell, it's me. Jim's had more chest pain. He's being taken to Lancaster hospital and Marg and I are with him in the ambulance.'

'Oh no!' She jumped up to her feet without thinking and Mitch had to steady her so she didn't lose her balance. 'I'll be there as soon as I can. Tell Marg and Jim I love them and I'm on my way.' She disconnected the call. 'I have to—'

'I heard,' Mitchell said. 'I'll drive you to the hospital.'

CHAPTER SEVENTEEN

'Someone to see you at the bar, boss,' Simon told Mitch.

'Another reporter?' he queried, looking up from where he was going through some accounts. There'd been a few reporters who'd visited the hotel today because some photos of Mitch and Stella at the fair together had made their way onto social media accounts.

'If so, she's the prettiest reporter I've ever seen.' Simon winked. 'No, boss. It's Stella.'

Mitchell stood up immediately with a grin on his face. 'Thanks, Simon.'

She certainly was pretty, he agreed as he saw her talking to Bill at the bar and giving Bill and the other patrons an update on Jim's health.

Her hair was swept back into some sort of hair clip contraption and that served to draw attention to her neck, making him want to get close enough to smell the scent of her perfume and nibble the flesh of that sensitive skin, right up to the delicate little shell of her ear.

There'd always been that one little spot right just below her lip that'd drive her crazy with ecstasy when he'd kissed her there.

'Hey Mitch.'

He couldn't admire her unnoticed anymore, so he moved forward.

As he did, his breath whooshed out of his lungs and his smile of greeting turned to one of pride.

Stella, his Stella, was the bravest woman he knew.

His heart swelled. 'You look gorgeous. I love the dress.'

For a second, she looked away from him before sending him a self-conscious smile. 'It's definitely cooler and much easier to get into than trousers.'

'You look a picture, Stella,' Bill told her.

'You certainly do,' Mitch agreed.

Surprisingly, and very satisfyingly, she walked towards him to kiss him.

It wasn't a kiss on the lips, but it wasn't a kiss on the cheek either.

'You tease,' he murmured for her ears only when she kissed him tantalisingly close to the corner of his mouth.

Her eyes laughed up at him. 'You going to buy me a drink?'

He looked at his watch. 'A little early in the day for that, isn't it?'

'I'll settle for an orange juice.'

'Simon, can we have an OJ and a root beer – er – sarsparilla, please?'

'Coming right up.'

'Root beer!' she scoffed light-heartedly as he led her away from the bar and over towards a more secluded table near the front window. 'Is this the same guy who impressed me with his Australian turn of phrase just a few days ago?'

He shrugged off her teasing. 'You can take the boy out of America, but maybe you can't completely take America out of the boy.'

'I like you as you are. Don't try to alter anything about yourself,' she told him.

He raised his eyebrows. 'Sounds like flattery. What are you up to, Miss Simpson?'

'Nothing in particular.' She reached out across the table and took her hands in his.

'I'm proud of you for being brave and wearing the dress, Stella,' he said. 'Never doubt I find you stunning.'

'Thank you. You've given me the courage to do it.' She shrugged. 'Besides, this is who I am now.'

'You're every-inch-beautiful.'

Dimpling at him she said, 'If you say so, I guess it must be true.'

Wanting badly to pick up where they'd left off last night reminded him to ask, 'Any more news about Jim?' He'd left her at the hospital this morning and gone home to be with Kade, but she'd called to let him know that Jim was being kept in hospital in Lancaster before a bed was found for him in the cardiac unit in Melbourne where he'd undergo some tests and be examined by specialists.

'I was just telling Bill that Morgan flew Jim to Melbourne a couple of hours ago and he's already been assessed by the cardiologist.'

'That was quick. What's the verdict?'

'Marg said that Jim needs a coronary angioplasty – where they insert a balloon catheter into the blocked blood vessel to widen it. Then he'll have a stent inserted to decrease the chance of it narrowing again.'

'When's all this going to happen?'

'The procedure's scheduled for the day after tomorrow. He'll have an overnight stay, then he'll be straight back home.'

'Wow.' It never ceased to amaze him how quickly patients were discharged these days. 'So, it's all fairly straightforward then?'

'The doctor outlined a whole lot of risks, but said Jim's fit and otherwise healthy. He told Marg he doesn't feel there's any need for them to stay in Melbourne once Jim's discharged, but Marg's decided she's not taking any chances.'

'Are you wanting to drive down to be with them?'

'Yes.' Stella nodded. 'Morgan and I are going to drive down together when she finishes her shift tomorrow after lunch. I won't go to the hospital as it's likely to turn into a media circus if I'm spotted, but I'll at least be in Melbourne. Then, we'll all stay with Callie for a few days.'

"Are you okay?' He loved the feel of her hands in his. 'Would you like me to come with you?'

The way her throat worked up and down as she swallowed told him she wasn't feeling great. 'I'm worried about Jim but I know he's receiving expert attention and I believe he'll be okay.' She rubbed one of her thumbs against the back of his hand. 'I could use some company before I leave though. Your company. I've missed you today.'

'I'm glad you came.' He raised her hands to his lips.

'You said on the phone that Liz has taken Kade into Lancaster to see some new Transformers movie?'

'Yep.' He rolled his eyes. 'Is this another Liz set up?'

'Oh! Maybe. She did call me to ask about Jim, and she told me they were going to the movies, then bowling, then to a burger bar for dinner.' She grinned as she said, 'Liz also said that they wouldn't be home until late and to tell you to look after yourself for dinner because they'd have already eaten and she'd be bringing Kade home and putting him straight to bed after a shower.'

'In other words, leaving the coast clear,' he chuckled.

Stella's eyes widened but it was in mock realisation and Mitch knew straight away that Liz's machinations had played right into Stella's plans. 'Oh. Is that what she meant?'

Just as well, because he couldn't have planned it better himself.

'I thought Liz was bad enough. Is she turning you into a schemer, too?'

'Here we go,' Simon said as he presented them with their drinks.

Mitchell was pleased that Stella didn't let go of his hand. They'd already been seen at the fair together, so the locals would've noted their level of intimacy but she had to know that her visit to him today and every bit of physical contact they shared would be noted and relayed around the place in no time flat.

It was part and parcel of living in a small community but it was easier to cope with because it was such a caring one.

'Thanks, Simon.'

When they were alone again, Stella's hazel eyes definitely contained more than a hint of mischief. 'There are schemers and then there are schemers. Some schemes might be fun.'

His voice emerged a little gravelly. 'Tell me your plan and I'll tell you what I think.'

'Life's short, Mitch, and we've already lost so much time. I think we should pick up where we left off last night.' She didn't need to convince him but continued, 'In fact, the second I got back from Lancaster, I packed a picnic basket and I've got it in the car. I'm hoping to spirit you away from your work this afternoon for a late lunch-cum-early dinner.'

Mitchell ran his finger around the rim of his glass. 'Just as well I have a drink. My throat just got very dry.'

They were both temporarily distracted by huge hoots of laughter coming from Bill and a few other old-timers who must be exchanging wild stories at the bar.

'You up for a picnic at our favourite spot by the creek?' Stella asked as she looked back at Mitch.

Oh, he was up for it alright.

Mitchell leaned further forward and whispered, 'As long as I get you for dessert.'

God, but her dimples were so beautiful.

He'd never get tired of her smile or the enchanting, faint blush that coloured her cheeks.

A loud cough distracted him and Mitch glanced over to where Bill had got up off his bar stool and had walked over to the old juke box. Mitch was a bit perplexed as the old-timers were looking at him and sniggering away at some private joke, but he refocused on his beautiful Stella. 'I vote we finish these drinks quickly and get going.'

Stella frowned a little as she looked over towards the men who were now chuckling away more quietly.

Following her gaze, Mitch saw the men had now stopped chatting and were looking straight at Stella and him.

Perplexed, but continuing to ignore them, he said, 'I can't wait to be alone.'

The juke box started up and Mitch finally understood what the joke was that had the old men sniggering away.

Turning towards them, he raised his hands towards them and asked with a grin, 'Seriously, gentlemen, are you pushing seventy or seventeen?'

The men erupted again with huge guffaws of laughter.

'We thought it might be appropriate,' Bill said.

'What are you on about?' Stella asked, obviously having missed the whole thing.

Mitch filled her in. 'The song on the juke box.'

Tipping her head a little as she listened to it, she finally got it. 'Oh very funny!' she said as her cheeks became a darker shade of red. 'Everyone's a comedian!'

The Starland Vocal Band's harmonising of *Afternoon Delight* filled the hotel's bar area.

'Well, why not make their day? Let's show them,' she said before getting up from her chair, walking around to Mitch, arranging herself on his lap and proceeding to deliver a kiss that had his whole body humming along to the harmony, and pleasure spearing through him all the way to his toes.

The men hooted and clapped.

'Looks like we might have another celebration coming up in the old hotel!' Bill said.

'Don't go getting ahead of yourselves,' Stella admonished.

'You've really started something now, sweetheart,' Mitch said.

She looked back at him. 'Do you mind?'

'Not at all, but I think you'd better stay where you are without kissing me for at least the next ten minutes or I might be mighty embarrassed.'

Her little laugh was pure naughtiness because she had to be aware of his arousal that was pushing against her thigh.

'How about I get up and sit back down and you just swing your chair around really quickly? I don't think the men are going to be checking out your trousers.'

She moved quickly, giving him no option but to do exactly what she'd suggested.

* * *

They lay together on the picnic blanket, enjoying the peace of the afternoon and the warmth of the dappled sunlight that peeked through the canopy of sheltering leaves from the paperbark tree.

'Mitch?' Stella ventured slowly, raising her head away from where it'd been resting on his chest, listening to his heartbeat.

'Hm?' He said lazily, while one hand still played with her hair.

She took a deep breath, propped herself up on one elbow so she could look down into his eyes as she made her announcement. 'I think it's time for dessert.'

He lifted his head and turned on his side to face her. 'You sure?'

'Absolutely.'

A slow grin spread over his face and sent her insides into an instant meltdown. 'You don't know how desperately I've been wanting to hear you say that!'

She got no right of reply because a second later he'd moved so fast, she was on her back and he was leaning over her and claiming her lips.

These were the kisses she remembered.

The kisses she'd hungered for.

Oh, their other kisses since she'd returned to Hope Creek had been tantalizing and sweet and had slowly built up to being hot, but these kisses were an instant inferno and blazing passion that seared through her, making her throb with the need to join her body with his once more.

'Not here,' he said, as he broke away from her.

'Yes, right here,' she insisted. 'We've walked away too many times from this very spot unfulfilled. I want to remember our reunion right here under this tree.'

They'd had some heavy sessions in this very spot as teenagers, but they'd never made love here and she'd always regretted it.

'But we're not teenagers now and I want you to be comfortable,' he added.

'I'm comfortable and I want this, Mitch. Right here. Right now.'

She saw the conflict in his features.

'I want it to be good for you.' His lips brushed over hers and he cupped her face tenderly in his hands. 'I want it to be perfect.'

'It'll be sensational.'

She raised one hand to pull his face down to hers for more kisses. The other hand was greedy to reacquaint herself intimately with the firm bulge below the button of his waistband – to relearn the shape and texture of him.

The next few minutes they may as well have been innocent teens again with their fumbled flurry of fingers.

Stella had forgotten how stubborn jean buttons could be to push through denim fabric and when Mitch had to help her, she felt his hand shaking. Despite his quivering fingers, there was nothing inexpert about his actions when he helped her out of her dress then hooked his fingers under the elastic band of her lacy knickers and eased them down her thighs.

The familiar, firm feel of his touch on the sensitive skin of her thighs was divine and she basked in it.

Oh.

He reached the end of her right leg and she tensed.

'Relax, my darling. Every inch of you has always been beautiful to me, Stella, and it always will be.'

Before she could start to feel awkward, Mitch lowered his head to kiss her again, his tongue sweeping over her lips and accepting her invitation when her tongue delighted in dueling with his.

'It's been so hard to hold back,' he breathed between kisses.

'No more holding back,' she panted as her hands ran along the hard, sculptured muscles of his back. They were harder than she recalled. He was stronger and perhaps a bit broader than she remembered after all his intense training and all his efforts on the football field.

But still, the feel of him was so achingly familiar against her fingertips and, even though the afternoon was warm, she reveled in the heat that radiated from his body.

Was this still as familiar to him as it was to her?

Oh, yes, he remembered.

His lips left hers and trailed across her cheek, pressing warm, delightfully sensational kisses along her cheek before they explored her jaw line.

Small nips of his teeth and flicks of his tongue right at the sensitive spot where her jaw joined her neck had her hips arching upwards.

'You were always so sensitive there,' he murmured before taking her earlobe prisoner with his mouth and subjecting it to sinfully torturous sensations that made her fingers spear through the thickness of his hair, wanting to hold him there to continue the pleasure that almost bordered on pain.

Her limbs went limp and heavy when he pulled away intent on delivering another level of pleasure altogether. He unclipped her front-fastening bra and drew one nipple into the warm cavern of his mouth.

Stella cried out as he laved at it with his tongue, bringing it to a hard peak.

She was so ready for him, but when she reached down to guide his thickness to the place she needed him most, he jerked away from her touch.

'Darling, don't. I burn to be inside you but if you touch me, I won't last,' he rasped. Kissing down the skin of her tummy and smoothing his hands over her flesh, all the way to her hips, he urged them apart. 'I want to know every inch of you again. I need to taste you.'

As good as his promise, his mouth pressed against the damp heat of her need, making her catch her breath as his tongue teased the sensitive nub of nerve endings and his fingers worked in perfect accord to build her tension higher in the promise of a spectacular release. Seconds after his fingers and mouth swapped zones and his tongue delved intimately inside her, she gripped his shoulders hard with her hands, rode out the storm of sensation and reached that release in the most earth-shattering orgasm she could remember.

He slowed his lapping, reaching up to caress her breasts with his palms before easing himself back up her body until he was able to look into her eyes.

It wasn't her imagination.

She saw the love in his eyes.

Did he see the wonder in hers?

His voice was low and gravelly with emotion as he told her, 'There are a lot of things I'm not sure about, but I'm absolutely certain we're meant to be together, Stella.'

Her lips quivered as she smiled up at him. 'Be mine again, my darling Mitchell.'

He wasted no time in taking a condom from his wallet and rolling it over his length.

This was it.

Nothing else was as important in her life as making love with Mitchell.

Anticipation skittered along every nerve ending, energising limbs that had been heavy and languid after her mind-blowing orgasm.

Hoping he wouldn't refuse her this time, she encircled his hard, heavy penis with her fingertips, parted her flesh and settled it at her entrance.

For a moment, he hesitated as he looked into her eyes, then kissed her mouth.

Then, gazing back into her eyes, he thrust into her.

'Yes,' she sobbed, relishing in his possession – overcome with pure joy because she'd never believed she'd know such perfection again.

The weight of her new foot felt odd and heavy as she raised it to wrap her legs around his waist, wanting to feel every inch of his flesh against hers and wanting him to know how gladly she welcomed him home.

Thank you, God.

Thank you for helping us find our way back to each other.

Their bodies had never forgotten their lovemaking and automatically fell into rhythm, adjusting in perfect unison because they sensed when to quicken and when to pause to deliver every ounce of pleasure to each other.

She reached her climax quicky, spiralling over the edge of reality and into euphoric ecstasy, and Mitchell followed her – the veins and muscles in his neck straining then relaxing as his divine body shuddered over hers.

Both breathing hard, they looked at each other in wonderment.

'Amazing.' His voice seemed to have lowered an octave and he cleared his throat. 'It was always incredibly amazing between us.'

She bit down on her lip to try to staunch her tears. 'What took me so long to find you again?'

'Darned if I know!' He flashed his killer smile at her and winked. 'But I've got to admit it was worth the wait.'

Moving away from her, he disposed of the condom and laughed.

'Don't look now but we've got an audience.'

Horrified, she sprang up, reaching out for her dress to cover herself before she registered that his tone had been amused.

Stilling her movements, she followed Mitchell's gaze and

saw that a mob of wallabies had taken up residence while they were in the throes of passion.

'Thank goodness!' she said quietly so she didn't startle the creatures who were all standing up straight and alert and looking directly at her. 'For a moment, I thought we had *human* company.'

'Would've been your fault if we'd been sprung,' he accused, sounding awfully like the teenager she'd fallen in love with.

She reached out to thump him on the bicep and her sudden movement was enough to spook the wallabies so they bounded away along the edge of the creek.

Mitch grinned. 'Only in Australia.'

Opening her eyes a little wider she said, 'In America it might've been a grizzly bear or a cougar, so I'm glad we didn't get together again there.'

He reached over and pulled a gum leaf from where it had fallen and been tangled up in her hair. 'Would my wild woman agree to packing up and taking this indoors now?'

'She would.' Feeling ecstatically happy she got to her feet too quickly and stumbled.

Mitch caught her before she could fall. 'I've got you.'

She was embarrassed and couldn't meet his eyes. 'Sorry. I… I still forget sometimes.'

Mitch put his fingers under her chin to force her to look up at him. 'When we go inside, I want you to be completely comfortable, sweetheart, and if that means taking your prosthesis off, then do it.'

'Making love with my artificial foot attached was kind of strange,' she agreed.

He guided her hand to feel the proof that he was already ready to make love to her again. 'Nothing,' he shook his head for emphasis, 'Nothing is going to give me any relief from this painful throbbing I get whenever I'm near you, but to come deeply inside you over and over again. So if you think you can turn me off because you've lost a foot, you can think again.'

Wrapping her arms up around his neck, and burying her head into the solid comfort of his chest, she hugged him tight. 'I love you, Mitch.'

'Love you too, Stella. I always have and I always will.' He gave her a searing kiss. 'We were meant to be together.'

'When will we let Kade know?'

'How about we tell him together when you get back from Melbourne?'

'Sounds good to me.'

Mitch grinned. 'I think it'll sound even better to him.'

'Liz will be over the moon.' She rolled her eyes. 'You know this is only going to encourage her romantic streak even more?'

'As long as she doesn't name her next characters after us!'

They both laughed, although Stella had a few misgivings as she and Mitch packed up their picnic and made their way to the cottage, because she wouldn't put it past Mitch's aunt to base a whole book around their romance.

CHAPTER EIGHTEEN

'It's so good to have you all here,' Callie told them as they finished dinner out on the terrace.

Callie lived in the Richardsons' Melbourne home which was located only five kilometers southeast of the CBD in the city's wealthiest suburb.

'Good to be here with you, Callie, but I can't say I enjoy the hustle and bustle of city life,' Jim said.

'I know you've said often enough that we should sell this home and downsize,' Marg said to Callie, 'but it's been convenient over the years and it's come in handy again now.'

It'd been great for Stella. Only a ten minute drive away from the Australian Open Tennis Championships at Rod Laver Arena, the house had been somewhere the whole family had been able to stay rather than at a hotel.

Jim stood up. 'I'm going to love you and leave you all and head for bed.'

'Are you feeling okay, darling?' Marg voiced instant concern.

'I'm fine. Just tired,' he said as he kissed all his girls goodnight.

'Night my beautiful girls.' Marg stood up.

'Good night,' they chorused.

'I'll leave the cleaning up to you tonight and go to bed too and read for a while.'

'Not one of Liz's books I hope,' Morgan said with a toss of her head.

Stella exchanged looks with Callie. They'd both decided they were going to tackle Morgan tonight about her broken romance.

'No comment on the grounds that I might incriminate myself,' was Marg's only response as she walked inside.

Callie and Stella chuckled as they stood and began clearing the table. Morgan didn't share their humour.

'Jim seems to be doing well,' Callie said, 'but I'm not in any hurry to see them rush back to the station.'

'Blue might be,' Stella said. 'He told me tonight on the phone that he's missing Marg's cooking.'

'I've been talking to the doctors from work,' Morgan told them, 'and they've said that the main risks once he's discharged would be from clotting within the stents—'

'Yes, but he's taking anticoagulants for that,' Callie put in.

'—and bleeding from where the catheter was inserted. They also said there could be associated kidney problems from the contrast dye.'

'None of those seem to be a problem. The nurse told Marg to look for any bruising around the catheter site and she said it's fine. He was also told to stay well hydrated and he has,' Callie added as she started wiping down the bench tops while Morgan and Stella stacked the dishwasher.

Stella bit her lip and hoped there wasn't going to be a disagreement about Jim's medical condition. Callie and Morgan seemed to be more argumentative as adults than they ever had been as kids – or maybe it was just because it'd been so long since she lived with them that she noticed it more now?

'I didn't say I thought there was a problem, Callie,' Morgan said firmly. 'I was simply outlining the risks I'd been told about.'

Callie opened her mouth, then closed it without speaking.

'Good that he seems to be doing so well,' Stella put in quickly as she finished loading the dishwasher.

'Glass of wine anyone?' Callie asked.

Stella hardly drank, but she decided tonight would be an exception. 'Yes please.'

'May as well,' Morgan said. 'I'm not flying tomorrow.'

When they were all settled with their wine out in the comfortable chairs on the terrace, Callie took the tiger by the tail. 'Morgan, I know you're still not happy about Stella's relationship with Mitch, even though she's told us all the truth of the situation and that Mitchell was never unfaithful to her. I'm really disappointed you can't be happy for her.'

Stella had confided everything Mitch had told her to her sisters and Marg, but hadn't said anything to Jim yet because she didn't want to cause him any concern during his recovery.

'I don't want to see Stella hurt again. Fool me once, shame on you but fool me twice and... you know the rest.' Morgan sat forward and placed her glass on the table. 'No offence, Stella, but can you really be certain it's you he's interested in? Hope Creek's a pretty small community. It's not exactly as if he's spoilt for choice.'

'Is that how you feel, Morgan? Do you think you were used because there wasn't anyone else available around?' Callie quizzed gently.

'Yes. No. I don't know.' She shifted restlessly, picked up her glass again and took a long drink. 'Dean asked me to resign and follow him to Sydney.'

'Then, he must've wanted the relationship to continue,' Stella said.

'Or, maybe he just knew I'd say no?' Morgan asked cynically. 'Having me say no to his suggestion meant I was the one who effectively broke up with him rather than the other way around. He was let off the hook.' The wine glass was placed back on the table with a little more force than necessary. 'I really don't want to talk about it. I'm getting over it and talking about it only reminds me.'

'That's fair enough, Morgan,' Stella said. 'Just know that we're here for you if you want to chat.'

'What about your love life, Callie?' Morgan asked.

'A complete drought,' Callie said emphatically.

'Really?' Seeing the way Callie had looked away when she replied, Stella wasn't certain she believed her.

'I'm sensing that's not quite true,' Morgan agreed.

Even in the soft light of the terrace, it was obvious that Callie's cheeks had coloured.

'Out with it, Callie!' Stella pushed.

'Well... er... Okay.' Her shoulders slumped. 'I met a guy at a nightclub.'

'Go on,' Morgan encouraged.

'I... did something very out of character.'

'Oh my God! You didn't sleep with him, did you?' Stella asked.

'Shush!' Callie hissed, immediately looking back inside the house to check Jim and Marg hadn't somehow magically appeared and overheard them.

'You did sleep with him!' Morgan said.

'Well, yes.' Callie squirmed as her fingers played nervously with the stem of the wineglass.

'Who is he?' Stella asked.

'I don't believe it,' Morgan declared. 'What happened to saving yourself for Mr Right?'

'Well, gee, Morgan. Haven't you been the one shoving it down our necks lately that there's no such thing as Mr Right?' Callie shot back.

'I think it's fair enough we're shocked, Callie,' Stella defended. 'What made you change your mind?'

Callie replied with a vague wave of her hand. 'Basically, it just seemed like a good idea at the time. You know, a kind of a life is short, let's go-with-the-flow type moment.'

No. Stella didn't know. This didn't sound like Callie at all. 'Are you seeing him again?'

'No.'

'Who is he?' Morgan probed.

Callie bit down on her lip. 'I don't know.'

'You don't know?' they both demanded simultaneously.

Callie shrugged. 'I have no idea. I don't know who he is and I doubt I'll ever see him again.'

'You're kidding?' Morgan's shocked disbelief echoed Stella's.

Callie had a fairly risqué sense of humour at times, but she was the super conservative one when it came down to it.

'You went all the way with a stranger?' Morgan asked.

'Don't judge me, Morgan.'

Morgan threw her hands up. 'Hey! I'm not judging here, I'm just totally, completely blown away by your very un-Callie-like behaviour.'

'You went all the way with a stranger for the first time?' Stella was probably even more horrified than Morgan.

'I know.' Callie looked away from them and took a large drink of wine. 'I know I always said I wanted to be in a meaningful relationship but maybe I just got tired of waiting and started feeling old.'

'So, you picked up some guy at a nightclub?' Morgan asked in total confusion.

'He picked me up, actually,' Callie said in defence. 'But it didn't take a lot of convincing.' A small smile played around her lips. 'He was completely hot and… well, let's just say that I'm glad I didn't wait any longer to discover the joys of sex.'

'But you're not seeing him again?' Stella asked. 'He's not married, is he?'

'Of course not!' came the instant denial. 'Well, at least, I don't think he's married. He wasn't wearing a ring.'

Morgan groaned. 'Oh God, Callie. How easy is it to slip off a wedding ring? Please tell me you insisted on him using a condom.'

'I didn't need to. He took care of that – although, of course, I would've insisted if he hadn't already been all over it.'

Stella and Morgan sat open-mouthed as they each regarded

Callie with wide eyes. Then, Morgan turned to Stella, 'This can't be our sister. This has to be an alien who's taken over her body.'

Stella was inclined to agree. 'Do you know anything at all about him?'

'Well…' Callie's expression became a little starry-eyed. 'He's from interstate. Classically tall, dark, handsome and very, very sure of himself.'

'How old?' Morgan asked.

'Hm. Mid to late thirties at a guess.'

'Did you tell him you were a virgin before you slept with him?'

'No, Morgan,' Callie answered a little waspishly. 'It didn't exactly come up in conversation.'

Morgan groaned again. 'How did he react when he found out?'

Callie's jaw firmed and Stella decided he hadn't been very impressed. 'It doesn't matter. I'm an adult and it was my decision. He got what he wanted and so did I and, anyway, I'm not going to be seeing him again.'

Stella wasn't certain what more to say and she could tell, by the way Morgan suddenly sat back in her chair and shook her head, that she felt the same way.

Who would've thought?

Conservative Callie.

The guy must've been a knock-out.

It was a shame they'd never get to meet him.

'Now you've had hot sex with a complete stranger, please tell us you're not planning on making a habit of it?' Morgan pleaded.

'I haven't changed that much,' Callie insisted. 'It was a one-off. I doubt I'll ever meet anyone so irresistible again.'

'Oh dear.' Stella wasn't sure what to think.

'Changing the subject which is never to be revisited,' Callie said a little awkwardly, 'are you and Mitch going to tell Kade tomorrow that you're together?'

'That's the plan.'

'He's a great kid,' Morgan said. 'From the few things he said to us when we had our baking day, he could use all the love he can get. I just hope Mitchell can give you the love you deserve, Stella.'

Stella raised her glass. 'Let's drink to Jim's speedy recovery.'

'And that Marg and Blue and all of us continue to enjoy good health,' Morgan said.

'And,' Callie chimed, 'to lasting love for all of us.'

'I'll drink to that,' Stella said as she clinked her glass against her sisters' glasses.

'Not so sure about the lasting love, but I'll certainly drink to our health,' was all Morgan contributed.

CHAPTER NINETEEN

Mitch closed his laptop and dropped his pen on the pile of invoices that were now stacked neatly on his desk. He'd brought paperwork home earlier this morning rather than working on it at the pub, as he'd promised Kade they'd take a trip into Lancaster this afternoon to the local animal shelter. Apparently, there were a pair of alpacas that needed re-homing and Liz had thought they might be a nice addition to the fast-growing menagerie that Kade loved.

Checking his watch, he realised he'd told Kade to be back up from the goat pen in ten minutes so they could get cleaned up, have a quick bite to eat and head into town. Kade was usually pretty good at keeping track of time, but Mitch would need to go and get him if he wasn't punctual because he wanted to leave by twelve-thirty.

After their trip into Lancaster, Mitch wanted to go over the managers' monthly reports and figures from his two remaining nightclubs. He'd scheduled the monthly video conference calls for tonight because he was expecting Stella to return from Melbourne tomorrow and he wanted his desk cleared so they could spend time together.

Hopefully he'd sell the last two nightclubs soon and then he'd only have to concentrate on the pub and the farm.

He'd be meeting with one manager after the other during the night because they were working on their time zones.

Still, the videoconferencing beat having to travel back and forth across continents. Mitch had no wish to jump on another airliner any time soon.

He was making his way through to the kitchen when there was a sharp, almost imperious knocking on the door.

Rounding the corner, he stopped abruptly in his tracks.

And, of all the cheek... she didn't wait to be invited in. She took one look at him, opened the fly screen door and let herself in so she stood right in front of him.

Bile rose in his stomach as he took in the image.

Coiffed, peroxided hair; fake tan; make up that must've been piled on with a trowel; and a low cut over-bright orange dress that worked hard to keep her implanted breasts contained.

'Hello Mitchell,' she purred through her thick, Botoxed lips as a shudder of revulsion ran through him. 'Better close your mouth, honey, or one of these revolting Australian flies will be exploring the inside of it before you know it.'

Panic pummelled through him and made him speak more sharply than she probably deserved. 'What the hell are you doing here?'

'That's hardly any way to treat your wife, Mitchell.'

Uh-oh. 'Ex-wife.'

'Be nice. With transits and delays, I've just travelled over forty hours to get to this God-forsaken hole.'

Bloody hell!

He was still shocked to the core that she was here.

Whatever had motivated her to come, it couldn't be good.

'As far as I'm concerned you can go right back to where you came from.' His hands rested on his hips and he was aware the distance between his feet had widened a little – as though he was prepared for battle and standing his ground. 'We had a deal, Deanna and you've broken it. You've got no reason to be here.'

'I've got a very good reason and you know it.' Slowly and blatantly she looked around the simple living room with its country-style décor and ornaments, then she sniffed disdainfully before turning her attention back to him. 'There's the small matter of my son. Dear Lord, Mitchell! I had no idea you'd intended to drag him to Boonyville.'

'*My* son.' He said pointedly, choosing to ignore the rest of her insulting words and behaviour. 'I have contracts which outline that you gave me complete custody.'

'You mean that bunch of documents you forced me to sign?'

He took a step forward as he pointed angrily at her. 'We spoke about this, Deanna. You agreed it was in Kade's best interest to move from the States and out of your father's radius.'

If he hadn't been so concerned at her turning up unannounced on the doorstep, the tossing of her head in dismissal of his statement would've been almost comical. Not a single hair on her head moved because Deanna always used at least half a can of hairspray to keep every strand in place. Then again, she'd been raised that way by her mother who thought that spending hours at the beauty salon was the best way to keep up appearances.

Another movement caught his eye.

A mobile phone protruded from the arm of Liz's favourite, wide-backed arm chair and he could just see the tips of Liz's fingers holding it. The chair was wide enough and high enough that the rest of her was completely obscured.

He had to stop his smile and he almost felt sorry for Kade's mother as he guessed his aunt had chosen not to reveal her presence but was videotaping every word.

Oh, Deanna. You have no idea who you're up against!

'My attorney thinks I was under duress when I signed that document.' She raised one finely plucked eyebrow at him and challenged, 'Can you prove I wasn't?'

The fingers of his right hand curled into his palms, forming a fist at his side.

'Don't mess with me, Deanna. This is Kade's life we're talking about and I won't let you screw it up.'

'I wouldn't be so dismissive if I were you. I could ruin your father's political career—'

'Like I give a damn about my father!'

'—when word gets out that you forced me to sign away my rights to my son and then you kidnapped my darling boy and whisked him out here in the sticks in the hope I'd never find him.'

Mitchell felt sick.

Surely she was making empty threats? She'd agreed Kade should leave. She'd acknowledged she didn't know how to care for him – that it'd be a relief to her for him to go. But, if she was here to play hard ball, no way in hell could he afford to feel any sympathy for her.

'Think again, Deanna. Both your lawyer and mine witnessed us both signing the legal paperwork granting me full guardianship to Kade. You said our arrangement would see you cut off from your parents and I agreed to pay you the sum you demanded in compensation. Now you're bound to honour your end of the deal. No challenges. Complete confidentiality unless you choose to challenge this, then all bets are off.'

She stalked a few paces away from him and placed her designer handbag on the coffee table. 'I might've signed away custody and agreed that you'd set the terms for visitation when Kade was older. I might even have sworn I wouldn't tell the world you weren't Kade's father – all under duress – but I didn't say I wouldn't tell the world just who I did sleep with nine months before he was born.'

Did you keep a logbook? He didn't voice the contemptuous thought.

He had to get her to leave. He hated the way her overpowering perfume polluted the air in the room and he wanted her gone before Kade saw her here.

Mindful of Liz's recording, however, he knew it would be better if he could get Deanna to incriminate herself and their fathers.

'Are you trying to blackmail me, Deanna? You should know I don't give a shit about my father, but I wonder how your father would feel if the truth comes out that he lied to me about the DNA test? I doubt he'd look too kindly on you for forcing me into the position where I had to tell the whole sordid story of his and your deception.'

'Your father gained the most,' she flung back petulantly.

'And he'll lose the most. But, like I said, I don't care.' He shrugged. 'If the shit hits the fan, he's well and truly had it coming and I'd probably be doing the American people a favour by blowing the whistle on how low his morals are.'

'You wouldn't d—'

'If you're really here for custody, there's the security tape I have that proves your infidelity. I doubt any court would consider giving you custody of Kade when the tape shows you were carrying on an affair in the room next to where Kade was watching cartoons.'

Finally, she seemed to understand he was serious.

Her jaw dropped open and her eyes widened. Dressed in orange as she was, she reminded him of a pop-eyed goldfish that'd just jumped out of the goldfish bowl and was now gasping for breath. 'You're serious?'

'Absolutely.' His tone softened then when he said, 'Deanna, why don't we arrange to meet this evening and you can tell me what's really behind this?'

'No.'

He wouldn't cave to blackmail but he wanted to get to the heart of the matter. 'Did you come here for more money?'

'This isn't about money.'

'Then tell me. What's this about?'

She adopted a hurt expression. 'I gave birth to Kade. He's my son. You have no right to take him away from me. I… I want him back.'

'No. He's not a toy, he's certainly not a bargaining chip and you've done enough damage to his psyche already.'

'He needs his mother.' Her eyes misted – just enough to

glisten but not enough to be in danger of tears spilling over and ruining her mascara.

It was incredible how this woman could cue her tears, but he wasn't just out of his teens now, and he'd shared the same house with her for long enough to know how well she could turn it on and pretend to be all warm and hurt when it suited her.

'You told me yourself you didn't know how to be a mother.'

Pathetically, she raised a finger in a pretence of wiping away tears. 'When did you get so cruel, Mitchell?' In the blink of an eye her demeanour changed. The finger that'd been so busy wiping at the imagined tears now pointed at him and any mask of civility vanished. 'You listen to me, Mitchell Scott. If you don't hand him over right now, I'm calling the police.'

Mitchell took his phone out of his pocket. 'Not only did you sign legal documents granting me full custody and accept money from me to do so, but you were also quite clear about your thoughts.' He took his phone out of his hip pocket, tapped a few times on the screen and Deanna's strident voice burst forth from the speaker.

'At least Kade's been worth something to me!' she said. 'Knowing how much you love that kid, I probably should've pushed for more money from you.'

Mitchell's voice played through the phone's speakers next.

'He's nothing more than a bargaining chip to you, is he Deanna? You don't love him at all.'

'I'm not about to apologise for not being maternal. Not everybody is, you know. Just because I gave birth to him doesn't mean I can love him.' There was a slight break in her voice before she said, 'I don't know how to love. Nobody ever loved me.'

'Deanna, please see a counsellor. It's not too late. If you can get some guidance, you might be able to enjoy a relationship with Kade one day.'

There was a dramatic sigh. 'I can't understand women

who get off on being with some utterly dependent, screaming kid all day. If I'd known what motherhood would be like, I would've aborted him. I almost did. I would have if Daddy hadn't provided me with the opportunity of palming the kid off as yours. I thought it'd be good to be married to you. I thought that the sex, at least, would be good.' She huffed. *'I didn't realise you'd be impotent during our marriage.'*

Mitch hadn't felt the need to refute her claim.

'I feel sorry for you. Don't you feel anything for him at all?'

'I wanted to,' she said slowly. *'I thought if I had a baby it would be someone who'd love me. I thought you might love me but… that didn't happen. Kade never really loved me.'*

'He didn't know how to respond to you. You said some awful things to him, Deanna.'

'My parents said awful things to me, but I still wanted them to love me.'

'Deanna—'

'Well, you paid me millions for him, so I guess it hasn't been all bad.'

Mitch tapped again on the phone. 'Heard enough?'

Amazingly, a crimson tide managed to fight its way through all her make up as it swept up her neck and rose to her cheeks. In a flash of fantasy, he imagined that any moment now, her hair might steam up as well, melt all the starch and stand on end.

'You had no right to record our conversation!'

'Maybe not, but there it is.' Mitch tucked the phone back in his pocket, securely. 'I doubt any judge or jury would give you custody.'

'It'd be inadmissible in a court of law!'

'Hm. Maybe. But…' He decided to call her bluff because he wasn't sure how else he could get through to her. 'There'd be tabloids who'd love to print every word you uttered, and who knows if the recording would end up mysteriously finding its way onto a social media platform and going viral?' He tried to hide his abhorrence at the awful scenario because he couldn't afford to let her see he'd never sink to such a low. With a shrug of his shoulders he said, 'You know how impossible it is to keep jurors away from tabloids. If evidence fell into the wrong hands, you'd definitely be tainted. I imagine all those social doors that opened through Kade being at his posh school, would start shutting firmly in your face.'

She whisked her right hand up to cover her heart and attempted to adopt puppy eyes. 'Are you blackmailing me, Mitchell?'

'No, Deanna. I'm not making any threats at all.' He ran a hand through his hair. 'What I want is for you to see a counsellor because you have problems that I can't help you with – problems that will still be there even if you did have your son living with you.'

'Another two million dollars, Mitchell.'

Bloody hell! She couldn't have spent the other millions so quickly, could she?

'Are you in some sort of trouble?'

'No.'

'Are you on drugs?'

'No, I swear I'm not. Please, another two million and I promise I'll be out of your life and his for good.'

Absolutely no way. As well as a signed legal document, surely Liz had enough on video now to stop Deanna returning. 'Not a dime more.'

'Mom?'

Mitch's heart plummeted as he heard Kade's tentative voice.

Had his son been there long?

How much had he heard?

Instantly, Deanna's bitter expression was masked – a beaming smile taking its place before she pouted. '*Daarling*! Sweet boy!' She stretched her arms out wide. 'Come and give your Momma a big hug! I've travelled so far to see you because I've missed you so, so much.'

Kade was slow to respond. When he finally opened the flyscreen and moved stiltedly towards his mother he asked, 'What are you doing here?' It was clear he subjected himself reluctantly to Deanna's stiff hug. There was nothing natural or warm about the kiss he planted on her proffered cheek.

Jax growled from outside the door.

'Dad didn't tell me you were coming.'

Mitchell watched him closely.

Sure, he looked uncomfortable about seeing his mother there, but there were no questions in his eyes that indicated he'd overheard any of their conversation.

'We wanted to surprise you – a bit of an early Christmas present! We want you to be the first to know that we're getting married again and the three of us are going back to Los Angeles—'

'Deanna!' Mitchell protested firmly even as his gaze flicked to Liz's phone to make sure she was still recording everything.

'—and we're going to be one happy family again. How does that sound? Wouldn't you love to move back home and for it to be the three of us again?'

What the hell planet was she on?

'Oh.' There wasn't a single note of jubilation in Kade's single word response. 'I... but I thought...' He looked at Mitchell with dull eyes. 'Aren't you and...? I'd hoped... I like it here at Hope Creek.'

'Nonsense,' Deanna told him as she gave him a little shake. 'This was only a holiday. You can come back here for holidays any time you like, but your life is in LA. Your friends are in LA.'

Jax started scratching at the flyscreen and alternated between whining and growling.

He obviously had Deanna's measure.

'Mom, I don't want to go back to LA.'

'Kade's friends are here and his life is here,' Mitchell said firmly as he went to stand by Kade's side and placed a reassuring hand on his shoulder. 'Kade, your mother is making a joke that's in very bad taste. I won't ever be re-marrying her and you and I won't be moving back to the States.'

He felt Kade's shoulder relax under his hand.

'Would you mind excusing your mother and me for a bit?'

'Sure.' Mitch didn't blame the boy when he went back out the door to Jax as fast as he could and disappeared without uttering another word to Deanna.

'You've turned him against me!' Deanna shrieked.

'I've done nothing of the sort,' Mitchell said quietly but firmly. 'He's happy here, Deanna. He's never been as happy in his life as he is here. You said you wanted for him to be happy.'

'You can't keep him. I'm his mother. More to the point, *you're not his father.*'

'Be quiet! You've said enough.'

'I haven't said nearly enough.' If it wasn't so serious she'd look comical the way she was huffing and puffing with her cheeks inflating and deflating as though she was playing a tuba. 'I'll fight you for custody and prove with a DNA test that you're not his real father!'

Bloody hell!

'Have you forgotten I already have a DNA report from your pregnancy?'

'We both know that was doctored by your father and mine. You know you're not his father. What fantasy are you living?'

Geez.

'I'm his father in every way that counts.'

'You don't love him,' she accused bitterly. 'You're using him to score points from me.'

This from the woman who'd just demanded another two million dollars from him! Mitchell had had quite enough of her waspish behaviour and her lying comments. 'Get out now, Deanna. Go. Leave Hope Creek and don't ever come back.'

'I'm not going without my son.'

'You're going to have to. Not a court in the world would

return Kade to your custody. The evidence is piled way too high against you.'

'Just because you're rich and famous and think you're somebody doesn't mean you can kidnap my son.' Her voice got louder with every word she uttered. Darn it all, everyone on the neighbouring properties was likely to hear her if this kept going much longer. 'Wait until I tell Kade you're not his father. Do you think he'll want to stay with you then?'

Every fibre of his being wanted to physically eject her from the cottage, but he knew he had to stay calm. If he laid a finger on her, she'd be screaming assault. 'If it's a choice of you or me, then yes, I think he'll stay with me.'

'What's your game here, Mitchell? Why did you really come back to Hope Creek? There have been photos of you with that one-legged woman in the news and on social media – the one who used to play tennis? Is it true you've become so desperate you've been screwing her?' she spat out scornfully.

* * *

'One foot actually, not one leg.' Stella chose that moment to make her presence known.

Thank God she had returned early, and thank goodness she'd told Liz she was back.

She'd received a text from Liz that Deanna had arrived and that she should get to the farm house as quickly as possible, but when she'd come in through the back door, she'd been too shocked by all she'd heard to enter the fray – and she'd thought it was better not to get involved. But having heard Deanna's insult…

'Grizella,' Deanna said disparagingly. 'The little Aussie girl who couldn't keep her man.'

Stella merely raised her eyebrows at the overpainted, overdressed woman with the hideously Botoxed lips and walked to Mitchell.

'Hi, darling.' She put her hands on his shoulders and stood

up on her tiptoes to plant a kiss on his lips before turning and standing at his side so they faced the demon witch together.

'You think he's your darling? Forget it sweet honey-pie. Mitchell's coming back to the States. We're going to re-marry and be a family again for Kade. He was just telling me how he's never stopped loving me.'

Stella shook her head and let out a short sound of amused incredulity. 'I love Mitchell, Deanna.' She shifted, perhaps none too subtly, so she stood directly in front of Mitchell. 'I lost faith for a while, but now I know that true love does endure and we're not going to lose faith in each other again.'

'Oh baloney!'

'Deanna, if you want money for counselling, I'll pay the session fees directly,' Mitch offered.

'Mitch has told me what an awful childhood you had,' Stella said, 'I realise you—'

'You don't realise anything!' Deanna marched to the coffee table then reached into her oversized handbag. Producing a document she announced, 'This is the original DNA test, Mitchell. This is the proof that you're not and never have been Kade's father.' She brandished the document in front of her as though she was holding a revolver.

In Deanna's hands, Stella supposed this document was like a weapon.

For a moment, Stella's confidence faltered when Deanna delivered her ultimatum, 'You want Kade in your life – you want to be in his and save him from his wicked mother, then you'll play this the way I want.'

Once before Mitchell had chosen Deanna – well Kade, really – over Stella.

Would he do it again if his hand was forced?

He had warned her he'd do anything he had to so Kade would have a happy, stable life.

Stella stiffened a little and found herself holding her breath as Deanna continued her rant.

'Move any other piece on the board and you'll never

see Kade again and never know what sort of life he's living under my *care*.' She tossed her head. 'Imagine all the tortured, sleepless nights you'd have wondering how his life is going and knowing you're powerless to intervene. Much better to do as I ask.'

'This isn't a game, Deanna.' Mitchell put his hands on Stella's shoulders and she realised it was his way of showing Deanna that they stood together.

'Oh, but it is, and I'm playing to win.'

'Each year of marriage to you was a year of hell. I'm not stepping back into that prison,' Mitch declared. 'I've tried to support you, but you take me on and you're the one who'll lose the legal battle. No judge or jury in their right minds would award you custody of Kade and he's old enough to speak for himself now, too.'

As Deanna opened her mouth – no doubt to spew forth more venom – Stella was amazed when Liz stood up from where she'd evidently been sitting, unseen, in her favourite high-backed leather armchair that faced away from the doorway and away from they were standing.

'Bravo, Deanna. That was quite a performance and one I've preserved for prosperity on video on my phone!'

Stella's heart lifted as Liz came to the rescue.

'Gotta love modern technology,' Liz said with a wink in Mitch's direction. 'And, with the marvels of instant technology, I've also been able to send the video to our local police with a text message asking them to come straight away,' Liz's smile of satisfaction broadened. 'Unless you want to be forcibly removed and interrogated by the police, I suggest you leave right now.'

Deanna regarded the phone, then shot a death stare at Liz. The daggers in her eyes zeroed in on Stella and Mitch. 'You haven't heard the last of this.'

'For all our sakes I hope we have,' Mitch said a little wearily.

The second Deanna grabbed her handbag and flounced out

of the house, Stella collapsed against Mitchell, whose arms wrapped around her.

'Oh Lordy!' Liz exclaimed. 'I couldn't have conjured up a viler character in one of my books. She's been truly inspirational. It makes me want to get straight back to my keyboard and write it all down.'

'You're incorrigible, Liz, but I have to admit my spirits lifted when I noticed your phone and knew what you were up to,' Mitchell said.

'You knew Liz was there?' Stella asked.

'I noticed the phone. I also know that's Liz's favourite spot to sit. Thankfully, Deanna didn't see it.'

'Oh, my next villain is going to be a doozy! Maybe I should dedicate my next book to Kade's mother?'

Mitch groaned. 'Please don't.'

'I pity your poor hero and heroine,' Stella said.

'I pity Deanna.' After clearly having tried to lighten the mood, Liz had become serious. 'The woman obviously has mental health issues, Mitchell. I know you mentioned counselling just now but has anyone seriously tried to get her into therapy?'

'Tried and failed,' Mitch said. 'Sadly, even when people need help, they can't be helped unless they want to be helped. With the full backing of her father, Deanna's got away with manipulating people and lying to people for way too long. It is sad but it's one of the reasons I was desperate to get Kade away from her.'

'Regardless, we need to do something to get her some help because she is Kade's mother,' Liz declared.

'And, presumably, she's alone here in Australia,' Stella added. Biting her lip for a moment she suggested, 'Mitch, maybe you should go after her and try to talk to her again without all the emotion?'

Mitchell sighed. 'You're right. She's really messed up. I'll phone around and see if I can find out where she's staying.'

'Where is Kade?' Stella asked.

'I asked him to give Deanna and I some time. I imagine he's taken Jax for a walk, but no doubt he heard her leave and will make an appearance shortly. We're supposed to go into Lancaster and pick up some alpacas.'

'Is it true?' Liz asked. 'Are you Kade's father or not?'

Mitchell's lips twisted. 'Depends on your definition of the word 'father'. Biologically? No. We don't share the same DNA.'

Liz raised one hand to her brow. 'I can't believe it. Why didn't you tell me?'

'I—'

'She said your father knew the truth?' Liz questioned.

'Yes. He lied about the DNA result.'

Liz shook her head. 'Please don't tell me my sister was a party to the deception?'

Mitch pressed his lips together and Liz covered her eyes with one hand. 'I know she was never maternal, but... I can't credit she was part of the lie?'

Mitch merely nodded.

'How on earth...?'

'Long story and not one I want to go into right now, but I will sit down and tell you when Kade's gone to sleep tonight,' Mitch promised.

'Would Kade have overheard any of the conversation?' Liz asked.

Mitch looked thoughtful. 'I hope not, but maybe I'd better go and find him before I make those calls about Deanna.'

'You do that,' Liz said. 'His demeanour will tell you straight away whether he got the gist of it. He's pretty easy to read, that lad.' She turned to Stella. 'While he goes off, I'm going to put the kettle on. I'm most definitely in need of one. Want to join me?'

Stella sighed. 'Absolutely. A cuppa sounds great.'

'My sister and I have always been polar opposites and I knew she wasn't a good mother to Mitch. I stayed in touch with her primarily so I'd have a relationship with Mitchell.

Since he went to Stanford, she and I have only exchanged Christmas cards. Too bad I've already sent mine this year. I can tell you she won't be getting one next year.' She shook her head again. 'Poor Mitchell.'

'You know, Liz, tea is great but I wouldn't say no to something stronger after that showdown.'

Liz winked at her. 'I think we can manage that. After all, it's six pm somewhere in the world and I'm reeling from the encounter and from what I've learned!' Her lips compressed and she looked sad. 'I should've had more faith in Mitchell.'

'You're not the only one who's guilty in that department.'

Liz gave Stella a hug. 'We can both make it up to him from now on.'

CHAPTER TWENTY

'Coo-ee! Anyone home?' Jim called out from the front door about five minutes later.

'Come on in, Jim,' Liz invited. 'I've just put on the kettle.'

And they'd both downed a Scotch while they'd been waiting for it to boil.

Stella went to give Jim a hug. She was still rather shaken from the encounter with Deanna and took solace in his hug. 'Hi. Marg not with you?'

'No she's not, and thanks, but I won't stay. Just came to say hello to Liz and thank her for her wishes while I was in hospital.' He tilted his head and looked more closely at Stella. 'Is that Scotch on your breath?'

'Yes,' she admitted sheepishly.

'Are you okay? You look rather pale.'

'Well…' Stella looked at Liz then back at Jim. 'It'd be fair to say we've had some drama here just now.'

'Would that have anything to do with the maniac who drove out of here like she was being chased by the hounds of Hell, then almost ran poor Blue off the road?'

'Ah, yes. It would,' Liz replied.

Stella was instantly concerned for the elderly ringer. 'Is Blue okay?'

'He's shaken but okay.'

It must've been a very close call for Blue to have been shaken.

'He was on his way over to let Mitch know he saw Kade running with Jax a short time ago. He wasn't close enough to say for certain but he was worried because he thought Kade was crying.'

'Oh no!' Stella exclaimed.

Liz cursed and the normally faint lines across her brow deepened with her concern. 'Which direction was he headed?'

'South. Towards the creek.'

Liz whipped into action straight away and had her phone out. 'I'll call Mitch straight away and tell him.'

'Not good?' Jim asked quietly as Liz spoke to Mitch.

Stella shook her head as she worried at her lower lip with her teeth. 'The maniac driver was Kade's mother. She turned up completely out of the blue, wants Kade back and she's just had a slanging match with Mitchell. She had a DNA test that proves Mitch was never Kade's father and said she plans to pursue legal action for custody. If Kade was upset there's a good chance he heard what she said.'

'Don't jump to conclusions.' Liz had hung up and obviously caught the last of Stella's fears. 'Deanna made it known in front of Kade that she wanted him to return to the States with her. It could be that Kade didn't stick around to listen to anymore and that he's upset about that prospect.'

'I hope so.' But she couldn't help but feel a huge sense of foreboding.

'Mitch said to thank Blue,' Liz said. 'He's changed his course and will head in that direction.'

'I think I might hang around and have that cuppa after all,' Jim said. 'I'd like to make sure young Kade is okay and hear the rest of this story.'

'Cuppa coming right up,' Liz said as she bustled off.

'Are you okay?' Jim asked Stella.

Stella covered her hands with her face for a moment before she said, 'Kade's mother is really tragic. I can only imagine the hell Mitch went through in living with her for all that time.'

'What about what she said – that Mitch isn't Kade's father? Is there any truth in that?'

Letting out a long sigh she nodded. 'Yes. Mitch had already told me the truth – that it was a set up between Stella's father and his that worked to his father's political advantage.'

'Say again?'

Stella was too on edge to go through it all now. 'It's a long, convoluted story and I don't think I'm up to going through it all right now, but basically Mitch was well and truly stitched up.'

'And his father was in on it?'

'Yes.'

'Son of a bitch!'

Stella's eyes widened because she'd never heard Jim use such language before.

'Does Lizzie know?' he asked.

'She does now, but I think I'm the only one Mitch has spoken to about the whole story.' And she admired him for his reasons. 'I told Marg, Callie and Morgan while we were in Melbourne, but I didn't want to stress you out with all the details.' The truth was unfathomable. 'Mitch didn't want it to be out there because he regards himself as Kade's father and didn't want Kade to find out from anyone before he was at an age that Mitch was going to be the one to tell him.'

'Fair enough. It isn't anybody else's business, but it's certainly affected your life.'

'It has, but Mitch's life was affected more. Thankfully, we're good now, Dad.'

It was only when Jim looked shocked that Stella registered what she'd said.

Dad.

Smiling up at him she said, 'Should have started calling you that years ago. I've certainly thought of you as my dad for long enough.'

He pulled her to him and she was wrapped in his big bear-like hug.

'I didn't mind you calling me Jim – still don't – but it's nice to know you think of me as your father and I won't complain if that word slips out every now and then.'

'You're my father and Marg's my mum in every way that matters, the same way Mitch is Kade's dad.' She shrugged. 'I used to think it was just a title, and I guess it is because Deanna's Kade's mum but there's no way she's earned that title. You, Marg and Mitch – you're all everything parents should be.'

She was astonished to see the big, gentle bear of a man go all glassy-eyed.

'You can call me whatever you like. No title will ever change the way I feel for any of my three girls.'

He was one in a million.

'That looks good, thanks,' he told Liz as she came back carrying a steaming hot cup of tea.

'Strong and black, just the way you like it,' Liz said.

It struck Stella how Liz hadn't needed to ask Jim how he had his tea. The friends and neighbours must've made hundreds of cups of tea for each other over the years.

Conversation turned to the inconsequential. Neighbourhood gossip. The price of stock and the recent cattle yard sales Jim had attended in Lancaster just prior to the fair.

All the while, Stella kept looking at the clock and wondering when Mitch and Kade would return.

Forty-five minutes later, there was another knock at the door.

'You home, Liz?'

'Oh, Crikey.' Mitch's aunt jumped up from her chair. 'Gary! Rick! I'm so sorry. I'd forgotten I called you. Come on in.'

Stella had also forgotten the police were on their way. 'The immediate crisis is over, but we still should fill you in.'

'We're just having a cuppa and a chin wag,' Liz said. 'Will you join us?'

'Don't mind if we do,' Gary said before both men wiped their feet on the mat and proceeded to come inside. 'Seems there's a lot to talk about.'

'Just hang on while I make a fresh brew,' Liz said.

Jim stood to shake their hands and greetings were exchanged all around. The officers asked after his health while Liz went back to the kitchen to boil the kettle.

'You didn't happen to book a mad American woman who was driving like a maniac did you, boys?' Jim asked.

Rick, the shorter and stouter of the two of them, grinned from ear to ear. 'As a matter of fact, we did!'

'What was that? You booked Deanna?' Liz asked as she poked her head around the corner.

'Recognised her straight away from the video you sent us,' Gary told her. 'We would've been here earlier but we saw her doing about a hundred and forty clicks in the seventy zone going toward town and we had to turn around and pursue her.'

'She didn't stop?' Jim asked.

'Nup.' Rick shook his head and spoke excitedly as he told them, 'Poor Mavis nearly got run over crossing over on the pedestrian crossing in the main street!'

'Is she okay?' Jim asked as Liz and Stella gasped.

'Yeah,' Rick said. 'We stopped on our way back through town and checked up on her. She was at the pub telling everyone about it.'

Great.

The news would be all around town in no time flat that it was Kade's mother. That would set the gossips' tongues wagging and there'd be no end of questions to face.

'It was like a scene from the damned *Dukes of Hazard*!' Gary told them before amending, 'Mind you, we're not incompetent like those officers were.'

'Of course not,' Liz said with a smirk.

'We had the sirens blaring and the lights flashing for about five kilometres and we radioed ahead to Lancaster to see if they had a patrol in the area that they could send our way.'

'Good grief!' Jim exclaimed. 'Did they have to cut her off?'

'Nope. It didn't come to that. But the only reason we caught up with her in the end was because there was a train at the Miles Crossing and she had to stop.'

'What did you do with her?' Liz asked.

Stella spoke at the same time. 'Where is she now?'

'We thought it was best if she spent some time cooling off in a cell,' Rick said.

'Had a mouth from the gutter, swearing like a trooper,' Gary put in.

'Too right. Anyway, we handed her over to the boys from Lancaster. She can swear all she likes now in a cell in Lancaster and we'll decide what we do with her in the morning. She's broken a half a dozen laws and could also be charged with reckless endangerment.'

'You certainly deserve a cuppa!' Liz said.

Stella could hear the kettle boiling in the kitchen. 'How about you sit and I'll get it this time, Liz.'

'Thanks, Stella love.'

For all that Liz had been annoyingly meddlesome, she was extremely kind-hearted and empathetic. Stella heard her saying to the police officers, 'You heard the way Deanna behaved on that video clip I sent you. I know she's a foreigner, and to be perfectly honest I'd rather have her booted out of the country as quickly as possible, but I truly believe she needs a psychiatric assessment. Is there any chance that could be arranged? If she goes back to America, I don't believe she'll get the help she needs.'

The officers agreed with Liz's assessment and said they'd look into it.

Stella didn't interrupt the conversation to ask how Gary and Rick had their tea, deciding she'd just bring the pot, cups, milk and sugar out on a tray and ask them as she poured.

They were still relaying details of their car chase to Jim and were clearly excited by it.

Golly! She doubted Hope Creek had ever seen such drama.

She could imagine Mavis's excitement in relaying the story to anyone who'd listen and saying, 'That's what happens when an outsider comes to town!'

Serving tea as she rejoined the group kept Stella occupied for another five minutes. Liz was filling the officers in on the unannounced arrival of Deanna, what had transpired that afternoon and a bit of the history between Deanna and Mitchell.

Stella was painfully aware of the passing of time and kept looking at the clock then at the front door, hoping to see Mitch and Kade standing there.

'It's been an hour and twenty-five minutes now since Mitch left,' she announced to them all when there was a lull in conversation.

'Don't fret,' Jim offered sagely. 'If Kade's upset, Mitch might be needing to have a heart-to-heart talk with him.'

'He might've even taken him somewhere to show him something to brighten him up,' Liz suggested. 'Another cup of tea for anyone?'

'I will,' said Gary. 'We might hang around for a little while longer to make sure everything is okay.'

'Good idea,' Rick agreed. 'I don't expect there'll be any other maniac drivers to arrest on Hope Creek's roads this afternoon.'

Another hour later and Liz's phone rang.

'Mitch. Have you found him?' She paused. 'Just a moment and I'll put you on speaker phone. Jim's still here with us, and Gary and Rick have arrived – but I'll tell you about that later.'

'I'm getting worried,' Mitch told them. 'It's not like Kade to take off this far or to be gone for this long. I might be concerned over nothing, but it's getting later and I'm thinking…'

'You want us to organise a search party?' Jim said.

'Yeah.'

'We're on it,' Gary told him before he said to Rick, 'Good thing we stayed.'

'Hold off on that for a bit. Let us look around the farm first, closer to the house in case he's come back and he's just down with the goats or something simple,' Liz said. 'If the five of us don't find him in the next fifteen minutes, then we can galvanise the troops into action.'

'Okay.'

Stella felt sick.

'It's four fifteen,' Rick said. 'Let's split up and meet back here at four thirty.'

They each had a section of the farm to look around, with Stella going back to her place to see if he might've taken refuge there with Jax.

Fifteen minutes later, they'd all drawn a blank.

It was time for the community of Hope Creek to swing into action.

CHAPTER TWENTY-ONE

Ordinarily, the town convened at the hotel when there was any urgent situation to confront. This afternoon, however, knowing Kade had last been seen here, everyone came to Hope Farm.

Gary and Rick ran everything like a well-oiled machine, organising all the able-bodied men and women into groups and giving them areas to search.

Mavis and her neighbour, Pamela, had stopped off at the store on the way and bought up all the supplies to feed the hungry hordes, in case of the worst-case scenario where a search might go all night.

There was a current of unease running through the gathering, and everyone was serious, but each person knew they had a role to play and they set to it.

Jim and the older men were to monitor the radios and keep track of everyone's movements.

The older women, including Marg, Liz and Mavis, boiled the water for the urns; buttered the bread that Mavis and Pam had picked up on the way, and started to make sandwiches to hand out to the searchers before their groups set off by foot.

Mavis had spoken briefly about the near 'hit and run' as she described it, but was too concerned about Kade to dwell on it.

Stella phoned Mitch and asked him to come back briefly to

collect supplies, let Rick and Gary know where he'd already searched, and to join a group.

When Mitch was reluctant, Stella handed the phone to Gary.

'We need you to come back in, mate.' Gary said. 'You can let us know where you've already been so we can chart it, then we need you to join a group. The last thing any of us need is for a solitary searcher to get lost or injured in the dark and make matters worse.'

Half an hour later, Mitch arrived back and Stella had never seen him looking so fraught with concern. She went to him straight away and gave him a quick hug, but knew all he wanted at the moment was to find his son, and that he was anxious to get out there again.

'He'll be found, Mitch.' She willed him to believe it. Willed it to be true. 'You have to know that we're all with you and nobody here will stop looking until he's found.'

He gave her another tight hug and brushed his lips over hers. 'Everyone here deserves a medal. Thank you. Make sure you let them know how grateful I am.'

Liz thrust a jumper and a torch at him and Mavis called out, 'Don't forget the spare batteries. I've got them over here.'

Then he left with the last search group who'd all been waiting for him to arrive.

Time dragged.

Every time someone radioed in, Stella and everyone in the room snapped to attention, ears straining as they hoped to hear good news.

Each time they'd been disappointed as the calls had only been position reports.

'Why don't you get some sleep?' Marg asked her. 'I can call you the minute we hear anything.'

'No. I won't be able to sleep until I know Kade is safe and sound.' She rubbed her arms in a comforting motion. 'He must be getting cool out there.' The days were hot but it was cool at night.

'He's got Jax to cuddle,' Liz said. 'They'll keep each other warm enough.'

Stella sighed and rubbed the back of her neck. Tension had wound her muscles into a series of tight knots all across her shoulders and up her neck.

'I'm not going to sleep but I think I'll go home and have a hot shower.' Standing under the hot water would help relax the muscles. If she didn't, she'd end up with a headache from the muscle tension and then she'd be no good to anybody.

'Good idea, darling,' Marg agreed. 'Take your phone with you and we'll let you know the minute we hear.'

'Actually, that's a good point. My phone is nearly dead so I'll grab my phone charger while I'm there.' She gave all three of the other ladies a kiss on the cheek. 'I won't be long.'

'Take as long as you need to,' Liz encouraged. 'Now that everyone is out there and we've done the next round of sandwiches, we should probably roster ourselves off two at a time for a rest. As much as we're all stressed and probably unable to sleep, we should at least all have a lie down for a shift. We can spring back into action if necessary.'

Stella heard them agreeing that Marg would go for a lie down now in Liz's spare room as she left the farmhouse.

She looked up at the night sky and was grateful for the almost full moon.

Oh, Kade. Where are you, darling?

Please be safe.

Although she took extra care with her footing, every step back to her cottage was as heavy as her heart. She could only imagine the desperation Mitch was feeling and wished she was out there searching with him. She would've been if it hadn't been for her blasted foot! She'd known if she joined a search party, she'd only slow them down.

When she reached her cottage, she operated on automatic as she walked through to her bedroom to select a fresh change of clothes.

Her throat was dry and scratchy too.

She needed to stay hydrated.

Dumping her clothes in the bathroom, she went to the kitchen for some water.

There, on the bench, right next to another bunch of flowers that he'd brought for her, was Kade's sketch book. He'd left it there some time last week when he'd come to keep her company. Stella had been looking over the architectural plans for the cabins and main office and writing up some notes for the builder on a few changes she'd decided to make. Kade had been great company, sketching by her side.

He'd been going to show her the sketches, but Marg had phoned and asked her to come over to the homestead to help her turn over a heavy mattress that needed airing, so Kade had left the sketch book there and said he'd show his work to her next time. There hadn't been an opportunity since for him to show her the sketches and she knew he'd wanted to show them to her himself rather than have her look through them without him.

But now… Now she wanted to feel close to him.

Picking up the book, Stella turned to where the pencil had been inserted at his last drawing.

Wow!

Kade had sketched Jax as he lay in the sun by the back screen door.

The picture was fantastic.

Mitchell hadn't been kidding when he'd told Kade he had genuine talent.

Feeling lightened, and connected to Mitch's son through his sketches, she kept turning the pages.

Wow!

There was a sketch that was unmistakably Mitch, and Stella marvelled at the likeness. Kade had pictured Mitch's strength and determination and Mitch's boy hadn't even hit his teens yet. He was a brilliant artist.

Kade had drawn a paperbark tree. Another image showed the nanny goat with her three kids.

Ah, she remembered he'd said how much he loved drawing the Australian birds. Flipping through the images she saw a kookaburra, a cockatoo, a willy wagtail. Then there was…

Oh my God!

The mine shaft!

A surge of adrenaline had her sucking in a huge breath as her fingers tingled against the paper.

He'd never spoken about it, but he'd obviously been there to have sketched it, and it wasn't very far away from the farm's southern border with Hope Creek Station.

Optimism that she might have discovered Kade's whereabouts turned to terror.

The mine was dangerous.

It'd been boarded over years ago – if not a century ago – yet Kade's sketch showed an opening in the boards – an opening that was big enough for a young boy of his size to get through.

Trepidation beat through her as she dialled Mitch's number.

'Stella? Have you got some news?'

'Maybe.' Oh Lord, she didn't want to worry him and didn't want to divert their search if it was a wild goose chase. 'I've just found Kade's sketch book and seen a picture he's drawn of the old mine shaft. Has anyone checked there?'

'Shit!' She heard the dread in that single syllable. 'Are you certain it's a picture of the shaft? He's never spoken about it.'

'It's a very clear sketch.' And, the voice in her head warned, wouldn't it be a boy thing to do – to think he was on a grand adventure, finding his own special place? A place he could go to if ever he needed some space or was hiding from the world. A place to lick his wounds. Kade must have known it was dangerous and that if he mentioned having been there he'd be told not to return. But if Kade had thought of this as a bolt hole, he'd keep his find to himself, wouldn't he?

'I'll radio in and see if there are any teams in the area, but given that I'd already been south initially, I think the teams are concentrating their searches in other areas.'

She knew it was true because she'd just come from the room with all the maps. 'There are no teams close by.'

'I'm a good forty minutes away.'

'I'm not.' It was only about ten minutes from her cottage to the mine shaft – maybe a little longer given her slower pace due her right foot. 'I'll head out now and you can meet me there.'

'No, sweetheart. You stay put.'

'No way. I love him too, Mitch.' And as tears sprang to her eyes, she knew she loved Kade deeply.

The little boy she hadn't wanted to know.

The boy whose mere existence had cast a shadow over her happiness for so many years was a boy she'd now grown to love.

'No. Listen to me. I—'

Whatever Mitch had been going to say, and she could guess he was demanding she stay put, was cut off as her mobile battery went dead.

Grabbing her backpack, she threw in some water, muesli bars, a spare coat and towel, spare torch and… hell… what else would she need? Rope? No, she didn't have any.

Just get going. Mitch won't be far behind you and he'll have anything else you might need.

She didn't want to waste time going back to the farmhouse to tell the search controllers where she was heading. She'd told Mitchell and she was certain he'd relay the information on to them.

If Kade was in the mine shaft, it was vital someone get to him as quickly as possible. There was no telling what danger he might be in.

Shit.

It was an effort to hold herself back – to remind herself that she couldn't run down the verandah stairs or set a cracking pace through the bush.

One foot in front of the other.

One step at a time.

Hold on Kade, I'm on my way.

After what seemed like an eternity, but a quick check of her watch told her had only been fourteen minutes, she finally arrived at the mine shaft.

Her heart sank when she saw the impression of the sole of a sports shoe right at the entrance to the mine.

'Kade!' she called desperately. 'Kade? Are you there? Can you hear me?' Her ears strained but there was no response.

What the hell did she do now?

Did she put herself in danger by venturing into the mine when he might not even be there?

Common sense decreed she stay put and wait for others to arrive.

Then, she heard barking.

Jax.

'Kade,' she called again. 'I can hear Jax. I know you're there. Are you okay?'

'I'm not coming out.'

Oh, thank God! He was alive!

Damn that her mobile phone had run out of charge and she couldn't let everyone else know the fantastic news.

'Are you hurt?'

No answer.

She guessed it was a stupid question. He might not be physically injured but if he'd heard Deanna saying that Mitch wasn't his father, then he'd be cut to the bone.

'Please don't make me come in to get you,' she pleaded. 'It's not safe in there for either of us.'

When he didn't respond, she knew there was nothing else for it. She'd have to go in.

It'd been safe enough for him, so hopefully it'd be safe for her.

The space that'd been created by ripping two boards off the entrance didn't look quite large enough for her to fit through. One more would have to go.

She grabbed a plank and pulled. It moved a little, but she'd have to keep trying. The original boards that'd sealed off the mine entrance were obviously newer than a century old or they would probably have rotted and the nails would've rusted through.

Shifting her position she pulled at it again and again until finally it gave way… and she landed back flat on her butt.

Ouch!

Picking up her backpack and slinging it over her shoulder, she paused.

She should leave something at the entrance. In case disaster struck, she needed to leave something so Mitch would know she'd gone in.

Her necklace.

She took it off and clasped it around one of the remaining boards.

Nobody could possibly miss it and Mitchell would recognise it as being hers.

About to call and let Kade know she was coming in, she hesitated. If he realised she was on her way, that might make him venture deeper into the shaft and into an area that was less stable.

Decision made, she ventured into the dark, eerie mine shaft as quietly as she could.

So far, so good.

But as she descended, she knew she'd have a hard choice to make because when she'd been growing up, Jim had told her and her sisters that there was a labyrinth of tunnels down here. She hoped she had enough inconsequential things to leave at each point so she could mark her trail and find her way back.

Stella shivered.

The deeper she went, the chillier it got.

The air was danker as well.

It couldn't be healthy for Kade to be down here.

She reached the first point where the shaft split in two directions. Now, she really had no choice, she had to alert

Kade to her presence. 'Kade, please come out. I'm getting scared.'

Jax barked.

Yes! Good on you Jax. Keep barking.

As she turned to enter the shaft where the barking was coming from, Jax came running forward and almost knocked her off balance.

'Hi boy!' She patted him as he kept jumping up at her enthusiastically. 'Where's Kade?'

The puppy was more interested in greeting her than in taking her to Kade, and she guessed he was probably very hungry.

Not much further along, she saw Kade huddled against the wall, red-eyed and shivering.

'Oh sweetheart, we've all been so worried about you.' Overcome with relief, she took off her backpack and got out the blanket and water bottle she'd brought with her. 'Here, put this around you, have a quick drink and let's get out of here.'

'I'm not going,' he said with a miserably defiant tone, even as he took the blanket she offered and wrapped it around his shoulders.

'Your dad's on his way.'

On a huge sob, Kade's features scrunched up in sheer, undisguised despair. 'He... Mitch isn't my dad, Stella.'

Never had Stella loathed a person in her life with the intensity that she loathed Deanna right at that second.

'He is your father and he loves you very much,' she said calmly.

'No. You don't understand! I... I heard Mom,' he said between sobs. 'She said he's not my father. She said she can prove it and he said...' His features seemed to crumple in even more misery. 'I think she sold me to him.'

Sensing his sadness, Jax whined and went to Kade's side.

'Shh.' She sat on the other side of Kade and drew him against her as she stroked her hand over his head. 'It's all going to be okay. You'll see.'

'No! She's going to... She said she's going to take me back to America with her, but I don't want to go. He promised me I'd never have to go back. He told me I'd have a choice if I wanted to visit and that I'd never have to live with her again.'

'Your mum is missing you but Mitch isn't going to let her take you anywhere,' she tried to assure him. '*I'm* not going to let her take you anywhere and nor is Aunt Liz. In fact, I can tell you right now that there isn't a single person in Hope Creek who'd stand by and let her take you away from us, because we love you and this is where you belong.'

If anything, her words seemed to cause him greater distress because his sobbing intensified.

'Please, Kade, have some water.' He was probably dehydrated if he'd been crying all afternoon.

He did as she asked, drinking thirstily from the bottle before handing it back to her.

'You don't understand. She's mean to me.'

Stella steeled herself because she was afraid of what she'd hear. 'Well,' she sought to distract him, 'I think she has had a pretty tough life and maybe she doesn't realise she's hurt you.'

'But how can I stay here with Da... with Mitchell when he's not my real dad?'

Stella had to wipe her own eyes with the back of one hand and swallow down on her emotions before she was able to respond. When she did, she pulled away from Kade a little and said, 'Look at me, Kade. Mitchell loves you more than you'll ever know. As far as he's concerned, you're his son and I can tell you, without any doubt, that you're the most important person in his world.' As she said the words, she knew she was right. Surprisingly, she wasn't jealous. She believed that Mitchell loved her but knew that it was right, when push came to shove, for him to consider his dependent child's needs above hers. She also knew there was room in his heart and in his life for both of them.

Looking away from her and gathering Jax up on his lap, Kade asked, 'But how can he love me when I'm not his son?'

'The same way Jim and Marg love me and Morgan and Callie like daughters. Just because they're not our real parents doesn't make them any less loving. In fact, you're privileged in the same way that my sisters and I are privileged.'

'How?'

'Because Mitchell didn't have to be your father. He chose to be your father.'

'Like Mr and Mrs Richardson chose to be your parents?'

'Exactly. They took responsibility for us and I feel their love for us every day.' She reached out and placed her hand on his shoulder. 'If you look inside your heart, don't you feel Mitchell's love for you every day?'

He sobbed again as he nodded.

'And can you tell me that you love him any less now that you know he's not your birth father?'

He shook his head. 'I do love him. That's why it hurts so much. Why didn't he tell me?'

'I know he meant to tell you when you were a bit older, but to be perfectly honest with you, I don't really believe he thinks about it much. I think that to him you are his son and that he probably forgets that really you're his *chosen* son.'

She could see him absorbing her words and turning them over in his mind.

Jax looked up at Kade and licked him on the chin as though he was telling him to trust that everything was going to be alright.

'When he realised you weren't happy he and your mother both agreed that you should come here to Hope Creek. Your mother's had a change of heart because she's missing you but right now, your dad is worried sick about you. Everyone is worried sick about you. The whole community are out of their warm beds and searching high and low for you. How about we get out of here and let them know you're safe and well?'

'I'm sorry. I didn't mean to worry everyone.' He sniffled loudly. 'I didn't know everyone would be out looking for me.'

'Come on.' Stella started to haul herself up. 'Let's get you home.' Jax jumped up and barked. 'I think we need to get both of you fed, too.'

'Stella! Kade!'

Stella just about wept with relief when she heard Mitchell's voice.

'We're here! Don't come in. We're coming out!' she yelled as loudly as she could.

'Dad's come,' Kade wept.

'Of course he came, you big goose,' she said as she squeezed his shoulder. Reaching into her backpack, she handed him her spare torch. 'You go first. I'll be right behind you but I have to go a bit slower and watch my steps with my foot.'

'We're coming Da... Dad!' Kade yelled as they got to the point where the shaft split into different directions.

'We're coming Da... Dad!'

'We're coming Da... Dad!'

Kade's words echoed eerily through the shaft.

'Wow, that's pretty cool,' he said more quietly to Stella. 'I didn't know there'd be an echo if I yelled.'

She frowned. 'Maybe you shouldn't yell?'

'I'm coming in,' Mitchell yelled back.

'No! Don't!' Stella called back. 'We'll be with you in a few minutes.'

This time Stella's words echoed.

'Only a few minutes, Dad!'

'Only a few minutes, Dad!'

'Only a few minutes, Dad!'

Stella was about to tell Kade not to yell anymore when a loud rumble echoed through the mine and the walls started to tremble.

'Get out!' Mitchell yelled. 'Now!'

'Run, Kade!' Stella urged. 'As fast as you can!'

Rocks and debris began falling from the ceiling,

Terrified, Stella looked up. But, in looking up, she forgot she should be looking down. As she took her next step, she lost her footing, stumbled and fell heavily on her knees.

Hearing her cry, Kade turned back towards her. 'Stella!'

She heard the sheer terror in his voice.

'Go, Kade!' she commanded.

'But—'

'Keep going and don't stop!'

The rumbling intensified.

As she pushed herself back to her feet, it seemed she was being pelted with larger clumps of dirt and pieces of rock. As she grabbed her torch again and shone it on the path ahead, light bounced back off the dust particles that were dancing in clouds and making her cough.

Ahead of her, the light from Kade's torch told her he'd done as she bade and pushed on ahead.

Surely he was nearly at the entrance?

Almost to safety?

And it couldn't be many more steps for her…

Creak.

Groan.

A God-almighty roar and the shaft caved in and blocked her path, trapping her behind Kade.

Oh God, let Kade have made it to the other side of the cave in.

Stella felt a sharp blow to her forehead as a rock fell.

Instinctively, she crouched low and lifted her backpack up over her head in case there was more falling debris.

A slow trickle from the site of the pain and down to her brow told her the rock had broken her skin. But it hadn't knocked her unconscious, the thundering had stopped and Mitchell knew she was in here. It wouldn't be too long before they mounted a rescue operation to free her.

And surely Kade had made it to safety by now?

Coughing hard, she lifted the neck of her top up over her

nose and mouth to try to filter out the dust from the air she inhaled.

Apart from the faint sound of small amounts of dirt falling from the roof of the shaft, there was silence. Cautiously, Stella lowered her backpack and retrieved her water bottle. It was almost empty after Kade's thirsty swigs, so she only allowed herself to have a few small sips to lubricate her dry, dusty throat, then screwed the cap back on.

She didn't need her torch now, either, so she switched it off to save battery power.

With darkness surrounding her and in total silence, Stella drew her coat closer around her and huddled against the damp chill that started to seep into her bones.

This darkness – this silence – feels like a tomb.

No. She refused to panic and give into negative thoughts and elected to take the only control she could and close her eyes so the inky blackness wasn't so oppressive.

They would come.

The people of Hope Creek wouldn't let her down.

Outside, they would already be organising her rescue.

I could run out of air down here.

Worse, I could be breathing in toxic gases right now.

Or, there could be another cave-in and I could be buried alive.

Clamping her teeth together she vowed not to give into hysteria – vowed not to think about the dangers she faced.

But time became a distorted concept and doubt sent its chilling, ghostly fingers down her spine.

Her forehead started to throb and she began to feel lightheaded and disoriented.

Mitchell.

Kade.

Jim and Marg.

Morgan, Callie and Blue.

One by one she made herself focus on the faces of all those

who loved her – all those she knew would be worried out of their skulls right now.

Weariness assailed her and, even as the thought crossed her mind that perhaps she was losing consciousness due to poisonous gases in the mine shaft, she couldn't fight it any longer...

CHAPTER TWENTY-TWO

A tap, tap, tap awakened Stella from her exhausted slumber.

She opened her eyes into pitch darkness and was, for a few seconds, completely confused. The cold earth against her back and under her backside soon reminded her where she was and what had happened.

Tap, tap, tap.

At first, she thought they were trying to communicate with her and she fumbled for her torch so she could find something she could use to hit back with. Then, she realised the striking and its eerie echoing through the mineshaft was the sound of a pickaxe.

She drew in a deep breath, only to start coughing again.

Miraculously a feeble beam of light shone through a gap right at the top of the barrier of the cave-in ahead of her.

'Stella?'

'Yes!' Relief washed through her.

'I'm Dan, commander of the rescue team,' came the unknown, authoritative voice. 'Are you hurt?'

She crawled forward and pulled herself up to where the beam of light shone through. 'Only a blow to my head. Is Kade okay?'

'Yes. He made it out unscathed.'

'Stella!' Her eyes stung and her lips trembled in sheer

relief as she recognised Mitch's voice even though it was shaky with emotion. 'Thank God you're alive.'

'You don't get rid of me that easily,' she rasped and became aware of how very dry her mouth was.

'You shouldn't be here,' she heard Dan tell Mitch. 'You need to wait outside.'

'Sit tight, my love. The rescue team is coming to get you out.'

My love.

Stella scrunched up her eyes as tears began to scald her eyes and the skin across the bridge of her nose and under eyes felt as though it was being abraided by the sharp points of pins and needles.

On a half-sob and half-laugh she said, 'I'm not going anywhere.'

'Stella,' Dan spoke again. 'I'm going to feed two tubes through this opening. The one coming through now is one you can drink from.'

'Thank you,' she croaked as she took the tube gratefully and began to drink.

After a moment Dan said, 'Do you have a torch?'

'Yes.'

'Good. Now, I'm going to feed another tube through. It has a small camera on the end.' Every word was calm and instilled her with confidence that he knew exactly what he was doing. 'I need you to shine your torch all around the walls and ceiling of the shaft as you direct the camera around. We need to get a good idea of the structural integrity of this part of the mine before we break through any further.'

'I can do that.' She located her torch and did as he said.

Time dragged as she performed the task. Every now and then he'd tell her to move the camera closer to the wall, or to go back to a spot again so he could take another look.

Finally, he said, 'Okay. That's it. We're going back outside now to get some different equipment, but we'll be back in five minutes.'

Pathetically she wanted to ask one of them to stay and talk to her so she didn't feel so isolated, but she knew they had work to do so she bit down on the request that stemmed from her fear. But as the light was withdrawn and her section of the mine was plunged into darkness again, she called out, 'Please...tell Mitch I love him.'

'You can tell him yourself in the next half hour,' Dan told her.

Stella sank back down awkwardly to the rocky floor.

Only half an hour.

I can do another half an hour.

It probably was only five minutes, but it seemed like an eternity until the pickaxe started up again – in fact now there were two that were striking away at the rocks in a symphony of determination and perseverance.

Every now and then the striking would stop and she'd hear male voices but not be able to make out what they were saying.

The gap at the top gradually broadened and more light shone through to illuminate her surroundings.

'Stella, we're starting to remove the stones from the top and pulling them to this side, but you might get some falling down on your side,' Dan told her calmly. 'We need you to move back two metres or so. Can you do that?'

'Yes.'

'Make sure you're forward of the main support beams.'

Trepidation ran through her at his command because she understood why. When she'd been steering the camera around the mine, she'd noticed the huge crack running down the middle of the beam. She realised it could give way and she needed to be closer to where the rescuers were digging and definitely not under the beam itself.

'I'll put my backpack over my head,' she told Dan then realised as soon as she'd spoken just how ineffective that would be against a tonne or more of dirt and rock falling on top of her.

'Shouldn't be too long, now,' he said.

* * *

'How much longer?' Mitch asked one member of the specialist mine rescue team who'd been flown from Ballarat by helicopter to take part in the rescue operation.

'It's hard to say, but not long. At least there's airflow in the shaft now so she's in less danger.'

The rescuers had been concerned about possible asphyxiation or poisoning from toxic gases, but even knowing that was no longer a threat, Mitch wouldn't relax until he could hold Stella in his arms again and know she was safe.

'They've done a sterling job,' Jim said from beside Mitch. 'I was concerned it would take much longer.'

'We know she's a fighter,' Marg said. 'She's already proved that too many times in her young lifetime.'

'I'm amazed at the efficiency of the whole set up.' Blue shook his head. 'I know they're trained specialists and they have to be efficient, but seeing them in action has been something else to watch.'

It had been a process to behold.

The minute they'd arrived at the abandoned gold mine, the commander and his team had been all business. They'd pored over the only known map of the shaft that Rick had procured; had spoken to Kade to get an idea of Stella's position; and they'd swung into action to assess the structural integrity of the shaft.

There were miners, two engineers, a geologist and paramedics who formed the rescue team.

A command centre – in the form of a tent – had been established quickly at the opening of the shaft, and the tight-knit community of Hope Creek had stood by on the fringes, gathered in anxious clusters and collectively awaiting news of the successful rescue.

A small cheer had gone up when Mitch had emerged from the shaft and announced that the team had broken through and ascertained that Stella was alive.

Throughout the harrowing ordeal, being surrounded by all the locals from the community had provided a small balm to soothe over Mitch's heart which had been caught in a vice-like grip of fear. Their turnout – first to look for Kade, and then staying through the long night awaiting news of Stella – was a testament to the love, the hope and sheer togetherness that defined the Hope Creek community and demonstrated how they coped with the most daunting trials they faced.

As one.

While most of the mothers had left at some point to get children to sleep, every family was still represented. Those remaining sent news updates back home as the darkness of night had lightened, a faint indigo glow had appeared on the horizon then given way to orange hues and fingers of soft pink.

Now the day had truly arrived and the sky was clear blue, but Mitch had no idea of the actual time.

'You men need to go and get yourselves some breakfast,' Marg ordered. 'Rumbling stomachs won't do Stella any good.'

'Not hungry.' It was probably the first time in his life Blue had uttered those words but Mitch could totally relate.

'I insist,' Marg said. 'You too, Jim. Bad enough that you've been out all night so soon after your surgery. Get yourselves over to the BBQ and make Bill, Mavis and Pam feel their efforts are appreciated.'

Mitch stayed where he was. Anxiety and helplessness had his gut churning.

The evening had been a see-sawing of emotions.

Even while he'd known utter relief as Kade's torch light had become visible and his son had collapsed against him all dusty and grimy but in one piece, his guts had been hollowed out as his eyes had strained into the dusty darkness behind Kade in search of Stella.

'Stella?' he'd asked.

Kade hadn't been able to speak. The wail of grief he'd let out before he'd sobbed against Mitch's chest would haunt

Mitch forever. He was torn in wanting to comfort Kade and wanting to shake information from him – had Stella been trapped under the debris from the collapsed mine, or had she at least been further back and been miraculously spared?

'We've got to get out,' Rick had told him. 'This whole mine could collapse.'

He'd known Rick was right and they all had to get to safety, but he'd had to go further into the mine. He had to see for himself that Stella wasn't lying incapacitated somewhere he could reach her.

When he'd reached the blockage, he'd called Stella's name as loudly as he dared.

The silence had been almost too much to bear.

'Mate,' Gary had followed him in. 'You need to get outside.' And, when he still hadn't moved, he was told, 'Kade needs you.'

It'd been impossible to keep his voice devoid of fear when he'd emerged from the mine and comforted Kade.

'This is my fault. It's all my fault,' Kade had cried as the local ambulance officers had checked him out. 'I'm so sorry.'

'We know you were upset, son. Stella will be okay.' Mitch prayed it was true as he crouched down in front of Kade. 'I love you, son.'

'I love you, too... Dad.'

'The mine rescue team are on their way from Ballarat,' Gary had told him.

Liz overrode Kade's objections when she told him, 'Come on, darling. Let's go back to the house and get you cleaned up.'

'They must've reached her,' Morgan said now when a couple of the rescuers picked up a stretcher and headed into the mine.

Mitchell heard the hopeful note in Morgan's voice. Earlier she'd buried her hostility towards him and given him a hug as they'd waited for news of Stella.

'I can see how frantic you are, Mitch,' she'd said.

'I love her, Morgan.'

She'd nodded. 'She loves you, too. She'll get through this and you'll be together at last.'

'With your blessing, Morgan?'

'Yeah, Mitch. As long as you make her happy, I'm happy.'

'I plan to do just that.'

Now, Mitch and Morgan began moving closer to the entrance of the mine.

'The second Stella's out safely, I have to call Callie,' she told him.

Callie had driven up from Melbourne as soon as she'd heard the news, and she'd arrived as dawn had broken, but she'd headed up to the farm house a short time ago to check on Liz and Kade and to pick up some more supplies for the breakfast BBQ.

Liz's partner, Connor, had also driven up from Melbourne to support her when she'd phoned him to tell him Kade was missing. It felt as though there was a cast of thousands hanging on the news of Stella's safety.

Mitch hoped Liz had managed to get Kade to sleep last night. He was going to have to talk to Kade about what he'd overheard. While he hadn't spoken for long enough to Kade to confirm it, he was convinced Kade had run off because he'd overheard Deanna saying that he wasn't his father.

'They've got her!' Morgan cried out joyfully before she joined Mitch in dashing towards the stretcher as it emerged from the mine.

Mitch looked at Stella through eyes that swam in unstoppable tears. Unable to form words, he reached out and encased her hand in his.

'I love you,' she rasped as she squeezed his hand.

'Thank God you're out!' Morgan told her.

Jim, Marg and Blue all converged to see for themselves that Stella had survived the ordeal.

'Just give us some room, folks,' Dan told them all. 'Let the medics do their jobs and you can say all you want to say in due time.'

The others fell back but Stella didn't let go of Mitch's hand and Mitch sure as hell wasn't going to let go of hers any time soon.

'That's a pretty nasty blow to your forehead, Stella,' one of the medics told her after they'd cleaned some of the dust and dirt from her face and examined the wound. 'We're going to have to take you to the hospital at Lancaster for some tests.'

She nodded and said, 'Thank you,' before sending Mitch an exhausted smile.

'I'll come with you, sweetheart.'

She shook her head. 'Kade will need you. Have you spoken to him yet?'

'Not yet.'

'He knows, Mitch. He heard Deanna.'

'Liz and her partner are with him. He'll be fine.'

'No, Mitchell.' She turned her head a little and said to the medic, 'Please, can Mitch and Kade both come with me? It's important for us all to be together right now.'

The medic smiled. 'We can accommodate that.'

Mitch's heart squeezed. Even after all she'd endured, that Stella could be so considerate – so aware of Kade's needs – was just one of the reasons he loved this woman. 'Thank you.'

'The three of us are going to be a family, Mitch. Families stick together.'

CHAPTER TWENTY-THREE

At the hospital in Lancaster a couple of hours later, Mitchell sat and spoke to Kade while Stella went off to receive a thorough examination.

Wrapping his arm around his boy's shoulder, Mitchell pulled him close and planted a kiss on his forehead. 'I know you overheard what your mother said, Kade.'

'It's true, isn't it?' Pained eyes looked up at him.

'What's true is that I love you and I'll always regard you as my son, even though I have found out that another man got your mother pregnant.'

'When did you find out?'

'After the accident you had where we rushed you off to the emergency department in LA.'

'You still brought me to Australia with you. You didn't leave me behind in the States.'

'Of course I didn't. That should tell you all you need to know, Kade.' Mitch shifted so he knelt down in front of his son. 'I'll never leave you. I have custody of you because I want to take care of you.'

'I bet she was happy not to have me with her.' Kade's eyes were awash with tears.

Yes. She had been. She'd only argued about the sum of money she required for the custody, but he would never admit that to Kade.

'Your mother didn't have good parents and she didn't know how to be a parent herself,' he replied with a shrug.

'I don't want to see her again Da— er…'

'One day, we'll talk more about it, and there might come a day when you can understand her and forgive her.'

Kade hung his head for a moment before he looked back at Mitchell. 'Can I still call you Dad?'

'I hope you will. As far as I'm concerned, I'll always be your dad.'

Kade smiled just a bit before he frowned. 'I mean it. I don't want to see her again.'

'If that's what you want, I'll do my best to make sure she stays away, but…' He didn't want to make excuses for Deanna's inexcusable behavior, but she was still Kade's mother. 'Your mother has never felt loved.'

'What do you mean?'

He let out a long breath. 'Well, she came from a wealthy family but there wasn't any love there.' Mitch was, once again, so thankful that when he'd been growing up he'd known love from Liz, the Richardsons and the Hope Creek community in general. 'Her parents pretended they had a loving family when they were in public, but they were far from loving and your mother rebelled against them. I think she's spent most of her life looking for love, but she's gone about it in the wrong way.'

'I would've loved her, Da—' His voice broke. 'She didn't want *my* love.'

Mitch held Kade tight as his body was wracked with sobs.

'Even though she wants to be loved, she doesn't understand what it's all about. You're going to grow up knowing you're loved and that'll make it easier for you to love others.'

Kade pulled away from him and scrubbed at his eyes. 'I'm like Stella. She said I was lucky because you chose to be my father just like the Richardsons chose to be her parents.'

'I think we're all lucky because we have each other.'

A nurse walked by, then turned back. 'You're both here with Stella Simpson, right?'

'Yes,' Mitch agreed.

'You look really exhausted,' the nurse said to Kade. 'Are you the boy who was missing in Hope Creek?'

Kade's head dropped and he looked at his feet, nodding with absolute reluctance. Mitch knew he felt guilty about the whole community being out looking for him, and for Stella having been trapped in the mine.

'How about I set up a bed for you so you can get some rest?' she asked.

Kade shifted a little closer to Mitch, but Mitch thought it was a great idea and said, 'That would be wonderful, thank you.'

'Leave it to me. I'll be back soon,' she said before she walked away.

'It's okay, Kade. Nobody is blaming you for what happened.'

He stared at his feet for a bit longer before he finally looked up at Mitch. 'Dad, about Stella...'

'She'll be fine.'

'Yes, I know, but... you know how you said we were lucky we all have each other?'

'Yes.'

'Dad, do you think you could marry her so she could be my mum?'

Mitchell ran his hand over Kade's head. 'I think that's a brilliant idea.'

'You love her, don't you?' his son asked.

'I do.'

'And she loves you?'

'She does.' He knew it with absolute certainty.

'I'd be really happy if you both got married,' Kade said. 'You should ask her and see what she says.'

Mitchell couldn't keep his small laugh contained. 'Did Aunty Liz put you up to that?'

'No, but I did ask her last night about you and Stella and she said she'd be super happy for the two of you to get married, too.'

There'd never been any question about Liz's feelings on the subject.

'She also said Stella loved me a lot or she wouldn't have risked her life to come down the mine shaft to rescue me.'

The nurse reappeared before Mitch could reply.

'I've got that bed right ready for you now if you'd like to come and have a lie down,' she said. 'There was a spare room a few rooms down the corridor from where Stella is going to be, so I've set up a recliner chair that doubles as a visitor bed, and I've made it up for you.'

Kade stood up. 'Thank you. I am kind of tired.'

'I checked with radiology and Stella will be about another half an hour, then she'll be brought back to her room,' the nurse told Mitch. 'The doctors have said they want to keep her in overnight for observation.'

'Thank you for looking after us all so well,' Mitch said. 'I really appreciate it.'

He saw Kade settled and wasn't surprised his son was asleep within five minutes of his head hitting the pillow. Then, he headed back to Stella's room to wait for her.

She'd barely been wheeled back into the private room before she fell asleep.

Mitch sat on the bed beside her, holding her hand and thanking God that both Stella and Kade had come through the whole disaster relatively unscathed. He was exhausted too, but he had too much going through his mind to be able to sleep.

Perhaps he squeezed her hand a little more firmly as he vowed he'd lose no more time in making her his, because Stella's eyelids fluttered open.

'Mitch,' she said sleepily. 'I love you so much.'

'I love you, too.' He framed her face in his hands and simply couldn't hold back his proposal any longer. 'Marry me, Stella.'

The happily sleepy expression was gone and she pulled herself up against the pillows and beamed at him. 'Considering I'd already said you and Kade and I were going to be a family, it's just as well you asked.'

He laughed. 'Will I take that as a 'yes' then?'

'Absolutely! Oh Mitch, nothing would make me happier than to be your wife.'

'About bloody time,' Blue said from the doorway as Jim cleared his throat from behind him and Marg squealed her delight.

Mitchell shook his head at the trio. 'Talk about timing.'

'Congratulations to both of you,' Marg said.

'Well, this is the best news,' Jim said. 'Fantastic. We always thought you two belonged together.'

'Blind Freddy could see it,' Blue added.

'Come on Jim, Blue,' Marg urged, 'we're intruding. We'll come back a little later.'

'No,' Mitchell said a little grudgingly. 'Please stay. I know you love Stella as much as I do. It's only right you're here.'

'We love Stella and we love you,' Marg told him before rushing into the room and giving him a big hug before she bent to Stella in the bed and kissed her as she repeated, 'Congratulations, both of you!'

'A good thing to walk into your hospital room to happy news,' Jim said. 'But, please, make this the last time we ever have to visit you in hospital again, love.'

Mitchell hoped it wouldn't be the last time. Although they hadn't spoken about it for over a decade, their plan had always been to have children. He hoped Stella still wanted that, but he wanted to be with her even if she'd changed her mind about kids.

She and Kade were all the family he needed.

Blue followed Jim in, giving Stella a congratulatory kiss and shaking Mitchell's hand. 'Callie and Morgan will be here shortly. They just stopped in at the hospital shop.'

'And we saw Liz and Connor trying to find a park as we walked in, so they won't be far behind us,' Jim added.

'It'll be quite the party then,' Stella laughed.

'Where's young Kade?' Blue wondered.

'A nurse popped him in a spare room down the hall and when I last checked in on him he was fast asleep,' Mitch said.

'Knock, knock.' Gary and Rick appeared at the door. 'Whoa! There's a party happening and we weren't invited?'

Mitch laughed, 'Come on in! Did you bring the rest of Hope Creek with you?'

'Only their well wishes,' Rick told them.

'Do you have news of Deanna?' Jim asked.

'We do.' Gary looked around him and asked quietly, 'Um… is Kade around?'

'Little tacker's fast asleep,' Blue said.

The police officers both nodded, then Gary continued, 'We've just been down to the station and found out Deanna was released from jail this morning. She was charged with traffic offences, resisting arrest and a number of other offences, but apparently she has friends in high places because we were told the US Ambassador stepped in and the Lancaster police were ordered to drop all charges and let her go. They were told that to make her face court could cause an international incident.'

Jim swore.

Mitch swore too, but for a different reason. He'd hoped to sit down with Deanna and have a deep and rational conversation with her.

'Friends in high places, huh?' Blue said.

Mitch gritted his teeth together being well aware of the identities of the friends in high places. Her blasted father and his.

'Where is she now?' Stella asked hesitantly.

'Heading back to Melbourne to catch a flight back to the USA.' Gary looked out in the hospital corridor before he said, 'Even in the light of the appalling way we saw her behave yesterday on the video Liz sent us, we asked the officers in

Lancaster to let Deanna know about Kade's ordeal. We thought she might want to come and reassure herself that Kade was okay. Apparently she,' he shifted uncomfortably on his feet, 'was… er… very quiet when she heard the news. She apparently made the comment that Kade was better off without her and she… er… passed on a message for you, Mitchell.'

Mitch steeled himself.

It was Rick who said, 'The officer I spoke to said she appeared to be remorseful – that she seemed to realise she'd set off a chain of events that'd placed two lives in danger. She said to tell you that she wasn't making any promises but she might send you a bill for the appointments you suggested.'

Mitch hadn't realized he was holding his breath until Rick finished speaking.

Finally.

He hoped with everything he had in him that in hearing about the ordeal at the mine, Deanna would finally have been shocked into action.

He wanted her to heal.

Kade needed her to heal.

He looked back at Stella and she must've sensed his need for reassurance because she sent him a hopeful smile. 'Miracles can happen, Mitch.'

'They can. I just wish we all hadn't had to go through so much drama to achieve one.'

Stella laughed, 'Well, hell, Mitch. I went through one hell of a drama before we found our way back to each other!'

'No more drama,' he decreed.

'Wow! Didn't know there was a civic meeting going on!' Callie said from behind a massive arrangement of flowers.

'Any room for us in here?' Morgan asked.

'We'll head off,' Rick said. 'Just wanted to let you know what's happened.'

'Thanks Rick. Gary,' Mitch said.

'Oh, and the team from Ballarat blasted the mine shaft entrance this morning after your rescue. There's no way anyone will ever get trapped down there now because there's absolutely no way in.'

That was a relief.

'Should've done it years ago myself,' Jim muttered.

After the officers left and a bit of reshuffling took place so the sisters could kiss Stella and set up the flowers on the small cupboard beside her hospital bed, Liz and Connor arrived with yet another massive bouquet.

Liz took one look at Stella and Mitch and beamed. 'Congratulations you two!'

Stella sent a questioning look at Mitch. 'Did you – ?'

He raised his hands in protest. 'I didn't say a thing. How could I? You'd no sooner said yes than we were inundated with visitors!'

'You're engaged?' Morgan asked.

'Yay!' Callie did an excited happy dance. 'You said yes!'

'Liz told me last night she was certain you'd propose at first opportunity, Mitch,' Connor told him.

'I write romance,' Liz said smugly. 'I have a sense for these things.'

Amid all the excited congratulations and chatter that followed, Mitch ran a hand through his hair – frustrated that he couldn't get any alone time with his gorgeous fiancée, even while he enjoyed all the warmth and love that surrounded them both.

It was a couple of hours before the nurses shooed everyone away, but Mitch and Stella had spent barely any time alone before Kade came in to join them.

'Hello,' he said awkwardly from the front door.

'Hey, buddy,' Mitch greeted. 'Come on in and join us.'

'You had a long sleep,' Stella said.

'Mm.' He moved closer to Mitchell and in a stage-whisper asked, 'Did you do it yet, Dad?'

Mitchell chuckled, knowing exactly what he was referring to. 'I did.'

'And?'

'And she said "yes".'

Kade let out a loud whoop and jumped up and down on the spot before throwing himself into Mitch's arms and then racing to Stella to hug her too. 'You're going to be my mom – I mean my mum!'

'Yes,' she told him happily.

'And do you think I'll get some brothers and sisters, too?'

Mitchell looked at Stella and frowned because her smile disappeared and her body jerked back against the pillows. 'Um. We'll have to see about that, Kade.'

'Hey, Dad. I'm kind of thirsty. Do you reckon I could get some money and go and buy a soda from the vending machine down the hall?'

Mitchell smiled at the blend of Aussie and American terms. 'I think we can let you have a celebratory soft drink.'

Kade took the change eagerly and raced out of the room.

'Mitch, I didn't just lose my foot in the accident, I had some internal injuries and I lost an ovary.'

His head jerked back. 'Oh sweetheart, I'm so sorry for all you've been through.' He couldn't help but think he should've gone with his initial gut reaction and flown to Paris to be there for her.

'I hope we can have children, Mitch,' Stella said. 'I haven't been told it's impossible, but there's a reduced chance now.'

He winked at her. 'I guess we'll just have to try twice as hard then.'

The slight blush of pink along her cheekbones was visible before she lowered her head and he realised that even though they'd been lovers previously, there was still a little shyness in Stella as they began their intimacy again. It was quite adorable.

'Seriously, my darling, while I hope we can have children together, but you and Kade are all I need to be happy.'

Stella looked up at him lovingly. 'I'm so thankful we've found our way back to each other.'

'With a little interference from Aunt Liz,' he acknowledged.

Stella closed her eyes and tilted her head towards Mitch as he lowered his head for a kiss.

Divine sensation flowed through her as their mouths met.

Divine sensation that she was going to enjoy for the rest of their lives.

After so long apart, she was finally going to marry her best friend and the man she'd never stopped loving.

The future stretched before them.

They'd fallen in love at Hope Creek.

Their lives had been blown apart by manipulation and lies, but now they'd returned, they'd healed and she knew instinctively that their love was more mature, and stronger than it had ever been. It would withstand whatever challenges life threw their way.

Despite all the adversity, she was so fortunate she'd found her way back to Mitchell.

Now, she prayed her sisters would find similar happiness.

Maybe she should have a word to Liz?

'This is going to be a very special Christmas,' Mitch told her.

Stella sighed. 'Nothing compares to being at home for Christmas.'

'Christmas at Hope Creek,' Mitch said with a nod. 'I like the sound of that.'

'So do I,' Kade said as he rejoined them. 'I can't wait!'

'Come here, Kade,' Stella urged. 'I'd like a group hug with both my guys.'

They obliged enthusiastically and Stella knew that they'd face any challenges that lay ahead together with love and optimism.

Thanks for reading *Return to Hope Creek*. I hope you enjoyed it.

If you liked this book, you might like to read my other books. These are *Five Dates with the Billionaire*, and my **The Billionaire's Baby** series – *Seduced by the Enemy*, *Seduced by the Stranger*, and *Seduced by the Billionaire*. You don't want to miss out on *The Magic of Christmas* and you might also love my **Royal Affairs Series** – *The Defiant Princess*, *The Irredeemable Prince*, *The Formidable King* and *The Irresistible Royal* collected together in a new four-book collection A Royal Affair. My other books are *Roses for Sophie*, *Echoes of the Heart*, and *Mistaken Identity*, collected together as *The Billionaire Meets His Match.*

Printed in Great Britain
by Amazon